DAUGHTER *of* NO WORLDS

THE WAR OF LOST HEARTS: VOL. I

CARISSA BROADBENT

Copyright © 2019 by Carissa Broadbent

Cover Illustration by Ina Wong: artstation.com/inawong

Typographic & Interior Design by Carissa Broadbent

Editing by Nick Bowman.

Editing by Kate Bowie: katebowiewrites@gmail.com

Additional developmental editing by Noah Sky: noahcsky@gmail.com

For my Writing on the Wall crew.
This book is yours, and it would not exist without you.

PROLOGUE

It begins with two souls who find themselves suddenly, utterly alone.

Evaluate. Judge. Act.

    The young man let the words echo like a second heartbeat.

He did not allow himself to acknowledge the possibility that he was going to die here. Not even as he slipped on blood, stumbled over bodies, mentally counted the men and women that had followed him into the city but would not follow him out. Not even as possibility crept closer and closer to certainty.

He was twenty-one years old. He had been in too many battles to count. But this? This wasn't a battle. This was a slaughter.

Evaluate. Judge. Act.

He pressed his back against the outer wall of a townhome, peering around the corner down a narrow city street. The roads were densely populated with crooked little houses that squished up against each other. Terrified faces peered from within them.

Mothers tore their children away from the sight of steel and magic and fire mingling in a terrible, deadly dance.

Deep beneath his thoughts, the voice chuckled.

Shut up, he told it, and launched himself back into the fight. He flew through the streets, whispering to the flames beneath his breath, coaxing them to him. They complied eagerly, furling around his hands and up his arms in spirals. He yanked them out of houses and off the streets, away from thin skin and fragile bones.

But there was too much. It consumed his energy and his focus. So much so that he didn't even have time to evade when a sharp pain split his back. The warmth of blood melded with stinging, salty sweat.

Act, act, act.

He grit his teeth and spun in a well-practiced counter before the rebel could land another strike. The body hit the ground in a clumsy tangle of limbs. He didn't look at her face, grateful that it was covered by a mass of curly brown hair.

As if awakened by the smell of fresh blood, the voice leapt inside of him. *{Kill it!}* it hissed, throwing itself against the surface of his thoughts like claws gouging at a door.

No —

He paused a split second too long. A force collided with him, knocking him back into an alley. Instinct kicked in. His hands were already drawing his blade, poised at his attacker's throat before he even turned his head to see —

"Don't you dare kill me." A warm, familiar voice murmured against his ear. "There are hundreds of rebels here who would love to do that instead."

That voice. It was, in that moment, the most beautiful thing the young man had ever heard.

He exhaled a silent sigh of relief, dropping his dagger as he turned. "Where the hell did you go?"

The young woman greeted him with an unwavering, steely gaze. Her irises were so fair that they melted into the whites of her eyes, leaving pinpoint dark pupils watching him in an assessing stare. Soot and blood painted her cheeks, her white braids tangled and dirty. A coat hung from her shoulders that had once been blue. Now it was so spattered with red that it edged on purple, the stains crawling over the crescent moon insignia on her lapel.

The sight sent his heart lurching to his throat. "How much of that is yours?"

"How much of *that* is yours?" The woman grabbed him by the shoulders and turned him around.

"That bad?"

"Very bad."

"Wonderful," he grumbled. He'd hoped the wound wouldn't be as deep as it felt.

She turned him around, hands still gripping his arms, her face inches from his. "You're bleeding a lot. You don't feel that?"

Not anymore. He shook his head. The movement tilted the floor, as if the world was a ship preparing to capsize. He imagined the sun on the back of his jacket cleaved in two by whatever blade sliced his back, the halves sliding with him, separating in the sky—

"Hey." Her fingers were at his face, snapping in front of his eyes. She looked angry, but he knew her well enough to know that it only masked her fear. Just as she had been when they had ventured into the forest for the first time as children, when they had wandered around lost for hours until—

"*Wake. Up.*" This time she shook him, too. "Stay with me."

He felt something encroach at the edge of his thoughts — a brush of her presence. Her magic reaching into his mind. "Don't do that," he growled.

The voice chuckled something disgusting, far away.

"I'm just checking on you." Her presence retreated as the line between the young woman's eyebrows deepened. "I went to the west end of the city. So many dead."

So many dead.

The young man blinked away the image of the little faces peering from shattered windows.

"We have to retreat," he said. "There are too many towns-people here for this. I can take the fire as we go."

"Their leadership is here. Retreating isn't an option. Too good of an opportunity."

He almost laughed. Bitter and ugly and humorless. *"Opportunity?* No, this is—"

"They chose to start this here, in one of their cities," she spat. "If they want to shit in their own beds, they can lie in it."

The words hit him like a strike to his gut. He wasn't sure if it was her callousness or the blood loss that made his stomach clench with nausea.

"These are still civilians," he shot back. "Rebellion or no. These are *people.*"

"We have options."

"Not with what I've seen."

"We have *you,*" she whispered. One hand traveled to his face, hovering over the muscles that clenched his jaw. *"We have you."*

A shiver shuddered through his deepest recesses. He stood there, lips parted but unable to conjure words strong enough to match his revulsion.

The best he managed was, *"Hell* no."

Her mouth thinned. If he had been paying attention, he might have noticed her caress migrating to his temple, pushing aside strands of black hair.

"We don't have a choice," she whispered. "Please."

"No. We're in the middle of a city. And—"

And what? And so many things. Too many to encapsulate in words. Just the thought of it prickled shards of icy horror in his veins.

"I'm sorry," he said, quietly. "But the destruction would be—and I–"

It was probably the first time he had ever failed to do what was in the Orders' best interest. But all he could think about were those little faces in the windows.

She looked for a moment as if she might push further, but then something shifted, softened, in her expression. Her lips twisted into a sad smile. "That bleeding heart will get you killed one day, you know."

Maybe, the young man thought.

{Likely,} the voice whispered.

There was a long silence. And then, finally, she simply said, "I am your commanding officer."

He almost questioned his sanity, questioned whether he heard her correctly. "You're — what?"

A laugh skittered through his thoughts, jeering at the dread that clenched his heart.

"Targis is dead. I saw him." She looked up at him with bright eyes. Reflections of flames glittered in their dampness — the only sign of emotion. "With him gone, I am your commanding officer. And I command you to utilize the full extent of your abilities."

Her words split him in two, a pain so sharp that it felt as if someone had grabbed the top of his spine and ripped it through his skin. *"Nura—"*

"I command you to do it."

And that was when he noticed her hand at his temple. When he noticed her magic reaching further than that, into his thoughts, to that door that he had slammed shut, nailed shut, *bolted* shut—

"No."

The word was the only thing that he could choke out in one ragged gasp, the rest dying in his throat as he felt her reach deeper into his mind.

It was the one thing she swore she'd never do.

He threw whatever remaining strength he had into reinforcing his mental walls, but he would never be as strong when it came to these things as she was. Her magic was born in the world of thoughts and shadows, while his was far more suited to brighter, more immediate forces. Especially now, with more and more blood rolling down his back, and that creature fighting desperately to get out.

"Stop—" A burst of pain blinded him. He felt her pry open that door, crushing it, discarding it.

5

Her lips formed the word, "Sorry," but if she said it aloud, he didn't hear it.

{So sweet,} the voice whispered, so near and so real that goosebumps rose on the crest of his ear. *{You always try so hard.}*

Fuck you.

His hands dropped from her arms. Fingers stretched. Then clenched, releasing a cacophony of cracks.

If he was capable of speaking, he would have told her that he would never — *never* — forgive her for this.

But he was not capable of speaking. He was not capable of anything but hurling himself against his own mental wall, over and over again, in a desperate attempt to regain control.

Even as it slipped further from his reach.

Even as his palms opened and he was blinded by fire and fire and fire.

ACROSS THE SEA

The little girl was amazed by how quiet it all was.

The slavers had come in the middle of the night, yanking her little village from a deep slumber. Like most of her kin, many of her nightmares revolved around this moment. At some point, it had become an omnipresent danger constantly lurking in the back of her mind.

But the real thing was different than the nightmares.

She had always imagined that there would be more noise — more screaming, more shouting, more drawn-out fighting. But the men in the wide-brimmed hats and their team of mercenaries had struck the youngest and strongest men first, hobbling them in their beds before they had a chance to cause trouble. And even the ones who did fight back were surprisingly quiet, their battles little more than muffled grunts and blunt steel, ending shockingly quickly with trembling final gasps.

The girl's mother, their leader, had not spoken to her as they were woken by the sounds of horses' hooves and crying wives. Her only comfort was a quiet hand on the child's shoulder. When they had stepped outside the door, she had taken one look at her village — her people, or what was left of them after such a swift destruction — and offered terms to the slavers.

The girl was no more than thirteen, but she knew that her mother was trying to save her people from the inevitable. She also knew that it wouldn't work. Aside from her mother's brief, hushed commands, no one said a word.

That is, until the little girl stepped forward, looked up at one of the slavers and those glinting dark eyes, and said, "You can get a better price for me."

The words slipped from her teeth before she even fully realized what she was doing. The slaver was less intimidating than she had imagined. He was short, and fat. His long leather coat was wrinkled and strained to contain the pudgy width of his shoulders, and strained further still as he shifted to look at her. She knew that he was taking in her unusual appearance: her skin and hair that was totally white, completely sapped of color, while splotches of what would have been her natural deeper coloring crawled across her skin. One green eye, one white. Streaks of dark mingling in silver hair.

Behind her, she heard her mother take a step forward, as if to stop her.

She didn't turn.

"You can get a better price for me," she said again. It took every bit of her strength not to let her voice crack or tremble. She focused on the wobbling of the fat slaver's lower chin. One tendril of her mind reached out towards his, listening for glimmers of his thoughts. His greed smelled like sweat in the air.

"Maybe if you were complete," he grumbled, after a moment. He took a strand of white hair between his fingers, then lifted her chin, turning her cheek, examining the swath of tan that encroached on the right side of her face. "But this —"

"What?" Another slaver joined the first, his black hat crumpled in one hand as he wiped sweat from his brow. This one was thin, all knobby joints and gaunt cheeks. The girl forced herself to recognize how funny they looked together. Fat and thin. Tall and short. Like clowns. Not monsters.

"Look at this one."

"She's Fragmented. Not a real Valtain. And too young to whore anyway."

The fat slaver shrugged. "By some standards."

Even with her magic, the girl rarely felt even a hint of her mother's tightly-held emotions. But at this, a shock of furious panic shook her like a thunderclap.

Still, she did not turn.

"She's not worth anything," the thin slaver said. "Maybe if she was complete."

Words tangled in the girl's throat. The men were starting to turn away from her, looking to their soldiers, who shackled the men at the front of the village. In a panic, she opened her palms and a butterfly of light flew from her hands, batting through the air until it collided with the fat slaver's face.

"Look," she said, desperately. Another butterfly. And another. "I am a Wielder. I can perform. You can get a good price for me. Better than the mines."

The two slavers watched the butterflies rise into the sky, disappearing against the unbroken silver moon. They looked at each other, communicating wordlessly.

"She'll be pretty, eventually," the fat one said, slowly. "Young, but... you ever buy unripened fruit at the market?"

The thin slaver crossed his arms over his chest, surveying her in a way that made her skin feel as if ants were crawling up her spine.

"She can cook, too. Clean. Very obedient." Her mother's voice came from behind her. Suddenly, it become so much more difficult to remain composed.

Now both slavers crossed their arms. The little girl's eyes flicked between them.

"Fine." The thin one let his arms drop, yanking his hat back onto his head. "Take her. We'll sell her in En-Zaheer to one of those peacocks."

"Wait!" the girl cried, as the slaver grabbed her arm. "My mother must come too."

The slaver scoffed, as if this didn't even dignify a response.

"Please. I need her. She—"

The thin slaver's eyes flashed, and the girl felt his anger curdle in the air like rotten milk. He opened his mouth, but before he could speak, her mother was at her side, hands clutching her shoulders.

"She is young and afraid," she said, quickly. "She doesn't know what she's saying. I understand that I cannot go with her."

Her mother spun the girl around to face her, hands still braced on her shoulders. For the first time since this horrible nightmare began, the girl allowed herself to meet her mother's eyes directly. They were bright amber-green, identical to the little girl's colored right eye. In that split second, she took in her mother's familiar face — high, regal cheekbones, dark brows that framed a piercing, calm gaze. She had never seen her mother visibly scared or shaken. Even today, that did not change.

"None of us can follow where you go, Tisaanah. But you have everything you need to survive. And listen to me — *use* it."

The girl nodded. Her eyes burned.

"Never look back. And never question stepping forward and saying, 'I deserve to live.'"

"*You* deserve to live," the girl whimpered. The mines were a death sentence. Everyone knew it.

A glimmer of sad uncertainty rippled across her mother's features. "None of that," she said, flicking away the girl's tears before they fell. And that was all she offered, before she pressed her lips to her daughter's forehead in one final goodbye kiss.

She straightened, lifting her chin as she looked from one slaver to the other, then back to her people, who lined up bound by rope and chain. In that moment, she had never looked more a queen, noble and breathtaking even as she offered her hands for binding.

The fat trader took the little girl away, dragging her into the back of their cart, while the thin one led away the rest of her village. She sat among bags of grain and boxes of kitschy merchants' goods, back pressed to the splintering boards. Soon, her friends and family were silver-dipped silhouettes in the distance — one long line, backs straight, chins raised, the unmistakable form of her mother at the front of them all.

Behind them, the village burned in smears of garish orange flames.

She never thought it would be so fast — so quiet. It took less than an hour for her entire life to change, disintegrating into the night like one of her shimmering butterflies.

"No tears for your mother, huh?" One of the mercenaries peered over his shoulder, letting out a scoff. "Cold."

"They're always like that," the slaver said, matter-of-factly. "Unsentimental."

You did this, the little girl wanted to scream. *You refused to take her with me.* She wanted to shout, she wanted to sob. She wanted to let herself collapse on this dirty cart floor, pound the wood with useless fists, weep until she vomited.

But instead, she was still, her back straight and her chin raised, pantomiming her mother's stone strength. She bit down so hard on the inside of her lip that warm iron flooded over her tongue. The echo of her mother's kiss burned on her forehead.

You have what you need to survive, her mother had told her. The girl had no possessions other than her sweaty nightgown, but she knew she had tools. On that long, dark ride to the city, she counted them, over and over again. She had her unusual appearance, looks that might one day turn into something worth desiring. She was a good listener and a fast learner. She had her magic — silver butterflies and pretty illusions, yes, but more importantly, she had the ability to *feel* what people wanted of her.

And, most valuable of all, she had the gift that her mother had given her: permission to do whatever it took to survive, without apology, without regret. She would do absolutely anything, except cry.

PART ONE:
WINGS

CHAPTER ONE

EIGHT YEARS LATER

1*, 2, 3...*

When I danced, I never stopped counting.

The truth was, I was a terrible dancer. I wasn't sure that I believed in the concept of talent at all, but even if I did, I could recognize that I didn't have any. At least not when it came to dancing. But talent, I had learned, was optional. It could be substituted with long nights and early mornings, bleeding feet, obsessively memorized footwork.

No one needed talent when you had brute force. And, despite my willowy size and my unassuming doe-eyed smile, I had more brute force than anyone.

...4, 5, 6...

Twirl.

And — fire.

I smiled at the merchant man seated in front of me, opening my palms to let blue fire unfurl from between my fingers. The audience, Esmaris's party guests, *ooh*-ed and *aah*-ed appreciatively. There were several hundred people mingling about the large marble room, all dressed in their finest clothing. Lots of gold thread and floaty, sheer chiffon. Lots of white. Rich people loved white, perhaps because it proved that they had the money to spend on a small army of slaves to keep it clean.

All of those white-clad bodies bent towards me in that moment, rapt, as I unleashed a wave of my signature translucent butterflies into the air. Four dozen of them fluttered to the high ceiling and disappeared, unraveling into puffs of blue smoke.

All except for three.

Three fluttered to three separate men in the audience, circling their necks, flitting against their cheeks before they disappeared.

Every one of the men flinched as the butterfly approached, then laughed with varying degrees of enthusiasm when they realized they felt like nothing but air. Their gazes had been glued to me this entire time, and I could tell that they were itching for the opportunity to throw coins in my direction, if I used what I had correctly.

I focused on the youngest one first, a merchant man perhaps only a few years older than myself. He had something to prove. New money. I danced closer to him, and as my fingers reached out to flirtatiously touch his shoulder, my mind did too — tasting the air for his thoughts, his preferences. This one, it turned out, had no preference for me at all. In fact, I could feel his attention being constantly pulled toward Serel, one of Esmaris's handsomer bodyguards, who lingered in the far corner of the room.

That was fine. He didn't have to want to screw me to serve my purposes. If anything, it made things easier for me — he would be overly eager to prove his virile interest in a scantily-clad dancer like myself, rather than a scantily-clad guard like Serel. And he wouldn't try to get me alone once the dance ended.

The strings of the harp plinked on, but there might as well have been no music at all. My dance was memorized. My feet didn't stop moving as I coiled my arms around the merchant's neck. "I left something over here," I purred, pulling my fingers from behind the edge of his jaw and revealing one of my twinkling butterflies. "She likes you. Would you like to keep her?"

The young merchant smiled at me. He was handsome, with

curly brown hair and big amber eyes framed by lashes so long that they made me jealous.

He and Serel would make a beautiful couple, really.

"I would," he said, staring at me too intently, even though his thoughts told me that he had no interest in keeping her at all. What he *did* have an interest in was showing that he could hold his own in this room of wildly rich and wildly successful people — even against Esmaris himself. He lifted a hand as if to take the glowing butterfly from me, but I twirled backwards, smirking at him coyly.

"What will you give me for her?"

I caught a glimpse of Esmaris over the young man's shoulder. He was clad in a shock of color — bright red — which stood out in a sea of white. He didn't need to prove his wealth or status, after all, with his choice of clothing. But even beyond the shade of his shirt, there was still something about him that separated him from the crowd. A certain cool, authoritative air, like he strode through the world expecting it to bend to him. It usually did.

He was engaged in a conversation with one of his guests, looking vaguely bored. His hair — black but streaked with grey — was bound back in a low ponytail, with one unruly strand that he kept sweeping behind his ear. Mid-movement, he glanced up to meet my eyes. Our eye contact lasted for a fraction of a second before he looked back to his guest, unconcerned.

Good. He wasn't usually possessive, but better to be careful.

"You already have my admiration," the young merchant said, and it physically pained me not to roll my eyes.

"Valuable indeed," I cooed instead. "But so is she, isn't she?" The butterfly's wings trembled against my fingertips. I closed my fingers around it, and when I opened them, a little glass version of my illusion sat in my palm. For a moment I couldn't help but admire it, proud of myself. This was a new addition to my routine.

The merchant's eyebrows arched, and I felt his impressed surprise rippling the inches between our faces.

"For you."

"That is incredible." The man's pleasant smile split into a full-on grin. In that awestruck gaze, I could see what he might have looked like as a child, enthralled by some circus acrobat or shiny bauble. When those beautiful eyes met mine again, we shared a moment of genuine connection.

And then he reached into his pocket. "For *you*." He took the glass butterfly from my hand, and in its place, dropped five gold coins into my palm.

Five.

Gold.

I blinked down at them, momentarily speechless. I wasn't a fool — I knew that there was a reason why he dropped the pieces so loudly into my hand, why he was doing this while everyone's eyes were on us. It was bold, even rude, of him to give me money without so much as seeking a glance of wordless permission from Esmaris, never mind money like *this*. Many did not like their slaves to have money at all, and more still did not like that money to come from other men. In both of these ways, Esmaris was quite liberal, but *five gold* was skirting the bounds of respectability by any measure.

One thousand and two.

I wasn't expecting to hit that number that night, or the night after, or after that. I was lucky if I left one of Esmaris's parties with ten silver pieces.

One thousand and two. One thousand and two.

"Thank you," I choked out, forgetting to be coquettish. I closed the coins in my palm, relishing their weight as I slipped them into the tiny silk purse at my hip. "Thank you."

The man smiled and nodded at me, oblivious to what he had just done for me.

Excitement and elation bubbled up inside of me. For a moment, I was lost in it. Then the sound of the harp came roaring back, and I realized that I almost missed my cue.

I wanted to jump up and down and spin around and laugh.

But I had hours of performing left to do. So I began to count again.

1, 2, 3, 4…

Before I twirled away, I ran my fingertips along the merchant's cheek, through his admirable thick curls. And I smiled, and smiled, and smiled. As I cascaded across the marble floor, Serel caught my eye from across the room and cocked his head, asking me a silent question. In response, I only grinned. Perhaps he would know what it meant.

One thousand and two.

One thousand gold was the price of my freedom.

CHAPTER TWO

"One thousand." Serel echoed the number that had been circling my thoughts all night, letting out a whistle of amazement. He ran a hand through blond hair, pushing it away from his face. "You did it. How did you even manage that?"

"Eight years," I murmured. Mostly to myself, because a part of me still couldn't believe it. "Eight years of work."

I folded my hands over my stomach, blinking up at the ceiling. Serel and I lay splayed out on the floor of my modest bedchamber, exhausted. The party had gone on until the small hours of the morning, and while Serel had clearly been ready to retreat to his own room and crawl into bed, I dragged him to mine. I had to tell *someone*, and Serel was the only one I trusted enough.

I wouldn't sleep that night, I already knew. I was so excited that my hands still trembled now, hours later. It killed me that I couldn't meet with Esmaris tonight, dump that pile of gold on his desk, and walk away. It would probably be another day or two before he had the time to arrange a private meeting with me.

"He never told *me* I could buy my freedom," Serel grumbled.

"I asked him."

"Of course you did."

"Well... demanded, I suppose."

"Of *course* you did."

I let out a small chuckle. Esmaris had owned me for perhaps a year at that point, and I recalled feeling rich the first time I performed at one of his parties, where guests tossed a few silver coins at me here and there. Over the course of the year, I hoarded them until I had a grand total of fifty silver pieces — half a single gold piece. To me, a little girl from a village that dealt mostly in trade, that was a mind-boggling amount of money. The moment I got my fiftieth piece, I marched up to Esmaris, thrust the pile of coins into his hands, and announced that I was buying myself back from him. "Surely this is a good price," I had told him, careful to sound much more confident than I felt. I had already learned by then that everything in this life needed to be a performance.

I was lucky. That stunt probably would have gotten me whipped with any other owner. Now, I looked back and cringed because I didn't even realize how lucky I was — lucky that Esmaris was, and had always been, genuinely fond of me. He had looked down at me then with a smile twitching at the corners of his mouth, even as his dark gaze remained typically sharp.

"You are worth far more than fifty silvers, Tisaanah," he had said.

"Seventy-five, then," I countered, and he had sat back in his chair and crossed his arms over his chest.

"You are worth one thousand gold," he told me, at last. "That can be the price of your freedom."

At the time, I couldn't even comprehend that kind of wealth. Even all these years later, that was still a struggle — even now that I physically had it in my possession.

I watched the slave trade closely in the years since. I now knew that one thousand gold was actually grossly over-value for what I was. I had seen real Valtain, with uninterrupted albino skin and pure silver hair, go for nine hundred. No matter how hard I worked at my magic or my dances, I was still Fragmented.

That one green eye and splotches of golden skin reduced my value significantly. But I wanted my freedom more than anything, and if Esmaris wanted one thousand for that, well then, I would just have to make it happen.

And I did. Somehow, I did.

"He was handsome," Serel mused. "That guest. You should have found him afterwards and thanked him." He caught my eye and grinned, winking.

I scoffed. "That was all for show. He was more interested in you than me."

"Really?" Serel sat up, shocked. "Why didn't you tell me earlier? That never happens."

"You don't want to get tangled up in that."

"Yes I do!"

"Fine. I'm sorry. I was distracted." I turned my head to meet his tired blue-eyed stare. "At least now you know for next time he's here."

"He probably won't be invited back, after that display," he sighed. What both of us knew but didn't say aloud was that it was probably for the better. Dalliances with the wealthy were extremely risky for people like us. I had learned that the hard way, once, and was rewarded with a broken heart and ten lashes to the backs of my thighs. I could still count every individual strike in the scars.

If Serel was ever caught with a wealthy *man?* Death. No question.

There was a long silence. I had thought that Serel had finally dozed off, until he asked, quietly, "So what now? The Orders?"

I nodded. "The Orders."

"I'll be honest," he whispered, "I never thought it would happen."

Neither did I, I wanted to say, but as a rule I didn't dignify uncertainty out loud.

"I'm proud of you, Ti. If anyone deserves it —"

"You deserve it. All of us deserve it."

Deserve. I hated that word, even though I had spent so much of my life clinging to it.

"We'll get there." He said it so simply, so matter-of-factly.

I sat up, swinging my legs beneath me, looking down at him as he lay there with his hands behind his head. It was always so easy for him to assume the best in people, in life. At first I had thought it was a mask he slipped on, the way I slipped into my flirty dances and practiced my confidence until it was a begrudging part of me. But soon I learned that he really meant it — really *believed* it. Even though his story was just as bloody as mine.

I had recognized that kindness in him the very first time I saw him. I had traveled with Esmaris on a short business trip to a neighboring city, and I had sat behind him and watched as rows of slaves were marched through the marketplace. It was awful. The pain and terror in the air were unbearable, tearing through my head and my muscles as if I was experiencing the worst day in the lives of dozens of people, all at once — and on top of that, vividly reliving mine, too.

But even through that tangle of emotions, Serel had caught my eye. He had stopped to comfort a young girl beside him — younger than I was when I stood in her place — and even though it had earned him a shout and a vicious lash from the slaver, he had still offered that child such a genuine smile. Serel was tall and muscular, but all I could see were those big watery blue eyes, those features that were so kind and delicate that they were almost childlike.

If Esmaris did not purchase him, he would have been bought by a mercenary faction. He would have become one of the men that yanked my family from their beds that night, years ago. And I couldn't bear to see that happen. "What about that one?" I had whispered to Esmaris. "He is just what you're looking for."

If Esmaris had given thought to why I had such an interest in this one handsome young man, or had any assumptions about why that might be the case, he didn't show it. After a moment of thought, he raised his palm, and Serel was his.

I had spent a long time in his bed that night, as if he expected compensation for ceding to my request. But it was worth it, because Serel quickly became the best friend I had ever had — before slavery or after.

Now, I watched my friend with a lump rising in my throat, suddenly emotional for reasons I couldn't explain. For a moment, the idea of giving him my money — buying *his* freedom — crossed my mind. He was better than I was. Deserved it more.

"I'll come back, you know," I murmured. "For all of you. I'll have connections, I'll have resources —"

He reached up and patted my knee, as if he understood the guilt churning through my stomach. "I know you will."

EVENTUALLY POOR SEREL couldn't take it anymore and wandered back to his own room to get some much-needed sleep, leaving me alone in mine. I was exhausted, but I knew there was no use even trying to rest. Instead, I paced.

This was a slightly dizzying endeavor, considering that my room was only barely larger than my bed. Still, it was clean and well kept, with nice furniture and a few decorations. Esmaris sometimes brought me little gifts from his travels, which lined the shelves around my room. But my most treasured possessions were the ones that came from Ara.

Ara, a little island thousands of miles away, primarily known as the home of the Twin Orders: the Order of Midnight and the Order of Daybreak.

Ara, the place I would be going the minute I purchased my freedom.

That thought — or the pacing, or exhaustion, or all three — began to make me nauseous. I dropped to the floor, yanking a worn wooden box from the bottom of my bookshelf. In it were some pieces of junk (a stone from Ara's beaches, a few pieces of paper with circular markings scribbled on them) and several books. I pulled out the one with the plain blue cover, unmarked other than the silver moon and gold sun insignias foiled on the front.

The symbols of the Orders.

I threw it open and flipped through its pages. My fingertips traced over the pictures, the raised ink, the still-unfamiliar writing, as I practiced my Aran beneath my breath. I paused at one sprawling illustration that covered a set of facing pages: a drawing of founders of the Order of Midnight and the Order of Daybreak, Rosira and Araich Shelaene. Blues and purples swirled around Rosira, framing her white hair against a moon silhouette, while fire circled Araich. Their palms touched across the seam of the binding.

Rosira represented the Valtain, magic Wielders with albino skin and white hair, who comprised the Order of Midnight. And Araich represented the Solarie, non-Valtain magic Wielders who comprised the Order of Daybreak. Their magic complemented each other even as it contradicted, like two sides of the same coin.

The book, along with all of my trinkets from Ara, had been a gift from Zeryth Aldris. He was a traveler from Ara and a high-ranking member of the Orders who would stay at Esmaris's estate as a guest for a few days at a time. I was immediately fascinated by him. I had never met anyone who looked anything like me before, even though, unlike me, his colorless skin and white hair were uninterrupted — a full Valtain. I took to following him around like a lost puppy, but he was kind to me and seemed to enjoy indulging my curiosities. I would listen to him for hours as he would tell me in fractured Thereni about the Orders and their history.

And then, during the days, I watched as Zeryth mingled with Esmaris and his nobles. I observed the way people smiled at him, deferred to him, looked at him with the same fearful respect that many reserved only for Esmaris himself.

Something had clicked into place, then. As a member of the Order of Midnight, Zeryth had resources. He had support. He had protection. And most importantly, he had power.

Everything I needed to make my survival worth what it cost my family. Everything I needed to *become* something.

"Could I become a member of the Orders?" I had asked Zeryth, later, eyeing my hands and the splotches of sand-colored skin that crawled across two of my fingers.

"Certainly," he replied, giving me a dazzling smile that made my fourteen-year-old self melt. "Fragmented or no, you are still a Valtain."

Well. That was all the encouragement I needed.

I threw myself into it from that day on. I researched the Orders obsessively. I practiced Aran in whispers at night, teaching myself what I could of their strange, frustrating language. Zeryth would visit several other times over the years, and with each return, he would bring me little gifts from the Orders and put up with my incessant questions.

He had promised me that if I made it to Ara, he would introduce me to the Orders. I hoped he was ready to make good on that promise.

A shiver ran through my body, and I looked down to see that my hands were trembling around the yellow pages.

No. No sleep tonight, that was for sure.

Instead I stayed awake until the beginnings of dawn seeped through my curtains. I read every book Zeryth had given me, cover to cover. I practiced every Aran phrase I knew, and repeated ones I didn't until they sounded secure on my tongue. I filled my brain with plans until there was no room left for fear or uncertainty.

Hours. Only hours remained, before everything I knew would change.

I hoped they were ready for me.

I hoped I was ready for them.

CHAPTER THREE

One would think that after all these years, I would have stopped finding Esmaris so breathlessly intimidating. I had lived with him for seven years, and I had perhaps seen him in more — one could say — compromising positions than likely anyone else had. But still, sometimes I would walk into a room and be momentarily stunned by him, by the way that it seemed like all of the air in a room bent towards him.

This was one of those moments.

I watched his back silhouetted against the window of his study. Like the night of the party, he wore red, though this time his jacket was a deep burgundy brocade. His hands were clasped in front of him, the line of his shoulders perfectly broad and square. The man never slouched.

He didn't look at me.

I told myself that I had nothing to be nervous about. This was a straightforward business transaction. Nothing more. Nothing less. Serel was stationed outside the door, as Esmaris's favored bodyguard, and I clung to the memory of the brief, encouraging smile he had given me as I walked into the room.

Still. My palms were drenched in sweat.

Say something, I willed Esmaris.

"One thousand." As if he heard me. He still didn't turn around. "That is significant."

"Significantly more than the fifty silver pieces I offered you the first time," I replied lightly, letting my smile seep into my voice but, to my relief, none of my anxiety.

"Indeed." Esmaris turned at last, appraising me with sharp, dark eyes. That single unruly strand of peppered black hair hung in front of one eye. It was the only thing out of place in his appearance. Everything else, from the fit of his clothing to the edge of his cropped beard to the smoothness of his bound hair, was impeccable. He had to be nearing sixty by now, but he had the stance of a much younger man.

I reached a tendril into the unspoken words between us, feeling for his reaction, his thoughts. He was always difficult to read, stony and unyielding. Still, I could occasionally catch glimmers from him, especially when he was pleased with me.

Now, nothing.

"I actually have one thousand and two," I added. "But I'm willing to give you the extra, since you've done so much for me." Riding the line between a joke and the truth, flirtation and gratitude, stroking his ego and reminding him why he liked me.

No reaction. A hurt that I didn't want to examine too closely flitted through me — a small, small part of me that, for whatever reason, had wanted him to be impressed.

"You have it?" He jerked his chin toward the bag I had brought with me, which rested near my feet. It was surprisingly heavy. It turned out one thousand gold coins was a lot of metal.

"Yes."

"Show me."

I did as he asked, bringing the bag to his desk and opening it. As soon as it touched the table, he yanked it upside down in one movement, dumping the coins over the desk. If I had closed my eyes, they might have sounded like bells. Some tumbled off the desk and onto the floor.

We stood in agonizing silence until those twinkling sounds finally quieted.

"Should I make you count them?" he said.

"I will if you wish. It's all there."

"This is a significant amount of money. How did you earn it?"

How did I earn it? What didn't I do? I did whatever I had to. Whatever I could. "I made myself valuable wherever possible," I said.

And look at what I did. Even the moments I weren't proud of were worth it, for this. A pleased smile crept to the edges of my mouth.

"And what," Esmaris hissed, "does that mean?"

My smile promptly disappeared.

Shit.

"I learned from you," I said, smoothly, pacing forward. "Business is just a matter of—"

"You whored for this money."

His revulsion — his *fury* — split the air so violently that I felt like I had been slapped across the face. The ugliness of the word, the way he hurled it at me, left me momentarily speechless.

I had never even said it that way to myself. It hit harder than I thought it would.

"No, I—"

Only once. I pushed away the whisper, reminding myself that I had no regrets about what I had done.

"You and I both know that I am not *stupid*. You could not have gotten this money any other way."

"I worked for it. Whoever who would hire me. Danced, conjured, scrubbed floors—"

That was the truth. I did work for it. And only one hundred of those coins came from that single night. The rest of it was hours and hours of sweat.

"Coppers, maybe. But this?" He let out a scoff so violent that I felt flecks of spittle dust my cheek. "I let you earn your silvers for dancing. But I never allowed you to whore for it. To embarrass me that way."

"I would never do that to you," I replied, acting insulted at the thought.

"One thousand gold pieces should have taken you fifteen years," he shot back. "Twenty, even."

Fifteen years.

I realized in that moment that Esmaris had never intended for me to earn his absurd price — at least, not until I was either too old for his tastes or he was too old to make use of me anyway.

His anger pounded in my ears, my head, beneath my skin, but it was slowly being replaced by my own.

"I met your price. You can buy a real Valtain with that money, if it suits you. One more beautiful and more talented than me."

"Slaves don't have the luxury of bargains, and I don't need your money," Esmaris snarled. "You forgot what you are."

My stomach fell through my feet.

"Are you aware of how well I treat you?" He straightened, eyes narrowed, clasping his hands behind his back. Silence. He expected an answer, but I suddenly didn't trust myself to open my mouth.

I don't need your money.

I had one plan. One goal. He had kicked out the foundation, and I felt that at any moment, my soul would topple.

"Are you?"

"Yes, Esmaris."

"And yet." His voice lowered so slightly that the change was barely audible. "You've gone through such lengths to leave."

All at once, it hit me. The air stank of it — the hidden under-current twining with Esmaris's anger:

Hurt.

We stared at each other. I watched the single wrinkle between his eyebrows. The one sign of guarded vulnerability.

This was the man who gave me so many scars, who took away my freedom, who crushed me and bent me and beat me. But he was also the man who remembered my favorite color, who once stayed up with me for hours after a bad nightmare. Who had smiled down at me with an odd sort of pride the day I had demanded my freedom from him.

I leaned forward until my palms pressed against his desk, those cold gold coins sticking to my sweaty skin.

And I just said one word: *"Please."*

He looked at me for one long moment, and I could hardly breathe.

Please, do this for me. If any part of you has ever cared for me. Please.

Then, I felt a door slam, a blanket of ice silencing Esmaris's tenuous conflict.

"Get off of my desk. Kneel."

I don't need your money.

Gods, what was I going to do?

"On your knees."

I dropped so hard that the polished wood floor bruised my knees.

I don't need your money.

His voice and the shattering of my goals echoed so loudly in my ears that I could hear nothing else.

I didn't hear Esmaris's boots walk across the room, or return, standing behind me.

I don't need your money.

I didn't hear the lethal snap crack through the air.

But, even through my haze, I certainly *did* feel the pain tear across my back, splitting me in two. My throat released a gasp, a whimper.

Crack.

Two.

Crack.

Three.

And it kept going, and going, and going.

Crack. Crack. Crack.

Five. Ten. Twelve. Sixteen.

I don't need your money.

What was I going to do?

I refused to allow myself to scream, to cry, even though I bit so hard on my lip that it drew blood. Just like I had that night, years ago — the night when I had abandoned my family, my mother, because she believed I could do something more. *Be* something more.

Crack.

Twenty.

But she had been wrong, because Esmaris was going to kill me.

This thought solidified slowly into certainty through the fog of my fading consciousness.

He was going to kill me because I had made a critical miscalculation. I had naively thought that his twisted, confusing affection would help me escape. Instead, it would crush me, because Esmaris only possessed or destroyed, and if he couldn't do one, he would do the other.

I wondered if Serel could hear this, through that thick door. I wondered if he would try to help me. I hoped he wouldn't. He'd be punished for it.

Crack.

Twenty-five.

Esmaris was going to kill me.

That *bastard*.

A fire lit within me. As I heard the whoosh of Esmaris raising his arm over his head, I flipped myself over, ignoring the agony that ignited as my back touched the ground.

"If you want to murder me," I spat, "you're going to look me in the eye as you do it."

Esmaris's arm was above his head, the whip slicing the air behind him, a cruel, stone wrinkle of disdain over his nose. My blood flecked his shirt, melting into the burgundy brocade. Something barely visible wavered in his face. His eyes lowered from mine.

"*Look* at me!"

I didn't make it this far just to flicker out in the night like a stifled candle. I'd *haunt* him.

Look at me, you coward. Look at my eyes, look at the eyes of the little girl that you met eight years ago. The little girl you saved and then destroyed.

Esmaris only sank deeper into his sneer, as if he could silence me by wiping me from existence.

Crack.

Twenty-six. I brought my arms up to cover my face, but didn't blink, not even as that barb nearly tore the tip of my nose.

"*Look. At. Me.*"

You will see my eyes in the darkness every night, every time you blink, every time you look at the girl who will replace me…

Twenty-seven. My forearms were on fire. Darkness blurred the edges of my vision.

LOOK AT ME.

And then, everything stopped.

Esmaris's chin snapped towards me. His arm froze. That dark gaze met mine in one jerking movement, as if pulled by a string that I held twisted around my finger, as if I had reached out with a pair of invisible hands and *forced* him to see me.

I realized, with surreal amazement, that I could feel his mind perched within my grasp. And for a single fractured second, I saw something raw, *felt* something raw, in his gaze.

There were a million moments that I might have seen in his eyes, then. Moments that I shared with a captor, or a lover, or a father, or some warped combination of the three.

Maybe I might have felt something.

But instead, I just thought about how fragile he felt beneath my invisible grasp. How sweet his fear tasted on my tongue as he realized — as we *both* realized — that I was capable of more than little butterflies.

His fear transformed into rage. His arm broke free from me, the whip lifting, the barb slicing —

And before I realized what I was doing, I yanked on that thread between us as hard as I could.

A deafening crack split the air. I cringed, thinking that it was the whip, but the pain never came.

A crash. I opened my eyes to see Esmaris stumble over a chair, toppling to his knees in front of me.

I pushed myself upright as he fell, nearly colliding with him. His extended hand almost swiped my cheek, but instead grabbed a fistful of long, silver hair, clutching it with a strength that eluded the rest of his body.

I was numb as he yanked me down to the ground with him, my palm instinctively bracing against his chest.

Look at me, my command echoed.

We both obeyed. I didn't blink, didn't look away, as I watched the fury drain from his face, leaving behind a raw sadness that stripped my flesh more viciously than those twenty-seven lashes.

"*Tisaanah —*"

I hardly heard Serel's gasp. When I raised my head, my friend was standing in the doorway, hand on the hilt of his sword, gaping at me in horror.

I must have been quite a sight: soaked in blood, my back shredded, holding the dead body of the most powerful man in Threll.

CHAPTER FOUR

"**B**anished Gods, what did he do to you?"

Serel's hands were at my shoulders.

I didn't hear him. I was still looking at Esmaris's lifeless eyes. They stared through me, past me.

"Look at me, Tisaanah."

Look at me. Look at me. Look at me.

Warm, calloused fingers tilted my chin. Serel's big, watery blue eyes were the opposite of Esmaris's in every way, and the sight of them was a gulp of fresh air that rattled through my soul.

I said the only thing that came to mind: "He's dead."

Serel flicked his gaze to Esmaris. He didn't ask me what happened. Perhaps the scene — the pile of coins on the desk, my blood, the whip, the crash that had drawn him into the room — told him everything he needed to know. But he didn't so much as flinch at the sight of the body. Sometimes I forgot that my sweet, kind friend was no stranger to death.

"Can you stand?"

I nodded but didn't move. Esmaris's clenched fist still tangled in my hair. With shaking fingers, I pulled it free. His hand was so warm that I thought he could grab me at any moment.

I killed him.

I killed Esmaris.

Me.

The terror hit me like a wave, knocking the breath from my lungs.

Serel helped me stand up. The movement set my back on fire, and I let out an involuntary whimper. Tears stung my eyes, though I refused to let them fall.

"I know," Serel murmured, voice clenched. "I know."

"What am I going to do?" I whispered.

I always had a plan, always had a goal. Even in the darkest moments of my life, I could count my options. Now I couldn't even think. Couldn't breathe.

I would never have my freedom.

Esmaris was dead.

They would know that I killed him.

I would be executed.

And so would—

My eyes shot to Serel. "You shouldn't be here. They'll know, they'll—"

"Sh," he murmured, a small, comforting noise. He was looking from Esmaris, to me, to the whip, mouth drawn into a tight line.

Think, Tisaanah, I willed myself. *Think. This isn't where it ends. It can't be.*

But my thoughts were mush. I just kept seeing the look in Esmaris's eyes as he fell. That whisper of betrayal.

I was so consumed that I didn't realize what was happening as Serel drew his sword and plunged it through Esmaris's chest. The sound it made wrenched me back to reality. A sickening, wet crunch that I knew, even in that moment, I would never be able to forget.

"Serel, what—"

"The blood could be his. Anyone could have killed him. Now they won't know who." Serel yanked his blade from Esmaris's body. More blood spurted onto the floor.

I gagged, swallowing acrid bile. Serel picked up the whip and coiled it tightly, hanging it at its place inside the closet as if it had never been touched.

The puzzle pieces began to assemble in my mind. I realized what he was doing. What *we* were doing.

I caught Serel's wrist, my fingernails digging into his skin. "This is dangerous. You shouldn't be here."

"Of course I should. We are going to fix this." He offered me a smile that, despite the blood on my back and the body at our feet, managed to be so effortless, so genuine. It boggled me. Then he looked me up and down. "Your clothes. You need something else. If you stay here, I'll go to your room—"

I looked down at myself, realizing that I was practically naked. The shredded silk of my dress barely held together. Blood ran all the way down the backs of my legs.

"I have some jackets here. In his closet."

What I didn't say: *Please please please don't leave me here with him.*

Serel nodded. He went to the closet and selected a coat that would be long enough to conceal most of my body, and, hopefully, thick and dark enough to hide the blood.

Esmaris had kept my clothes in his office, alongside his own. Another strange intimacy. I barely held off the urge to vomit again.

Serel stood behind me, coat in hand. For a moment he surveyed me in silence. "I'm going to have to bandage your back, Tisaanah. And then I'll put this on you." The pained, apologetic tone of his voice said that he knew exactly the scale of what he was asking of me.

Oh, gods.

Just the movement of putting my arms behind me knocked the breath from my lungs, made my vision go white. And that was just moving, just slightly — never mind sliding that stiff fabric over whatever was left of my skin. Never mind pulling *bandages* around it.

I can't, I can't, I can't. I never ever uttered those words, but all that damned fabric almost broke me.

"Just do it," I muttered instead, bracing myself against the edge of Esmaris's desk.

"Sorry." Serel's whisper was punctuated by the tearing of fabric.

And then, pain.

It took everything I had in me not to scream. My knees buckled, but I clung to the stability of that desk as Serel wound his makeshift bandages around my torso.

Ara, I reminded myself. *The Orders. Freedom. You will do this. You have no choice.*

The agony was so intense that I almost didn't hear Serel when he told me, what felt like ages later, to straighten. I swayed as I extended my arms so he could slide the stiff fabric of the jacket over my skin.

I was going to vomit. I was going to collapse. I was certain I would do at least one of those things, or both.

By some miracle, I didn't.

"You did it," Serel whispered, at last. "You did it."

If I could do that, I could do anything.

I still thought I might faint, but I forced myself to focus on standing straight. My eyes fell on the coins, still piled on Esmaris's desk. "We'll need some of those," I said, hoarsely.

At least they wouldn't go to waste.

Serel complied, grabbing a couple of handfuls of gold and putting it in my silk bag. Then he knelt down at Esmaris's body and unfastened the brooch at his lapel: a silver lily, his sigil.

"Smart," I wheezed, swaying. That pin served as Esmaris's blessing in his absence. He would give it to slaves or servants to represent his approval when they needed increased access.

Serel shot me a concerned glance. "You alright?"

"Yes." Maybe I could will it into truth.

"Just a little longer." He straightened, but for a moment he didn't move, staring down at Esmaris's body.

"Serel—"

"One thing."

A sneer cracked the bridge of Serel's nose as he lowered his chin and spat. The spittle rolled down our master's — former master's — cold, unmoving cheek.

"Now we can go," he said. And together, we slipped out the door.

———

I WAS NOT NORMALLY the type to unquestionably follow, but I had no choice but to trust that Serel knew what he was doing as he led me through the familiar halls of Esmaris's estate. Simply remaining upright consumed all of my focus.

"Do I look normal?" I whispered to Serel, after we nodded a greeting to another passing slave.

"You're doing great."

I felt blood rolling down the back of my legs. I wondered how long I had left before it began to pool in my steps.

"Hurry," I said, and we quickened as much as I could bear.

Soon I realized where Serel was taking me: the stables. One of Serel's fellow bodyguards, Vos, was stationed at the entrance. He grinned a greeting as we approached, which I returned as enthusiastically as I could muster. Vos was a friend, and I prayed that our relationship would be enough to distract him from how suspicious I surely looked.

"We have some terrific news today, Vos," Serel said, proudly. "Tisaanah is leaving us. She just bought her freedom."

What a good actor he was. I, on the other hand, only barely remembered to hold my smile.

Vos's entire face lit up. He'd always been like that: his emotions took over every feature with breathless enthusiasm. "Really? You finally did it?"

I nodded, faking a beam. "Told you I would."

"You sure did. Wow." Vos shook his head, visibly amazed. His happiness for me twisted a knife in my guts. I wondered if he would be punished when it was discovered that Esmaris was dead — and that Serel and I were missing.

"That's wonderful news," he said. "You'll be missed."

"You will too," I replied, meaning it. The world tilted. Serel's fingers tightened around my shoulder, disguised as an affectionate pat.

A breeze pressed my clothes to my body, and I realized that dribbles of blood were crawling down my calves. I couldn't stand here much longer.

"I need to go before sunset," I said to Serel, who immediately got the hint.

"Yes, she's too good for us now." Serel held out his palm, showing Vos Esmaris's silver lily. "He said one of the lesser horses is fine. Not the pure breeds, of course."

Vos barely looked at the sigil. "Of course, of course, just go talk to the stablemaster," he said, then looked at me and grinned. "Congratulations, Tisaanah. Good luck out there."

"You too, Vos. Good luck."

He would need luck. I tried not to think about what Vos's back would look like if he was punished for letting us go. What his body would look like hanging from the gallows.

Pull yourself together, I hissed at myself. *That isn't helping anyone.*

We didn't see the stablemaster, of course. Instead we went straight to the stalls where the workhorses were kept — the ponies and mutts that no one kept a close eye on. It was empty. Late in the day for a lot of stable hands to be around. It turned out, in a twist of bitter luck, I had picked a terrific time to accidentally murder my master.

I steadied myself against the wall as Serel selected a horse and threw a saddle over its back. After he bridled the animal and quietly opened the stall door, I held out my hand.

"I'll hold him as you get yours," I whispered.

Serel paused for a fraction of a second before nudging me out of the way. "I can't go, Tisaanah," he said, as if he were rejecting an invitation to lunch.

He and the horse continued down the hall, but I froze.

"What?"

"Sh." Serel looked at me over his shoulder. "You don't have time to waste."

"Of course you're coming."

I wasn't about to leave him here. That was simply not an option.

I hobbled after him, struggling to catch up until we were standing at the back door of the stables. I glanced outside, at the palms and ferns giving way to an unbroken blue sky tinged with the beginning of sunset. Glimpses of rippling golden grass peeked through the leaves. The famous Threllian plains.

Miles and miles that way, beyond the grasslands, there was the sea. And then across that sea was Ara.

The Orders.

I turned back to Serel, who was tightening the strap over the horse's ears. "Of course you're coming," I said again, definitively.

"Everyone knows that you wanted to buy your freedom, but I have drills in an hour. If I'm not there, they'll go looking for me. It's not enough time. Besides, we've now established that I escorted you here, leaving Esmaris temporarily unguarded. I'll go back and discover him. He had so many enemies. I could claim I saw anything."

"That will never work."

"It will work better than us both making a run for it. Someone would realize what happened within hours. This way, they might not even look for you. If they do, I can buy you at least a day."

Buy me a day. At what price? Just like Serel, always believing the best, even in the face of a much harsher reality.

"Stop being a martyr and get on the damned horse."

"You don't have time for this."

"You're right, we don't."

"You deserve every possible chance to make it. I'm not going to ruin that. I'll be fine here. I promise."

Deserve. I *hated* that word.

Serel was not the type to raise his voice. Every word he

spoke was always light and calm, and these ones were no exception. But I felt his resolve, a solid wall between us.

"Please," I begged, pulling his fingers into my palm, clutching them. I could never let them go.

I can't, I can't, I can't.

"I'm going to put you on the horse. Ready?"

I wasn't, but he did it anyway, gently lifting me by my waist. My hand felt cold where his skin used to be, and my body writhed in pain from the movement. By the time I was on the horse, the world was spinning.

"Here." He handed me his sheathed dagger, strapping its belt around my waist. Then his hand squeezed mine. "If I find out that you died in those plains, I'll kill you."

I looked down at him, at those clear eyes, more striking than ever now as they glittered with tears that wouldn't quite overflow. I thought of the day I met him for the first time. I knew now what that little slave girl must have felt like. How precious that gift of bittersweet, gentle comfort was.

There were so many things I wanted to say to him. So many that the unspoken words strangled me.

"You've got to go," he said, and pulled my face toward him, pressing his lips against my cheek. "Say hello to Ara for me."

I can't.

He sent my horse cantering, yanking me away before I was ready. The tangle in my throat released just enough for me to choke out, "I love you," but the words were lost in hooves and wind and almost-sobs that I smothered in my lungs. I would wonder countless times if he had heard me. If he, my friend, my *brother*, knew all that he meant to me.

His kiss burned on my cheek, joining the one my mother had left on my forehead all those years ago — twin scars branding me as someone who left behind the people most important to her.

I pushed through the ferns and the grasslands opened up in front of my vision, blurring from blood loss. I didn't look back. I couldn't. Otherwise I would turn around. Even as it was, a powerful part of me was dragging her fingernails into the ground, trying to crawl back to Serel, screeching in my ears, *You can't leave him, you have to go back, you can't leave him.*

But the hoofbeats quickened.

It would be worth it. I would *make* it worth it — make myself worth the sacrifice, not just to Serel, but to everyone.

And I inhaled the tears that clawed at me before they reached the surface.

I had everything I needed.

I had a handful of gold coins in my purse, enough to buy or bribe my way to Ara.

I had a power within me that was strong enough to kill one of the most feared men in Threll.

I had twenty-seven fresh scars that would never let me forget what I was capable of surviving — and I *would,* I *would* survive.

And, most powerfully of all, I had a debt to repay. I would do whatever it took, except cry.

CHAPTER FIVE

My name is Tisaanah Vytezic. I am from Threll. I am friend of Zeryth Aldris. I must speak to him.

I practiced those words obsessively, rolling the round Aran sounds on my tongue over and over again.

I whispered them to myself as my horse and I galloped across the plains in a frantic attempt to outrun the sunrise and my blood loss and the constant, looming possibility that Esmaris's forces would come searching for me.

I muttered them under my breath as I fought fever dreams, when I was at risk of collapsing, tucking myself beneath rocks and into tiny caves that hardly fit my body.

My name is Tisaanah. I am from Threll. I am friend of Zeryth Aldris.

They echoed from the plains into the forests, where my poor horse tripped and snapped a leg, and I was forced to put the beast out of its misery. I ate what I could of it that night, apologizing to it profusely the entire time.

They circled through my brain as I staggered through the forest on foot, pressing myself to trees at any sound of voices or footsteps.

I repeated them as a distraction, a reminder, during nights when I would stare at the blood on my fingers with growing concern, binding my bandages tighter and tighter to quell the bleeding.

And they shouted in a cry of triumph when I finally, days or weeks later, dragged myself out of the forest to see the beautiful, vast, powerful sea for the first time. They were momentarily quieted as everything inside of me went still at the sight.

I am friend of Zeryth Aldris. I must speak to him.

Those words lingered in the back of my mind as I stumbled through awkward interactions with nearly every sailor at the docks, trying to find someone who could take me to Ara. They spoke a different dialect of Thereni than I did. If it wasn't so frustrating, it would have been funny that I could understand them better if they were speaking Aran.

My name is Tisaanah Vytezic.

But then, they danced like a song when I finally boarded a boat, as I watched the Threllian shores shrink into the distance and let the salty air comb my hair.

I practiced them between bouts of vomiting when I grew relentlessly seasick.

I comforted myself with them when I dreamed of Serel, of the betrayal in Esmaris's dying gaze, and woke up in sweats.

When those sweats grew hotter.

When a fever overtook my thoughts, plunging me into delirium.

My name is Tisaanah, and I have abandoned everyone I love.

And I am a killer.

And I am going to die before I make it to Ara.

But I didn't die.

I was close by the time that ship docked in Ara's harbors. I only vaguely recall dragging myself out of the boat and staring up at those glistening glass towers — one of silver, one of gold — in awe.

I must have barely made it to the Orders' gates.

I'm told I collapsed when the door opened. That I choked

out, in raspy, fractured Aran, "My name is Tisaanah. I am from Threll. Friend of Zeryth Aldris. I must speaking him."

I remember the way the woman's silver hair caught in the waning sunlight, how I let out a weak, shuddering cry when she touched my back.

But that's all.

CHAPTER SIX

Chattering.

The sound circled around me, like bells twinkling the rise and fall of music.

I opened my eyes to see a silver brocade pattern through streams of light. It took a moment for my eyes to adjust enough to realize that I was looking at a patterned wall.

Gods, my neck hurt.

I was lying, mercifully, on my stomach. My body was cradled by white blankets that were thicker and softer than anything I had ever felt in Threll — though then again, in Threll, it was so hot that we would have no need for such things.

I blinked. A groan creaked from my lips.

The sound stopped. It was only when a plump woman's torso, clad in a simple blue blouse and a long, billowing skirt, entered my vision that I realized it had been a voice.

I lifted my chin, ignoring the stiff pain in my neck, just as the woman bent down to look at me. She was perhaps in her mid-thirties, with white skin and silver hair that was piled messily on top of her head, leaving some curly tendrils hanging around her round cheeks.

A Valtain.

All at once, I realized that I must be in Ara.

At the Order of Midnight.

The woman said something to me in Aran, but she spoke so quickly and my mind was so fuzzy that I let her words slip through my fingers without translating them.

The woman smiled at me, her eyes crinkling with concern.

"Tisaanah?" she said. Her voice was high and light. No wonder it sounded like bells. "Your name?"

She spoke slowly, emphasizing every word in a manner that might have been patronizing if she hadn't seemed so aggressively kind.

I nodded. "Yes."

Her smile broadened. She placed her palm on her own chest. "Willa."

"Hello," I whispered.

"Hello, de-ehr."

De-ehr. De-ehr. I prodded my brain, searching every Aran word I'd ever read. It was so much easier in writing.

Slowly, it clicked. *De-ehr. Dear.* Term of affection.

I could do this. The corners of my mouth turned up.

This small sign of comprehension was, apparently, all the encouragement that Willa needed to launch herself back into a chirpy onslaught of words. I had to force myself to follow her sentences.

"—been out for quite some time. I needed to come in here to heal you three times a day at first. You had a bad infection." She shook her head. "Very bad."

In-fect-shun.

New word. But I could gather what it meant.

I moved my arms, bracing my hands to push myself upright. I expected the movement to be met with a wall of pain, but it wasn't. Soreness, yes — but nothing compared to what I had endured for the last few weeks.

Incredible.

"I'm sure that still hurts." I looked up to see Willa staring at me with a wrinkle between her eyebrows.

"Not bad," I replied. "Thank you."

She made a small, sucking sound with her teeth, something caught between sadness and disapproval. "You poor thing. Your back was awful."

A slight, cold breeze drew my gaze to the right side of the room, which was essentially a wall of glass windows, floor to ceiling, selectively covered with layers of dusty-blue chiffon curtains. One window was cracked open slightly, allowing the sea air to slip in.

The room was small, but impeccably clean. The only furniture was my bed, a large mirror, and an armoire. All of them were simple in construction but clearly expensive, crafted of deep mahogany with silver hardware. That hardware, in fact, was the only decoration. Each piece — every knob or pull — was a little silver moon.

Another breeze. I shivered, clamping my arms around myself. It was only then that I realized, to my embarrassment, that I was shirtless.

My sheepishness must have shown on my face. "Don't worry. Naked bodies are nothing new to me," Willa said. "But I do have some clothes for you. I assume that you don't want *that* anymore."

She gestured to the armoire, where my jacket hung from a hook on one side. My tattered, dirty, *bloody* jacket. A jacket that could have only been worn by someone who was close to death. Someone who had seen and experienced terrible things, who had closed her eyes every night wondering if they would open again in the morning.

I shuddered.

No. I did not want it. I did not want to even look at it ever again.

But now, the sight of it reminded me with a tight pit at the base of my stomach why I had come here to begin with — made me wonder what Serel was going through right now. If I could speak to Zeryth, maybe he could help me rally the support of the Orders and go help him. I couldn't imagine they would stand for this, and with their firepower —

"I need speaking to Zeryth Aldris," I told Willa, who had opened the armoire and was rummaging around inside. She peeked out, holding a blue cotton dress. Her lips thinned.

"Oh yes," she said, almost as if to herself. "They did say that, didn't they…"

She hung the dress on the side of the armoire, covering my dirty jacket. "Here. Not the most stylish, but let's keep it loose for now so we don't irritate your wounds."

I only understood roughly half of that sentence, but I was too impatient to care. "Is Zeryth —"

"Yes, yes. While you get dressed, I'll go get someone who would like to speak to you."

Willa went to the door, her skirt floating around her feet. Even though she was short and relatively squat, she moved with a grace that I watched with faint envy. My dancing had been crafted out of practice and sheer force of will. Willa's movements were all natural poise.

"Willa," I said, as her hand touched the door handle. She paused to look at me. "Thank you."

She gave me a little, warm smile. "You are very welcome, my dear. I'm sure I will see you again soon."

And then she floated out the door, leaving me alone in the tower of the Order of Midnight — a place I had dreamed about for years.

I still didn't quite know how. But I had made it.

———

I SLIPPED OUT of bed and wandered a circle around the room, taking a moment to peer out the window between those light, flowing curtains. When I looked down, the floor seemed to tilt beneath me, and my throat released an involuntary gasp. I was probably hundreds and hundreds of dizzying feet above the ground. Only glass separated me from the sky.

My window overlooked the famous Aran cliffs, and the thrashing sea beyond them. If I tilted my head and pressed my cheek against the glass, I could barely see the Tower of Daybreak — headquarters to the Order of Daybreak — standing beside this one. It was identical to this tower, except its glass was lined with burnished gold instead of silver. Fitting.

Beyond it, perhaps a mile away, the Palace loomed against the cliffs. It wasn't nearly as tall as the Towers, but it sprawled against the curvature of the earth. The gold that lined its every angle glittered beneath stormy, sea-tinted clouds. Peaks accented with violent spires stabbed the sky.

A lump formed in my throat.

The ink drawings in my books and Zeryth's descriptions did not do any of it justice.

I turned around and went to the armoire, grabbing the dress that Willa had produced for me. Three layers of straight, loose cotton, dusty blue like the curtains, with billowing sleeves that hit to the elbow.

My nose wrinkled. Was this what Aran women wore? Did they *like* to pretend they didn't have waists, or…?

Well. I wasn't here to be beautiful.

I unhooked the dress and turned around, and in that movement, I caught a glimpse of myself in the full-length mirror.

I had to stop myself from dropping the hanger.

Gods. Was that *me?*

My hair hung in dirty tangles over both shoulders, my cheeks sunken, ribs protruding. Two angry, pink scars sliced across my chest and abdomen. They cut across my forearms, too. If I held my arms the right way, I could see the unbroken lines that the whip had sliced in my flesh when I shielded myself. But when I turned, my *back* —

My back was completely covered in deep, ferocious gouges. Some still bled, some had scabbed, and some were stitched together like a hideous patchwork quilt. No wonder I had been in such agony. I practically had no skin left. And it was already clear that magic healing or no, these scars would mark me forever.

Crack!

Twenty-seven.

The image of Esmaris's dying face flashed through my mind. And for the first time, the thought of it didn't inspire even a hint of guilt. I was *glad*. Glad he was dead, and glad I had gotten to kill him.

For one fractured moment.

Then I thought of that sadness that had stripped his features, that whisper of betrayal. The guilt followed like a wave crashing on the shore.

I shuddered, turning away from the mirror and slipping into that ghastly shapeless dress. I felt another ache at my wrist, and when I looked down, my brow furrowed.

Strange. There, on the inside of my wrist, was a crimson-splotched bandage. It was clearly fresher than my other wounds, small and neat and very deliberate-looking. How had that —

The thought was interrupted as I heard the door open behind me.

I turned to see another Valtain woman standing in the doorway.

She was a little younger than Willa, and much slimmer and taller. Her clothes were entirely white, blending with her skin and hair and flattening her to a colorless silhouette. She wore tight pants and a stiff coat that buttoned up to the neck, following her lithe body until it nearly touched the floor.

I looked down at my dress, relieved that this was not, apparently, what all Aran women wore.

"I'm glad to see that you're awake." The woman closed the door behind her. The movement revealed a large, dark-grey moon emblem across her back. "We were all worried about you."

"I am much better."

"Good, good." She stepped into the room, hands clasped, and

flicked her hair behind her shoulder. It was long, nearly reaching her waist, and braided into countless tiny strands.

She regarded me with an icy, stripping stare. Gods, those white eyes were so disconcerting. I felt like she was staring straight through me.

I met that stare, matching her intensity.

"I need speaking—" *To speak,* I reminded myself. "I need to speak of Zeryth Aldris."

"Can I ask what about?"

I hesitated. "If you get him, I will tell you both."

An echo of a smile quirked the edge of her mouth, as if something about this statement was amusing. I didn't know what. And I could *feel* nothing from her, not a hint of thoughts or emotions, or even the nebulous shape of her aura. When I reached out with my mind to find hers — try to sense something that might help me adjust my strategy — I was met with nothing. Just a blank wall.

"Zeryth isn't here right now," she said. "Actually, he's in Threll. Maybe you two passed each other in your travels."

Threll? My mouth went dry. I wondered if Zeryth would have stopped at Esmaris's estate, like he always did during his visits to the area.

"I received this letter from him last week, actually." The woman lifted her hand, and suddenly, a piece of parchment appeared between her fingers. She held it up, reading. "'As planned, I stopped at the home of Esmaris Mikov only to find out that he was, in fact, dead. He had been murdered mere weeks before I arrived. His city, needless to say, had fallen into turmoil.'"

She looked at me and raised her eyebrows. "Do you need me to translate that for you?"

Translate — as if to imply that she knew Thereni and chose not to speak it. I knew a power play when I saw one. Besides, I understood enough — enough for my mouth to turn to ash at the word "turmoil." I knew that word. I had read it in the books Zeryth had given me, in descriptions of war and brutality.

"I understand."

"Do you also understand why it might seem slightly suspicious that a Threllian girl with a whipped back collapsed at our doorstep just after Esmaris Mikov was killed?"

I bristled. "I left because I purchased my freedom," I said. "Fair."

The truth, if an extremely partial one.

"It's not my place to care whether you killed him or not. I saw what your back looked like. I wouldn't blame you if you did. However." She dropped the letter, which disappeared into a lazy spiral of smoke, then crossed her arms over her chest. Strangely enough, she reminded me of Esmaris — those same commanding, uncompromising movements. "The Orders are politically neutral. If the Threllians find out that we have knowingly harbored a wanted woman, we might ruin our relationship with them. Or worse, start a war."

Noo-trul. Har-boor-ing.

I filed the words away, along with my murky understanding of their meaning.

"We need to send you back to Threll," the woman said, slowly, as if she saw me struggling.

My fingers curled at my sides.

I went through all this, *dragged* myself here, and she was trying to tell me that they were going to send me back there? She saw what that place did to me, and she wanted to send me *back?*

No. That was not how this worked.

"I am not Threllian," I said.

The Valtain woman opened her mouth to respond, but I cut her off.

"I am not Threllian. I am Nyzrenese. My nation was destroyed by Threllian Lords when I was very small, my people killed and enslaved. And eight years ago, they caught me, too. They murdered my family and took me. I was beaten. Whipped. Raped. Others had worse. I nearly *died* to come to here."

I had prepared for this moment. I had specifically learned the

Aran terms for all of those awful things — condensed my life into little, terrible words — because I knew I would need them.

I opened my palms and sent a stream of silver butterflies rising to the ceiling.

"If you send me back," I said, "you send me to death. Zeryth said me that I could join the Orders, even though I am Fragmented."

I turned the butterflies to glass. They fell, shattering against the marble floor. The woman didn't flinch. "Nice," she said, flatly, eyeing the shards on the ground.

"This is why I come. Because my people need me. And for helping them, I need the Orders."

The woman and I stared at each other, her expression shuttered.

"I mentioned your arrival in my last letter to Zeryth," she said, at last. Then she opened her palm and produced another letter, reading aloud. "'I have met the Fragmented girl many times. She is intelligent and driven. She may be ill-trained and inexperienced, but she has undeniable potential, and it would be a deep shame to see that wasted.'"

She glanced at me. "I assure you that Zeryth doesn't always provide such praise to young women who collapse at our door mumbling his name."

A warm satisfaction unfurled in my chest. I may not have needed Zeryth's help to cross the sea, but I had needed it in this room. Silently, I thanked him for it.

"I will give everything I have to the Orders," I said. "I would be best Wielder it has seen."

I opened my fingers and whispered to the shards of glass, calling them to me. They slid across the floor and rose to my hands, where I closed them in my fists. When I opened them again, the glass had become a frosted, mottled circle.

The moon.

For the first time since our conversation began, a real expression crossed the woman's face — a bemused smirk clinging to the corners of her mouth. "That's a tall commitment from someone Fragmented, but I can appreciate the sentiment."

She opened the door. "Walk with me. And, I didn't introduce myself. My name is Nura."

NURA WALKED FAST, and didn't appear to notice or care whether I kept up. Still, I matched her pace step for step. It felt good to be able to move again, despite the tugs of sharp pain across my back. Whatever Willa had done for me had *worked*.

"Zeryth was right. There is no rule against Fragmented Valtain joining the Order of Midnight. It's not common, but…" Nura shrugged, lazily raising her palms. "I have no objection to that."

This was actually happening.

I craned my neck as we glided down the halls, taking in the tall ceilings, the white floors, the silver accents doused in sunset light through enormous windows. A few other Valtain passed us, some giving me curious looks. I tried not to gawk back at them. While most wore some kind of moon insignia somewhere on their jacket, none were as large as the one on Nura's back, and no one else dressed entirely in white like her. I wondered if she held a higher rank.

"We do have one problem, though." We took a sharp turn, arriving at a circle of cerulean blue carved into the floor, surrounded by a delicate silver gate. Nura stood in the center and motioned for me to join her. When I did, she placed both hands on the rail. The platform shuddered.

I let out a tiny gasp as I felt the floor begin to lower beneath me, resisting the urge to jump away from the edge. Nura shot me an amused glance. "There are many uses for our magic. Imagine how long it would take to climb these stairs."

So *she* was doing this? Lowering us, and the floor?

I watched floor after floor of the Tower pass as we dropped, smearing glimpses of bustling activity. "You do, however, have a problem," Nura said. "Apprenticeships were assigned six months ago. There are not as many Valtain as there are Solarie. I don't believe we have anyone to train you."

Uh-pren-tish-ips.

I didn't understand that word. But I *did* understand her last sentence.

"I do not need training."

Nura snorted, as if this was a ridiculous thing to say. "Yes, you do. Every Wielder, Valtain or Solarie, must complete an apprenticeship to join the Orders. No exceptions."

"Apprenti—?"

"Apprenticeship. Young Wielders train with a teacher for six years."

Six years?!

"I do not have that time," I blurted out. "People in Threll do not have six years for waiting for help."

Nura glanced at me, narrowing her eyes thoughtfully. I desperately wished I could sense her thoughts.

"And what kind of help, exactly, do you want us to provide?"

"Send small group of Wielders to Threll, with me." I didn't hesitate. I had thought this through many times. "Give me twenty men and Order protection to go to Esmaris Mikov's city and—" I stumbled for the Aran equivalent of the word "negotiate," groping through my mind to no avail. "—And discuss for the freedom of the slaves there. Give me money or power for making deals for their release. And if this does well, we can go further in Threll. But for now, I only ask of you twenty."

The platform came to a stop, touching the ground, but neither of us moved nor spoke. The silence was agonizing.

"You're ambitious," Nura said. "I don't know if that's a realistic plan. But we will see what we can do, maybe, after you complete some training. Nothing I do can get around that requirement."

She stepped off the platform, continuing down the hall and waving me along. "Follow me."

———————

THE GROUND FLOOR of the tower was more open than the spiraling hallways above, and so blindingly bright that I had to squint. The lobby was bustling with activity, full of people who looked like they all had very important business to attend to — Valtain with their white hair and albino skin, and Solarie, who looked like any other human but wore the sun emblems of the Order of Daybreak.

My gaze ran to the other side of the room and then stopped.

The mural that adorned the back wall was so intimately familiar, and yet so different from the version of it that I knew. The massive painting of Araich and Rosira Shelaene was the same image as the ink drawing in my well-worn book — the two of them framed by the sun and the moon, their palms touching. And right there in the center, where their hands met, the building itself changed, accents turning from Rosira's silver to Araich's gold. The Tower of Midnight and the Tower of Daybreak shared the same ground floor, and this was where they converged.

I didn't realize that I had stopped walking until Nura paused beside me.

"You know the story of our founding?" she asked.

"Yes. Very well."

I traced their faces. Araich's tilted down, his eyes looking straight at the viewer, while Rosira's gazed out over the sea through those great glass windows. I wondered if she had dreamed of my world the way that I dreamed of hers. If she had, she may never have gotten to see it. Five hundred years ago, the world had been without magic, and its resurgence was so chaotic and unpredictable that it threatened to destroy every-thing. As the stories were told, she and Araich had given pieces of their very souls to mold magic into something sustainable. And then, they had founded the Orders to be a beacon of stability in a new world of dangerous power and great possibility.

I swallowed a sudden swell of emotion.

That was, at least, what they had always been to me. A beckoning promise.

I was so entranced that I almost didn't notice when Nura began striding away. "Come," she said, and waved me along

I followed her into a smaller room lined with desks and bookcases that smelled strongly of the comforting scent of paper. Willa sat behind one of the desks in the corner. On the other side of the room, a woman and a man shuffled through papers. They wore gold sun insignias on their lapels — Solarie.

"You're moving well!" Willa said, giving me a grin I could not help but return.

"Willa. We need to find a teacher for Tisaanah." The moment Nura opened her mouth, Willa closed hers, giving her undivided attention.

Yes. Nura had to be important. Probably not the Arch Commandant — the leader of the Orders — but certainly highly-ranked.

Willa frowned, shuffling through a few pieces of paper on the desk. "I'm afraid that no one who is open to taking an apprentice is free now, since the assignments happened months ago—" She squinted at me. "How old are you, dear?"

"Twenty-one."

"*Twenty-one?*" Willa arched her eyebrows, looking to Nura. "She's three years older than apprentices are when they *complete* their—"

"Age has nothing to do with it. If she wants to join the Orders, she must complete at least some training. The laws are clear about that." Nura crossed her arms, tapping impatiently with her index finger. "I know we have to be unconventional."

A wrinkle formed on Willa's forehead. She pulled out a scribbled stack of bound parchment and began flipping through it.

"Look up where Maxantarius Farlione is living these days," Nura said.

Willa stopped mid-movement. "*Really?*"

"I told you we were going to have to be unconventional."

"But are you sure that he's the right—"

"Look it up, please."

A pause. Willa looked like she might retort. But instead, she flipped through her books, produced a small piece of paper, and handed it to Nura.

"Thank you." Nura glanced down at the parchment. "And how much longer do you think Tisaanah needs to recover before she can begin?"

Recover? I didn't need to recover any more. I wouldn't let them force me to train for *six years*, that I knew for sure. And that meant I had no time to waste. If I could drag myself thousands of miles while on the cusp of death, I could certainly put up with whatever this Maxa-whoever could throw at me. "I want to begin now."

Willa looked startled. "Tisaanah, dear, you're still —"

"I have waited eight years to come here. I am recovered. And I want to begin."

"But —"

"We can't fault her impatience." A tiny smile curled the edges of Nura's mouth. "She likes to get things done. I can respect that."

Respect wasn't quite what I saw in the amused gleam of Nura's pale eyes. But that was fine. I'd been given my chance to earn it, and a chance was all I needed.

"Let's go, then." Nura looked down at the paper Willa gave her, then flipped it over. She took a pen from the desk.

"Hold onto my arm." I obeyed as I watched her draw a circle. Then add lines and shapes winding through its center —

And then, suddenly, I was no longer standing in the Tower of Midnight, but blinking into a blinding midday sun.

"Nura." A strained male voice. "What, exactly, do you want?"

CHAPTER SEVEN

The earth shifted and slid beneath me, and I struggled to stay upright. It took me too long to realize I was still, embarrassingly, clinging to Nura's arm.

"Tisaanah, this is Maxantarius."

I tore my eyes from the bright sun, blinking at our surroundings. Nura and I now stood in one of the largest gardens I had ever seen. It sprawled in all directions, flowers and greenery consuming every inch of earth. Nestled in the middle of it all was a little stone cabin. And there, crouched among wild white rose bushes, was a man who stood to meet us, sharp features pinched beneath the shadow of tousled black hair.

Black hair.

He wasn't a Valtain.

This had to be a mistake. Now I understood the confused wrinkle on Willa's forehead.

"Maxantarius? Really?" He rolled his eyes, letting out a scoff. His purple silk jacket — which struck me as horribly impractical clothing for gardening — rippled under the sun as he crossed his arms across his chest.

His gaze settled on me. It was the brightest, iciest blue I had ever seen, so unnervingly stark that it edged on inhuman. "Can you tell me why you're bringing strange girls in nightgowns to stomp my irises?"

I looked down at myself, forcing myself not to be embarrassed by this shapeless cotton thing. Then looked down further, to the little blue flowers crushed under my toes.

To be fair, it would have been impossible *not* to crush *something*.

Nura only answered, icily, "You haven't shown up to the Towers for any mandatory appearances."

Maxantarius lifted one long, straight finger. "One. That isn't your concern, is it?" Then another. "Two. As you know, I am retired."

"You're still a member of the Orders."

He uncrossed his arms, jerking his sleeve up in one sharp movement, making a show of examining the inside of his right wrist. I caught a glimpse of a small, gold-colored tattoo. The sun. "I've been meaning to get rid of this thing."

Nura didn't react, save for a small tightening of the muscles around her eyes. So slight that I would have missed it if I wasn't desperate for signs of communication, desperate to latch on to something other than the Aran words that I struggled to understand.

She gestured to me. "This is Tisaanah. She has been assigned to be your apprentice."

I armed myself with the most dazzling, bright-eyed smile in my arsenal, inclining my head in a greeting.

Maxantarius's eyes danced from me to Nura and then back to me, black eyebrows raised ever so slightly, sharp words dangling in the air.

And then, he laughed.

"That's ridiculous."

"You didn't take one six months ago, so here you are."

"Retired. That was the agreement. And besides..." His arms dropped, gesturing to me, then flailing into something like a shrug. "I mean— *honestly*? Do I have to *say* any of this? Where do I even start?"

During that last question, his gaze flicked over me with an incredulous disgust that made my teeth grind together.

"What are your reservations?" Nura retorted.

"What are my *reservations*? You bring me a Fragmented *Valtain* who's practically *geriatric* and ask me what my *reservations* are?"

Geh-ri-act-rick.

I didn't know what it meant, but I was sure it was an insult.

I steeled myself with a face of charming, earnest pleasantness. "It would be honor to train with you— ah—" I didn't even know how to approach attempting to say Maxantarius's name. Instead I awkwardly cut myself short, offering a doe-eyed beam in its place, before turning to Nura. "But maybe better if I could find Valtain?"

He arched a brow, unamused by my practiced charms. "And she's *foreign*. What is that, Thereni?"

"There are no Valtain in the Order of Midnight who are available to apprentices right now," Nura snapped. "You are Tisaanah's only option."

Gods. Well, that was just terrific. If it was even true.

Maxantarius and I glanced at each other, and in that moment, I was certain that we had to be thinking the same thing.

He snorted. "As much as I love being a last resort, this is ridiculous. How old are you, anyway?" Before I could answer, he shook his head, turning back to Nura. "I won't bother. This doesn't even justify a response. You know it, I know it, and I'm sure she probably knows it, too. You already know where I stand on involvement with the Orders."

I glanced from Maxantarius to Nura, reading the taut hostility in their stances, the sharp edge in the way that they looked at each other. And I tasted the thread of tension in the air that lingered between them, one that seemed drawn from something deeper than this conversation alone.

There was history here.

Old rivals, maybe. Or…

I watched their unbroken stares, heavy with that distinctive blend of familiarity and resentment.

Or…

…Former lovers, perhaps. I tucked this theory away. Knowing these kinds of things about people always turned out to be useful, one way or another.

Details aside, one thing was certain: I strongly suspected that this argument was about more than just me.

"It's been eight years, Max," Nura snapped. "It's time to do something with your life."

"Your concern is touching, but I've given you an answer."

"You are a member of the Orders, whether you like it or not. I wasn't asking you for an answer."

"Of course. Holding true to pattern."

Silence. Nura and Maxantarius looked at each other with combative stares that were only barely shy of outright glares. The sound of birds flitting through the trees was suddenly deafening.

"I'm not doing this," he said, at last. "I'm sure you've just been *itching* for an excuse to put me in my place. But it's wrong for you to use *her* to do it."

"That's not— I already told you." Nura straightened, letting out a puff of exasperated air through her nostrils. She turned to me. "He's just being a child. He's more than capable of teaching you."

"I am not," he retorted. "Don't lie to the poor girl."

I looked at Maxantarius's stubborn, steady gaze. Then Nura's set jaw and icy eyes — equally immovable. I wasn't sure exactly what I had stepped into, but I knew that if I brought up finding another trainer, Nura wouldn't give in. Not after this whole argument.

I could do this, I told myself. I was an expert in making stubborn men do things that they didn't realize they wanted to do. I wrapped Threllian Lords around my fingers like they were made out of putty. And how different could this petulant Solarie possibly be?

Besides, I didn't *actually* need training. I could teach myself anything I needed to know. All I had to do was appease the Orders' technicalities, force myself through their requirements as quickly as possible, then convince them to help me get back to Threll.

Hopefully before Serel—

I didn't let myself finish the thought.

"He'll come around," Nura said to me, quietly, then turned to Maxantarius, who had crouched down to observe his roses.

"Don't you dare leave her here," he said, without looking up.

I *hoped* she was leaving. Every minute she spent arguing would make my job more difficult later.

"It's time to do something, Max. You're too young for this." A faint, tenuous warmth stretched in her voice, far beneath her words. It was only just audible enough to make him glance up, the wrinkle above his nose softening only slightly.

Oh, *definitely* former lovers. My suspicion became a certainty.

"Good luck," Nura said to me. "I'm sure I will see you soon."

And before I had the chance to stop her — before I had the chance to ask any of the dozens of questions thrashing in my lungs — she scribbled two jagged strokes onto her little scrap of parchment and simply disappeared.

Leaving me here.

"*Damn* it, I told her not to do that," Maxantarius grumbled.

A breeze rustled the garden, making the flower petals tremor like butterfly wings, pressing the fabric of my ridiculous dress to my back and offering a sharp, jarring reminder of my wounds. Whatever pain relief Willa had given me was starting to wear off. At least the ache sharpened my thoughts.

I watched Maxantarius, who diligently ignored me.

Docility was probably not the best option. I could already tell that approach would neither endear me to him, nor help me make any progress. Normally, I would take a more flirtatious approach, but that seemed risky, too. He had only scoffed at my attempts at charm before.

"Eager protégé" might have potential. Maybe.

I just needed to figure out what I had to work with.

I watched Maxantarius's back, mentally reaching into the space between us, searching for any faint whiff of his emotions, his thoughts, his preferences—

A sharp, startling pain rang out in the back of my head, as if my fingers had been slammed in a door. Maxantarius whipped his head around to glare at me. "Do *not*," he hissed, "do that to me. *Ever.*"

My jaw snapped shut, and I swallowed a rush of embarrassment.

Nura had clearly shielded her mind, hiding it from my abilities. As a Valtain, she would have a mastery of thoughts that would allow her to do such things. It hadn't occurred to me that a Solarie could do the same thing, though now it seemed obvious that such protections would be necessary, living in this world—

"I apologize—" I started. "I only—"

But Maxantarius rose without so much as looking at me. "Fucking Valtain," he muttered. "Sneaky bastards."

He strode to the door of the little stone cabin. I started to follow him, but he whirled around in the doorway, blocking it and sneering at me down the bridge of his nose.

"I'm not participating in this," he said.

And before I could respond, the door slammed so forcefully that I felt the wood reverberate at the tip of my nose.

I SHIVERED.

My back throbbed.

Maxantarius had not opened the door again after slamming it in my face. For a while, I had paced around the garden mulling over my options. The way things looked from where I stood, I had very few.

At first, it had been difficult to curb my anger, which grew more and more potent with every passing minute. I dragged myself across the plains, across the ocean, to get here. I hunted and bartered and hid. I nearly *died*. And — in a thought that still clenched shuddering guilt in my chest — I killed.

All of that, so that I could be discarded outside the locked door of some petulant "teacher" who refused to train me.

Gods, he wasn't even a *Valtain*. I didn't know much about Solarie Wielders, but I knew that even though they could, theoretically, do most of what Valtain could do, the way they used their magic was very different than the way I used mine.

But.

I breathed in my anger, and exhaled resolve.

If they were going to force me into this situation, then fine. I'd make everything I could of it.

I wasn't sure what Maxantarius expected to happen, but I didn't leave. Instead I sat down just outside the door, crossing my legs, waiting. He had to come out eventually. And when he did, I'd be here. Besides… it wasn't as if I had anywhere else I could go.

Minutes passed — thirty, forty, fifty. Then hours. I watched the flower petals grow brighter and brighter under the waning sun, then reflect the warmth of sunset, then curl and fold in on themselves in dusk.

It was cold. Threll didn't get cold, and I didn't particularly enjoy the unfamiliar sensation.

The flower leaves gently curled, like an animal getting ready to sleep. I wondered if he had put some sort of protective spell on them to shield them from the chill. My teeth chattered.

And then, finally, the door opened. I jolted so abruptly that my back screamed.

Maxantarius stood in the doorway.

"You look freezing," he said, matter-of-factly.

"Yes." I saw no point in denying it.

"Are you planning on going anywhere?"

"I have nowhere for going."

I tried to sound very pitiful.

He sighed. "Figures she'd leave you here on the coldest spring night we've had in years," he grumbled. Then he stepped back from the door, eyeing me warily. "I'm inviting you inside, but only because if I let you freeze out here, I'd have to relinquish my moral superiority."

I didn't understand what any of that meant, except for the important part. I pulled myself to my feet, wincing slightly as my back straightened and offering Maxantarius my most charming, grateful smile. "Thank you, Max-an-tar-ee-us."

I was very proud of myself for correctly stringing together all of those syllables out loud.

He rolled his eyes as he stepped aside, holding the door open for me. "Max, please. Otherwise we'd spend half our damn lives saying that ridiculous name."

Thank the gods.

I HAD NEVER SEEN SO many *things* packed into so small a space.

I stepped through the door and immediately stopped short. It took palpable effort not to let my jaw drop. My eyes didn't even know where to look first.

Max's home was tiny, but every single wall — *every* one — was lined with shelves that held trinkets and tools and art and sculptures and little strange whirring metal things. One shelf was devoted completely to what looked to be a very wide variety of sizes, shapes, colors and types of wine bottles. Four different rugs covered the floor, all overlapping each other at various angles, each a different color and texture.

A fireplace bathed all of this in flickering orange light, reflecting off little metal pendulums and curious, circling devices. A couch and two armchairs sat near the fire — none matching — and a dining room table with five different styles of chairs occupied the middle of the room. Around a corner, I caught a glimpse of a small kitchen, and a narrow hallway with a few closed doors.

"These are all very useful and important things," Max said, somewhat defensively, as if he saw my eyes widen when I walked in.

I nodded. *Sure.*

There was no possible greater opposite to Esmaris's vast, minimalist estate. At least it was clean in here. Cluttered, but clean.

"Are you hungry?"

Max disappeared into the kitchen. As if answering for me, my stomach rumbled.

"Yes."

He emerged with a bowl of soup and a teacup, which he placed at the table, motioning for me to sit. I did, and he slumped into the chair across from me. He replenished a mostly empty wine glass from a bottle that was also mostly empty, and leaned back in his chair.

I sniffed. The soup Max had given me was different than anything I had ever eaten before — thicker, and heavy with the still-unfamiliar smell of the ocean. I would have inhaled it even if it was disgusting, but it was good. *Spicy*, but good.

"Thank you." I was so ravenous that I barely remembered to say it.

Max had shifted to leaning on the table, his chin propped against his knuckles, watching me in silence. I returned the favor, regarding him warily between bites.

He was younger than I might have expected. Perhaps late twenties, though there was a certain sharp, observant quality to his expressions that made him seem like he could be older. High cheekbones doused in flickering firelight. A flat, straight nose. Delicate, upturned eyes beneath creaseless lids that only emphasized their unnerving, cloudy blue. Up close, they looked even more strange. I knew an old man in Threll who had cataracts that looked a bit like those, though certainly not in such a striking blue. Somehow I doubted that Max had eyesight problems, though. His gaze seemed too deliberate, too piercing, for that.

"So," he said, at last, "you're from…?"

"Threll."

"And how old are you?"

"Two-ten—" I realized my mistake, too late, and corrected myself. "Twenty-one."

"Twenty-one," he echoed under his breath, shaking his head — as if this was a ridiculous answer. "Apprenticeships are complete at eighteen. Do you realize how peculiar this entire situation is?"

I tried not to let Max see that I didn't understand, but apparently I failed, because he added, "Strange. Unusual."

"Enough."

"To be clear, *all* of this is very, very strange."

"Nura said of me that I cannot join Orders without training. Even though I'm too old."

I didn't bother to hide my irritation.

A smirk flitted across Max's mouth. "I'm glad you have enough sense to be frustrated by that bureaucratic stupidity."

"I did not come here to be sent back away."

"'Here,' to Ara, or 'here,' to my house?"

"Both."

He let out a breath of a chuckle, as if this answer were simply an amusing joke, and finished his glass of wine. Poured another.

"Sorry, how rude of me." He lifted the bottle. "Would you like some?"

"No, thank you." My gaze flicked to the walls, and the empty wine bottles that lined one of the shelves.

Noted.

But I needed more information about this man, if I was going to understand what he wanted. If I was going to figure out how to make myself invaluable.

I put my spoon down and took a sip of tea. Even that was spicy, making my nose burn. "How are you knowing Nura?" I asked, with calculated casualness. "Is she a friend?"

Max snorted. "She's the second-highest-ranking member of the Orders. Everyone knows Nura."

Oh, I did hear that bitterness. I smiled slyly at him. "You know her another way, I think."

"We fought together during the war, if you must know." Max straightened, narrowing his eyes. "But you're awfully bold for someone who dumped herself at *my* house and refused to leave."

"I can't leave. What war?" I knew very little about Ara's recent history.

But Max ignored my question. "You *can* leave. You can do anything you want."

I paused. All at once, it hit me: for the first time in my life, that statement was *true*.

But then, that realization drowned beneath an onslaught of images. Esmaris's dying face. Serel's goodbye eyes. The incriminating burn of his departing kiss on my cheek.

Guilt clenched in my stomach. No. I wasn't free. Not really. Not yet.

"I need to join the Orders," I said. "Nura says I must be here for doing this. So no, I cannot leave."

"Bad goal. For two reasons." Max raised a finger. "One, because you shouldn't join the Orders. I wish I hadn't." Another finger. "And two. Because I'm not going to train you. It's not personal, it's just a matter of principle."

Beneath the table, my nails clenched against my palm. "I can help you in other ways. I can clean, or cook—"

Max let out a choked laugh, brow furrowed. "Are you implying that I look like I'm in desperate need of domestic help?"

I glanced around the cluttered house and refrained from following up on that particular line of conversation.

"There must be *something* I—"

"I don't need to be harassed in my own home." Max stood up, stretching, then took my empty bowl and teacup. "You can stay here for tonight. *Just* tonight, and then tomorrow we'll figure out what to do with you."

I stood, too. Exhaustion sank into my eyelids, my bones, my muscles. Whatever Willa had done to heal me was miraculous, but she had been right: I was still not fully recovered.

"Washroom?" I asked, and Max's arm waved from around the corner of the kitchen to gesture me down the hall.

That was a relief, at least. I had no idea how common such things were in Ara, and during my journey I had relieved myself in enough disgusting or embarrassing places to last a lifetime.

I splashed some water on my face and then looked at myself in the mirror. It was an unusual piece — clearly very old, framed with tarnished gold that twisted into a morass of little creatures. Bugs, dragonflies, lizards, snakes. My face reflected in the middle fit in far too well. Just another thing that looked like it would be rolling around in the dirt.

I grabbed a handful of my knotted hair, which I had still not managed to fully untangle. But in that touch, all I could feel was Esmaris's hands clutching it, dragging me down to the ground with him.

Suddenly, the sight of it made me ill.

I peered out into the hallway, where Max was shuffling around the living room.

"Do you have— um—" I racked my exhausted brain, searching for the right Aran word. "Um— It says—" I held up my two fingers, bringing them together, making "*snp snp*" sounds with my tongue. "This thing?"

Max gave me a look of deadpan confusion. "Huh?"

"It says *snp snp*," I repeated, frustrated, bringing my fingers together again.

He stared at me like I was insane.

The Thereni word, of course, was screaming in my ears, even as the Aran one was nowhere to be found.

"*Oh.*" Max snapped his fingers in realization, then opened a drawer and held up a pair of gold shears. "Scissors."

I'd try to remember that and save myself some humiliation next time. I took them and returned to the mirror. And I did not hesitate, not even for a second, as I hacked my hair off in handfuls between my chin and shoulders.

I had kept it so long, after all, because Esmaris liked it that way. I didn't have to care about that anymore. And by cutting it

70

all off, I could release myself from his final touch. Cleave away the last place he grabbed me.

A satisfied smirk curled the corners of my mouth.

I could feel Max's gaze as he leaned against the doorframe. "You're going to wish that you left it a little longer."

Another handful. I disregarded Max's statement. It felt good to have the ability to disregard the opinion of a man.

I shook my head, feeling the lightness, watching my shortened hair bounce above my shoulders. "Is good this way," I said, handing the scissors back to Max.

He shrugged. "You're going to have a hell of a time keeping it out of your face. Long is fine, short is fine. It's this in between stuff that gets you into trouble." He tucked the scissors into his pocket and jerked his chin towards the basin. "Not my problem, though, as long as you clean all that up."

I did as he asked. And I had never seen anything so beautiful as the fireplace flames claiming those tendrils of black and silver, shriveling them, reducing them to ash.

CHAPTER EIGHT

Bright, midday sun flooded through the curtains by the time I opened my eyes. I was once again awoken by that musical, chattering sound. This time, I recognized it instantly as Willa's voice.

That got me out of bed quickly.

I threw my single shapeless dress back on — uncomfortably. I'd had to sleep naked simply because I had no other clothes. I hurried out into the living room, where Willa and Max stood somewhat awkwardly. There was a new, nervous tinge to Willa's voice.

"—And you know how it is, things are just so tense with the invasion of Tairn and all the hostility in Vernaya. Ascended only hope it won't go to war— Oh!" Willa stopped short. Two sets of eyes turned to me. "Tisaanah. Good morning."

"Good afternoon is more accurate," Max said.

"How are you feeling? Oh, your hair…" Her voice trailed off. I wondered if it was good or bad that my shortened hair was enough to reduce Willa to silence.

"Good morning," I said. "I am much better. Thank you."

"I meant to make it here last night, but with everything that happened…" She let out a breath, her small, plump mouth thinning.

Something was off.

"What?" I asked.

"Our oh-so-great Queen Sesri's paranoia cost a lot of people their lives last night," Max said.

"Paranoia?" Willa's brow furrowed. "These are difficult times, Max. We can't dismiss it as paranoia. She's doing the best she can, under the circumstances."

Par-uh-noy-uh.

I knew nothing about the queen of Ara — until now, not even her name. The most recent history that my books covered was more than two decades old at this point. Still, I understood what Willa was saying before I walked into the room: war. War could destroy all of my plans.

Or… it could be a chance to advance faster than I would otherwise.

That thought put a nauseous pit in my stomach, and I hated myself for considering the possibility. I was very young when the Threllian Lords conquered Nyzerene, but some echo of my memory still recalled the smell of the capital burning, the chill of the night as my mother and I fled. War destroyed my home. Scattered my people to the plains. Sent me into slavery.

But it also presented an opportunity. I didn't have the luxury of ignoring that.

Before I could ask more, Willa shook her head as if to clear the unpleasant thoughts and spoke again. "Anyway. *That's* not what I came here for. I wanted to bring you some clothes and take a look at those wounds again since you left so suddenly, and all. I wasn't really expecting her to take you away right then and there, if I'm being honest. That's — not normally how things are done."

"Don't bother," Max cut in, before I could respond. "She's not staying. In fact, this is an excellent opportunity for you to take her back to the Towers."

Ugh. I didn't understand why he had to be such an ass about it.

Willa's fingers played around each other. Max, I realized, made her *nervous.* Interesting.

Max gave her a deadpan stare. "I'm serious, Willa."

"Well— this poses a problem—"

"The only problem anyone should be talking about is the fact that I already told Nura *no.*" He threw up his hands. "How come no one ever discusses *that* problem?"

"I don't care who trains," I said, growing increasingly irritated with this discussion. "I will train with anyone. I only want to join the Orders."

"See? Anyone could do it."

Willa picked more ferociously at her fingernails. "Apprenticeships were assigned six months ago, Max, and with everything happening right now, there's no one else available who—"

"There's no *way* that's actually true."

Willa looked so startled at being outright accused of lying that I felt bad for her. "It *is* true. I checked."

Shit. I had still been holding out hope that Max wasn't *actually* my only option.

"If you don't do it," she went on, "then no one can, at least not for another five months when the current crop of senior apprentices—"

"Then she can wait for five months."

I shook my head, fiercely. "I *cannot* wait five months."

"Both of you need to calm down." Willa's voice took on a tone that sounded as if it was meant to soothe cranky children. "I spoke to Nura about this before coming here. Tisaanah, because of your unusual situation, we're willing to let you do your first round of tests early. The other apprentices have their evaluations in five months. You test with them, and from there, we can see whether you're fit to move forward more quickly."

If this was supposed to be good news, it didn't feel like it. I nodded and tried not to show how tight my jaw was, or the way my fingernails dug into the flesh of my palms. Who knew where Serel would be in five months? Where *any* of my friends would be by then? And that was only the *start…*

Calm down, I told myself. *You'll prove it to them. You'll find a way. You always do.*

"This still doesn't change the fact that I won't train her."

Gods, I wanted to *throttle* him.

"After five months," Willa said, somewhat pleadingly, "we can see about switching things around."

"I told Nura no."

"Well, Maxantarius, as you know…" She continued to fidget, her voice halting, as if she was very much dreading saying what she was about to say. "You are still beholden to the Orders. You know what the penalties are for failing to uphold your duties. Especially because of *your —*"

Max raised a palm. Fury seeped into every line of his face, drawing harsh wrinkles of tension around every feature. "Right, I see where this is going. You're saying I don't have a choice."

"All of us have obligations," Willa said, apologetically.

He let out a scoff, then turned those inhuman eyes on me. "They picked an unusual battle in *you,* didn't they?"

I returned his glare with a sweet, accommodating smile. "I will be *excellent* apprentice."

Max crossed his arms and went outside without another word, leaving Willa and me staring at each other. I picked up her bag. "Thank you," I said, then grabbed the skirt of my shapeless dress. "I'm glad to rid this thing."

That was good news, at least.

WILLA STAYED FOR A WHILE LONGER, helping me unpack the clothes she had brought. In this case, "unpacking" simply meant trying to find a clear surface upon which to place them, but I didn't mind. I was just thrilled to be able to get out of this hideous dress. Instead, I changed into a pair of close-fitting trousers, paired with a blouse that wrapped around my body and tied around my waist, both rendered in shades of dusky blue. Simple, but worlds better than that awful chiffon thing.

Before she left, Willa looked at my wounds and seemed pleased with how they were healing. She had me lay on my stomach while she hovered her hands over my bare back, muttering under her breath. Whatever she was doing itched, but didn't hurt, even when she touched open wounds directly.

"Could all Valtain do this?" I asked her.

"No, just some of us," she chirped. "Everyone's abilities manifest a bit differently. Certainly, it is a useful skill to have."

Then, before she left, she took my wrist and removed the bandage that I'd noticed when I first arrived, revealing a tiny, neat wound.

"I'm sorry, dear. This will sting."

I winced as she took a small knife and opened the wound just enough to coax forth a few drops of blood, which she captured in a glass vial. I resisted the urge to pull my hand away.

"What is this?" I asked.

"Just for tests," she said, as if it were nothing. Then she replaced the bandage. "There! Now, what's left…"

Max didn't come back inside at all during this entire encounter. Before Willa departed, she pulled me against her in an unexpected embrace.

"Don't worry," she whispered into my hair. "Everything will come together."

"I know," I answered, if only because I wouldn't allow myself to consider any other possibility.

And then, Willa was gone, leaving me alone again in this house where I was clearly so unwelcome.

But, there were worse things to be than unwelcome. At least now I had a goal, a plan. And a teacher who, at the very least, couldn't kick me out.

I found Max out in the garden, clipping dead blossoms from a shrub. He didn't even look at me as I approached.

This would be so much easier if I could sense his thoughts. Still, I didn't need magic to feel the anger that surrounded him like a cloud, tainting the air.

"Why do you hate the Orders?" I asked.

"Because they're archaic and controlling and power-hungry."

He didn't look up. *Clip*. A blossom fell to the dirt.

"I only need for you to tell me what I need to know for the test. Only this."

Clip.

Max laughed.

"*Only* this," he repeated, shaking his head.

"Please," I said, making my voice small, sweet. "I need your help." Men loved that voice. All tiny and helpless. Over the last eight years, I'd honed mine to perfection.

Max's eyes flicked to me only briefly, with a removed coldness that told me he was neither fooled nor moved by my performance.

"I went through a lot to gain my freedom from the Orders. I'm not about to turn around and hand it right back to them. I don't want to get myself thrown into Ilyzath, so I'm not kicking you out, but make no mistake, I don't plan on making this easy for them."

"Ilyzath?"

"It's a— prison. That's beside the point."

Clip.

Max scooped up a handful of browned, wilting blossoms. He didn't even look down as fire rose from his skin to consume them in his palm.

It took me a few seconds to find the Thereni translation for "prison" stored in my mind, but when I did, I wondered what Max did to be in such precarious standing that *I* could get him locked up.

"You can do what you want," he said, "but I'm not participating."

I stood up. Crossed my arms. "Fine."

"I'm glad we understand each other." He did not look at me.

I didn't need him anyway.
I had five months. That was more than enough.

CHAPTER NINE

I began by raiding Max's bookcases, sprawling the tomes all over the floor and chipping through words I hardly understood. Something in here had to help me, or at least give me a hint as to what would impress the Orders. But reading them felt like wading through sludge. Aran words blurred in front of me, little more than a tangle of letters. Tucked between books were pieces of parchments with circles scribbled on them, similar to the ones I'd seen Nura draw, but I had no idea what they did. The books didn't help with that, either.

Max regarded me through all of this, ignoring me except to remind me not to touch something or to clean up whatever I had misplaced (I refrained from pointing out that "cleaning up" was an awfully relative term, in this house). Eventually, he went into the kitchen and soon, aromas that made my stomach rumble filled the house. He emerged with two plates, motioning for me to sit.

I slid into a chair, not even really bothering to look at what I was eating before inhaling it. I was that hungry.

Max eyed the pile of books at the center of the floor. "How far did those get you? They're not exactly easy reading."

I pushed my rice around my plate. Before I could find a way to tell him exactly how far they *didn't* get me, the door swung open.

I looked up to see a man standing in the doorway — tall and straight-backed, hands tucked into the pockets of a well-fitting bronze jacket. He was perhaps Max's age, with dark skin, cropped black hair, and quiet eyes that slowly moved from me to Max and back again.

Max looked over his shoulder. "You should knock. One of these days you're going to walk in on something that you don't want to see."

The newcomer's brows rose, just slightly. "Is that what I'm doing now?"

"Not that kind of scandal, sadly."

He shot Max a questioning look, then took a step forward and leaned over the table, extending a hand to me. "Sammerin. Whom do I have the pleasure of meeting?" His voice was low and smooth, deep but inviting and gentle.

It took me just long enough to be awkward to realize that I was supposed to grasp his hand. This was not a common greeting in Threll. "Tisaanah."

"This is my apprentice," Max said. He hadn't stopped eating through this exchange. "At least, so they tell me."

Sammerin straightened, his eyebrows jumping. "She's your apprentice?"

Every single word in that small sentence was emphasized in a different way, communicating a different meaning.

"*She's* your apprentice?" Translation: *She's a Valtain, and a Fragmented one for good measure.*

"She's your *apprentice*?" Translation: *She's way too old for this.*

"She's *your* apprentice?" Translation: *They got you to take an apprentice?*

It was oddly comforting, the way these things transcended language. And that I could hear those little nuances in Aran just as I did in Thereni.

Max sighed. "Yes, apparently."

Sammerin seemed stunned by this, his brow wrinkling thoughtfully. Then it smoothed as he offered me a small smile. "It's lovely to meet you, Tisaanah. I'm sorry that you've been saddled with such an unpleasant mentor."

I liked him.

Max jerked upright, leaning to peer around Sammerin's body at the doorway. "What did I tell you? No apprentices allowed in the house!"

"You just said that *she's* an apprentice," a wavering, lisped voice replied. I craned my neck to see a boy standing behind Sammerin, perhaps twelve years old, chubby with a mopped head of curly blond hair.

"This one won't leave, so it appears that I'm stuck with her. But if she broke as many of my things as you did, I'd banish her, too."

"I'm sorry about the spyglass, it was —"

Sammerin looked down at the boy. "Why don't you go outside and practice today's lesson? I won't be here long."

"But —"

"Moth." The patience in Sammerin's voice was so threadbare that it sounded within seconds of tearing.

The child sighed. "Fine," he huffed, then retreated into the garden. Sammerin shut the door behind him, letting out a low, exasperated breath as he sank into a chair.

"That boy. You have no idea."

I had some idea.

"I have some idea," Max said.

"Five and a half years left." Sammerin eyed the bottle of wine. Max poured him a glass and slid it across the table.

Sammerin straightened as he turned back to me, as if he was trying to shake off his frustration. "So, Tisaanah. Tell me about yourself." He was so soft-spoken that I found myself leaning closer in order to hear him. I wondered if this was intentional.

"Nura just *left* her here yesterday," Max grumbled.

"My question was not directed at you." Sammerin gave Max

a withering look, then turned a much more pleasant gaze to me, waiting politely.

Yes, I decided, I definitely liked him.

"I must apprentice for joining the Orders. Max is the only one who can do it. So I am here."

"Hm." A flicker crossed Sammerin's face, gone before I could identify it. Then, "You aren't from Ara, are you?"

Oh, he was pretending that my accent wasn't that noticeable. Very cute. "I came from Threll."

"That is a long journey."

I nodded.

Sammerin's fingers hovered at his chin, thoughtfully brushing his cropped beard. "And you came just for the Orders?"

I nodded. "I met a Valtain, Zeryth, who teach me about them. He said he would introduce me, but…"

Sammerin and Max exchanged a look. Max sat up straighter, suddenly attentive. "Zeryth *Aldris*?"

"Yes." I flicked my eyes between the two men across from me, my own interest piqued by theirs. "You know him?"

"What was Zeryth doing in Threll?" Max asked.

"He said — Order things." I tried not to look too interested. "Why?"

Silence for a second too long. "We're just curious," Sammerin said.

"How do you know him?"

"It's a long story. We—"

"Sammerin, I don't mean to interrupt you but—" Max stood up, peering out the window. "Your apprentice has set my rose bushes on fire."

Sammerin jumped to his feet, muttering a word that I didn't understand but was spoken with the violent enthusiasm of a curse. "That boy. You have no idea."

I have some idea, I thought.

"Five years, four months, and twenty-six days." Sammerin paused at the door, his voice softening into a honeyed tone that, I suspected, was reserved only for attractive young women. "It was lovely to meet you, Tisaanah."

"And you." I unleashed my most well-practiced, charming smile.

I wondered if Sammerin would be open to taking a second apprentice. He seemed far more agreeable.

"What about me?" Max said. "Was it *lovely* to see me, Sammerin?"

Sammerin placed a sarcastic hand over his heart. "Always, Max."

Then he slipped out the door, leaving it to slam behind him. In the distance, we heard his voice. "Moth! By the Ascended, what are you *doing?*"

"I was just—"

"You can't just wander around throwing those sparks—"

The voices stopped abruptly. I wondered if they had disappeared like Nura had when she brought me here.

Max and I sat in silence for a moment, looking at each other.

"You could have *that* apprentice," I said, at last.

A smile quirked at the corners of Max's mouth, though it looked like he was fighting it desperately. "True," he replied.

And then, at the same time, we both chuckled.

CHAPTER TEN

Two weeks slipped by, and Max still refused to train me.

This was especially frustrating because I wasn't even asking much of him. I only needed him to tell me what would be on the Orders' evaluations. Those tests, I figured, were my best chance to prove to Nura and the rest of the Orders that I was capable of membership — and not only that, but to convince them of my cause.

And to do that, I had to do more than pass. I had to be *remarkable.*

Max's books, as he seemed to suspect they would be, were unhelpful. The language was too archaic for me to understand, and more philosophical than instructional.

So, I did what I could. I tried to force my body physically back into prime shape, rising at dawn to run as far as I could force my legs to carry me, pushing my lungs until my breaths came in shaky, ragged gasps. I was so *weak.* I used to be able to dance for hours on end without letting my flirty smile waver. Now, my body sputtered at a fraction of its previous capability.

Max would watch me as I returned, gasping and heaving, usually leaning back in a chair with a book in his hands or crouched among the gardens. "That looks hard," he would remark, and I glared at him as I panted and shoved another pin into my hair (as he had, frustratingly, been right about the length).

"Would be less harder if I knew what to study," I snapped, between gasps.

"Running around in circles is probably not on the Order's evaluation."

I practiced every scrap of magic that I knew. Conjuring, bending the breeze around my hands, sucking droplets of water from the earth. I even tried drawing some of those circles on the ground, mimicking the ones I had found in Max's study. I didn't know what they were intended to do — which, I supposed, could have gone very poorly — but for me, they did nothing at all.

Once, while I was copying what had to have been my fifteenth circle, Max stood behind me and peered over my shoulder. "Hm," he remarked, cocking his head, before wandering away.

That one sound made me want to snap him in two.

At least I was doing *something*, unlike Max, who seemed fairly committed to doing absolutely nothing, ever. On a particularly cold day, he stepped outside, shivered, looked up at the sky, and declared, "I'm not made for this," before wandering back into the house. I quickly learned that Max was apparently only "made for" an exceptionally narrow set of environments, temperatures, activities, and interactions.

I wished Sammerin would come back. Maybe I could have gotten more help from him.

But the weeks passed, and it was just me and Max, mostly ignoring each other. I never let him see anything but determined, steadfast confidence. But at night, curled up in my small bed in that ridiculously cluttered room, sleep taunted me. Every time I closed my eyes, I saw the betrayal in Esmaris's dying face. I saw the affection in Serel's goodbye, felt his kiss on my cheek. I heard Nura's voice reading Zeryth's letter.

And I had the same dream, over and over again.

In a terrible way, it was funny. When Esmaris beat me, I had vowed to haunt him — cursed him to see my eyes every time he closed his. Now I was the one who saw him in every shadow. *You forgot what you are,* he had spat at me. Well, I never forgot now. Every time I came close, there he was – reminding me of everything I had left behind, and everything I would carry with me forever.

The days ticked by.

And then, one morning, Willa returned to look at my wounds. She was friendly and chipper as she informed me that everything was healing nicely. For a while, it was nice just to be around someone who was at least relatively pleasant.

Then, I asked her, "Do you have any new letters from Zeryth? About Threll?"

Willa's silence plunged my heart into ice water.

"He says that things are a bit..." Her voice trailed off, the musicality flat. "Things are a bit complicated there."

My fingers tightened around the bedsheets.

"Complicated?"

"I suppose with that Lord dead, there's been some struggles..." Willa coughed. I wanted to yank the words from her. "But it's just a period of change. Things will calm down."

I did not trust myself to open my mouth.

All I could think about were Serel's sweet eyes, and the sound that his sword had made in Esmaris's chest — a crunch, a squelch, a reminder of how soft and breakable a human body really was. It didn't matter whether it belonged to the most powerful man in Threll or a slave boy with a kind, gentle smile.

CHAPTER ELEVEN

T hat night, I collected every scrap of paper I could find that
had those circular symbols scribbled on them. I lined them
up outside, looking at them. Every single one was different —
the markings going through their center in different shapes and
orientations.

I still had no idea what they were, or what they did, other
than that Nura used one to bring us here. And that they were the
most concrete example of *something* important that I didn't know
how to do.

So, for whatever reason — perhaps simply because I needed
a solid goal to latch onto — I channeled all my energy into
understanding them. I copied every single one, imitating each
stroke with exact accuracy. In some cases, I even layered the
paper and traced them, stroke for stroke, line for line.

Hours passed. The sun set. I lit lanterns. I wouldn't go inside
because I didn't trust myself not to slap Max if he snickered
at me.

I repeated those symbols over and over again, the same way I
had practiced my dancing steps for hours and hours, forcing
them, hammering them, shattering them and myself until we

were melded together. I would do the same damn thing with these stupid symbols.

I *had* to.

I wasn't sure how late it was by the time I heard the door open behind me. By this time, I was surrounded by paper, stacked up all around me in piles, like a gate locking me in.

"Not that it's my business, but do you plan to stay out here all night?" I heard Max ask.

I didn't turn around. My steady hand did not waver as it traced another circle. Calm. Methodical. I had a system — combining each symbol with each type of ink. "If I must."

"I'm exhausted just looking at you."

I had no response to that. Anger simmered deep beneath my skin.

"Do you even know what those are?" he said.

My fingers tightened so hard around my pen that I nearly snapped it in two. "No. And I think you probably will not say." The words came out in a low snarl.

"The Orders probably won't ask you about them."

Before I could stop myself, I jumped to my feet, whirling to him, the pen still clutched in my hand. "I *know*. I need to— need to—"

The Aran words eluded me, driving my frustration to thrash up against my surface. I glared at Max, who leaned against the doorframe.

I wanted to scream at him. I wanted to ask, *Who has ruined you so badly that you can't do anything but stand in the way of people who have actual important things to do? Why do you feel such a pervasive, petty need to shove your petulance in the Orders' faces? And why the hell do you need to bring me down with you, too?*

Instead, the Aran words that came out sounded something like, "What so many hates do you have?"

"Huh?"

His confusion, understandable as it was, *infuriated* me. I let the pen drop violently to the ground. I hammered every Aran word home, slowly. "*Why* do you *hate* the Orders? *Why* do you hate *me* so many? *What* is *wrong* with you?"

"I don't hate you," Max replied, which made me even *angrier*.

"That is not true!" I shook my head. "That is *not true*. I don't care if you hate me — hate me here." I touched my heart. It was the only way I could think to convey what I was saying. "Or here." I pressed my fingers against my temple. "But you hate me in what you *do*. Why? What wrong did I do to you?"

"It's not about you." Something shifted, softened, in Max's expression. But I was past looking for scraps of kindness.

"It *is* about me! This is my life, not only yours." I blinked and all I could see was Esmaris's body, Serel's face, hands and skin of every man I danced for to earn the money to leave. "I was slave in Threll. Did you know?"

He didn't answer. Just stared at me, with one deepening line in his brow.

"*Did you?*"

"No," he said, quietly.

"I did many things to come here. I *killed* for coming here. My friend —" I didn't have the vocabulary to describe what Serel had done for me, given for me. "I left my most important people. They *need* me. I cannot fail them. To help them, I need this." I thrust my open palm down to the piles of drawings. "I have nothing without the Orders. No power. *I need this. They need this.*"

I didn't *make* myself all of these terrible things — a whore, a killer, a traitor — just to be ignored and discarded before it could be *worth* something.

Max's mouth thinned. I couldn't read him, and I did not try. I was long past caring what he thought. In that moment, I didn't care what *any* of them thought — all of these people who, my entire life, had used me as a part of their stories, had assumed that I was a set piece in *their* lives. Like Esmaris did. Like every lord I seduced. Like Nura, using me to get under Max's skin. And now, like Max, who saw me as a representative of some petty grudge and not an actual *human being*.

"This is *not* only *yours*," I spat. "So *tell me* what is on *stupid* test."

Silence.

My rage receded, slightly, like a wave falling back after crashing on the shore. In that brief reprieve, I cursed myself for losing my temper, wondering if I had forever ruined the ability to mold my relationship with Max by showing him something so raw and impulsive.

He just stood there. Staring at me.

"You were a slave," he repeated.

I paused, taken aback by the look on his face, still exhaling the remnants of my fury. "Yes," I answered, at last.

"And your plan is to join the Orders and then use their influence to help the other slaves in Threll."

"Yes."

He tucked his thumbs into his pockets, letting out a breath that was too long and slow to be a sigh. The unforgiving hardness of his features cracked, shifted. Just slightly. "It won't work."

"I will make it work."

"That's not how it goes. It's not that simple."

"I do not care."

"They aren't going to make this easy for you."

I scoffed. That was certainly already clear. "I know."

"The Orders are..." He paused, shaking his head. "They aren't *good*. Maybe once they were used to accomplish great things. But now, they're a tool used and run by very flawed people."

Those bright eyes went far away, as if lost in the past.

As much as I wanted to deny it, I was sure that in some ways, he was right. Perhaps the Orders were not the benevolent organizations that they once were. But I *needed* them.

And maybe, in a way, they could need me, too. Maybe I could make myself into something valuable.

"Perhaps they could do great things again," I said.

A bitter laugh slipped between Max's teeth. "Maybe." He didn't sound convinced.

"I have no other choices."

He looked down at his feet, hands in his pockets, and there was a long, long silence.

When he lifted his head again, his gaze met mine with a stronger determination, fragile but fierce, like a sheet of cracked glass. "You're really going to do this? Force the Orders to do something worth doing?"

"Yes," I replied, without hesitation.

"I don't know why I believe you."

But I could see in his face, in that eggshell hope, in the near-invisible bob of his throat, that he did.

"Well." He shook his head, then turned to the stacks of papers. "These are Stratagrams. They're used to direct magic for more complex spells. Kind of like instructions."

I looked down at them, rustling in the breeze around my feet. "I've seen them only one time. On Valtain slave. Complete Valtain, not like me. On her arms." I extended my forearm, demonstrating where I had seen the marks tattooed up and down the woman's albino skin. I had tried to talk to her, then, excited to meet someone else like me. But she had only looked at me with dead eyes.

A muscle twitched at the bridge of Max's nose. "If she was a slave, it was probably meant to cripple her power, direct her magic away from being anything useful. Imagine tying a cow's head to its tail. But as a tool, they're more commonly used by Solarie, since our magic is so much more external than yours." When we looked at each other again, the corners of his lips were curled in a confident smirk. As if that brief of flicker of vulnerability had never existed. "But, these are very advanced. We won't start here."

We won't start here.

My heart leapt. I nodded eagerly, so grateful to have an ally — *any* ally — that I didn't even care that he was overwriting my plans.

91

"Come inside. Get some rest. If you're done littering up my garden, anyway." He opened the door, stepping aside for me. "We'll have a long day tomorrow."

I went to the doorway, then stopped before I entered, turning to Max and regarding him in silence. Shadow doused the hard panes of his face, but his features were so sharp that they sliced through the dusk, meeting mine with equal determination and wary curiosity. We stood only inches apart, each allowing the other to peer into a rare, guarded honesty.

The urge to thank him lingered at the tip of my tongue. *Don't thank him for doing what he should have done to begin with,* a snide, colder part of me hissed.

I don't know why I believe you, he had said. But I knew. He believed me because he *wanted* to believe me — wanted to believe in the possibility of something better, however unlikely it was.

And that?

That was something that sank into my soul like water after miles and miles of parched, desperate desert.

"Thank you," I said, and went inside.

CHAPTER TWELVE

"That's it? That's what you've got?"

Max sat cross-legged among the tall, rippling grass, watching my silver butterflies rise into the sky.

"'That's it?'" I echoed.

"I mean — that's it?"

It was impossible not to be insulted by this reaction. "Not only these," I said, gesturing to the butterflies. "There was also fire and—"

"Sparks, honestly. It's just all very...performative."

"I know thoughts also," I offered.

"Right. No need to demonstrate that, I saw that one first hand." His teeth clamped down on the end of his pen, looking down at the stack of papers he had brought with him. "And when you do that — what do you typically do, exactly?"

"What do I *do*?"

"Do you speak, or just listen?"

I stared blankly at him. His eyes flicked up at me from the parchments.

"What I mean is, how closely can you understand what

people are thinking? Words, or just feelings? And how much do you control them?"

"Control?" It came out like a gasp. Could Valtain *do* that?

Max let out a humorless chuckle. "Ascended, you really are new to Ara, aren't you? This is why you need to be careful here."

I shook my head, putting aside that line of questioning for later. "I hear what they feel," I said. "Not words. Just…" I couldn't decide how to explain it in Aran, so I placed my hand over my heart. "Big things here."

He nodded, as if he understood this perfectly.

My thoughts shot to Esmaris, the way his mind felt withering and suffocating beneath my own, the look on his face as he fell to the ground. But I said nothing about that.

"Fine. Good." Max placed the pile of papers on the ground, staring down at them. I was fairly certain that he did not sleep last night. When I went to bed, he was scribbling frantically at the table, not bothering to so much as look at me as he bid me goodnight. And he was in exactly that same place when I got up again in the morning, except surrounded by substantially more paper and with eyes bracketed by darkness. Still, he was exceptionally energetic when he greeted me and almost immediately whisked me outside to begin.

No objections from me. In fact, this was the most encouraged I'd felt in weeks.

"No one taught me. I learned what I must. To—" The word eluded me. I settled on, "To dance."

"Dance?"

"Yes." I snapped my fingers as the word I was searching for came to me. "*Perform*. In Threll."

It took a moment for understanding to flood across Max's features, dimming some of his enthusiasm with a shade I couldn't quite identify. "I see. It makes sense that you would be self-taught."

He grunted as he pushed himself to his feet. I did the same, if only because I didn't like the idea of him staring down at me.

"More than anything," he said, "The Orders care about

control. That was why they were founded to begin with, to make sure that Wielders weren't going to accidentally wreak destruction simply because they didn't know what the hell they were doing. And to the Orders' credit, they fulfill that role very well. When Wielders wreak destruction, it's usually because they want to. Unless we're talking about Moth and my roses." Max glowered at the scalded flowers for just a moment before turning back to me.

"You seem to like conjuring, so let's start there. And, there's potential with that. That thing you do, turning the butterflies into glass? That's impressive for a Valtain. They struggle with physical things like that."

I must have looked pleased with myself, because he raised a finger.

"Don't get too full of yourself. Your accuracy is still a mess." He picked up a flower — a little yellow one with layers and layers of tiny, long petals. "Let's start with this. I want you to make me a copy of this flower."

Easy. I began to smile, but again, he raised that finger.

"No. Get that cocky smirk off your face. I'm not asking for what you *think* this flower looks like. This *exact* flower. Every little detail the same."

I looked from Max, to his raised hand, to the little yellow flower — all of those layers and layers of petals. I was sure I could do it. But was it really any more impressive than my own tricks? People liked performances. They liked to be *dazzled*. And I would certainly need to dazzle the Orders to accelerate myself.

"This will really help me impress in tests?" I said, skeptical.

"Are you implying that I'm leading you astray?"

The look on my face must have betrayed that I knew almost none of those words.

Max let out a breath through his teeth. "Listen. Many people believe that Fragmented Valtain are less capable. The idea being that Valtain magic bleaches hair and skin, so by that logic, someone like you…"

Someone like me would be inherently less powerful. I

nodded, glancing down at my hand and my two tan fingers. Those patches of gold had hurt my value as a slave, and now they hurt my value as a Valtain, too.

"It's not proven. The point is, many people, especially full Valtain, will be expecting you to fail. They'll be looking for a reason to prove that you're not capable of doing this. We'll make sure that you knock their moon-obsessed robes off, absolutely. But when you do it, you need to be technically *perfect*."

We'll make sure. Apparently, there was a "we" now.

I had to admit, I was pleasantly surprised — if somewhat perplexed — by how quickly Max had gone from trying to drive me away to being so deeply invested in my success.

"I will be," I said.

"You'd better. I have other things I could be doing. Make it worth it." Max handed me the flower. "Remember. *Exact*."

It turned out that my little assignment was harder than I thought it would be.

My first flower came easily, hovering, silver and translucent, between my hands. But Max took one look at it and shook his head.

"What did I tell you? That's not *this* flower. It's *a* flower. Or worse, what you *think* a flower looks like. There's nothing real about that."

It took only one more long look at what I had created to realize that he was right. My creation was too perfect, formed in rows of tear-shaped, identical petals that looked real from a distance but revealed themselves to be eerily fake up close.

I nodded, letting the flower dissolve into the air. Then tried again.

And again.

And.

Again.

Too big. Too small. Too perfect. Too symmetrical.

"You're duplicating petals," Max pointed out.

"I know," I muttered. I didn't mean to duplicate, but it was so hard not to. My mind felt too thick and clumsy to create all of that detail. My head *pounded*. But I offered no objection, no complaint.

Hours passed. My conjurings began to take longer and longer, flickering and writhing in the air like smoke. Soon Max and I both had to squint into blinding sunset light.

"We can stop for the day," Max said, rising to his feet. "Even experienced Wielders would struggle with this. You don't have to get it tonight."

But I didn't look away from my translucent flower as I replied, "No."

"What?"

"No. We do not stop."

He paused mid-step, looking perplexed. "This isn't typically the context in which I'd like to hear that. But my answer is the same nonetheless." He turned back around, slumping back to the ground, quirking one eyebrow at me in a skeptical challenge. "If you can do it, I can do it."

Oh, I could do it.

So, we resumed — me creating flower after flower and Max telling me all the ways in which it was wrong. By this point, I knew before he opened his mouth exactly how it was lacking, and I was already letting it dissolve by the time the words left his lips. By then, all final dregs of sunlight had long ago disappeared beneath the horizon, leaving us in darkness. Max opened fire in his palms and placed it on the ground, where it hovered in an eerie, self-contained ball.

"Could I do that?" I asked, without looking away from my five-trillionth flower.

"I don't know. Can you?"

I flicked my eyes to the fire ball. Fire had always been difficult for me, like it was speaking a language I didn't quite understand. *Sparks, really,* Max had called it. He wasn't wrong.

But I said, casually, "I'm sure yes," as if it were nothing.

He chuckled.

Flowers and flowers evaporated into the night. Max's responses grew slower and less enthusiastic. Eventually, he stood up and stretched. "Alright. I'm done. Sleep." He said it as if he couldn't conjure the energy to create more complete sentences.

"You go. I will stay."

A brief, surprised pause. "Are you sure?'

"Yes."

"Ramming your head against the wall will probably get less effective over time."

"I don't know what that's meaning."

"It means, don't kill yourself. But then again, I'm in no position to judge, I suppose." I heard the door open, even as my eyes were unwaveringly focused on the petal I sculpted. "Good luck."

A bitter smile twisted the edges of my mouth. "I do this so I don't need luck."

"I can't decide if that response is charming or terrifying."

And with that, he closed the door, leaving me in silence, singularly focused on my work.

It was comforting in a way to have something to fight for, to push myself beyond the shadow of talent and forge my success out of something stronger. There was a certain meditative quality about throwing myself against a stone wall again and again, chipping away at it. I could feel it cracking beneath my fingers, even as I felt it cracking *me*. At the end, one of us would be left standing. And I wasn't about to let myself break.

I eventually began conjuring each petal individually, figuring out how to hold the others in my mind as I moved on to the next one and the next and the next. And then, after that, I forced myself a step further: figuring out how to turn it into glass without letting all of those separate petals slip through the grasp of my mind.

The sounds of the nighttime bugs and creatures faded. The sky turned purple. My vision blurred, my head grew leaden, throbbing behind my eyes, ears, temples.

Tisaanah.

It was Esmaris's voice at first, accusing and pleading all at once.

"Tisaanah." The murkiness dripped away, peeling back the memory of my former master's face, his betrayal.

I opened my eyes to see a bright sky, tree branches and green leaves encroaching on the edges of my vision. And a pair of angular, bright blue eyes looking down at me from beneath perplexed brows.

I had fallen asleep.

"I told you that slamming your head against the wall wouldn't work," Max said.

My head sure felt like it had been slammed against *something*. It throbbed so intensely that the colors of my vision grew brighter and dimmer with every rhythmic beat of pain. I reached to my side, my fingers groping in the dirt, closing gently around something hard.

"It didn't?" I smiled at him as I opened my fingers to reveal a glass flower — every petal different, perfectly imperfect, an exact replica.

I'd never tasted anything sweeter than the quiet, muted surprise on Max's face as he took the flower from me, turning it around in his fingers.

"Good," he said, finally. There was a hint of a question mark at the end, as if he wasn't quite sure what to make of it.

I let my throbbing head fall back into the grass, allowing the flowers to hide my grin. Gods, I forgot how wonderful it felt to exceed expectations.

CHAPTER THIRTEEN

T he fish burned my throat.

I'd never really had much of a home, so I, perhaps naively, thought I would be immune to homesickness. Not true, it turned out. There were many things I missed about Threll, even about the Mikov estate, the only home I had known for my adult life. Near the top of that list was food that didn't hurt to eat. Arans, apparently, confused "taste" with "pain." Or at least, Max did.

He kept turning that glass flower around and around in his fingers as I ate. To my delight, he had nothing bad to say about it.

"Now you just have to learn how to do that in seconds instead of hours."

"I will," I replied, even though the prospect of it seemed dizzily daunting. "We will continue after eating."

I said this very casually, even though my stomach clenched at the thought. The floor felt like it was shifting beneath my feet, like I was back on that wretched boat with my infected back.

Max scoffed. "Like hell we will. You need at least a few hours to rest."

"I feel fine."

Untrue. But I had no time for rest. And besides, the thought of lying there with nothing to occupy myself but my thoughts seemed far more intimidating than forcing myself through exhaustion.

Max gave me a narrowed stare that pierced my lie. "You pushed yourself too hard. Wielding expends a lot of energy, and you've been doing it nonstop for the last twenty hours."

"It worked."

"This time. You won't always be so lucky." He shifted in his chair, opening his mouth as if he were about to speak. But before he could, the front door swung open and Sammerin stood there.

"Thank you, as always, for knocking. So very polite." Max cast a glance over his shoulder, though Sammerin offered no response other than a smirk and a delicate shrug. "Did you bring our favorite apprentice-sized ball of destruction? Because if so, he's not allowed in the house. Or the garden. I suppose he can sit very very still in a corner somewhere, touching nothing."

"Moth is visiting his mother." Sammerin slid into the chair beside Max. "Thank the Ascended."

"And you choose to spend your precious freedom with us? How sweet."

"Limited freedom. I have a client soon." Sammerin's gaze settled on me, pausing for a moment. I wondered if he heard it too — the "us." "How are you, Tisaanah? You look a bit—"

"I'm fine," I replied, at the exact same time that Max said, "She spent all night making this."

He handed Sammerin my glass flower, who examined it thoughtfully before glancing from Max to me. "Good work."

"Thank you," I said, at the exact same time that Max remarked, "It's acceptable."

"Hm." Sammerin looked from me, to Max, back to me. I was not typically one to be self-conscious, but I had to resist the urge to squirm beneath the assessing weight of his gaze.

"Client?" I asked.

"Sammerin is a healer," Max said. Frankly, it was a relief to hear that answering for others was not just something he did to me.

"Like Willa?"

"Not quite," Sammerin said. "The result is the same, but the process is different."

"Valtain are internal. Solarie are external." Max said this as if it was a self-contained explanation, but I was left turning those syllables around against my tongue.

In-turn-ul. Ex-tern-ul.

"What does that mean?" I finally asked. I hated the taste of every word, suddenly too aware of the thick tang of my accent.

"Valtain are..." Max chewed, thinking for a moment. "When Willa heals you, she is, in a sense, talking to your body. Encouraging it to grow and heal, feeding your life force from within." He jabbed his fork toward Sammerin. "When Sammerin does it, he's physically moving flesh, patching it together and melding it at a small, small level. The end result is similar, but the approaches are massively different. Sammerin's way hurts much more."

"But, it's far better for serious injuries like broken bones," Sammerin added, with a faint tinge of defensiveness. "And faster."

"When things get particularly nasty," Max said, "it's best to have both."

I wondered if he knew from experience.

"I see." At least, I somewhat did. The boundaries would become more clearly defined, I was sure, the longer I spent in Ara. I had met a Solarie only once — a beautiful raven-haired woman who had attended one of Esmaris's parties. She was the wife of a Lord, but was unusually kind to me for a noble, enhancing my performances with conjurings of little dancing lights and making the gold statues undulate as if they were moving with me. It was clear to me then that she used magic differently than I did, but I didn't fully understand how.

"Anyway, with that little lesson..." Max stood up and started down the hall towards the washroom, leaving Sammerin and I in awkward silence. I chewed the final forkful of my scalding fish.

Sammerin spoke first. "It looks like his attitude has changed since I was last here."

"No choice. There was no one else."

I said this matter-of-factly, as if we didn't both already know it was far from enough to change Max's mind.

"It takes a great deal to convince Max to do something," Sammerin said, stroking his beard. "But when he does it, he *does* it. For example…"

He gestured at the window and I followed his gaze. I realized that he was referencing the gardens, sprawling out from the cottage in every direction.

"He made the whole thing?" I asked.

"Planted every single flower. It was obsessive. But he does nothing halfway."

"He could be good teacher." I paused, then added, purely out of pettiness, "Maybe."

Sammerin shook his head slowly, his eyes crinkling with an intrigued smile. "There is no could. Max *will* be the best teacher you can find anywhere in Ara." He leaned back, head poised in a thoughtful tilt. "Curious."

"MAX! Did you know that there's a beautiful woman asleep in your house?"

I snapped my eyes open to see a mass of curly golden hair hovering over my face, fingers sweeping my hair off my forehead.

I let out a wordless yelp, jumping up in bed. A stunning young woman, bright face framed by wild golden curls, perched at the edge of my bed. She smiled at me in unfettered admiration.

Holy gods, was I dreaming?

My window revealed a sky that was only barely tinted purple, the room hazy with the dusky light of almost-dawn. I had crawled into bed early that night and fallen into a sleep so deep that it seemed only a shade away from death. It did not seem out of the question that I was having some sort of strange, waking dream.

"Hello," the woman said. Her fingers traced my cheek, following the edge of my patch of tan skin.

A Thereni greeting sat at the tip of my stunned tongue, tangling with the word "hello," but I was too shocked and disoriented to spit out either one.

"I thought living in the middle of nowhere meant that I didn't have to lock my doors. What did I ever do to make my house so welcoming?" Max's voice, rough with sleep, approached from the hallway. "I really tried to be as unpleasant as possible."

He appeared in the doorway, and I glanced at him before quickly looking away.

He stood there leaning against the frame, patting hair that stuck up at the back of his head. Crumpled linen pants rested low on his hips, and he was shirtless, lean muscle shifting across his stomach and chest as he yawned.

He looked... *different* than I would have expected, considering that his main hobbies appeared to be drinking and enthusiastically doing nothing.

I noticed this and then promptly tried to un-notice it.

"Max." The woman's voice was a gasp of amazement. She moved from my bed to the doorway, where she ran her hands through Max's hair. Her simple white dress floated around her ankles. She was barefoot. "You look *beautiful*."

A lover, perhaps? Somehow that didn't seem quite right.

"Thanks, Miraselle." His voice was flat. He winced, pulling away from her hands. "Haven't seen you around here in awhile."

Miraselle didn't even appear to hear him. Instead she looked back at me with the amazement of a child, pressing her palms together. "Look at her. Isn't she *lovely*? Look at that eye! It's the same color as the sun through the leaves! Did you notice that she's two different colors?"

Max and I glanced at each other. I pulled my knees up to my

chest and wondered if I should be alarmed that he was so un-alarmed.

"I did, in fact, notice that." He sighed and rubbed his eyes. "Where have you been?"

"I traveled the coast all the way to the Capital."

"I told you that wasn't a good idea."

Miraselle spread her arms out. "The wind just *took* me, Max!"

Every word she spoke was a sing-song note, breathy and amazed. It seemed… off. And the more I watched her, the more something seemed strange about her stare, as if it looked past me, past Max, past everything that touched her delighted gaze.

Max sighed. Then he placed a gentle hand on her shoulder, nudging her out the doorway. "It's not even sunrise yet. Let's go."

They padded down the hall. I slid out of bed and followed, too curious to remain in my room.

When I reached the living room, the door was already open and Miraselle swooned against it, face tilted to the garden. "Oh, how I missed the flowers here."

"Rightfully," Max said. "They're worlds better than the fussy terraces you saw in the Capital."

A lovely smile spread across her face. "I missed you, Max. You are so *nice*. I always loved that you're such a *nice* person."

If I hadn't been so perplexed, I would have laughed at that characterization.

"Thanks, Miraselle," he replied, unaffected.

And then, she spun to face me. "And you…You're just so *lovely*, Tisaanah. Truly *beautiful*."

"Thank you," I replied, because I wasn't sure what else to say.

It took me a moment to realize that I had never told her my name.

"Don't get into trouble," Max said to her, but by then, Miraselle had floated out the door, transfixed by the flowers.

He closed it behind her and let out an exasperated sigh. "Ascended. What a way to wake up."

"What is… wrong of her?"

"What makes you think anything is wrong with her?"

I gave him a look that silently reprimanded him for having the audacity to think I'm stupid.

"She's harmless," he said. "She just wanders around. She's a little strange, but I suppose that makes sense, since she wasn't always human."

Wasn't always *human?* "What was she?" I asked, immediately fascinated.

"A hummingbird."

I blinked blankly at him. He picked one of the many gold figurines off the mantel and tossed it to me. "Like this."

I looked down at the image of the bird in my palm — the pointed wings and long beaks. We had them in Threll, too, though of course the Thereni word was different. My nose scrunched up. "A *huhm-ing-berð*," I repeated, practicing the word.

I got the distinct feeling he was teasing me.

"Yes," Max replied, a little too casually. "She wanted to be a person, so I made her into one."

"You *made* her—"

"Yes."

"You can—"

"Yes."

I glanced at the figurine, then at Max, who looked far too pleased with himself. "You are lying," I said. "Making joke."

"Me? Never. I'm thoroughly humorless." He yawned. "Anyway, I'm sure we'll see her here more often. She likes the flowers. Understandable, I suppose."

Roughly three-fourths of me was sure that he was messing with me. The other quarter thought that he was, at the very least, heavily exaggerating.

"It's too early. I'm not made for this." Max began slinking back towards his bedroom. "Hopefully I can get a few more hours of sleep without anyone else wandering into my house, since that is, apparently, the fashionable thing to do these days."

I stood in the living room for a few minutes longer, the bird figurine still in my hand, thinking about the emptiness behind

Miraselle's features. Then I rose my gaze to follow Max's bare back sauntering down the hall. A long, angry scar slashed across it, starting at his right shoulder and falling all the way to his left hip, slipping beneath the waistband of his pants.

Interesting. Interesting, indeed.

CHAPTER FOURTEEN

S ammerin was right about one thing: when Max did
something, he *did* it.

We launched into training with a zeal that could only be
described as ferocity, and every second of it delighted me. I found
a certain euphoria in the exhaustion that came with relentless
pursuit of my goal. And I knew that Max enjoyed it, too. He didn't
show it — at least not as openly as I did — but a life in servitude
had taught me how to see between the cracks. Max's were few and
far between. But the energy that seeped from them fed my own.

We rose every morning at dawn to begin work. Max insisted
that I relearn everything that I already knew, despite my
protests. "You can't give those bastards any opportunity," he
pointed out, constantly, "so your basics need to be flawless."

And though I had been skeptical at first, I soon had to
begrudgingly admit that he was right. After a lifetime of self-
teaching, I had learned to cut corners that I didn't know existed.

So, I sculpted flower after flower, shaving minutes off at a
time. I ended every day with a throbbing head, trembling fingers,
and usually, some clipped, sparse words of praise from Max.

But, though I relished the fact that he approached our training sessions with enthusiasm that matched mine, our partnership was still far from perfect. Outside of our lessons, we did not talk much — mostly because I *never* wanted to be outside of our lessons. I pushed him constantly — another hour, and another, and another. One more set of lessons. One more round of practice.

Sometimes, he indulged me. Other days, he would roll his eyes, loosen some vaguely insulting quip, pour a glass of wine, and disappear into his room. No matter. I would practice on my own until I couldn't keep my eyes open any longer.

When they finally shuttered, I would be greeted with the same images, every night. Esmaris's face. Serel's eyes. The crack of the whip. The smear of blood on my fingers. I always knew, somehow, that it didn't all belong to me.

I tried to avoid sleeping whenever possible. It was, I told myself, a waste of time anyway. And for all Max scolded me about the necessity of rest, I knew he hardly slept, either. Too often, when I crept from my bed in the middle of the night, I saw the soft glow of flickering light beneath his bedroom door. Sometimes I would see his silhouette out in the garden, pruning dead blossoms in the middle of the night.

Surely, he must have seen me, too. But I was relieved that he never approached me. There were certain things I was not ready to let him see. And he seemed equally uninterested in indulging my curiosities.

Only one time, in those weeks, did he acknowledge me. It was a particularly brutal night for me, and I was plagued with nightmares so vivid that they curdled the blood in my veins. I couldn't practice, I couldn't study. Instead, I escaped out into the garden, pacing wide circles around the cottage, desperate to slow my racing heart.

Eventually, I grew so agonized and frustrated that I let my knees buckle beneath me, near tears.

You forgot what you are.

The words looped, over and over again. And all I wanted was for my mind to be quiet, for just one minute, one second.

I sat there, kneeling in the damp soil, head bowed, for what felt like hours. And when I finally, finally lifted my head, I caught a glimpse of a pair of blue eyes peering at me through the curtain.

My cheeks burned. Embarrassed, I dragged myself up, dusted myself off, and went back inside. I resumed my studies until, finally — mercifully — sleep took me over my books.

"Let's try something different today."

Max sipped his tea, his back to me as he stared out the window.

It had taken me a few minutes to scrape up the courage to even look at him the next morning, embarrassed that I had unwittingly let him see me in such a state. But once I did, I was careful to be a perfect picture of my typical everyday self.

I paused, my fork halfway to my mouth. "Different?" I echoed.

"I have some errands to run in the city. You've never been there, have you?"

"The city?"

"The Capital."

I shook my head, even though his back still faced me. "No." I had seen it from a distance, during my brief stay in the Tower of Midnight. But that hardly counted. I had read about Ara's capital city, and my books had made it sound so alive, so grand. A small part of me — fine, a large part of me — was eager to find out whether it was everything I pictured it would be.

But...

"When will we do today's training?"

Finally, Max turned. He took another sip of tea, giving me a long look that I returned with equal steadiness. "I think," he said at last, "that you've been doing plenty of training."

Self-consciousness prickled at the back of my neck.

"I only have five months," I said. "I cannot waste time."

He let out an exasperated sigh and pinched the bridge of his nose. "Fine. We will go to the Capital for a few hours this morning. And then we will continue with a lesson this afternoon. Does that satisfy your compulsive productivity standards?"

I paused.

Just one morning. One morning to think about something other than my upcoming evaluations. One morning to see the city — and not just any city, but the *Capital of Ara*. A place I only dreamed I'd witness with my own eyes.

A few hours will be alright. Just this once.

A smile yanked at the corners of my mouth, without my permission. "I think maybe that will be fine."

Max gave me a little, reluctant smirk, raising his teacup. "And thus, our Threllian princess has spoken."

CHAPTER FIFTEEN

After we finished breakfast, Max led me outside and I took his arm as he unfolded a little piece of parchment.

"A Stratagram?" I asked.

"Yes. It would take all day to travel there otherwise."

"When will I learn this?"

He arched an eyebrow at me. "I'm starting to think that you have a terribly one-track mind."

"My mind has many tracks," I retorted, as if I knew what his insult meant.

"Clearly."

I watched his hands as he drew a circle. Then one line, and another—

My heartbeat quickened in my chest, and my fingers tightened of their own accord.

"Is it amazing?" I murmured, the words slipping from my lips without my permission.

"Oh, no. It's horrible," Max replied. "You'll love it."

He drew the final line of the Stratagram, and the world snapped into a thousand pieces.

I was expecting it this time, but when we landed in the Capital, I still found myself clutching Max's arm much harder than I had when we left. I staggered against his shoulder as the ground seemed to rise up and slam against me. For a few horrible seconds, my senses smeared together in shades of grey. They returned one-by-one. Sound came first.

Specifically, the sound of Max snickering at me.

I released my grip.

"You alright?" he asked.

"Yes," I shot back, too quickly.

We stood in the corner of a bustling cobblestone square. Buildings lined narrow streets, packed together like mosaics. Decorations adorned even the smallest ones, stone lions peering over door frames or delicately carved vines creeping across windowsills. And the people...There were people *everywhere*. People in all styles of dress, wearing anything from torn up work clothes to floating chiffon gowns. People of every color, every age, all so densely packed that their shoulders brushed each other. If the crowd bothered anyone, no one showed it.

I raised my eyes further to see the Palace looming over it all — those knifelike peaks more striking than ever from down here, slicing into the faint mist of the hazy coastal sky. Just beyond it, the dual Towers lifted all the way into the clouds in two ethereal columns of gold and silver.

My lips opened, but I had momentarily lost my grasp on my new language. Words dissolved somewhere between my awe at the scale of it all and the panic that rose in my chest at the *much-ness*. I had never been so close to so many people at once. Ever.

"I know," Max grumbled, reading my face. "That's why I don't come here. That, and, in a city of a few hundred thousand people, it's only a matter of time until you run into someone you don't want to talk to."

His eyes lingered off somewhere in the crowd, and I wondered if he had already found one such person. There were probably a *lot* of people that Max didn't want to talk to.

"I'm not made for this. Let's get out of here. Ascended, I don't remember this square being *this* bad."

He started off through the crowd. As we moved through the sea of people, I smoothly slid my arm through his. I had done this for purely practical purpose, but the startled look he gave me was just so *delightful* that I pushed a little closer just because I wanted to see how he'd react. It was possibly the first time I had seen an expression on his face that went beyond either deadpan grumpiness or cocky satisfaction.

"What?" I smiled at him. "If I become lost, I will never be found again."

To my disappointment, that startled expression melted away as quickly as it had appeared. He merely narrowed his eyes and said, "Sometimes you're unintentionally poetic."

"Nothing unintentional," I replied, coolly.

Untrue, but he didn't have to know that.

The crowd let up somewhat as we skirted along the edge of the square and glided down a side street, so narrow that we disappeared into the shadow of the buildings on either side. The buildings changed as we walked, growing slightly less pristine and slightly less straight. The type of people we passed evolved, too — those elegant gowns were fewer and fewer, replaced by men in sloppy clothes leaning over easels or women in bright colors tending to potted flowers. One man that we passed wore a long, emerald green coat that nearly touched the ground, and a parrot the exact same shade of green — a *parrot!* — perched on his shoulder.

At that, I whipped my head around to look at Max, my face splitting into a grin. "Did you *see* —"

"It's not the strangest thing you'll witness in this city today." A little, amused smile crinkled the corners of his eyes.

He extracted his arm from mine. I was a little surprised at how much I missed it as my hands dropped to dangle awkwardly at my sides.

"Here." Max turned to a little storefront. At first glance, it looked closed. Dusty drapes covered the wide glass windows, the sign above them empty. Still, he didn't so much as hesitate as he opened the door, letting me go first.

The heels of my boots echoed on the dim wooden floor, the sound bouncing up to caress the rafters that cut across the tall ceiling. Light streamed through large, dirty windows, catching the dust that hung in the air like mist.

The space was large and mostly empty. At first, I thought it was unoccupied. That is, until my gaze fell to the far corner, where all of that emptiness and cool shadow gave way to a splash of warmth. Ostentatious couches and armchairs sat at haphazard angles, spattered with patches of color. In between them stood a long, dirty wooden table, which was covered with glittering metal pieces. Scattered throughout all of this furniture were various canvases and sculptures — faces and hands and eyes that stared blankly back at us.

And there, among all of this, were two figures. One of them, a short woman in a loose, paint-spattered white top and plain trousers, turned to us as we entered. Her eyes fell to me first, and she looked as if she were about to tell me where to go — nowhere good. Then, Max wandered in beside me and her expression brightened. "Max! I've been wondering where you've been. Was starting to think I'd be better off selling off everything I've saved for you."

"Fun things, or work things?"

As Max and I approached the living area, it grew harder and harder to pry my eyes off the sculptures that surrounded us. They were grotesque and beautiful. One consisted of dozens of gnarled, bodiless hands all reaching to some unseen point. A few of the less disturbing ones reminded me of some of the figures lining the shelves of Max's house.

The woman grinned, tossing a strand of long, auburn hair over one shoulder. Everything about her appearance looked lazy, like she could have rolled out of bed looking just as she did now. And yet, she was undeniably captivating. Not traditionally beautiful, exactly, but her features were strong and sharp, nearly as striking as her sculptures. White powder covered her hands, which left smears in her hair as she pushed it behind one ear.

"Both," she said. Then she looked at me. "This must be Tisaanah, the famous apprentice."

I tried to decide whether or not I liked being described in this manner.

One of Max's eyebrows twitched, asking an unspoken question. "Sammerin told me," the woman said.

"What a gossip," Max muttered. "Tisaanah, this is Via."

I greeted her, though I was still visibly distracted. I looked at the chunk of marble beside her — the one presumably responsible for the white dust smearing her hands and face. The bottom half was a pristine square, while the top chipped away to reveal a woman's head, chin lifted, face raised. "You made these?"

"Yes, though sometimes I'm not sure how I feel about taking ownership of them." She looked at her work in progress and scrunched her nose. "I'm not sure about this one."

"It's plebeian." A man who had been lounging on one of the couches swung his legs out, standing beside Via and placing a hand around her shoulder. He looked like he put a lot of effort into being extremely handsome and even more effort into not showing it. He was good at both, but eight years at Esmaris's estate made me an expert in spotting that kind of thing.

"You're capable of better," he went on. "Something more... raw. Soulful."

Via made a small, noncommittal noise, then waved a hand at him. "This is Philip."

Philip gave Max a smile that was more of a baring of teeth and completely ignored me.

"*Anyway.*" Via slipped from Philip's grasp and began striding away, motioning for us to follow. "Come to my workshop."

This wasn't her workshop?

She led us into a shadowy corner where a single, plain door stood nestled into the darkness.

"He's awful," Max muttered as Via opened the door.

"Oh, Max." She gave him a mischievous smile, stepping into a dim, golden light. "Would you judge a squirrel by its ability to swim?"

"I don't need to know where this metaphor goes next."

"What I mean is, he's no great conversationalist, but he's excellent at climbing trees."

Max groaned.

I didn't need to understand the specifics of Aran to understand her gist, and I chuckled. But only for a moment, because I stepped through the door and into stunned silence.

This room was the opposite of the dusty loft we had come from in every way: meticulously organized, with two smooth, clear tables in the center of the room perched atop neatly ordered shelves. The walls were lined with weapons. Swords, knives, spears, scimitars, daggers — and many others that were unlike anything I'd ever see before. They were all undeniably, lethally beautiful, their silver and gold and steel glinting in the flickering golden firelight.

Via shut the door behind us and began rummaging through a cabinet in the corner. I paced the walls, examining the weapons. Some, I noted, seemed oddly and intentionally incomplete. I paused at one sword that had a hollow center, delicate spiraling patterns cut into its blade.

Decorative? Or — perhaps they held some kind of purpose.

"Why is it like this?" I asked, pointing to one of the hollow swords on the wall.

She gave me a smile as sharp as her blades. "So Wielders can have more fun with it."

So... the space in the center was for magic? Interesting. I leaned closer, squinting at the designs.

"You like?"

"It is beautiful." An undeniable truth. "But beautiful is not enough. It needs to be both beautiful and—"

The word eluded me, but Max provided, "Functional."

"Yes," I agreed. "Beautiful and functional."

Via laughed, low and smooth. "Trust me, my work is always functional."

When I turned around again, Max was leaning over one of the workbenches, picking up the half-finished weapon on top of

117

it. "You're taking contracts?" He did not hide the disapproval in his voice.

Via emerged from the closet with her arms full of bottles, nudging the door closed with her elbow. "I so deeply enjoy when you come here and criticize everything about my life. Put that down, it's not finished."

He obeyed, but continued to stare down at the weapon with a wrinkle of distaste over his nose. "The Guard commission these?"

"I've got to make my money somehow."

My eyes settled on some stacked crates in the corner. The lid on the top one was askew, revealing piles of glinting steel.

There were probably close to a hundred weapons in those crates alone, if they were all full.

Max followed my gaze. "And business is good?"

"Business is mine alone." Via gestured to the small glass bottles on the table. "Now do you want these, or not?"

I joined Max beside the table. All of those little vials held black liquid — and yet, they were so oddly colorful, catching a glint of blue or purple or orange when the light flickered just the right way.

Max observed them for a moment. Then he chose three bottles: one that was so black it seemed to swallow the light completely. Then one that shimmed with a sheen of purple. And, lastly, one that sparked orange, as if it were reflecting flames even when it wasn't.

"Pick one," he then said, to me.

"What are these?"

"It will be more fun if you don't know."

"My fun or your fun?"

Via laughed. "Smart question."

Max smirked, his eyes glittering. "Depends on which one you pick."

I looked down at the table. My gaze settled on deep burgundy that flashed with brighter red. It reminded me of the spatters of my blood on Esmaris's deep crimson jacket — so much so that the sight of it brought a whisper of anger to my skin.

But anger was good. Anger was better than guilt. Anger was a reminder of why I was doing any of this in the first place.

"This." I handed Max the bottle. He held it up to look at it for a moment, furrowing his brow but offering no comment as he tucked it into his jacket.

"That's all we need," he told Via, who then packed the vials away and returned them to the closet.

She walked us out of her workshop and back to the front door. Max dropped a handful of coins in her palm.

"Too much," she said, pocketing it anyway.

"Do fewer contracts."

"Idealistic as only a rich man can be." She winked at him, and then her gaze slid to me. "Wonderful to meet you, Tisaanah. I'm sure our paths will cross again."

And then, she disappeared back into the dusty shadows of her apartment.

Max and I strode back down the street the way we came. We once again passed the man with the green coat and the parrot. This time, I couldn't resist. I stopped short, turning around and backtracking to him. He turned a calm, bespectacled gaze to me, and I offered him my most charming grin.

"I must ask," I said, "did you get the coat to match bird, or the bird to match coat?"

The man nodded seriously, as if I had asked him an extremely important question, and his voice reflected this grave nature as he bent down to whisper the answer in my ear. I felt both enlightened and satisfied as I quickened my steps to catch up with Max, a smile tightening my cheeks.

"What'd he say?" Max asked.

But I just placed a finger over my lips. "Is only for me to know."

WE TOOK a different route back through the city once we reached the main roads, Max leading me through wide, colorful streets. We were very close to the Palace now. I could see the golden stairs leading to its entrance in the gaps between buildings. Marketplace booths lined the sidewalks, hawking fruit or trinkets or gaudy jewelry. It was less crowded here than it had been where we first arrived, but I still struggled to adjust to the sheer number of people in my vicinity.

"Are you looking for something?" I asked Max, who paused to observe an extremely old-looking book at one of the stalls.

"Not particularly."

I brushed my fingers across a jeweled dagger. Pretty — but even I could tell it was practically a toy. Nothing like the elegant tools we had seen at Via's shop.

"The bottles." I nodded towards Max's pockets. "Are they weapons?"

"Not exactly."

"Is Via making so many weapons for war?"

"Let's not talk about that here." Max's eyes darted from one side of the street to the other, looking deeply uncomfortable.

But before I could respond, horns cut through the air, drowning out even the loudest voices in the crowd. Nearly everyone on this packed street silenced at once, all turning their heads to the Palace in unison that bordered on eerie.

"Shit," Max hissed. I turned to look at the golden stairs leading up to the Palace gates to see a procession of figures making their way down to the steps. Curiosity seized me, and before I could think, my feet were carrying me forward.

I knew nothing about Ara's politics, and I would have to remedy that. Whatever was happening up there, it looked important.

"Tisaanah—"

But I didn't even hear Max as I slipped through the crowd, pushing my way to the front of the group with my eyes drawn up to the stairs.

I got there just in time to see the first figures descend. There were eight of them, all entirely in black — tight-fitting pants, long jackets, hoods that covered their hair. The darkness was punctuated with shocks of gold in the buttons of their uniforms, the thick belts that encircled their waists, and, most noticeably, in the long, sharp spears that each of them held crossed over their bodies. Every single one of them, I realized, was a woman.

"Ascended, Tisaanah." I jumped, startled, as Max emerged in the crowd beside me. "What happened to, *'If I become lost I will never be found again'*?"

He was lucky I was too distracted to be offended by his imitation of my accent. "Well, you found me," I said, dismissively.

"I almost didn't. This place is a disaster. Let's go."

One of those hooded faces jerked towards me. She moved like a bird, with uncanny, abrupt leaps. When she turned to me, I had to strangle a gasp.

At first, the shadow of their hoods had obscured their faces so much that I didn't notice. But now...

"They have no eyes," I rasped.

Nestled into her eye sockets were only two neat, pink scars. And yet, she looked *directly* at us —

"We saw those—" The Aran word for "spear" evaded me. "Those pointed things. At Via's workshop. She made them?" I turned to look at him to see that Max looked so shockingly pale that I stopped short. "Are you alright?"

"Yes. But let's just—"

A shudder of murmurs ran through the crowd, and I felt their excitement, their fear, lurch into my bones. It crashed over and flooded my own thoughts, momentarily drowning me. I had to fight back to the surface of my own mind, forcing myself to observe every detail of this procession.

A smear of gold and blush descended the stairs — long sun-colored hair and a pink dress that trailed long behind its wearer. Disbelief stunned me, but there were no doubts who I was looking at. If any remained, the delicate crown atop that cascading hair put them to rest.

"*That* is the Queen?" I gasped.

"Yes."

"She's a *child*."

"That she is," Max muttered.

Queen Sesri could not have been older than thirteen, at most. Her round cheeks were completely still, enormous eyes unblinking, giving her the appearance of a porcelain doll. Her dress overwhelmed her tiny frame, swaddling her in layers upon layers of chiffon and gossamer. Beside her stood a Valtain man dressed in a fine but simple white suit. He stopped just behind her, flicking a plat of neat silver hair over his shoulder and regarding the crowd with flat stoicism.

The eight hooded soldiers parted and a finely dressed, portly man was forced to his knees on the steps.

"*Shit*," Max muttered, under his breath, "she's doing this publicly now?"

The tension in the crowd intensified, and for one terrible moment I forgot who I was, swept away by the overwhelming emotions of others. I nearly doubled over, then snapped back into my own head so quickly that I felt like I had walked into a wall.

Focus, Tisaanah. Focus.

The queen opened her mouth, and silence fell over the crowd like a suffocating blanket. "Lord Savoi. You are here to testify before your people. Do you look into the eyes of those you betray and continue to insist your innocence?"

"I have no traitorous intentions, my Queen," the man said. The slight waver at the end of his sentence was the only sign that he was afraid. But I could taste his fear, feel it seeping into my own skin and melding with the trembling tension of the crowd.

The Queen turned to look at the Valtain who stood beside her. He shook his head in one small movement.

"You are lying," she said to her prisoner. "You keep lying."

"I do not lie, my Queen. I do not."

I will die I will die I will die.

My fingers shot to my temples, a rough exhale escaping between my teeth.

"Are you alright?" Max's breath on my ear beckoned me back to my own head. I nodded, even though I knew I was leaning against him more heavily.

"You *do* lie," the Queen barked. "You're lying to all of us. Such traitorous intentions killed many more people than just my father. I'm sure your kin remember."

She gestured to the crowd. And I felt the memories ripple through them, and through me — flashes of blood and steel, the iron tang of panic.

The hooded, eyeless guard's face turned toward us again.

Max's other hand gently gripped my shoulder. "Let's get out of here."

The guard leaned over at the waist and whispered into the Queen's ear.

I nodded, turning away with Max to push our way back through the crowd—

But then the Queen's voice rang out. "Maxantarius Farlione."

Max froze. *"Fuck."*

CHAPTER SIXTEEN

My stunned gaze snapped to Max. Why would the Queen—?

"Step forward, Maxantarius."

He muttered a string of curse words beneath his breath. Then he released my shoulder and turned, pushing through the front of the crowd. I watched him with my heart lingering at the base of my throat, unable to shake the feeling that a dangerous shadow loomed over us.

It was only as I watched him approach the steps that I noticed Nura standing near the bottom of the stairs, hands behind her back. Beside her stood several other members of the Orders, each bearing the insignias of the Orders of Midnight or Daybreak.

I saw only the smallest hint of surprise glimmer across Nura's face.

The Queen smiled at Max. "I remember you. I have very good memory, you know."

Gods, she was such a *child*.

Max offered no response. I watched the stiff line of his back, shoulders square with his hands clasped in front of him.

"Do you know who this is, Lord Savoi?" the Queen asked.

"I— I do not, my Queen." The man peered over his shoulder. "I am familiar with the Farlione name, but—"

"Maxantarius Farlione is nearly solely responsible for the end of the Great Ryvenai War. Specifically, our victory at the city of Sarlazai."

No one made a sound, but the emotional response that tore through the air was so explosive that for one moment I forgot to breathe — as if I was being ripped in two, torn between stunned admiration and acidic *revulsion*. I clenched every muscle to keep myself upright.

I could have sworn I saw Max's shoulders shudder.

The Queen gazed down at him admiringly for a moment, and I recognized the look on her face, that adoring doe-eyed smile that I had practiced in the mirror many times at her age. Then, it soured. "You were invited to the Palace to be honored after the end of the war. But you didn't come."

"You were only six years old then, my Queen. I thought it would likely be past your bedtime."

A collective gasp. Mine joined it.

Stupid. *Stupid.* In Threll, such blatant disrespect could cost a man his life.

The remnants of the smile withered at the corners of the Queen's mouth.

"You will address our Queen with respect," one of the eyeless guards barked, her fingers tightening around that spear.

I vividly remembered the sound of Serel's blade piercing Esmaris's chest and my blood turned to ice, imagining that same wet crunch as the spear impaled Max—

I desperately, so desperately, wanted to grab him and yank him back into the crowd.

Max's face turned just slightly, only enough for me to see the edge of his profile over his shoulder.

"I was merely providing an explanation," he said to the Queen, who frowned. The she looked at the Valtain, who, in turn, stared at Max with a wrinkle between his brows.

"Don't even think about it, Tare," Max hissed. But the wrinkle on the Valtain's forehead only deepened, and Max's fingers curled at his temple.

When the Valtain glanced at the Queen and nodded, she let out a visible breath.

"You only have lenience," she said, voice wavering, "because of all you sacrificed for my father." Then, to Lord Savoi, who still kneeled on the steps, "Do you wish to look into the eyes of such sacrifice and lie to him, too, Lord Savoi? I'm sure you heard the fate of the Farlione family. After everything he did for this country, he lost his kin to traitors like you, just as I did."

It took me a moment to fully translate the words. When I did, my heart clenched.

Lord Savoi looked down at Max. "I do not lie," he said, pleadingly.

Queen Sesri turned again to the Valtain, who shook his head, his expression stone.

Her delicate hand curled into a fist. "You *do* lie. *Why?* After what such lies took from me? From heroes like Captain Farlione—"

"Firstly, I'm not Captain anything anymore." Max's furious voice sliced through hers. "I am no longer a member of the military. And secondly—"

The girl's face went blank, stunned. "You will not—"

"*Secondly,* my *Queen,*" he spat, "what happened to my family was a tragedy, not a political statement. And *this* is not what they or your father died for. He would be ashamed to see you using his death to justify this circus."

For one split moment, I was certain I was about to witness Max's death.

That is, until Nura darted from her designated place in the sidelines, sliding in front of Max and dropping into a kneel. "Please, forgive him, my Queen. The things he witnessed and lost during the war still linger, and his mind has never been the same. He does not know what he says."

I could only imagine the face he was making at *that* implication.

"I know exactly what I say," Max snarled.

"The insane always think they do," Nura said to the Queen, ignoring him.

"I know *exactly* what I say, and I will face the consequences for it if necessary."

No one needed my particular gifts to hear the dare in that statement.

Nura looked at Max as if he really *was* insane, and frankly, I was beginning to wonder, too.

The hooded guards' graceful bodies shifted in minuscule, lethal movements, like coiling cats.

The Queen's lips were pressed tightly together, her doll-like eyes glistening, fists trembling at her sides. For the first time, her Valtain companion moved. He stepped forward, placing one hand on her shoulder.

As if to silently say, *Don't.*

But she looked only at Max. "You cannot talk to me that way. I am the Queen. My father would be proud of what I've done to avenge him."

"Your father would—"

"Enough! *You*—"

The Valtain's hand tightened at her shoulder. He leaned forward to whisper in her ear. Then stepped back, leaving Queen Sesri standing there with her chest heaving, a furious internal battle warring across her face.

"I know you saved my father's life," she said at last. "So in his memory, I grant you mercy, *once.*"

I choked out a strangled breath.

But the Queen was not done.

She whirled around, lips curling into a furious sneer. "But *you.*" She pointed at Lord Savoi, who knelt on the steps. "*You* are a liar. *You* are a traitor. And I will not repeat my father's mistakes."

"Please, my Queen—" Lord Savoi touched his forehead to

the stone ground. His whole body shook. When I looked at him, a terror that did not belong to me flooded my veins. My vision was beginning to blur.

"I know you lie. I know you conspire."

"I do not—"

"*I know you do!*" Tears glided down her cheeks. "I am young. But I am not naive, and I am not weak."

"Please—" Max jolted forward, a hand outstretched.

But then, so quickly that their movement made time feel like it had skipped forward —

Two of those hooded guards drove their spears through the cowering man's back.

The world went silent as his blood spilled over the Palace's golden steps, dripping down in syrupy waterfalls. It pooled around Max's feet.

One of the guards used her boot to remove Lord Savoi's twitching body from her spear, kicking it down the stairs.

"Let this be proof," the Queen said, but I doubt anyone heard her. We all stood in silence as she and her soldiers and her Valtain ascended up the steps, that long, blush gown trailing behind her.

As soon as they disappeared behind the gates, I leapt to Max, who stood perfectly still as he watched the blood soak into the soles of his boots. I felt it soak through mine, too. Still warm.

Like Esmaris's had been. Like mine had been.

Before I could speak, Nura whirled to us, fire glinting in her colorless eyes.

"If you want to die so badly," she spat, "hang yourself like every other sorry bastard. I won't put myself in that position to save you again."

I was surprised at how quickly a barbed defense lurched to the tip of my tongue. I had to catch it in my teeth, reminding myself that I needed Nura's favor.

Max hardly reacted. "You're right, Nura," he said, flatly. "It must be hard to be so fucking selfless."

His hand slipped into his pocket and retrieved a piece of parchment, which he slowly unfolded.

Lord Savoi's lifeless face, just a few steps away, stared somewhere over my right shoulder. Behind us, the crowd began to dissipate.

"Max —" I wasn't even sure what I was going to say. I had so many questions, but I felt too ill to untangle them. All of my energy drained into separating my own thoughts from the fog of others'.

Max's gaze fell to me, and something in it wrenched, a wrinkle of concern forming between his brows. "Let's go home."

He tore two vicious lines through the paper, and the world began to wither and dissolve around us. I clutched his arm, tightening my fingers as I realized, with a start, that he was shaking. Or maybe that was me.

The gentle, melodic silence of the garden was almost eerie as we arrived back at the cottage. Max didn't say a word as we began striding to the house. The world was still spinning, and I think he knew that, because he didn't try to extract his arm from mine.

I wanted to ask him if he was alright, but that was a stupid question, because it was obvious that he wasn't. I wasn't sure that I was, either. So instead I said, "You were right."

Tired blue eyes slid to me. "What?"

"The man with parrot. Not the strangest thing."

Max hissed an angry, humorless laugh, and we barely spoke again.

I HAD DISCARDED my bloody boots and bathed several times over, but that night, I still could smell nothing but death and see nothing but that lifeless face pressed against the golden steps.

The sound had been exactly as I imagined it, too. Flesh and bone.

Max's history in the war, then, was more than I had thought. And his *family* —

His family —

Now, some things made more sense. Max's isolation. His cynicism. His bitterness. I knew how tragedy like that, no matter the circumstances, could so easily became a core piece of your being. Mine had. I just set it on fire and let it fuel me. It just as easily could have eaten me alive.

I slid out of bed and paced my room, peering out the window to watch the moonlight nestle into the delicate folds of flowers. I looked down at my hands, willing cool blue light to shudder from my fingertips. It folded into a butterfly before I even had to tell it to. Pretty. But too delicate, too fragile.

Whatever had happened at the city of Sarlazai had been polarizing. I had never felt such strong disgust. Such *hatred*. Whatever Max had done there had won the crown its war, yes. But it had come with a heavy price.

But then, that was the nature of war, wasn't it? I barely remembered the worst of the Threllian Wars, but I knew that even Nyzrenese victories left so many mourners. My most vivid memory of the time before the fall of the Nyzrenese senate was peering into my parents' bedroom at night to see my mother weeping, wrapped in the arms of an aunt or family friend that I no longer remember. Now, I didn't even recall who had died. But above all, I would always remember my distinct confusion. That day had been full of celebrations — more food than we'd been afforded for months, and the Strategasi himself climbing upon the capital balcony to speak of our valiant and crushing victory over the Threllian armies on some battlefront or another, to praise our honor and our hope, to assure us that peace and victory were imminent. I was five years old — I was just excited to drink milk, to eat pies baked with real sugar. I did not notice my mother's silence or her forced smiles. And that night, as I had watched her cry, I didn't understand.

We had won, the Strategasi had said. Weren't we supposed to be happy?

I was too young to know the truth then. That victory meant another's defeat, and sometimes our own defeat. That winning meant sacrifices, and sometimes ones that even our own people were not willing to make. That in war, someone always paid.

I thought of the Queen. The weapons piled high in Via's shop. The anticipation of the crowd.

If war came to Ara, what would I do? Did I have any choice but to use it to solidify my position? Use that position to help my own long-suffering people?

The ones who had sacrificed everything for me?

My butterfly withered, as if it was being consumed by flames.

I hoped I wouldn't have to make that choice. Perhaps because I knew what I would choose, and hated myself for it.

I slid back into bed, staring at the ceiling. Sleep felt so far away, but I closed my eyes anyway. In the darkness I saw the Palace steps, the Queen, Max's back. The blurry memory of my weeping mother. The blood running down those stairs again, and again, and again.

CHAPTER SEVENTEEN

T he shadows beneath Max's eyes the next morning told me
he had slept about as well as I had. And then his pointed
silence told me that he certainly had no interest in talking about
what had happened the day before.

I had so many questions — about the war, about his family,
about the Queen's father. But I'd spent enough time reading
people and massaging my interactions with them to know that
outright asking was not the best way to find out what I wanted
to know. So I had obliged his unspoken request, sitting in
silence, watching out the window bleary-eyed as the sun rose
over the horizon. It wasn't hard. I felt like I had been trampled
by a few dozen horses.

We were halfway through breakfast when the front door
abruptly swung open, revealing an unamused-looking Sammerin.

"I hear that you had a very exciting day yesterday," he said,
calmly, in place of a greeting.

Max grunted something wordless.

"You're lucky to be alive."

"Absolutely. So lucky."

Sammerin gave him a cold, hard look — one of those looks

shared between friends who knew each other well enough to speak silently.

Max shrugged.

"She's a child," Sammerin said. "You should have controlled yourself."

At this, my mouth went sour, the image of the blood rolling down the steps overtaking my vision. "A child?" I said. My voice was raspy with exhaustion, like my headache was seeping into my throat. "She *killed* that man."

"That isn't the first one, either." Max scoffed. "Someone had to say something."

"Very noble of you." Sammerin let out a silent breath, invisible except for the lowering of his shoulders. "If Tare had given her any other sign, it would've been your body kicked down those stairs."

Max laughed bitterly. "Good point. All those years ago, would you ever have thought Tare would be the one holding so many lives in his hands? *Tare?*" He shook his head. "Ascended above. What a time to be alive."

"The Valtain with her?" I asked. Max had addressed him by name yesterday, too, I recalled. "You know him?"

"The Orders are incestuous," he replied. "Everyone knows everyone, mostly because everyone has either screwed or screwed over everyone else. Sometimes both. Occasionally even at the same time."

"In-ses-tu...?"

"It means..." His brow furrowed, then he shook his head. "Nevermind."

Sammerin sighed. "Just tread carefully, Max. You won't get chances like that again."

Something softened in Max's expression, just slightly. "I know." Then he stood up, turning to me. "Are you ready?"

I blinked at him, trying to clear the cloud from my thoughts.

"You look like death. But you don't think you get a break because of this, do you?"

I had assumed, judging by Max's foul mood, that I'd be practicing on my own today. But this was a pleasant surprise. "If you can do it," I said, "I can do it."

A smirk glimmered at the corners of his eyes. "That's what I like to hear." Then, to Sammerin, "Excuse us, Sammerin. We have work to do. Besides, I'm sure that Moth is probably destroying something as we speak."

"Probably so," Sammerin muttered. His gaze went far away, as if imagining what he would go home to find.

Poor Moth. I hoped that they didn't talk about me that way.

Sammerin turned to the door, then paused for a moment and looked back at Max. "What were you doing in the city to begin with?"

"Just picking up some things from Via."

"And then you stayed? Some might dare call that out of character, Max."

Max shrugged. "And paid a price for it. Lesson learned."

"Hm." Sammerin gave us one of those quiet, unreadable looks, and slipped out the door.

───────

"THIS IS *AWFUL*," Max said, drawing his arm across his forehead and making a face of disgust.

I couldn't disagree.

Summer had come in the span of a few days, it seemed. I was used to the heat. But Ara's heat was a whole different beast altogether, so wet and sticky that I couldn't tell whether the slime on my skin came from sweat or from the air itself.

Neck craned, I watched Max stand at the top of a modest pile of rocks, wiping perspiration off his face and looking down at the lake below him. Water lapped at my bare toes.

We had stepped out of the cottage into this wall of humid heat, and Max had immediately announced, "I am not even *remotely* made for this." Then, after a moment of pondering, he led me off much further beyond the tree line than we normally ventured, deep into the woods. I was dripping in sweat and half eaten alive by bugs by the time we arrived at this spot: a break in the forest cradling a beautiful, idyllic-looking pond.

Max yanked his sweat-soaked shirt off over his head with one hand. As he curled his back in a stretch, the tree leaves above flickered light and shadow over the muscles of his shoulders. He crouched to kick the crumbled fabric out of his way and those delicate flecks were shattered by the brutal scar that sliced across his back.

I stared more intently than I meant to. The Queen's words echoed in my head: *Captain Farlione is nearly solely responsible for the end of the Great Ryvenai War.*

This was a body that was capable of things powerful enough to end a war. Powerful enough to commit whatever acts had inspired such intense, divisive reactions in that crowd, the awe and disgust that had shocked through me like lightning.

Gods, I had so many questions.

Max peered down only briefly before he hurled himself off of the rock in one sleek, graceful leap. His head bobbed back up a second later, shaking his wet hair out of his face. "Much better. Your turn."

I looked from the rocks to the water and strangled a whisper of uncertainty in my stomach.

I mimicked his path up the cliffs, then removed my wrapped shirt and trousers, leaving me in my undergarments — a chamois shirt and shorts. They were far less revealing than many of the things I wore every day in Esmaris's servitude, and even in those days, I thought little of having so much of my body exposed. Now, I didn't feel *self-conscious*, exactly, but I was acutely aware of Max's gaze.

That distraction, however, was far from my mind as I hung my toes over the edge of the rock and looked down.

Seconds passed.

"Are you afraid?" Max asked, at last.

"No," I lied.

The cliff was only about ten feet high. Not far.

"There is... very little water in Threll," I added, haltingly.

"You don't know how to swim?"

When I finally made myself look at Max, he was suppressing a smirk of amusement. "I promise I won't let you drown. Unless, of course, you'd rather not jump."

"Of course I will," I said, as if suggesting otherwise was outright ridiculous. And then, since I knew that that tone of voice meant I had to follow through...

I squeezed my eyes shut and then a moment later I was falling, falling, until the water slapped me.

And then I was sinking, surrounded by cold and darkness.

Fear seized me as my limbs flailed. *You said you wouldn't let me drown, you ass!* I wanted to screech. But of course, I couldn't speak, or breathe, or see—

Until I felt a force solidifying beneath me, as if the water itself was propelling me up and up.

My face broke the surface and I sputtered, coughing. My hands instinctively shot out in a wild flail, grabbing at Max or at anything that might keep me afloat.

"Relax, Tisaanah. Stop moving long enough to feel it."

Feel it?

And then I noticed: I was floating all on my own. The water pushed up beneath my feet, catching me and supporting my weight. I curled my toes, squirming as the current caressed them.

My head whipped to Max. "You can do this?"

"No." Ripples circled his shoulders as he treaded, looking pleased. "You can."

Me?

And, as if on cue, the current sputtered and I dropped. This time, Max's hands snaked out to catch me, and he guided me toward the shore until I felt the squishy relief of earth beneath my feet. I let forth a fit of coughs again when my head emerged from the surface.

Unpleasant. So deeply unpleasant.

"You alright?" Max's palm did not leave my arm, as if he were afraid I might float away. When I nodded, he said, "You'll get better, or at least more consistent, I'm sure."

I swirled my hand through the water, watching my spotted skin through the pulsating surface. I willed the water to move with me, and it did, running circles around my fingers. A satisfied smile twisted the corners of my mouth.

I had done little tricks with water before, for my performances. But nothing like this.

"You look far too pleased with yourself." Max beckoned to me. "Again, you have no control. Show me some of those butterflies you like so much and we'll see how much you earned that little smirk."

I obliged. The first ones were sloppy, heavy and dripping. But soon they grew more delicate, more controlled.

"Better," Max said. "It's like speaking another language. Once you learn the accent, it comes easier. I was curious how far you'd be able to go."

"Can you do this?"

"Water isn't quite a language I speak. The general rule is that water and air tend to be the domain of the Valtain, while Solarie are more attuned to the more physical elements like fire and earth."

I arched an eyebrow. "Really? *Nothing* with water?" I intentionally infused the shade of a dare into my voice. As much time as Max spent instructing me, I had never seen him perform much magic of his own. And now, after yesterday, I was more curious than ever.

"Some things." He looked at me like he knew exactly what I was doing. It was always the same skeptical look: pinched eyes slightly narrowed, mouth pursed towards one side.

"Like what?"

He paused, as if deciding whether to accept my challenge.

Then that wary look gave way to a more focused spark, and I knew I had him. He moved a few steps into more shallow territory, until the water lapped around his waist instead of his chest. Then he flattened his hands at the glassy surface.

At first, there was nothing. Then, bubbles started to rise around him, faster and faster, like the water was leaping to a boil.

Or…

A particularly childish image popped into my head and refused to leave.

I couldn't help myself. I pinched my nose. "Max!" I breathed, aghast. "In Threll, it is *very rude* to do that in front of others."

For a moment, Max just looked confused. Then realization swept over his face and his mouth flattened into a very tense, very straight line. "Tisaanah… Ascended help me, was that a *fart* joke?"

I just stood there, pinching my nose, grinning.

Serel and I had wielded this kind of immature humor with nothing less than mastery. And I hadn't known until this moment exactly how much I had missed it. Joking — even clumsily.

Max's mouth twitched. First the left side, then the right. And then, all at once, he burst into wild, unrestrained laughter. I realized then that I had never heard him laugh before, at least not in a way that wasn't some biting chuckle or a sarcastic scoff.

I could, I admitted to myself, get used to it.

"Sorry," I said, not meaning it. "I could not resist."

He shook his head, laughter slowly fading. "I don't know what impresses me more. That you made a joke or that it's one befitting of a five-year-old. Now that that's out of your system, will you let me focus?"

His final chuckles disappeared as a line of concentration formed between his brows. The bubbles rose more frantically.

At all once, a wall of steam burst from the surface of the water, temporarily blinding me in warm grey. Slowly, the cloud dissipated, and it took me a moment to realize what I was looking at: a massive serpent carved from cloudy mist. It rose and rose and rose, and I craned my neck to follow its ghostlike face, transfixed.

And then, it lunged for me, circling around my body in wet, warm heat before launching into the sky. It was nearly enveloped by the clouds when, at last, it dissipated into — and here, I could not help but smile — hundreds and hundreds of little butterflies. It must have been visible for miles.

When I looked back to Max, sweat glistened over his skin. He dunked his head beneath the water and came up pushing his hair away from his face.

"That's it?" I said, casually. "Is very… performative."

Fine. I was impressed.

"Throwing all kinds of words back at me today." He looked pleased with himself, even if he was trying to hide it. "I don't recall saying you could stop."

I managed a butterfly with wings so finely crafted that they were translucent and smiled at myself.

"Good," Max said, giving a little nod of approval. Then his voice grew slightly more serious as he said, "You're feeling better today?"

I'd managed to distract myself enough to forget about yesterday's events, at least for a few minutes. At the thought of it, self-consciousness burned at my cheeks. "Yes."

"You were having a hard time."

It wasn't a question. And — of course it wasn't. It had to have been obvious, how much the emotions of it all had overwhelmed me. Drowned me.

"I felt very much yesterday," I said, quietly. "The thoughts of the crowd. The Lord. The Queen. Very much."

Even that small admission of vulnerability nearly stuck to my tongue.

But Max's face softened, and his voice was surprisingly gentle as he asked, "Do you often struggle in large crowds of people?"

I thought of the day I first saw Serel, when I had choked beneath the emotions of the slaves in that pit. Torture. Absolute torture. "Sometimes," I admitted.

"It's a common problem for Valtain," he said. "There's another reason why I brought you here. I wasn't sure, at first, how I was going to help you with this. Totally unfamiliar to me, after all." His fingers skimmed over the surface, releasing tiny waves. "But as a Valtain, you're sensitive to what other people's minds release into the world. All of those… ripples."

A realization clicked into place as I watched his hands move over the surface of the pond. "Like water."

"Right." He gave me a faint smile. "The nature or degree to which individual Valtain feel and interpret them is very different, as I'm sure you're well aware, but we know how you feel them."

"Emotions," I said.

"Generally mild, as far as Valtain mental abilities go. And when it's just a few, there's nothing to be concerned about." As if to demonstrate, he dipped his fingertips into the water, releasing delicate circles across its surface. "But when you're looking at a big disruption..."

I lifted my hands and brought them down in a violent splash, spattering myself and Max in water.

He winced. "Exactly." He gestured to the surface, now shuddering with hundreds of indistinguishable ripples.

Right. It was simply *too much*, all of those waves of feeling clashing together until my mind was as disrupted as this water was. And that was almost exactly what it felt like: like everything that had once been clear and smooth, defined waves and circles, had become a tangled mass of movement.

"In Ara, it's a universal and necessary skill to learn how to shield your own thoughts as much as possible," Max said. "There are a lot of Valtain around, and no one, Wielder or no, wants them poking around their thoughts. I've always thought of it like putting up a wall... or, if we want to keep this metaphor going, a dam."

He gestured to the other end of the pond, where an old stone barrier extended towards the center, crumbling. Maybe once it had created a reservoir of some kind, though by the looks of it those days were long gone.

I thought of the one time I had attempted to so much as brush Max's thoughts. Whatever he did, it worked.

"But," he went on, "you'd probably require something a bit more... sophisticated. You need to cull what comes in, and what goes out."

An old memory whispered through my mind — my mother

and I, kneeling beside a muddy stream, thirst clawing at my throat. She held a swath of thin, delicate fabric in her hands, and together we ran the water through it until it came back clear.

"Like filtering cloth," I murmured.

A small smile. "Like filtering cloth."

I closed my eyes and imagined it — imagined draping a filter across my own thoughts and building a barrier between me and the world. The faint echo of Max's presence dimmed further, as did the thrumming presence of the birds and fish. My own head felt quieter.

I lifted it, felt those tiny awarenesses bloom back to life. Lowered it again.

I felt a smile begin to tug at my mouth.

"It'll take some time to master, like most things," Max said. "And you're probably always going to feel it to some extent."

"Good," I said — and meant it. I wouldn't want to cut myself off completely from that part of myself, even when it was difficult. As much as it hurt me to feel the overwhelming weight of all those slaves' emotions at the marketplace years ago, their pain was already mine. I would never want to turn that away.

And the fear and anguish and anger that I felt yesterday...

My gaze fell to a little waterfall above Max's shoulder. The water trickling over the stones reminded me so vividly of the blood on the Palace steps that I suddenly found it difficult to breathe.

Max followed my gaze, paled slightly. I knew we were both thinking the same thing.

"There are many things I must know," I said, quietly. And when Max's eyes found mine again, a resignation had settled into them.

He sighed. "I suppose there are."

CHAPTER EIGHTEEN

"Tell me about the war," I said, when it became clear that Max didn't even know where to start.

He lifted his chin toward my hands. "You keep going with those butterflies, and I will."

I obeyed. So did he.

"There is an area in northern Ara," he began. "A mountainous region called the Ryvenai territory. Traditionally, the region has always had some tension with the rest of Ara, even centuries ago. They have always been somewhat separatist. Over the course of Aran history, they've fought for independence no less than five times. But the war eight years ago was by far the worst, because it was the first big one since the rise of magic and the establishment of the Orders."

"Why worse?"

"Because an abnormally large proportion of Solarie are Ryvenai. In fact, many people believe that *all* Solarie are Ryvenai in some way, even if it was centuries back in their bloodline."

"Are you?"

He let out a humorless chuckle. "Enough to be stuck with one of those ridiculously long names."

"So you fought for—"

"I fought *against* the Ryvenai, not for them. It didn't make me very popular with anyone."

The more he spoke, the more his voice tightened, like a string drawing taut. I could tell this was difficult for him to discuss.

"Why?" I asked.

"I had been in the military since I was twelve. It wasn't even a choice for me. Besides, I would never throw away everything I had built."

Twelve?

At my blink of surprise, he added, "I wasn't a soldier then. It was what I did instead of a traditional apprenticeship. I was trained by the military. Honestly? I loved it there. But, it was different in peacetime."

A faint steam rose from the surface of the water around him. "Anyway," he huffed. "This is not about me."

"It isn't?" I pressed.

"It isn't." He eyed me. "Butterflies, please."

I obeyed, but my mind was far away. "Did Sammerin serve also?"

"Yes."

"As a healer?"

A pause. "No."

"Then—?"

"There were more useful ways to utilize someone with his mastery of flesh and bone."

I didn't know what that meant — not exactly — but the darkness that imbued his voice made me think of Sammerin's quiet, observing expression. It seemed so incompatible with anything that could ever be described in such a tone.

Max shook his head, like he was chasing away an image of his own. "Anyway. It was bad. Armies of Wielders hurling all kinds of terrible magic at each other left and right, and not caring who was caught in the crossfire. No one had ever seen that scale of destruction before, and no one knew how to handle it."

I thought of what I had done to Esmaris. Me, an inexperienced Fragmented girl — without so much as touching him. I could only imagine what trained Wielders were capable of. And in those kinds of numbers...

Max cleared his throat. "Butterflies, please." He sounded grateful to change the topic, even momentarily.

I looked down at the still water, my reflection glinting back at me from the glassy water. And I made another butterfly.

"How long did it last?"

"Two years," Max replied, bitterly. "There have been wars much, much longer. But none of them had even been half as bloody."

"And the Queen —"

"She was just a small child then. The war was nearly coming to an end, or so we thought. And then, the King was killed by his best friend. The person he trusted above anyone else. And that sent everything to shit all over again. Apparently..." His voice flattened. "She was there when it happened."

No wonder she was paranoid.

"But you won still?"

"*The Crown* won, in the end, yes." His correction was strained and firm. The Crown — not *him*.

Those words echoed again: *This is the man responsible for the end of the war. Responsible for our victory at Sarlazai.*

"Because of Sarlazai?" I whispered.

Max flinched, so slightly that I wouldn't have seen it had I not been watching his face so intently, tracing the tightening muscles around his eyes and jaw. "Yes," he said, and offered nothing else.

A victory — or a devastation — strong enough to bring triumph to a country that no longer even had a king. It had to have been something incredible.

He looked at me as if he were expecting me to press him for

more information, and was dreading it. And he was right in that the questions were rising to the tip of my tongue. But…

Something gave me pause. Something that lingered beneath the steeling panes of his face, something vulnerable that begged not to be prodded.

I recognized that hidden vulnerability. I nursed it in my own bones.

So, I didn't touch it. Not this time.

Instead, I said, "Now she kills men in streets."

"It's been less than a year since she received control from the advisors that ruled in her stead during her childhood. She had that power for weeks before she started getting tyrannical."

He said it with such disdain, and though I didn't know the word itself, I knew well enough what he meant. Especially when I thought of that blood spilling over the stairs, seeping at Max's feet.

But something didn't sit right. "What does she want?" I asked.

Max scoffed. "Does it matter? Power. Revenge. Who knows."

I shook my head.

I had been excellent at the role I played at Esmaris's estate, and it wasn't because I was the most beautiful girl or the most talented or the best dancer. It was because, every single time I turned my attention to a man, I asked, *What does he want?*

"Is more complicated and more simple than that," I said. "Always."

The man I whored myself to didn't want sex. Not really. He wanted to feel powerful. Specifically, more powerful than Esmaris. And once I figured that out, he was butter in my hands. *Oh no, I couldn't, he would be so upset, he would never allow it.* And that price went up and up and up.

"Once she starts slaughtering people in the streets, I don't care what she wants. I don't care that she's a child. It doesn't make those people any less dead."

I thought of the fear that ripped through the air when I looked at the man on the steps.

"I felt such *fear,* yesterday, when I looked at that man," I said. "Then, I thought it belonged to him. And some probably did. But..." I thought of the little girl watching her father die. Watching his death at the hands of someone she likely called an uncle. "Perhaps it was hers."

Max paused at this only for a moment. "People do all kinds of terrible things out of fear. It doesn't change anything. I know far too well what that kind of behavior leads to."

He was no longer looking at my butterflies. Instead, his gaze turned only to me.

I met it. "And your family—"

"—were war casualties."

He said it with a finality that I knew I couldn't challenge, and I didn't want to even if I could. He could keep his secrets a little longer. I knew how painful it could be to even acknowledge such memories, let alone force them to scald their way up your throat.

"We all have sad stories," I murmured, and Max simply nodded.

The ensuing silence was so heavy that it stifled my breath. I continued making butterflies, and long, wordless minutes passed.

After some time, I shivered. "I am cold," I announced, grateful for any excuse to break the tension, and pushed my way to the shore. The unrelenting warmth of the air was actually a relief at this point, lifting the water on my skin to steam.

I didn't even think to be self-conscious until I turned around to see Max standing completely still in the water. He looked like he wasn't even breathing, his searing gaze hurling an arrow through my chest — the intensity of it paralyzing me.

What?, I wanted to ask, but the force of his stare was so strong that the question died before it left my lips.

"I hope that whoever did that to you died a terrible, painful death," he said at last, words hissing like steam. "And I hope that if there is an underworld, they suffer there forever."

Warmth rose to my face.

My scars. I had managed to forget about them — at least for a few hours.

Did I hope the same? I wasn't always sure. *He would have killed you,* a voice whispered to me. But every time I thought of Esmaris, I thought more about the way his life felt draining from his body than the frenzied fury in his eyes as he beat me.

"We all have our sad stories," I said, content to leave my throat unscalded, and pulled my jacket over my shoulders.

———

THAT NIGHT, I sat in front of the fireplace, looking over my notes from our lessons with my legs crossed in front of me. Max slumped in one of the armchairs, a book in his hands and a pair of reading glasses perched over his nose.

It was an oddly peaceful moment, to the extent that any moment was peaceful, in my head — my head that was always reaching for the next thing, always thinking of Threll and Serel and my family. None of that was gone, but some of it disappeared in the crackling of the fire — in the chuckle that I had released as Max grumbled to himself while lighting it with a snap of his fingers, *Just like fucking Ara, the inside of an oven all day and then damn freezing at night.*

I raised my gaze from my books and watched the flickering firelight shudder over his features, imbuing the thoughtful lines of his face with intermittent flames.

"Max."

Nothing moved but his eyes, which flicked to me. "Hm?"

"What is it that *you* want? In life."

Only a very brief pause, and then he muttered, "Mostly, I just want everyone to leave me alone."

Exactly what I'd thought he'd say.

But then, I thought of the way that he had agreed to train me after he heard why I was here to begin with. Of the odd urgency in his voice when he had asked me what Zeryth Aldris was doing in Threll, or when he pushed Via to tell him more about her weapons contracts. And I thought of how he had stood there in front of the Queen, what he had said to her — and the way he had jerked forward, right as those spears dove for that man's back.

I answered slowly, "I think no."

He peered at me over his reading glasses, eyebrows arched. "You think no."

"I think you are better than that."

It took him a moment to respond with a quiet chuckle beneath his breath. He looked back down to his book and flipped a page as he said, "Well, thank you, not many people think so," and we lapsed back into a quiet, comfortable silence.

CHAPTER NINETEEN

I had one of my most vivid dreams yet that night. I awoke gasping, covered in sweats, the image of Esmaris's sneer and Serel's eyes burned into the pre-dawn darkness.

I threw the covers off my body, padded down the hall and out the front door, and practiced my magic until the sun crested the horizon. There was no time for sleep.

"I WOULD LIKE to write a letter to Zeryth," I said to Max in the morning. "How would I send it to him?"

Max placed his teacup carefully on the table before responding. "Zeryth Aldris, I take it."

"Yes. He is in Threll."

"Right. I do remember that interesting bit." He narrowed his eyes, just slightly. "Well. If you know exactly where he is, you could try sending it to him with a Stratagram. Or you could send a falcon and hope the thing is able to find him before it keels over in the plains."

So basically, he was telling me that I needed someone at the

Orders to send it for me, since they were the only ones I knew who had any idea where in Threll Zeryth was.

"Why do you need to write to him?" Max stirred his tea far too casually.

"I need to find out what is happening in Threll, with my—" I wasn't sure what to call Esmaris, or his estate, now that he was no longer my master and his home was no longer mine. "My friends."

"You should talk to Willa. See if she can help." Despite his helpful answer, his voice still held the unmistakable tang of disapproval. "How did you meet Zeryth, exactly?"

"He would stay at my—" I stumbled, but I had no other word. "— my master's home when he traveled. We became friends then."

"Your master," Max repeated. "Is he the one who gave you those scars?"

"Does that matter?"

"I think so. Yes."

A pause. I didn't know who I was protecting — why it pained me to confirm it. "Yes, he did." I watched Max pick at the wood grain of the table, his mouth drawn into a thin line. "You do not like Zeryth." A statement, not a question. Max was perhaps the least subtle person I had ever met.

"We have never gotten along. And…" A brief moment of hesitation. "He had the resources to have gotten you out, and chose not to."

"It was not his for doing. He could not free every slave he met in Threll."

I spoke casually, but the truth was, the first two times Zeryth came to visit, I dreamed that he would take me with him when he left. It took a few years for me to decide that my freedom would have to be my responsibility and no one else's. I couldn't fault Zeryth for not taking that upon himself, especially since he spent so much time teaching me and indulging my questions. Lighting that fire in my stomach was its own kind of freedom. At least, that was what I told myself.

Max shook his head. "That just isn't what I would consider a friend."

"You do not have friends," I tried to joke, but Max shot his answer back with decisive intensity.

"I have one excellent friend who is far better than I deserve. And if Sammerin was in that position, I would never, ever allow him to stay there."

His words slid between my ribs and twisted in my guts. In that moment, my mind was far, far away from Zeryth. No, my thoughts furled only around Serel. Around my mother.

My cheek and forehead burned, scars left by everyone I had abandoned.

"It is never so simple," I shot back, too quickly, too loudly. And perhaps the vehemence of my answer told Max that somehow, we had started talking about something different, because his face shifted in the beginnings of concern.

But I was relieved when a knock at the door rang out. Max hesitated briefly before standing to answer it, muttering, "I don't even know what that noise is, considering that no one ever bothers."

He swung open the door, and there stood Nura.

"How wonderful to see you," Max said, baring his teeth in a smile.

CHAPTER TWENTY

"What do you want?" Max demanded.

Nura gave him an icy smile. "May I come in?"

"If I say no, are you just going to wander in anyway? Because that seems to be how these things go around here."

"Yes, probably."

"You're that determined to lecture me?"

A low laugh unfurled from her breath. "Don't be so self-important, Max. I'm not here to see you."

I tried not to look surprised. They both turned to me — Nura with her mouth twisted into a little unreadable smirk, and Max with a hard glint in his eye that echoed of nervousness.

"Why?" he barked.

"Let me in and you'll find out."

Max hesitated, then stepped aside.

Nura strode across the room and slid into the chair near me. She was wearing a variation of the same uniform she donned every time I saw her — the long, white jacket buttoned all the way up to her throat, moon insignias on her lapel and across her back. I was once again struck by how graceful and deliberate her movements were, as if every muscle worked in perfect unison,

152

even in the tiny expressions of her face. She was actually quite beautiful. As she moved to sit down, her white braids fell over one shoulder, rippling light from the windows across her face in a momentary softness. Then she settled and that glimmer was replaced once again with steel.

"Is your training going well?" she asked.

"Very well." I would have given her that reply regardless, but I couldn't help but glance at Max as I answered — pleased I didn't have to lie.

"Good. I've come because the Orders request your help."

I blinked, refusing to allow myself to look surprised even though a wild hope leapt to my skin. This had to be good… didn't it?

"For what?"

"Lord Savoi's son in Tairn is refusing to abdicate power, even though his family has been removed from leadership. It's merely a tantrum. But we need bodies to march upon the city gates and scare him out of his hideout, and I would like for you to join. It will not turn to bloodshed. He simply needs to be scared."

"The Guard doesn't have enough people to do this as is?" Max cut in. "One Fragmented girl will make all the difference?"

"One Fragmented girl and one ill-tempered, moderately famous Solarie, if you're cooperative."

She said the word "cooperative" so drily that it cracked and scattered across the floor.

"But again, you're too self-important," she went on. "We're sending letters to many people in the area, since the Guard is preoccupied in Vernaya."

"The war hasn't even started yet and you're already over-taxed?" Max needled. "And what happened to the Orders being politically neutral? Or have you given up that farce now that one of your own is driving this mess?"

But I let Max's ranting fall into the background, watching Nura, thinking.

I would take any opportunity presented to me. I couldn't afford not to. But I didn't give up anything for free.

"I will go," I said.

Max, who had been mid-complaint, snapped his mouth shut.

"I thought you would seize the opportunity," Nura said, looking pleased.

"I will go," I repeated, "*if* Zeryth Aldris will bring my friend back to Ara with him when he leaves Threll."

I spoke smoothly, confidently, even though I felt just like I had when I was a little girl demanding my freedom from Esmaris with my fifty sad silver pieces. I was sure my presence at this city was nothing of value to them. But if it was, they wouldn't get it without giving me something in return. Not when there were so many things I still needed.

I carefully avoided Max's gaze, though I could feel it searing a charred hole in the center of my forehead — stark contrast to Nura's, glassy ice that glistened with faint sheen of amusement.

"Members of the Orders need to follow directives without the luxury of conditions," she said.

"Firstly, that does not seem to be true." I gestured to Max. "Secondly, you made very clear that I am not member of the Orders. Not yet."

Nura's eyes betrayed silent laughter. "Oh, Max. She really has learned a lot from you, hasn't she?" Then, to me, "Everyone in this room knows that you need us more than we need you. And yet, if I understand you correctly, you're asking me to inconvenience one of our most important members on one of our most important missions for you?"

"You ask for my help, so I ask for yours." I leaned forward. Max's words still pounded in my ears. *I would never leave him there.* Well, I wouldn't either. Never. "And this is not for *me*. This is for decency. You already denied thousands of people help. You said it was too much. Now I ask for one person. Is that still too much? Or are the Orders less powerful than they say to be?"

Silence. I half expected Nura to look angry, but she didn't. Instead, she peered at me with one shallow wrinkle of thought between her eyebrows, a faint smirk tightening the corner of her mouth.

"Fine. Give me a name and we'll see what Zeryth can do."

My heart lifted.

"And in return," Nura went on, "I expect to see you tomorrow at the gates of Tairn. Is this a deal?"

I did not hesitate. "Yes."

Max stood there in rare, conspicuous silence.

"Your friend is lucky to have you." Nura crossed her arms, tilted her chin thoughtfully. "Be careful, though, Tisaanah. It's easy to manipulate people who want one thing more than anything else."

I nodded solemnly as if this were new information, happy to be underestimated. But really, I knew this better than anyone. I just didn't have the luxury of choices.

THE SUN THROBBED at the back of my neck as I squinted at the cottage. Beside me, Miraselle cooed over some peonies, stroking the petals between her fingers. I had no idea where she went when she wasn't wandering around Max's garden, but she always seemed to materialize whenever I found myself outside by myself. This was fine by me — as odd as she was, I liked Miraselle. She was easy to be around and one of the few people who did not make me feel painfully aware of my accent, because she was the only Aran I'd met whose vocabulary was even smaller than my own.

Shortly after I made my agreement with Nura, she had turned to Max — who had been atypically quiet — and asked to speak to him alone. It was an obvious signal for me to leave, so I had retreated out to the gardens to practice on my own.

Still, I kept casting glances at that house as the minutes ticked by. My curiosity clawed at me.

Some time later, they emerged. Nura only waved her hand to me from a distance before whisking herself away, which I chose not to find insulting. Max didn't so much as look at her before marching toward me.

Miraselle leapt to her feet. "Good morning, Max! Isn't it a beautiful day today?"

"What. The *hell*. Were you thinking?" Max snapped his face to me with a set jaw, words sizzling out between clenched teeth.

"What was I thinking?" I almost laughed. "What else would I do?"

"That's not how this works. You think you won something in there?"

"No," I said. "Not completely. But I needed to try."

Miraselle crowded closer, her beautiful face drawn into overwrought concern. That woman had no sense of personal space. "Max, why are you so sad?"

Max put up his hands, gently pushing her away. "Miraselle —" he snapped, then stopped himself, letting out a breath. "Three steps, please. That's all I ask. Three steps of space."

Miraselle took one, two, three steps backward.

"What would you say I should do?" I asked.

"Say no. That's what I'd say you should do."

"I cannot do that."

"You don't make deals with the Orders. *Never*. And it's not even as if it's a blood pact or anything that would stop Nura from going back on her word. Not that she even *gave* you her word. *She'll try.*" He scoffed. "Please."

I regarded Max quietly. I would be lying if I said that his reaction didn't make me nervous. But nothing he was saying to me now was news. I knew that I had no guarantees. I had noticed Nura's distinct lack of promise. And I knew that I had bought myself — bought Serel — only a sliver of a chance, and nothing more.

Still, it was something. It was all I had.

"My friend needs even a chance," I said. "I have no other option. And even if Nura said no, still, I would have agreed."

I couldn't quite decipher the look Max gave me at that. "You shouldn't."

"I need to impress them. You know this." I jumped as

Miraselle's hands began combing through my hair, and I had to stop myself from slapping her fingers away.

"Miraselle—" Max sounded as if it were taking every effort he had not to snap at her. "Give us a minute."

Miraselle looked momentarily hurt before wandering back into the rose bushes.

"What's a blood pact?" I asked, once she was gone.

"A deal sealed in magic, so neither party can break the terms."

"What happens if they do?'

"They can't."

"But what if—"

"Tisaanah, this is beside the point. You cannot trust them. They will use you."

I was using them, too. And besides, what possible use could I be to the Orders, organizations populated with the most powerful Wielders in the world? "For what?"

"I don't know yet." Max looked at me with his strange eyes bright beneath the shadow of a furrowed brow, mouth twisted in thought, shoulders tensed. His concern settled at the bottom of my stomach and lay there, heavy.

"I can do this," I said, quietly.

"That's what I'm afraid of." He drew in a long breath, nostrils flaring as he let it out. "I hoped I'd never find myself on a battle-field again."

I blinked at him, surprised. "She said you must go too?"

Max snorted. "Nura? She could try and see how far that gets her. But if you're going, then I'm going."

"You—"

"I'm not letting you go out there alone, Tisaanah."

This realization — the realization that my goal, and the things I chose to sacrifice in my pursuit of it, no longer belonged to me alone — crushed me so suddenly that I could feel myself swaying beneath this new responsibility. I looked at Max in silence for a moment, lips parted, groping for words and finding none.

I had been nervous about marching on Tairn, but only in a resigned, distant way. Now something sharper lurched into my heart as I realized that, intentionally or not, I was dragging Max back into everything he fought so hard to escape.

"You do not have to."

"Don't be ridiculous. I did not graduate from the Zeryth Aldris school of shitty friendship."

"Max—"

"Not a discussion."

Max still regarded me with that pondering stare, and I just looked at him in silence, two realizations dawning.

The first was that I was not going to talk him out of this.

And the second hit me harder: the realization that something had shifted in the nature of our relationship, and I had simply failed to notice. But I understood with a resolve that settled deep in my chest that I had been given something precious in this fragile, tentative friendship. I closed my fingers around that delicate gift and drew it close.

"Thank you," I said, and Max just nodded. One look at his faraway stare, and I knew he was already on that battlefield.

CHAPTER TWENTY-ONE

Max peered over the edge of the bridge and clutched the metal rail as if he might topple into the murky water at any moment. I watched the white overtake his knuckles, cloudy skin betraying his lack of composure. I wondered if I had a similarly obvious tell. I tried to bury my fear so deep inside of me that no echoes would reach the surface, but it still felt like it screamed from my every pore.

Sweat pooled at the base of my neck, down my back, between my breasts. I tried to blame the stiff fabric of the Order of Midnight jacket that I wore — brutal in combination with the swampy heat — and not my own anxiety.

I drew my eyes up, over the rows and rows of shoulders lined up in neat streaks of color. Most were gold, denoting members of the Crown Guard, who were not Wielders at all. Then there were a few columns of blue, flashes of moon insignias across their backs. And green, marked with bronze suns. As I peered over my shoulder, I noticed a few sets of eyes flicking towards us, necks craning ever so slightly. Looking at Max, no doubt. Everyone, it seemed, was surprised to see him.

The city of Tairn loomed over us, dark and silent, backlit by the rising sun. It was nestled at the apex of three rivers, built up on a rocky hill. As a result, it was notoriously inaccessible — three bridges led to the main city, which itself was all centered around one circular building topped with a single silver spire: the Savoi estate, and the central hall of Tairn.

I squinted up at it. That building, apparently, held Pathyr Savoi, the man we were here to coax out of hiding. The son of the man whose blood had soaked through my shoes.

Sammerin stood beside me, following my gaze. He, too, it turned out, had been asked (or commanded) to join the march, as a member of the Orders and a former member of the Military — though unlike me, he didn't get a personal visit to ask him to do so, which still perplexed me.

We watched another dove fly over the wall, parchment clutched in its feet.

"Fifteen," Sammerin remarked.

The fifteenth dove. Fifteenth letter. Fifteenth attempt at negotiation. We had been here for hours. Max had spent nearly all of that time leaning over the railing, looking into the water.

I did not ask him if he was alright — he was awful at hiding his emotions, and it was clear that he wasn't. Instead, I crafted a little butterfly from the swampy lake below and drew it up to hover in front of our faces.

"How is it wrong?" I asked.

He hardly looked at me. "What?"

"What is wrong with it?"

Slowly, he turned. Then looked to my butterfly.

"So?" I prodded.

"Too heavy," he grunted, at last. With each word, his voice got a little clearer. "And you got sloppy with the movement. It's lurching like a—"

But then, there was a crash. We whirled around. I let my butterfly fall back into smelly water.

All faces snapped to attention as we watched Nura step back as the black-clad figures smashed their spears into the bottom of the gates. An orange glow crawled up the planks of wood, seeping into minuscule cracks, tearing them apart.

Max straightened, exchanging one of those looks of silent communication with Sammerin. He somehow managed to look even paler.

My heartbeat quickened, but I strangled my nervousness, forcing it down my throat.

"Those soldiers without eyes... They are Wielders?" I croaked, searching for distraction.

"The Syrizen? Yes. Solarie, sort of." His voice sounded far away. Then, he asked quietly, "Do you remember everything I showed you last night?"

I nodded. Later that evening, he had called me from my magic practice out into the garden, holding two daggers and handing me one of them. "If you're going to agree to do something stupid," he had said, "then you need to know how to protect yourself." We spent the rest of the night going over various defensive maneuvers — mostly movements meant to keep me alive if I ever found myself in a tricky situation and magic failed me.

Now, I watched the vestiges of those gates come down and prayed I would not have to use them. Still, I mentally rehearsed the movements. Just in case.

"I suppose this didn't scare him out of his tantrum after all," Max muttered. Sammerin shook his head, silent.

I closed my eyes, thought of Serel, and reminded myself why I was here.

And then we began to move.

The cold metal of the bridge was replaced with slippery cobblestones beneath my feet. The sun beating down on my face gave way to damp shadows, courtesy of the tall townhomes that crowded narrow, winding streets.

I peered back at the bridge over my shoulder, soon blocked from view by the soldiers behind me. I noted in a distant, matter-of-fact thought that we were now trapped on this island.

Max nudged my shoulder, as if he too shared my realization.

"Stay alert," he whispered, voice taut with caution, beads of nervous sweat dotting his nose. "And stay right here."

The streets of Tairn were so narrow and twisted, tight turns bathed in the shadows of the surrounding buildings. Max, Sammerin and I were packed nearly shoulder-to-shoulder. We were near the front of the group, only just behind Nura and the Syrizen, but even then, the city itself seemed to bear down on us.

To make it worse, every step brought us into a thicker and thicker fog, so dense every breath felt as if I was inhaling liquid. The bodies in front of us became little more than silhouettes. Ahead, Nura would lift her arms to push the swampy mist away like a swimmer parting water, only to have more arise steps later.

The hairs on my arms and the back of my neck stood, cold nausea turning in my stomach.

Something wasn't right.

"Something isn't right," Max murmured.

The city was completely silent. Shop booths stood empty — some even had fruit in them, flies buzzing around softened berries and oranges. I looked at the darkened windows, obscured through the fog, and my brow furrowed.

The silence extended beyond my ears, seeping into my mind. An unnatural stillness for a city of this size. A dangerous stillness.

I leaned towards Max. "Look at the blank windows."

"I noticed."

"I hear no one." I pressed a finger to my temple, shaking my head. "Nothing."

Then I raised my eyes to that central tower, perched at the top of the hill, silver spire poised to pierce the hazy circle of the sun obscured through fog. And when I looked at it, my mind erupted into a wordless mass of light and activity and iron *fear*.

I saw the back of Nura's head pause, turn, as if she too were noticing what I did.

"They're all *there*," I started to say—

But then, where there had been nothing, there was suddenly

something. The fog shifted, moved, changed, thickened and thinned at once, sculpting.

And I could see them, feel them — people everywhere, surrounding us, figures unfurling from the mist.

Nura let out a wordless shout of warning. She raised her hands and shadows roiled around her, around *us*, shielding us beneath a cover of darkness. The last thing I saw before darkness overtook my vision was the Syrizen's spears lighting up with warm, orange light, their bodies leaping into the air and flickering into nothing. Simply disappearing.

A deafening crash. Blue sparks barely penetrated Nura's blanket of shadows. I felt the cobblestones under my boots shift.

Smoke filled my lungs. My eyes groped frantically in the darkness, finding nothing but black.

But then something beyond sight — deeper than sight — sensed a presence beside us, sensed a blade lifting and swinging toward Max—

I didn't think before I grabbed his shoulders and pushed, sliding my body in front of his, grabbing onto the presence and twisting and pulling and snapping as hard as I could. A sharp pain sliced my hands, raised in front of my face—

Then I felt myself being yanked backwards, felt the ground shake, felt a sharp impact at the back of my head.

And then the darkness melted into something deeper.

I OPENED my eyes and the first thing I saw was blood. Blood dribbling through cobblestones, covering piles of wet, broken wood. Blood dripping into my eyes, covering my sideways vision, smearing against my cheek as it pressed to the ground.

My fingers touched something soft, and I almost jumped until I pulled it closer and realized it was a torn-up stuffed dog toy, stained crimson. My hand was soaked.

"That was stupid," Max's voice murmured. It was weak, nearly trembling. "Never do that again. I would have been fine."

163

I tried to sit up. Pain screamed in my palms as I pressed them against the floor, and the world spun, but I forced myself to steady. Max caught my shoulders, stabilizing me. When I raised my head, he looked at me with an abject fear that would have caught me off guard had I not been so completely focused on not vomiting.

Nura's shadows were gone, the harsh morning casting grotesque patches of gold over broken beams and crumpled stone. I was in what looked to be someone's home — or had been, once. The building had collapsed into rubble, leaving eerie fragments of some poor family's life scattered in stained sand. Max and Sammerin knelt in front of me. Sammerin rubbed blue dust between his fingers.

"Lightning Dust," he said, brow furrowed.

I turned my head and strangled a cry. Two outstretched hands reached from beneath a massive beam. The rest of the body — or whatever could possibly remain of it — was buried beneath a pile of rubble, the river of blood trickling from beneath that mass of broken beams.

Max said something, but I didn't hear him.

He tipped my chin with his finger, turning my face toward him, and said it again. "Are you hurt, Tisaanah?"

I shook my head, even though I wasn't totally sure if that was an accurate answer. I looked down at my palms, which were slashed so deeply I caught white flashes of bone.

Without speaking, Sammerin took my hands in his. I bit back a yelp as my skin began to burn.

"He blew up his own city?" Max crouched at the ground, peering at the blue dust. "Ascended above. That's fucking insane."

"Perhaps he thinks it's better than letting Sesri take it back," Sammerin replied.

I watched, rapt, as the skin of my palms crawled like hundreds of tiny spiders, threads crossing the chasm of my wounds and bridging flesh to flesh. It hurt fiercely, and the gory image of it was… nauseating. But when Sammerin released my hands, the wounds were replaced with smooth skin.

Sammerin stood, pulling me to my feet. The rubble around us was intact enough to form a shadowy shelter, albeit one that looked like it might collapse at any moment. Outside, the soupy mist had returned, obscuring the wreckage to silhouettes. But I could hear the sounds of dull, blunt fighting, shouts and grunts and moaning, of calls for help. Still, always quieter than one expects it to be. Just like the night the slavers came to my village.

Blew up his own city.

So that was why it was empty. But I couldn't imagine what his final goal could possibly be — how this could possibly end well for his people.

I peered out of a gap in the rubble.

Ghostly figures melted into physical forms only to melt back into the fog as if they were nothing at all, striking our soldiers with lethal, silent strokes.

I felt ill. Max's gaze flicked to mine and I could tell he did, too.

"They have a Valtain up there," Max whispered. "Probably several. Good ones, to cast a spell like this over so many of their soldiers."

"Everyone is in that tower," I said, pointing. "We need to—"

A crash shattered my sentence. A morass of shadow and fog, thrashing with a young soldier, smashed against our pile of rubble. Max yanked me back away from the opening, and the three of us held our breaths in the darkness until the Tairnian soldier's body was left twitching on the ground. And then Nura appeared, stepping out of the shadow, blood smeared over one cheek.

"You're alive," she breathed, panting. "Good. Can't believe the bastard would— would…"

She let out a sharp, shuddering breath, then shook her head. "Get to the estate gates. He and whatever traitors are doing this are hiding in the hall. They'll see how much they like to play with explosives when we bring down the building."

My heart stopped. I hoped I misheard her.

"You can't," I blurted out. "The whole city is—"

"It's the Syrizen's directive, not mine. And we don't have time to fuck around."

"Nura, even you can't think—"

She cut Max off before he could finish. "I don't have time for your judgement. Either we get in there and root out those rats or the Syrizen bring the whole damn thing down." Silver strands escaped her braids, echoing the whites of her eyes. A flicker passed over the icy determination in her face. "I tried to tell them — You don't know how many bodies I've yanked out of these buildings." Her throat bobbed. "Get to the gates. That is an order."

And then, she was gone, her white hair and skin and jacket melting into the fog like she was one of those cursed soldiers. I didn't notice or watch her leave. All of my attention was drawn to that morass of heartbeats that I could feel pulsating in my mind, thousands of people piled on top of each other beneath that building.

I looked down at the ripped-up dog toy.

Terror hardened into something sharper, stronger, in my veins. When I looked at Max, his stare was already meeting mine, mirroring my determination.

"If we get in first—" I started, desperately, and he returned it with a sharp nod.

"The Syrizen only care about their goal. If they've made up their mind, it's the only thing we can do. Besides." He let out a puff of air through his teeth. "As good a way to die as any, I suppose."

We both turned to Sammerin, who gave us a look of silent resignation. "We all know," he said, "that I'm committed." Then he poised himself at the gap in the rubble. "If we go, we go now. Ready?"

"Yes," I lied, confidently.

Max's answer was not nearly as reassuring. "Ready as I'll be."

And then, before there was another moment to think or doubt —

We were out and into the that mass of mist and blood and sweat, fighting our way to the tower. Fire leapt from Max's hands, curling up his forearms, casting grotesque red light into the mist and illuminating garish silhouettes for only a split second before they lunged at us.

I grabbed at those shadow minds in frantic fistfuls, pulling tight on the invisible threads that connected us, twisting, snapping. Half the time they slipped away before I could grab them. Other times, they stumbled long enough for Max's fire to catch their clothing or hair, crawl around them, yank them back into their fragile physical existence and send them careening to the ground.

But he never struck to kill. And once they were on the ground, out of our way, he pulled the flames back with him when we moved on.

Out of the corner of my eye, flashes of bright gold sparks alerted me to the Syrizen leaping into the air, flickering and disappearing mid-jump, then reappearing further into the sky — as if they were flying.

"Pay attention," Max grunted, as fire lit up my face, knocking one of those misty figures away from me. "Blades up, Tisaanah."

I would have laughed if I could catch my breath. My little daggers felt ridiculous in a battle like this. What good would these little pieces of steel do, against illusion and smoke and flames?

We fought our way forward, Max surrounded by fire, Sammerin wielding blades like mine. Neither of them had either explicitly told me that they fought together in the war, but now, that was beyond a doubt. Their movements silently coordinated even without looking at each other, as if one constantly had their hand on the other's pulse. I could only imagine what the two of them would be capable of if I weren't dragging them back.

Even still, we *flew*, slipping between bodies and battles, engaging only where necessary. Nura's words echoed in my head, and I was constantly aware of the flashes of the Syrizen's movements. With every pounding heartbeat I could hear the ever-present pull of all those people, drawing me forward.

By the time we reached the tower's solid, brass doors, there were so many soldiers hidden in the fog that we clashed every few steps. Our own men were far behind us. We moved slower as Max and Sammerin's practiced grace gave way to something choppier and more desperate.

I tripped as Max shoved me aside, warmth spattering my cheek. Too late, I saw a figure tear from the air, sword raised. Max staggered, flinging a vicious stream of fire before I could react.

I didn't see the body until it hit the ground. Max grabbed his shoulder. "I'm fine," he rasped. Blood seeped from between his fingers, but he only stared down at the listless body of my attacker.

He was not fine, but there was no time for Sammerin to do anything now. We were surrounded, our backs now pressed against the metal doors. My mind was as soupy as my vision, catching only glimpses of the people we could not see, fire illuminating their broad strokes.

Overwhelmed, I blinked, squeezed my eyes shut to clear my mind —

And in that moment, I could see all of it: spots of light in the darkness. Like I was looking at an inverted version of the world with each soldier, each life, each ball of thought clearly illuminated. In front of me, the invisible soldiers. Behind me, the people huddled beneath the tower. The Syrizen. Everyone.

It was so vivid that I snapped my eyes open again, plunging back into my normal, dulled senses, gasping. Without thinking, I raised my arms in front of me. An invisible force sprung from my arms, pushing the soldiers back, buying us precious few seconds.

"Good." Max's voice was a gasping grunt. His right arm was

soaked in blood. His left was still crawling with fire, creating a wall around us as he peered over his shoulder at the door.

I knew what he was thinking: we weren't getting through. Not by physical force. I could feel the faint magic pulse of someone holding it from within. Iron was not the only thing keeping it closed.

The ground rumbled. The Syrizen had begun to compromise the base of the tower, readying it for collapse.

No, I thought. *No, no, no.*

I winced, squeezing my eyes shut, and as I did the world once again lit up like a map in the darkness. All those souls, so close and yet separated from us by so much.

So close, *so* close—

All at once, an idea hit me.

I whirled to Max. "Can you send fire in without looking?" I asked, straining to raise my voice over the chaos.

He looked at me like I was insane. "Too dangerous. I can't go in blind."

"I can see," I said, pressing my finger to my temple. When he just stared at me, I said again, more urgently, "*I can see.* Let me in here." I brought my hand to his forehead. "And I can tell you where to go. We can push them out."

Max's face went hard as stone. "*No.* Absolutely fucking not."

At that moment, the ground rumbled again, this time accompanied by a bone-rattling cracking sound.

We were running out of time.

"We have no other ideas," I pushed, desperately, and Max winced — as if the truth of the statement physically struck him.

But again, he shook his head. "I can't," he said, more quietly. "I can't."

But I heard what was really hiding in the razor's edge of his voice, in the hard tension of his features. Before I gave myself time to think, I took his bloodied hand in mine, ignoring the startled jump of his fingers.

His fear was so intense that I felt it vibrating from his skin.

"Trust me," I murmured. A plea, a request, a command — I

wasn't sure which, or perhaps all three. Max looked like he didn't know, either.

He paused, grimacing, fire still springing from his other hand. He looked at the battlefield, then me, then his eyes lifted to the Syrizen at the base of the building.

And then his gaze fell back to mine, and even before he opened his mouth, I knew the exact moment that he made his choice.

"Sammerin—" he started.

Sammerin nodded. Somehow, the man still managed to appear perpetually unshaken. "I can cover."

He slipped his blades into his belt and lifted his hands.

And what I saw next had me transfixed, horrified.

The dead bodies piled around us began to move. Not in a life-like way, but in grotesque, skin-crawling lurches, their limbs dragging at awkward, sickening angles, heads lolling, clawing over each other to the base of the bridge that led to the tower. They were creating a wall of human flesh, slithering over each other into a twitching morass.

There are more useful ways to utilize someone with Sammerin's mastery of flesh and bone, Max had told me. Gods, he had been right.

"Tisaanah," Max barked, yanking my attention back. He opened his palms. A spiral of fire lengthened and broadened between them, creating a ball, then a tower, then something larger, more organic: a serpent, like the one he had produced out of mist that day in the water, but carved from searing flame.

It circled our bodies, so close to my skin that it could have scalded the hair of my arms. Still, it grew, until it was larger than either of us. The fire dyed the mist red, silhouettes through the fog looking like they were swimming through blood. Sammerin's growing wall of human bodies were reduced to broken, crimson shadow puppets.

"You need to tell me where to go." Max's arms were trembling, as if controlling this serpent took every ounce of his strength. "I've opened the door for you. Don't you dare poke around in there."

His mind, he meant. I nodded as if I knew exactly what I was doing, even though that couldn't be farther from the truth. And I allowed myself to drop my shield, squeezing my eyes shut.

The world lit up in a map of souls and flames. A pair of blue serpent's eyes opened in the darkness. I stepped into them, surrounding myself with Max's presence, slipping into a crevice of his mind that he had carved out for me.

I'm blind, I heard his voice echo. *Be very careful. For both of us. And for everyone inside.*

The muted terror in his exposed nerves twined with mine. I tried to send him shaky reassurance.

The civilians were beneath the tower, huddled in one giant mass beneath the earth. But a smaller group lingered near the top. This, I thought, had to be Pathyr Savoi and his commanders, who must have been overseeing the battle from the highest vantage point.

And if we cut them off... we'd be forcing their surrender.

Go, I whispered.

And the viper — Max — listened.

The wild path of flames raged through the winding halls, roaring past doors, around corners, scalding tapestries and paintings. And I inhaled it. *Became* it. Smoke filled my lungs. My stomach. My eyes.

I guided Max with seamless, wordless direction. His power was mine, and I could feel it thrash forward. I realized his muscles had been trembling not because he was pushing so hard, but because he was holding himself back. With every confident turn, every furious surge, it grew wilder.

Careful, he murmured in my ear. I could feel him tasting shadows of past memories, recoiling. Every heartbeat danced on a blade's edge between intoxicated power and agonizing fear.

We're fine.

Stop.

Not yet, I soothed. *A little further.*

Blood pounded in my ears. The lights grew closer, the smoke thicker. Door after door shuttered past my view.

Max's tension grew tighter, like a bowstring pulling further and further back. Control threatened to slip away. But he waited, his tentative trust still cradled in my hands.

Not yet, I whispered.

Doors. Smoke.

Now. Up!

The fire obeyed, the serpent roaring through every crevice of the floor, rising through the doors and windows and between stones.

And there they were: a handful of huddled, well dressed figures. They jumped, terrified, as the fire tore through the room, encircling them within a ring of flames.

A spell snapped in two.

And then —

A ragged gasp. My face against stone. Eyes snapped open into darkness, weak and dark and dull. My own eyes. Back on the bridge, back in my body.

Black boots and golden sparks flew by my blurry vision. Then a flash of white.

Dark hands pulled me upright. My shaky vision settled on Sammerin, then Max, slowly pushing himself up from the ground. And then the open brass door, flickering in firelight.

Open.

Nura and the Syrizen were running down the hall. Or perhaps flying would be a better term, the Syrizen's lithe bodies soaring into those leaps, flickering and disappearing and reappearing further and further and further like stones skipping across the surface of a pond.

Behind me I felt the warmth of flames. I glanced only briefly over my shoulder to see the city on fire before running after them, delving into those dim passageways and scaling the tower steps.

Didn't have to think. Didn't have to breathe. I knew exactly where to go.

Pathyr Savoi and his companion were at the very top of the tower, in a room surrounded by windows. The first thing I saw was Nura's back, stark and white. Despite the bright sky and open windows, the room was growing steadily darker, like she was calling shadows to her. A young man stood before her, his hands outstretched, shielding a small cluster of people behind him — including two Valtain.

"Your Queen murdered an innocent man," he snarled. "My father was no traitor. She is a tyrant."

The darkness leeched from the corners, clouding the windows, misting the air, forming an inky cape around Nura's shoulders. My breaths came quicker.

When I blinked, I could have sworn I saw Esmaris's blood spattered face. Saw Vos's body dangling from gallows.

"I have no concern for your father." Nura's voice moved like ink dissolving into water.

The shadows grew thicker. My heart beat faster, slipping from my control.

Distantly, I recognized that this was not natural. That the darkness that crawled from the shadows and writhed around us was no trick of the light. That the sudden panic surging in my veins was not entirely my own. That some terrible magic curling around Nura's fingertips was drawing it all to the surface.

But it hit me too quickly for it to make any difference.

My knees struck the marble floor with the force of dead weight. The white stone was cold beneath my skin. White like Esmaris's floor.

Crack!

Twenty-six.

I plunged into cold terror.

"It's not real." I hardly heard Max's voice. "It's not real, Tisaanah."

I could feel Esmaris's whip striking me, again and again, flesh opening across my back. I could feel his life cracking. Could feel Serel's hands sliding away from mine.

"I don't care if your father was innocent. You certainly

aren't." Nura, a silhouette of white in darkness, raised her hands. The Savoi man was on his knees in front of her, clutching his head. "Your people are dead because of your actions. Did you know that? Every last one. I hope you like how that blood looks on your hands."

I flipped my palms up to see crimson.

Perhaps I screamed. Terror suffocated my senses.

Max's hand slipped into mine. At his touch, I caught a brief, powerful flash of snake eyes and sheets of long black hair, echoes of a familiar face peering between them. And grief so sharp it split me in two.

Snap!

Deafening silence as the bodies hit the floor.

All at once, the darkness was gone. And so was that unnatural fear, leaving only sore exhaustion in its place. Blinding midday light slapped me across the face.

I lifted my head from the ground, watching the Syrizens' spears bury themselves into Pathyr's fragile flesh. They made quick work. The dozen people huddled in this room were executed within seconds.

The sound, I realized, was always the same.

Nura watched in silence, her arms crossed over her chest. When she finally turned, she only said, "Good work," before striding past us. Beside me, Max let out a rough groan and a shaky breath.

I slumped against the wall, so exhausted I could hardly lift my body. Ghosts echoed in my vision as darkness slowly overtook me.

CHAPTER TWENTY-TWO

Clean up was almost worse than the battle itself. In the frenzy of the fight, adrenaline had shielded me and numbed me. But afterwards, the brutality of what had been left behind was stark beneath the still midday sun. Every sight and smell, every remaining fractured moan, every shocked survivor's sob raked across my skin.

Still, I drew myself together as if with little pieces of twine and worked diligently, even though when I first pushed myself up from the ground, I thought that I might topple. Max and I had stared at each other for a moment, still standing in that room of dead bodies. I wondered if I looked as terrible as he did.

I was certain that he'd whisk us back home immediately, since he looked like he was dying to get out of there. But then he peered out the window, let out a heaving sigh, and said, "If we're going to be responsible for this, even indirectly, it's only decent to help deal with the aftermath."

I agreed. And, more selfishly, I didn't want to give the Orders any reason at all to go back on their commitments.

So, we threw our exhausted bodies into the cleanup effort, even when I thought I had nothing left to give.

"All this for what?" Max spat, heaving as he yanked aside a beam, nudging a pile of discarded clothes with pained, visceral anger. "For a big 'fuck you' to Sesri? All this for his personal revenge?"

I didn't understand either, and every time I looked at the shattered fragments of some family's life, fury careened into my stomach. But then I thought of Nura's lie — of the agony on Pathyr Savoi's face when she made sure he died believing that he had killed all of his people. Was he a man who truly didn't care about his city? Or had his rage and grief twisted his judgement so thoroughly that he believed he was doing the right thing?

It was amazing, the mental somersaults minds and hearts could do to justify their actions in the name of love.

By the time we were finally dismissed, it felt like the last several days hadn't even happened. The city was still in ruins, bodies were still left unburned — or worse, still unrecovered within the wreckage — and the Tairnian people were still wraiths, wandering lost.

But I couldn't take anymore, and I knew Max couldn't, either. Even Sammerin, who always exuded unwavering stability, looked like he was ready to collapse.

I had never been so grateful to smell the fresh, clean scent of those flowers, or to be greeted by the crowded warmth of the cottage. I waited until Max disappeared into his room before I went to the basin and let myself retch.

CHAPTER TWENTY-THREE

I barely even tried to sleep that night. The echoes of what I had seen in Nura's shadows were burned into me, so visceral that remnants of that panic sat beneath every breath. But even worse were the images that I saw when I closed my eyes, bloody scars from the battle and the aftermath.

I was so exhausted that my mind and body hurt. But I couldn't just lie there any longer. Eventually, I slipped from my bed and retreated outside into the garden, the cool dampness of the bare earth beneath my feet a relief. The flowers had exploded since the spring, thriving in the moist heat that had descended upon us in these last weeks. Vines and leaves tickled my ankles as I traced my steps through the paths.

Clip.

Clip.

Clip.

I turned my head to see a figure crouched in the garden. A gentle orange warmth illuminated Max's face, intently focused on the rose bush that he tended.

I crossed the path and settled next to him. My limbs screamed with every movement, and I knew Max still felt the impacts, too. I glanced at his shoulder. In the moonlight, I could see the darkness of old blood still seeping through his shirt. He'd refused to let Sammerin heal it, insisting he needed to save his energy for more dire patients.

Clip.

"You too, huh?" He plucked another dead blossom, then collected the wilting petals in his palm and consumed them with a gentle burst of fire, dumping the ashes into the dirt.

"Yes."

I watched Max's profile — moonlight and his intermittent fire illuminating the line of his straight nose and still, serious mouth. Max's mouth, I had noticed, was rarely still. It was always thinned in concentration or twisted in a sneer or curled in a sarcastic smirk. Not now, though. Now, he just looked tired, empty, as if the events of the last few days had peeled the muscles from beneath his skin.

And he went out there for me.

I drew my knees up to my chest, rested my cheek on my kneecaps.

"I know it was difficult for you," I whispered. I didn't need to say what I was referring to.

"It's difficult for everyone. That's just how it is." His eyes flicked to me, eerily bright even in the darkness. "And how are you?"

"Fine," I lied.

He looked as if he didn't believe me for a second. "Nura really hit you."

At the mention of her name, I could feel that razor blade of terror shoot through my veins — see Esmaris, Serel, Vos. Despite myself, I shuddered.

"And that was just overflow, what you and I got. That wasn't even close to full force." Max shook his head, letting out a breath of a humorless laugh. "Pathyr Savoi is lucky that they killed him. I've seen her lock people up like that indefinitely."

The thought made the hairs on my arms stand upright. "What *was* that?"

"She drowns people in the worst of their fears. Or usually, worse — the worst of their memories. Like a living nightmare, but more real. It's... bad."

Clip.

I thought of what I had seen when Max touched my hand — the snake, the girl with the long black hair. And the sheer, crippling force of his terror.

As if he knew what I was thinking, he said, "It was a two-way passage, you know." He paused. "I saw your master. With the whip."

Crack.

Twenty-seven.

I flinched, just as a wrinkle of a sneer sliced over the bridge of Max's nose. "Please tell me that man is dead."

Clip.

His fingers curled around the dead petals, and the ensuing flames felt slightly brighter, slightly more vicious, this time.

"He is," I said, hoarsely.

"I hope you did it, and I hope it hurt."

My stomach somersaulted. And Max's eyes flicked to me again, bearing a particular kind of knowing look that made me wonder what else he saw — whether he knew what I had done. "And I hope," he added, quietly, "that you don't regret it for a second."

He knew. He had to.

"He would have killed me," I whispered.

"He would have." *Clip.* Fire. "Fucking monster."

"Not always. He was..." My voice trailed off. How could I even describe what Esmaris was to me? All of the twisted, uncomfortable shades of our relationship? "He was kind, sometimes. I thought he cared for me, in his way."

And yet, that man who looked at me with such sparkling affection was the same one who stripped the skin from my back, lash by lash, with every intention of continuing until I was nothing but a lifeless sack of flesh. "But it was only at the end

179

that I realized," I said. "He loved me as a thing belonging of him. Not as a person."

It hurt more to say it aloud than I thought it would.

Max's jaw was so tight that I could see the muscles flexing even in the moonlight. "He deserved it." He cast me another sidelong glance. "And what about the blond man?"

Gods, how much did he see? My surprise must have shown on my face, because he gave me a tiny smile. "You weren't exactly mentally prepared, and you were still *in* my head. I had a front-row seat."

"My question now," I said, instead of answering. "The girl with black hair. Who was that?"

Max's expression hardened. He was silent for a long moment.

"That was my sister." *Clip.* He looked away as he spoke again, in blunt, removed sentences. "To answer your next question, yes, she died with the rest of them."

War casualties, he had said, with that same choppy finality. "You had more?"

"Siblings? Yes. There were seven of us. And my parents." *Clip* — faster and sharper. "It was a loud house."

Seven. How horrible and eerie it must have been, to go from a family of that size to... nothing. "Tell me of them," I said, quietly.

"About my family?"

"Yes. What were they like?"

I watched Max's hands pause, the corners of his mouth tightening ever so slightly. And I watched his eyes go far away, as if dipping his toes into memory. "Too much to say. My father was loud and friendly. My mother shy and reserved."

Cli-ip. More slowly.

"I had three brothers and three sisters. Brayan, Variaslus and Atraclius. And then the twins, Shailia and Marisca. And then Kira."

Six siblings. I imagined a young Max tucking himself into corners to get away from the ruckus or squabbling with siblings over everyday mundanities. No wonder he was so particular about his things. He probably grew up having to defend them constantly from a house full of people.

"You were probably…second most old," I guessed.

Old enough to hone the sense of protective vigilance that I caught hints of here and there. Young enough to have to prove that vigilance by joining the military.

He glanced at me, revealing a faint glimpse of surprise. "Good guess."

I pressed my finger beneath one eye, pleased with myself. "I see you, Max. You are no great question."

Only partially true. It was a nice sentiment, but there were definitely still many questions.

He gave me a smirk that said he knew this, too. "In that case, all-knowing one, I can stop answering yours."

"Tell me about the sister I saw."

The smile disappeared.

"Not in death," I added, quickly. "Tell me of her in life."

"That was Kira, the youngest." *Clip.* Instead of burning the dead blossom, he held it loosely in his hands as he folded them in his lap. "She was the strangest person. She liked — how else do I say this — gross things. Like spiders and things. Smart as sin. And she was just getting started. She was twelve when she died. No one got the chance to see what she'd become, or what she'd…"

He groped for words, then gave up and lapsed into silence.

As always, Max's thoughts were closed behind a curtain I couldn't part. But I could still feel his grief tainting the air between us, echoes of what I had felt when I was inside of his mind — echoes of what I felt in my own heart. I knew that loss.

"When the slavers came to my village," I said, "I left behind everyone I knew. My friends, my family. My mother. They were sent to mines. Only I was sold to the lords."

I could still remember the way they looked, their backs rod straight as they were led off into the night, dignified in those silver-dipped straight lines. And I watched them from that rickety cart, steeling myself in preparation for a new life.

"I'm sorry," Max murmured, and he sounded like he really meant it — like he felt it with me.

"I'm certain they must be all dead now. The mines kill quickly. Or perhaps they all killed themselves first." There was always talk of it among the adults, what they would do if they found themselves standing at the entrance of those tunneling coffins. It was not unheard of for entire villages to swallow poison hidden beneath their tongues rather than face a demeaning and inevitable death. I imagined those silhouetted lines collapsing, row after row. Blinked back the thought. Swallowed.

"The worst thing, though," I continued, slowly, "is to think that they are all buried somewhere in a hole, with so many other slaves. And I hate their deaths. But what I hate more is that there is no one left who remembers their lives."

No one but me.

My mother was powerful and wise. She was the center of the world to me and to the people of our community. And she had faded away to nothing but a clutched handful of my memories.

A warm breeze rustled my hair, sending a shudder through the leaves. I could feel the heat of Max's shoulder next to mine, even as we were both completely still.

"And who the hell are we," he finally said, voice low and thick, "to carry something so precious?"

One of the many uncertainties I did not dignify aloud, but that plagued my thoughts every day. I had no answer.

I heard the dull sound of the clippers dropping to the damp earth, Max's hands still. We sat there for a long time in silence, grief and memories twining into ghosts around us.

I wasn't sure how long it was before he spoke again. "How did you make it to Ara?"

"I do not remember most of it. I was very injured."

"You dragged yourself across the ocean with those wounds?"

"Yes." I let myself fall backwards into the grass. "My friend helped me go."

"The blond."

Shame ripped through my chest. The remnants of Serel's goodbye burned my cheek. "I left him," I whispered. "He helped me and I left him."

"You're going to get him back," Max murmured.

"I will. I must."

"He's fortunate to have you fighting this fight."

Maybe. Maybe not. There was only one me. And there were so many Serels.

The stars blurred. Gods, I was tired. "Thank you for coming with me to Tairn," I murmured. "And thank you for trusting me."

Out of the corner of my eye, I saw Max slump backwards too, lying beside me. The warmth of him was oddly comforting, radiating even though we didn't touch at all.

That same warmth infused his words as he said, "We made an alright team."

And we did not speak again as we lay there, grounded by the grass and earth and whispering night air, eyelids finally fluttering into a tentative sleep as the sun crept toward the horizon.

CHAPTER TWENTY-FOUR

"Well, this is cute."

I opened my eyes to the aggressive, blaring sun, which seemed like a personal insult to my throbbing head. I blinked again and a silhouetted form took shape, backlit to illuminate silver braids, arms crossed over her chest.

"Late night?" Nura asked.

"Just who I like to see first thing in the morning." Max's voice, still hoarse with sleep, came from beside me. I glanced at him only briefly as we pushed ourselves up from the ground. We hadn't so much as touched, though we had fallen asleep inches away from each other. Still, something felt uncomfortably — though not unpleasantly — intimate about the whole thing.

"Still? That's flattering, Max. Maybe a little sad." Nura watched us get up, not moving. Despite her quip, her voice was flatter than usual. Once I got to my feet and got a good look at her, it was obvious that she was exhausted. Purple shadows circled her eyes and the hollows of her cheeks. Whereas I had always thought she looked lithe and powerful, today that same body seemed thin to the point of frailty.

"Besides," she added, eyeing us, "it's actually nearly noon."

Max grumbled something wordless.

"But then, I can't judge you for doing whatever you have to do to get some rest after all that. You deserve it. I didn't get the chance to tell either of you how well you did." She looked from me, to Max, to me. "Clever idea."

"Someone had to figure out something that didn't involve crushing a few thousand people to death." Max rubbed his left eye with the back of his hand, glaring at Nura with his right. "But hey. They shit in their own beds, right?"

Nura visibly flinched. "It didn't come to that," she said. "Thanks to you."

"Thanks to her." Max jerked his chin to me. "Now what can we do for you, Nura?"

"I came to speak to Tisaanah." She looked me up and down. I crossed my arms over myself, suddenly very conscious of my cotton nightgown.

Taking that as his cue, Max grumpily excused himself. As he sauntered off to the cottage, he cast one glance over his shoulder, meeting my gaze for the first time since we woke up. There was something rawer and more honest in the look we shared.

"How has he been?"

I turned to see Nura staring after him as well, brows furrowed slightly, the corners of her mouth turned down. Her voice sounded so different in that shade of understated concern. But then, everything about her seemed so different. I almost wouldn't have recognized her.

"Fine," I said. Not entirely true — not all the time — but I knew it was what he would want me to say.

"A good teacher?"

"Yes."

A brief, faint smile tightened her lips. "I knew he would be."

Nura's gaze flicked back to me, and something grew more distant in it. "You did very well in Tairn. Better than I even thought you would, I'll admit. And beyond that, I owe you a personal thanks. So do the people of Tairn."

I thought of the ruins. That stuffed dog. The devastated looks on the residents' faces as they emerged from the basement of the tower. "Even still, they lost very much."

"Yes," Nura agreed, solemnly. "I'm sorry that you had to witness what you did."

I knew instantly, even with the vague phrasing of that statement, that she was talking about herself — her vicious, brutal display in that tower. Even now, it was impossible not to look at her and remember it, a silhouette of stark white in a room of darkness, emanating terror.

"Why did you lie to Pathyr Savoi?" I asked. "Before his death?"

Nura's face hardened. "It was only minutes away from being true. He was ready to make sacrifices that didn't belong to him for his own personal vendetta. I have deep sympathy for his loss and his pain. But I have no patience for such terrible, dangerous selfishness."

Right now, she looked like she had no patience left, period. Like whatever shields she had constructed between herself and the world were worn down.

"But I'm sorry," she added, more softly, "that what I did affected you, too. No one prepared you for that."

"No one ever does."

A biting, humorless chuckle. It reminded me eerily of Max's. "True." Then, she said, "You fulfilled your end of the deal. And we'll fulfill ours. Zeryth wanted me to give this to you."

She reached into the pocket of her jacket and pulled out a wrinkled letter, sealed with silver wax pressed into the shape of the moon. The outside said only one word, rendered in perfect, curling script: *Tisaanah.*

I turned it around in my hands. Despite the fact that it was stored in Nura's pocket, the paper was so cool to the touch that I nearly flinched.

"Thank you," I said. Nura didn't answer, and when I looked up again, her chin was tilted towards the cottage. Max had come outside again and was rearranging piles of firewood near the door. I couldn't quite decipher the expression on her face. I prided myself on my ability to understand people — but Nura remained such a mystery to me, visible only in blurry, broad shapes, like a figure lingering behind ice-glazed glass.

"He went out there for you, you know," she said. "So you wouldn't be alone."

"I know." I felt the weight of that responsibility, even though it was oddly warm and comforting in my chest.

Nura's eyes flicked back to me, a dull glimmer glittering as the corners of her eyes crinkled — the one sign of a small, distant smile. "I knew he would."

Then, before I had the chance to say anything more, she raised her palm, uttered a tired goodbye, and folded away into the air.

I WENT BACK to the cottage before opening the letter, reading it aloud as I paced around the living room. Max watched me with a cup of tea in one hand, the other loosely hanging into his pocket.

Tisaanah -

It made my day the first time Nura mentioned your name. I hear you have been trying to reach me. I offer you my deepest apologies for my absence and my silence.

I return to Ara shortly and I will not come back without every possible effort to fulfill your noble and well-deserved requests. You have my personal assurance, along with my deepest respect.

Always knew you had it.

- Z.

I LOOKED up when I was finished, catching the end of Max's exasperated eyeroll. I flipped the paper over. Folded it. Unfolded it.

That's it? A few sentences with a vague promise of... something?

"Zeryth and his personal assurances. I'm sure that was what you were hoping for." Max slurped the final sip of his tea, shooting a sardonic stare to the letter in my hands. "But at least he gave you that sweet, patronizing little bit at the end. I'm sure it was all worth it to know that the dazzling Arch Commandant always *believed* in you —"

I didn't even hear his bitter sarcasm. I nearly let the paper slide from my hands.

"Arch Commandant?" I squeaked.

Max blinked at me. "What?"

"Zeryth is Arch Commandant?"

"You didn't know?"

"How I would know?"

"How *would I* know."

"You would know what?"

"I was correcting your Aran." Max cocked his head. "You really didn't?"

I looked down at the letter again, brow furrowed. I never would have imagined that the man I had spent so much time with could possibly be the most high-ranking member of one of the most powerful organizations in the world.

"He never said."

"I'm shocked. I thought he'd start to melt if he went more than an hour without mentioning it."

I paused, silent, turning this new information around in my head.

On one hand: this was good. Just to be known by name by the Arch Commandant had to be a good thing. No question.

On the other...

I felt something bitter and acidic seep into my stomach. I had dismissed Max's anger on my behalf before, but now, to think that the damn *Arch Commandant* had befriended me in slavery and then *left* me there...

I clenched my teeth, allowing the tension of my jaw to cut off the rest of that thought. And I placed the paper on the table, folded neatly.

"It makes nothing different," I said, curtly. "We're late on training."

CHAPTER TWENTY-FIVE

I sat cross-legged in the garden, watching as Max dragged a circle in the dirt with a stick. Then, he punctuated his drawing with three lines, all running through the center at various angles.

I held back a grin of anticipation.

A week of delicate, tentative normalcy had crept by, and it had taken about that long for Max and me to slowly settle back into our own heads. When we got there, it was as if we both mutually looked at the calendar and realized, with a start, that my evaluations were only two months away. All things considered, that was not a lot of time at all. Which was why I was thrilled that Max had finally decided to tackle —

"Stratagrams," Max announced.

He dropped the stick, held out his hand, and various flower petals appeared in his palm, as if snapped to his skin by a magnetic force.

My smile faded. I looked at him, unimpressed.

"Only this?"

"*Only this.* Please." He spread out his fingers, picking through the flower petals. There was one lily petal. One hydrangea. One violet. And more and more, never more than one piece of any given flower. "What I just did," he said, "was provide instructions. I want one single petal of every type of flower in this garden. That requires magic to go in a lot of different directions at once, and it requires it to *think*."

"Think?"

"I need to tell it that I want one of every separate species of flowers, and it needs to recognize that. It may seem simple, and in a lot of ways, it is. But it does require magic to go in a lot of different places at once. Controlling it is easier with Stratagrams, though they aren't necessary. This is why most Wielders need to use them for travel, for example. They need to tell the magic where to take them, where to leave them, and how to get them there. Complicated to do mentally alone."

He reached into his pocket and a produced a small stack of paper. Then into his other pocket, revealing the bottle of black liquid I had chosen at Via's.

"It's ink," I said, in realization.

"In a sense. Ink with a little something extra built in." His eyes glittered and I got the impression that I was about to be on the wrong end of a joke. "Now, I want you to do what I just did. A petal of each flower. Since you find it so unimpressive, it should be easy for you."

I opened the ink and Max handed me a pen. I observed Max's circle, drawn in dirt on the ground. Then went to draw the same thing—

— And let out a yelp, tumbling backwards. And as soon as I touched the pen to paper, a shock ran up my hand, releasing a puff of sparks and smoke and slapping me in the face with a force that I was thoroughly unprepared for. By the time I got my bearings again, the first thing I heard was Max's laughter.

I glowered at him. "Thank you," I sniffed, sarcastically.

"You're so very welcome." Max composed himself, though the laughter remained in his eyes long after it faded from his mouth. "To be fair, you picked a particularly fierce one. Fitting, I suppose. Ready yourself for it this time."

I settled back onto my knees, steeling myself before I touched the pen to the parchment. When I was ready for it, I only jolted slightly, but quickly got a handle on the magic flowing from my fingertips — like I was grabbing the reins of an unruly horse.

"Good," I heard Max say, but I was too focused on glancing from his circle to mine from beneath a furrowed brow. I copied it stroke for stroke, and then I opened my palm in preparation for the flower petals.

…And nothing happened.

I flicked my eyes up to Max, who looked far too amused.

"I wonder why it isn't working?" he said. "Here. Let me demonstrate again." He used the stick to draw another circle in the dirt. And another series of lines. And just as before, a flurry of flower petals rushed to his hands.

But my brow furrowed. This circle was completely different from the first. They didn't even have the same number of lines within them, and the positions of the ones that remained were wildly different.

"I do not understand."

"Magic is just as much of a living being as you or I. So the way you direct it needs to change. This Stratagram is how I needed to direct it five minutes ago. But *this* one is how I needed to direct it thirty seconds ago. And if I were to do it again, that one would be different, too."

My lips tightened. I drew a circle, then paused. "But," I asked, "what do the lines *mean?* How do I read them?"

"Do you know what I hear, when you ask me that?" Max narrowed his eyes at me. "I hear, 'Max, how do I ram my head through this with unrelenting and methodical brute force?'"

"That's not what I meant."

It was, a little.

"Well, you can't force these," he said, smugly. "You just have to feel it."

I tried another circle, then another. Nothing.

"They do tend to be more difficult for Valtain," Max said,

after several failed attempts. "You magic is just more nebulous than mine."

"Does Nura use them?"

"Yes. I've seen her do some incredible things with them. For all her flaws, she is an exceptionally talented Wielder."

At the mention of Nura, I thought back to my odd conversation with her in the garden. There were many times when I almost asked Max the questions that lingered at the tip of my tongue. It never seemed like a good time — especially not when we were both still recovering from our time in Tairn. Now, my frustration made me bold.

"So," I said, drawing another circle. "Nura was your lover. Yes?"

"Excuse me?" Max let out a strangled chuckle. "What a topic change."

"It's true though. Yes?"

Another circle. Another set of lines. No response.

"Yes," he said, finally. "Long time ago."

It was no great surprise to me that Nura and Max had been together. But I still couldn't quite envision them as a couple, like they were two puzzle pieces that didn't quite fit. Then again, maybe that was because Nura was still such an enigma to me.

"You seem very different," I said.

A long pause. I kept my eyes trained to the paper, repeating circles.

"As much as it pains me to say this," Max answered at last, "Nura probably knows me better than any other living human being. I've known her since we were children. But when we were together, we were very different people, and far more... aligned."

Aligned. Hm.

"Why did it end?"

"Our views had become totally incompatible, and that became obvious in the most violent possible manner."

I glanced up at him, and he scrunched up his nose. "Don't give me that *look*," he said, "as if I owe you the dirty details."

I gave him a cloying smile. He rolled his eyes.

"And after?" I asked. "Other lovers?"

"Nosy, nosy."

My hand stopped. I pressed my finger to the tip of my nose, raising an eyebrow. "Nose-ee?"

Aran was a strange, strange language.

"It's a term for someone who sticks their nose where it doesn't belong. The definition might as well include your name."

I chuckled as I drew another circle.

Max's face brightened. "Look," he said, pointing. I peered over my shoulder to see a smattering of random flower petals scattered across the ground. "That's something."

"Not what I wanted," I scowled.

"Better than nothing. It'll work when you think about it the least."

I watched as the smile faded on his lips, though it still clung faintly to the corners of his mouth.

I would admit it: he was handsome, with those high cheekbones and, of course, those delicate, striking eyes that peered out from beneath his perpetually thoughtful brow. My gaze swept down, over the solid line of his shoulder, then following his arm and landing on the ropey muscle of his forearms.

Surely it wouldn't be difficult for him to find female companionship if he wanted to. But he never brought anyone home. Then again, bringing someone home implied that he left in the first place, which he didn't. Ever.

His eyes dropped. I wondered if I had been staring too intently. Too quickly, I looked back to my parchment.

"You did not answer," I said.

"I haven't had anything in a long time that went beyond the... uh... physical. Not that it's any of your business."

"Physical?" I echoed.

"Well — you know. More shallow romantic interactions."

"Shallow?" I leaned forward, doe-eyed. "How shallow?"

"Well — poor word choice." A slight but distinctive flush rose to his cheeks. "Definitely not *shallow*, but—" He stopped short as I struggled to contain my laughter, eyes narrowing at me in realization. "You shit."

I shook my head, still giggling, drawing another attempt at a Stratagram. I caught a glimpse of a flurry of directionless flower petals out of the corner of my eye. Not good enough.

"Why am I the one being interrogated here?" He crossed his arms. "What about you? How long have you been with your *lover?*"

He said the word "lover" in what I could only imagine was supposed to be an imitation of my accent — *loov-ear.*

"I have no lover."

"The blond?"

"Serel?" I laughed, shaking my head. "No. He would be more interested in you than me."

"Ah. I see." Max was silent for a moment. "So... no one?"

I didn't speak. A different reality flashed through my mind — a reality in which I was a normal Aran girl who lived an unremarkable Aran life, and could tell him a story of an innocent first love or a dimwitted ex-beau. And that false reality just seemed so... appealing. Simple.

Compared to my truth. My complicated, painful truth.

And yet, somehow I got the impression that he knew what he was really asking me. It was there in the gentle tone of his voice: an open door.

"Well. There was Esmaris. And the men I... performed for." I tried to speak as casually as possible, even though the words suddenly grew thick, like rancid honey. "But that was survival, not love. I knew my value, and I needed to use it."

I chanced a glance at him, and his lips were tight.

"That shouldn't have happened to you."

I shrugged, even though the movement was stiff, forced. "Many had much worse."

Are you aware of how well I treat you? Esmaris had asked me, minutes before he tried to kill me.

"That doesn't change anything." He shook his head. One

burning movement. "It doesn't make what they did to you any less terrible, Tisaanah."

His words hit on something within me. A wound that I had covered up, deep within my chest. I'd told myself so many times that I was lucky. I survived, after all, when the people I'd left behind had not.

And yet, I knew too that Max was right. I'd known it since the day Esmaris tried to beat me to death. I had seen such terrible things, *lived* such terrible things, that I mistook Esmaris's meticulous care for love. Even though he cared for me the way one cared for a prize horse: pampered it, groomed it, broke it and rode it, and discarded it when it began to kick.

After all, I was the *lucky* one.

"The day I tried to buy my freedom," I said, quietly, "he told me that I forgot what I was."

When I glanced at Max again, his jaw was set, his gaze sorrowful, contemplative. He did not speak.

"Perhaps in a way, he was right," I said. "But I forgot what he was, too. I forgot that he was someone who could never see me as more than a possession."

I had been just a child, when I met him. Just a child, and he had taken me in, told me I should feel grateful because he only beat me sparingly, because he waited a few years to rape me, because he didn't send me off to my death like he did to so many others.

Aren't you lucky, Tisaanah. Don't I treat you well.

My knuckles were tight around my pen. When I tore another vicious, mindless stroke over the paper, my fists were suddenly full of flower petals.

———

I SPENT the night drawing Stratagrams, though unsuccessfully, other than that one singular victory in the garden. Max and I had settled into a comfortable routine. I was in my typical spot near the hearth, crouched on the ground, paper scattered around me. And Max, as usual, draped himself over an armchair with a book perched in his hands.

The night ticked by, and in the flickering flames my ink was beginning to waver and blur in front of my eyes. Sometimes we both fell asleep like this, waking up to greet each other bleary-eyed in the harsh morning.

"Tisaanah."

Max's voice was hoarse with almost-sleep, so quiet that I almost lost it in my own exhaustion and the crackling of the fire. When I looked up, he peered at me from behind low, slightly crooked reading glasses, face taut and thoughtful.

"The way I look at it," he said, very solemnly, so quietly that his words slipped into the air like steam, "you didn't forget what you were. I think you remembered. And I hope no one ever again has the fucking audacity to tell you otherwise."

For a moment I blinked at him in silence. An odd, fleeting sensation rustled in my chest — like I had swallowed a handful of my silver butterflies.

"I know," I said at last, as it if were nothing. "I am wonderful."

Max shook his head, rolled his eyes. And in the dying scuff of his chuckle, we lapsed back into that quiet, comfortable silence.

CHAPTER TWENTY-SIX

Eight weeks.

That's all we had left until my evaluations. And Max and I, armed with this odd new intimacy that Tairn and its aftermath had created in us, surged toward our goal with renewed focus. Our training days lasted ten, twelve, sixteen, eighteen hours, or as long as it took until one or both of us collapsed into an armchair in exhaustion.

Something had clicked into place. And neither of us seemed to be able to identify what it was, but we both saw it in each other — in the growing ease of our conversation, in the unspoken understandings of our training sessions, in the safety and silence of our evenings at home.

Our life settled into a pulse, a heartbeat, a collection of breaths. In the silence between them, I memorized the cadence of Max's barefoot steps padding down the hallways at night, the way one single muscle in his throat twitched when he was stressed, the whisper of a laugh that always followed one of my quips (however unfunny). I learned that one side of his smile always started first — the left side, a fraction of a second before the right — and that he loved ginger tea above all else and the list of things he wasn't made for.

And, in turn, he quietly memorized me, too. I knew he did, because one day I realized he had long ago stopped asking me how I took my tea and that we mysteriously always had a never-ending stock of raspberries, even though I knew he didn't like them. And he would ask me, in quiet ways, about my life — always in the sleepy moments at the end of the day. *Tell me about Serel. Tell me about your mother. Tell me about Nyzerene.*

And for my part, I did the opposite: treaded carefully along the edges of questions with raw answers, pulling my fingers away from seeping, carefully hidden wounds. Max's past still held so many mysteries. But as much as my curiosity nagged at me, I saw those shrouded winces. I understood the value of the relief — the mercy — in leaving them unasked.

In this mutual understanding, we became each other's stability. On the nights when my nightmares woke me, prodded me out into the clean air of the garden, he always found himself mysteriously restless, taking a walk through the night and offering me some quiet company.

My Aran improved dramatically. Still, every so often, I would unleash a string of truly nonsensical words that butchered every conceivable rule of grammar. On one particularly exhausting day, I committed one such crime when asking Max where the Stratagram ink had gone. ("Has gone where... black water?")

Max hadn't so much as paused as he reached into a drawer and produced the ink. At Sammerin's look of somewhat horrified amazement, he shrugged and said, "After a while, you become fluent in Tisaanah-speak." And we looked at each other and exchanged a small, proud smile.

The days slipped by, one after another, blending together. Days stretched longer, then curled shorter. A bite nipped into the air, warning of distant autumn. The garden grew wild and over-grown, vines snaking over each other, blossoms curling over cobblestone pathways in beautiful, feral greed.

We practiced amongst those flowers one crisp morning, one

week away from my evaluation. I made some terrible joke and, in response, Max winced and shook his head. "Awful. Just awful."

"You say this now," I retorted, twisting air between my hands. "But what will you ever do when I'm gone?"

I meant it as a preening joke. But as soon as the words left my mouth, they landed like a thrown brick, striking us both with a blunt, unforgiving impact.

Max's grin had stilled and wilted. One wrinkle formed between his eyebrows. We stared at each other in startled silence, something palpable and indescribable thickening in the inches between us as realization careened through us both.

We had carved out these small, intimate spaces for each other in our lives, and by some miracle of human denial, neither of us had thought about what that would inevitably mean. Now, for the first time, I realized the breadth of the gaping absence we would leave in each other.

That, at least, he would leave in me.

"I suppose," he said at last, nudging a crawling vine with his toe, "I'll finally get this garden back under control."

I shut my mouth and feigned sudden interest in something on the ground, fighting an odd emptiness that suddenly caved in my chest. I had been so singularly focused on where I was going that I hadn't stopped to think about what I would be leaving behind. The thought of it filled me with words I wasn't ready to say.

CHAPTER TWENTY-SEVEN

A bead of sweat dangled at the tip of my nose, refusing to fall.

Max circled me, eyes razor sharp with militant focus as he barked command after command. My palms were open, juggling with air and water and sparks and illusions and, of course, those silver butterflies, leaping into the air in great desperate bursts.

Start. Stop. Hover. Higher, faster, smaller, slower — control!

I anticipated each word before it was out of his mouth, yanking illusions closer or pushing them further, sculpting water into perfectly formed likenesses.

"What's this?" Max barked, wiggling my loose, dangling elbow.

"Intentional," I gasped, between clenched teeth.

"Good. Trick question. Don't lock up. Show me those butterflies." And then, before I could move, "Seamless, please. Control."

The ball of water hovering between my hands was a perfect sphere — completely circular, without a drop escaping from its form, even as keeping it there took complete concentration. The water rushed in a circular motion, flowing within that sphere even as it never broke its bounds. With perfect fluidity, I peeled the butterflies from it — one first, then two, then five, then the sphere broke and gave way to a pack of them. First wet, flapping things, then shifting into blue, translucent light that rose into the sky.

"Call them back."

I did, yanking the butterflies back to my palms, circling them around my body. My hair rose with the breeze that swirled around my face, obscuring my vision. Still, that damn drop of sweat didn't fall.

"Back to your hands."

They gathered in my palms, cupped between my hands, pressing together.

"Now surprise me."

I smiled. Closed my fingers. When I opened them, the handful of butterflies were cast in glittering metal.

Max peered into my hands, a smile twitching at one side of his mouth. "What is that, steel?"

"Yes."

"Stronger than glass. Very poetic."

I shrugged, holding back my own smug smirk. I thought so too.

But Max straightened, that echo of a smile gone beneath layers of stone, his hands clasped behind his back. He regarded me with hawk-eyed intensity that seemed so unlike him that it might have made me laugh if I wasn't so focused. This, I thought, is what Max the soldier must have been like — this straight-backed, sharp-tongued, stone-faced captain.

Seconds passed. My stomach tightened.

And then, just as I was getting nervous, his face split into a grin. "Perfect." He raised his hands, palms open, as if bestowing a blessing. "Tisaanah, you are ready."

Nervousness quivered beneath my skin. My ensuing smile was short-lived. "Even without—"

"You don't need the Stratagrams. They won't be expecting that."

"But—"

"I'm far too pessimistic to tell you it's fine if it's not fine. There is no possible way they could look at that display and argue that you don't know what you're doing. *You're ready.*"

"I know I'm ready." My fingers fidgeted with each other. "But perhaps I should spend the night practicing for—"

"No. Not allowed. This is the cardinal rule: the night before an evaluation, you rest."

"Did you obey that rule?"

"No. But I didn't have a teacher as good as me." He reached out with his thumb and swiped the tip of my nose, looking at his fingers and making a face. "I've been waiting for that to fall for the last fifteen minutes. Couldn't resist." He turned on his heel and began striding back to the cottage, waving me to follow. "Go take a bath. You're disgusting. And I swear to the Ascended, if I see you sneaking Stratagrams like the most boring possible kind of addict, I'll wring your neck."

———

I RAN my fingers through wet hair, pulling it over one shoulder and twirling the damp ends around my fingers. It had grown significantly since the night I first arrived here and chopped it all off in Max's washroom. Funny how I didn't notice until now exactly how much. The passage of time slipped by like that.

With my other hand, I absentmindedly traced circles on the wood of the table. Then one line, and two—

"Tisaanah!"

I jumped. Max stood above me, arms crossed. "How disappointingly predictable."

"I wasn't really—"

"*Wasn't really.* Please." He scoffed, then slid a glass of red wine down the table to me. "Here. A much better coping mechanism for uncooperative nerves."

"I'm not nervous," I said. I took a sip anyway, enjoying the distraction of the bitter tang over my tongue.

"We both know we're past this bullshit." He pressed a finger below one eye, raising his eyebrows at me. "I see you, Tisaanah. No great question."

I laughed a quiet, uncomfortable chuckle — unsure of how to react to the way my chest tightened, the way my palms seized.

"Should I be — I don't know — taking you out on the town, or something?" He slid into the chair across from me, leaning back, his own wine glass dangling from his fingers. "Feels like we should be celebrating. And it occurred to me that maybe your idea of celebrating isn't sitting around at home with an unpleasant recluse like myself."

"It's too early to celebrate. Maybe we can go after I pass."

The truth was, there was nowhere else I'd rather be than here, drinking up these final moments of comfortable companionship. One way or another, pass or fail, I had the distinct feeling that everything would be different by this time tomorrow. And there was so much that I didn't want to change.

Max raised his glass. "Tomorrow, then. When we'll really have something to celebrate. I'm sure it'll be much more fun to go out with you than sitting in a corner watching ladies stumble all over themselves for Sammerin, anyway."

I snorted at that mental picture.

"It's something to behold, honestly." Max leaned over the table, making intense eye contact, lowering his voice in an imitation of Sammerin's smooth, quiet drawl. "'Oh, you're a hatmaker? How fascinating. I knew from the moment I saw you that you had an artistic spirit.'" He shook his head. "It's disgusting and, yet, riveting."

I could imagine it. And imagine Max glowering from a corner, watching unamused.

"And what about you?"

"I'm not made for that." He raised the glass to his lips, paused. "I'm referring to the social graces part."

"But the part after — you are made for that?" The response slid out of me so easily, in a voice that hadn't surfaced since my days dancing in Esmaris's court. I took another sip of wine, drowning my own mild surprise. Watched Max's mouth curl, ever so slightly.

"I receive no complaints," he replied smoothly.

A shudder rose to the surface of my skin. I tore my eyes from Max's face, traced the pattern of the wood grain. Dangerous territory. I didn't even know where that came from.

For a long moment we were both silent, the air taut as if we were holding our breaths.

"I have something for you," Max said, at last. The lightness to his voice snapped the thread of tension, and I exhaled. He rose from his chair and disappeared down the hall, emerging a moment later with a small, unassuming box in his hands. He placed it in front of me. Then he leaned back against the doorframe, casual and yet oddly tensed.

I looked down at the box. It was perhaps the size of my splayed hand, flat, neatly crafted from brown leather.

I flicked my gaze back to Max. I couldn't help it. A lump was already rising in my throat.

He barked a rough, uncomfortable chuckle. "Open it before you give me that look. It could be a terrible gift."

I obliged, and all I could do was sit there and blink at what was revealed, utterly stunned.

Inside the box was a golden necklace in a bed of black silk.

The back of it was an elegant thread of gold, which then widened into a beautiful, tangled mass of glimmering butterflies. Their wings were so perfectly crafted I could have sworn they quivered— the metal so delicate that it seemed like light refracted through it. Glinting vines and thorns and familiar blossoms twined between them, weaving them into a wild landscape. On closer inspection, I saw that there was one snake nestled in between it all, small and unassuming, curling off to one side.

He'd had this crafted for me. He must have. It was too specific.

My chest hurt.

"Flip it over," Max said, quietly. I obeyed. And there, where the metal would rest against my skin, were three tiny Stratagrams.

I didn't notice that he had moved until I felt his breath next to my face, leaning over my shoulder. "This one," he said, pointing to the first Stratagram, "will help you heal. Not a lot, but enough for little cuts and bruises. I had Sammerin help with it."

That thought touched me so deeply I thought my heart might fold in on itself.

His finger moved to the next circle. "This one will bring you warmth. Help you start fires. Again, limited, but—" He paused, letting out an awkward, scuffing laugh. "I thought maybe if you're traveling all over Threll, you might need that kind of thing."

I nodded, not trusting myself to speak.

There was a long pause. Max's hand hovered.

"What about this?" I said at last, pointing to the third Stratagram.

Max straightened. When he spoke again, his voice was lower, rougher, as if he were tethering something back. "That one will bring you here." He paused, cleared his throat. "If— if you ever wanted to return. It'll only work within a few miles, but…"

His voice trailed off and did not resume.

Gods.

At once, I understood. This was not about the necklace, beautiful and finely crafted as it was. He wasn't giving me another pretty trinket. No, Max — Max, the man who had taken such great care to carve out his own solitary corner of the world — was giving me what I'd never had.

The real gift was not the necklace. The gift was a home to come back to.

"Just… if you want to," he said, quietly, awkwardly.

My eyes burned.

I wanted to say, *Of course I want to return.* I wanted to say, *I don't even want to leave.*

But I didn't even smile, because I didn't know what would

come out of my mouth if I opened it. Instead I slipped the necklace into Max's hand, then lifted my hair, presenting my neck. As he fastened it around my throat, every brush of his fingers left little paths of fire along my skin, burning as they hovered there at the nape of my neck.

"Thank you," I murmured, finally. "It is perfect."

I let my hair drop. His fingers slid from my shoulders. "I figured you should have something both beautiful and functional, like you."

He said it so quickly that it almost didn't register. I whipped my head around to look at him. "Max," I breathed, touching my heart with exaggerated awe, "you think I'm functional?"

A dancing smile glinted in his eyes. "I think," he said, "that you are breathtakingly functional."

My fingertips brushed those butterfly wings as I swept my eyes over him — over the muscle twitching in his throat, over the twist at the corners of his mouth, the unruly wave of the strand of hair that fell across his forehead.

Honestly? I thought he was breathtakingly functional too. He was the most breathtakingly functional thing I had ever seen.

CHAPTER TWENTY-EIGHT

I couldn't crane my neck back far enough to see the top of the Orders' towers. They rose and rose and rose, like two walls of gold and silver, disappearing to misty clouds. I had been nearly unconscious the last time I stood at the entrance to the towers. Certainly not conscious enough to be amazed by the staggering height, staggering presence, staggering *everything*. Now, I had never felt smaller in my life.

Almost as a nervous tick, my fingers drew a circle on my palms, as if trying to capture the Stratagrams that still evaded me.

The four of us — me, Max, Sammerin, and Moth — stood in their shadows, anxious energy hanging between us.

"I haven't stepped through these doors in a very long time," Max muttered, eyeing them. Then Moth. "Nervous?"

Moth fidgeted. "Well," he said, with faux-confidence, "it took some work, but I think I've finally got energy distortion right. So, I think I definitely won't have any accidents."

Max and Sammerin exchanged a look, one of those silent ones that batted unspoken words between them.

"Moth has gone an entire week without destroying even one thing," Sammerin said. "We're all very proud of him."

"Except for the pitcher," Moth added, "but that wasn't really my fault."

Sammerin winced. "Except for the pitcher."

"Thankfully, I don't think they'll have any pitchers at the evaluations, so you should be in the clear there." Max looked at me. "And you?"

"Fine." My voice did not betray my anxiety, but I'm sure he knew how nervous I was. Normally, I found Moth endlessly amusing, but today I couldn't so much as crack a smile at his oblivious antics. At least for Moth, this was only one of six yearly evaluations he would be given. If he failed this one, he could redeem himself next year. I had no such luxury.

Sammerin and Moth began making their way to the doors, and I went to follow, but Max gently caught my wrist.

I spun around.

"I want you to know, Tisaanah, that I have complete and utter faith in your ability to do this," he said. "Now let's go show those bastards what you're capable of."

Even though I was so nervous that I quaked, a smile tightened my cheeks.

"Yes," I agreed. "I like this plan."

And with that, we opened the doors.

IF I HADN'T BEEN SO nervous, the first stage of the evaluations would have been utterly hilarious.

Max and I could not possibly have stood out more. Max was the only Solarie there, one messy splotch of color among a long row of pasty-skinned, white-haired Valtain teachers. And if the sheer peculiarity of a Solarie training a Valtain wasn't enough, his reputation took what might have perhaps just been mildly awkward and made it outright hilarious. No one seemed to know what to do with him. Every interaction was a tumble of awkward handshakes and confused raised eyebrows and hesitant, surprised greetings. During my personal favorite of these interactions, one Valtain said to him, "I thought you didn't do this anymore." When Max flatly provided, "What, Order bullshit?", the Valtain shook his head, flailed his hands weakly, and said, "I meant, well... the *world*."

I snickered through all of this, grateful to have at least one small sliver of my brain occupied by enjoying Max's highly visible, highly amusing social discomfort instead of my own nerves. Noticing this, Max prodded my ribs. "Don't get too comfortable," he grumbled. "Just you wait."

And oh, he looked like he was enjoying that grin when the evaluations began and I was rounded up with several dozen other apprentices.... all of which were, at *most*, twelve years old.

Needless to say, between the fact that I was nearly twice as old as my fellow students and my Fragmented skin (though, to my pleasant surprise, I did spot two other Fragmented students in the crowd), I earned just as many confused stares as Max did. But unlike Max, who glowered and squirmed through these interactions like a collared cat, I drank up the attention.

I needed to impress, after all. And if the eyes were already on me, that was only easier.

And impress, I did.

We were led through a series of structured exercises as a group, forcing us to demonstrate refined control of our abilities. And gods, it was *easy*. These exercises were simpler — more boring — than anything I did under Max's instruction on a daily basis.

So, I showed them what I could do.

Asked to manipulate water, while those around me struggled to maintain a smooth orb, I peeled out into perfectly crafted butterflies. Asked to conjure, I summoned two, three, four illusions at a time, twining them around each other in a — perfectly controlled, as Max would emphasize — dance. Asked to steel our minds against the sneaking tendrils of each other's thought-sensing abilities, I shoved out my partner, then turned around and echoed his own thoughts back to him.

Every request, met with an easy smile and a *"yes, and?"*

By the time the first part of the evaluations concluded, I was feeling very pleased with myself.

"I'm both disgusted and impressed by the delight with which you flaunt your superiority over a bunch of children," Max said, when I rejoined him between stages. "At least try to look like you aren't enjoying it quite so much."

"Why?"

"Some might call it distasteful."

I gave him a sly smirk. "But not you."

The corner of his mouth twitched. "No," he admitted. "Not me."

I knew he loved every minute of it just as much as I did. And just as there was no use in him denying that, I couldn't deny that his support curled around my heart and squeezed.

Still, I was nervous about what lay ahead. Too nervous, at least, to eat much of anything, so instead Max and I used the recess to slip across the lobby to the Tower of Daybreak and peer in on the Solarie evaluations. One look at Sammerin sitting in the spectator's area, sagging in his chair, staring through the windows with a look of what I could only describe as resigned horror, told me exactly how Moth's tests were going.

I grimaced. "Poor Moth."

Max chuckled. "Poor *Sammerin*."

We heard the faint echo of a crash, a flurry of activity from the next room, and whatever Sammerin was seeing made him put his head in his hands and let out a heaving sigh.

We took that as our cue to leave.

When we returned to the Tower of Midnight at the end of midday recess, Willa was waiting for us. Her face brightened as we approached.

"There you are! I wanted to congratulate you on those group evaluations, Tisaanah. You were terrific."

"Too early for congratulations," I said, but found myself suppressing a grin anyway.

She gave a cheerful shrug. "Well, still. I don't think anyone could argue. All that's left now is your individual evaluation. That's why I've come to get you, actually."

A knot tugged in my stomach. I had been particularly nervous about this part, mostly because I had no idea what to expect. My eyes found a group of other apprentices heading down a hallway, and I nodded. "I'm ready," I said.

I began to walk in that direction, but Willa's voice stopped me. "Oh, no, dear — yours will be somewhere else." She gave me a faint smile. "Come with me."

I hesitated. Exchanged a brief, nervous glance with Max.

A good thing, maybe, I told myself. I was clearly an unusual case. Of course, my test would be different.

"Alright," I said, and I followed her.

CHAPTER TWENTY-NINE

I was led into a large, circular room. Perhaps on typical occasions, it was a ballroom or some kind of event space. Today, it was stripped completely bare, devoid of decoration other than the moons etched into the wall and the glistening beauty of the white marble floor. Only four objects stood in it: three pedestals, each holding a simple silver sphere. And, in the center of the room, there was a large, smooth basin. Nura stood beside it, arms clasped in front of her, waiting for me.

The sight of her stirred a nervous surprise in my stomach. I wouldn't have expected someone so important to be here.

I looked over my shoulder, up at the balcony that curved over half of the room. Max learned over the rail, watching, fingers intertwined. When I looked at him, he gave me an uneasy smile. I suspected he had the same thought that I did.

Nura cleared her throat, and my eyes snapped back to her.

"This," she said, "will be your more advanced evaluation. You'll notice that there are three spheres in this room." She gestured to the three pedestals, arranged around the edges of the room in a triangle formation. "Your goal is to take each of these

spheres and deposit them in the basin at the center of the room."
She placed her hand on the curved lip.

My eyes darted between the three spheres. Then the basin. It
seemed too simple. And too... gamelike. I wondered if this was
normal — a standard part of every evaluation. Or if this was a
task cooked up just for me.

"Do you understand?" Nura asked. As always, she was
unreadable.

"I do," I said, with a nod. And in her returning nod, the
corners of Nura's mouth curled.

"Good. In that case, we begin..."

She raised one finger. Then two.

Three.

"Now."

Then she lifted her hands, and I was plunged into complete
darkness.

THE DARKNESS SWALLOWED me like a vat of ink, gargling in my
lungs. I had to remind myself to breathe. My heartbeat quickened in pulsing shivers at the edges of my vision.

Breathe, Tisaanah. This isn't your only sight.

I closed my eyes — out of habit, as the room was so dark that
it made no difference in visibility — and reached around me,
feeling the edges of the room with invisible hands, searching for
the spheres. In my mind's eye, they began to throb with a faint,
silver light. I caught their thread, and with it came a silent breath
of relief.

I have this. This is nothing.

I began to draw one of the orbs towards me, pulling it from
its stand. But the moment I did, it was immediately knocked
away, a violent force sending it careening across the marble floor.
I lunged after it —

—And was yanked somewhere far away, into a wall of cold.
Cold that surrounded me, inhaled me, settled deep into my bones

and guts. I blinked, and when I opened my eyes again, the darkness melted into endless, rippling grass and smeared stars.

I felt liquid run down my back — down the backs of my thighs. Scalding compared to the icy air.

My blood.

I was in the plains, in Threll. Wearing that dingy coat. With my dying horse.

A shiver of cold, of fear, of terror, ran up my spine. An illusion, I told myself. This was Nura. It wasn't real.

Isn't it?

I closed my eyes again. The backs of my eyelids revealed the same scene, the plains seared into my brain. My mind groped forward, searching for that thread of reality, dragging myself back to the tower, back to the room, back to those pedestals...

The plains flickered away, dissolving like sand in the wind.

The orbs glowed in front of me again. One of them slowly rolled across the floor.

I used magic to yank it towards me, snapping it to my fingers. It was pleasantly cool in my hands, firm and solid and *real.* I turned to drop it into the basin, smiling with satisfaction at the sound of metal against metal.

And then, suddenly, I was hit with a force. A wall of air so strong that it struck my body like a block of cement. Before I knew what was happening, I felt myself career across the room, felt my back slam against a curved wall. My throat released a muffled, wordless cry.

Darkness again, and as I slid down the wall, I dipped back beneath the surface of that drowning illusion. The marble beneath my hands and knees was the marble of Esmaris's study.

Crack.

Twenty-four. Twenty-five.

Esmaris's face flickered through the shadow, peering out from beneath a wide-brimmed, black hat. Terror drowned me.

You forgot what you are.

Not real. Not real. Not real.

It is real.

No. *No.*

I was stronger than   sliced through Esmaris's face, groping for reality. I pushed   elf to my feet only to feel the air knocked from my lungs again. But this time, at least, I was ready — I threw my arms up in front of me, like I did on the bridge in Tairn, and shielded myself. My whole body shook from the impact, but I remained standing.

In my mind, I sliced the remaining threads of Nura's illusions, unraveling them like a tattered tapestry.

Sweat rolled down the back of my neck. It took everything I had to shield myself both externally and internally, but I was doing it — somehow. I pushed forward towards the second orb. Reached out. Placed my fingertips against its cool surface.

I was just about to lift it from its stand when I felt something shift. I looked up to see a dim, gentle glow seep through the darkness.

And as the shadows danced away like a floating curtain, they revealed Zeryth Aldris.

CHAPTER THIRTY

Zeryth crossed his arms over a broad chest. "Hello, Tisaanah."

My fingers froze, struck with confusion — but it melted away with the heady warmth of his smile. The sight of it took me back to the evenings we had spent together in my little room at the Mikov estate. Some of my fondest memories there.

But, memories aside, it was borderline impossible not to be stunned by Zeryth's smile. Somehow, I had managed to forget the sheer impact of him. He was the kind of handsome that seemed almost offensive, the kind that leeched out into the air around him in a magnetic cloud. He wore a close-fitting white jacket, similar to Nura's, and with his white clothing and white skin and shoulder-length white hair, he stood out so starkly against the slithering shadows that I found myself squinting to look at him.

"Zeryth," I said, in a tone that couldn't decide whether it was pleased or confused or annoyed. I glanced back down at the orb, which sat between my fingertips. Were we done? I hadn't completed my task.

"Tisaanah," he said, "come here."

I removed my hands. Watched my fingers slide away from the metal. And I stepped forward, past the pedestal, towards Zeryth.

His gaze swept over me, starting at my feet and traveling slowly up until he reached my eyes. "You look different than the last time I saw you," he said. His teeth glittered. "Tell me, how long has it been?"

"A year and half, I think," I replied, and his grin broadened.

"Your Aran is much better, too. What a treat, to communicate so clearly with you now." He slid his hands into his pockets. "Tell me, do you like it here? In Ara?"

"I do."

"You've enjoyed training?"

"I have."

"Your instructor must be very pleased to hear that." He nodded up towards the balcony. "Turn around and wave to him."

I turned. Lifted my hand. Snapped my eyes up to the balcony. They settled on Max, and the look of hardened fury on his face snagged my slippery thoughts on something sharp.

Wait.

This was strange.

I looked at my raised hand. Curled my fingers.

There was something I was supposed to do. Something important. I was here for a reason. And somehow I'd just forgotten —

My thoughts solidified as I looked to my right, at the orb that still sat on its pedestal. I began to turn around, to walk back to it.

"Stop," Zeryth said.

My feet stopped moving.

"Look at me."

I turned back to Zeryth. He tilted his head. "Why do you want to leave?"

That was a good question.

I don't, my thoughts hummed. *I don't want to leave. I don't want to go anywhere.*

But I forced my mouth to comply. "There is something I must do."

"Nothing important."

Nothing important.

"Come here."

I did.

"Get on your knees."

Get on your knees, Esmaris had said to me.

I shuddered.

"No."

"Yes."

Yes, my mouth started to say, but at the last second —

"No."

No. No no no.

I realized what was happening. Realized that I had never seen Zeryth use magic before. Realized there was a pressure against my thoughts, a saccharine coating melting everything into one sticky, formless blob.

This was part of the test. The test I needed to finish.

"Get on your knees," Zeryth said again. My body froze halfway down. My thoughts slipped from between my fingers like handfuls of worms. But I grabbed onto my evasive thread of consciousness with painful ferocity.

I looked at Zeryth, straight into his white, expectant eyes.

"No," I said.

I'm not done.

Zeryth shot one brief glance at Nura, who stood a few feet away.

Then, everything went black again.

Black and cold. A living morass of all my greatest fears, all my worst memories. Gods, no — no, I couldn't — I was plunged into a terror that made what I experienced in Tairn look like child's play. I was being dragged through every fear I've ever had, everything I had ever had ripped away from me, every face I saw in the darkness at night, all rolled into blackness and blood and the crack of the whip, the searing warmth of Serel's lips against my cheek.

"Sit down," Zeryth's voice echoed.

Sit down, pretty butterfly. Rest. I know you're so tired.

I was so tired. So tired. But —

I'm. Not. Done.

I didn't know if I'd said it out loud, but I screamed it in my own head loud enough to drown out everything else.

I struggled to my feet, staggering like a newborn foal.

I'm not done.

I tethered that sentence to my heartbeat.

I whipped a string of magic from my hand to bring the nearest orb to me, but just as I did, a wall of wind bludgeoned me so hard that I went flying across the room. A sharp pain tore through my skull.

"Come back, Tisaanah," Zeryth purred. An offering of relief, of safety.

No.

I touched my head and felt warm blood over my fingers. My legs were already beginning to obey, crawling towards him. But I found it — the one sharp piece left in my brain. Clutched it.

I rubbed the blood between my fingers.

"Come here, Tisaanah."

Rest, little butterfly.

I drew a circle.

My legs still moved. Only my fingers still clung to the ground. A line.

I closed my eyes and I could see all of it, lit up like a map — me, the orbs, the three Valtain.

I'm not finished.

Another line.

"I won't say it again —"

No, I thought. *You won't.*

And I drew one final line of my Stratagram.

And then, all at once, there was a crash. Metal on metal and shocked grunts and a wall of light all converged into one beautiful, chaotic cacophony.

I opened my eyes just in time to see the final two orbs ricochet into the basin. To see Zeryth, Nura, and the third Valtain pushing themselves up from the floor. To look down and see my Stratagram smeared in my own blood beneath me.

And to hear a familiar voice shouting from the balcony:

"*What*. The *FUCK*. Was *that*."

I slumped back against the ground.

———————

WHEN I OPENED my eyes again, Max was leaning over me, hands on his knees. I saw his lips move but his words didn't register.

The events of the last few minutes hit me in flashes.

Nura. Zeryth. The shadows.

Get on your knees.

And the Stratagram. My *successful* Stratagram.

Max spoke again, each word hammered with sharp-edged intensity. "*Are you alright?*"

I did it.

I did it.

I touched the side of my head, still warm and damp. Pulled back my fingers to look at the red. I didn't realize that I was grinning until I started to wonder why my cheeks ached.

Max pushed back my hair, examining the wound. I hardly felt it. "Sammerin can take care of that," he said, but I couldn't care less about that cut.

Because *I did it.*

"Tisaanah, I need verbal confirmation that you're alright and that none of that turned your mind to custard."

I couldn't stop smiling. "I am very good," I said, hoarsely. "Very, very good."

Max dropped his head, letting out a sigh that started in relief

CARISSA BROADBENT

and ended in exasperation. "Ascended above. Get up. You look like a lunatic."

"Loo-nuh-tic?" New word. I hadn't found one of those in a while.

My head spun as Max pulled me to my feet.

"A crazy person. Like, for instance, one that rolls around on the ground grinning to herself while covered in her own blood."

Loo-nuh-tic.

I liked it.

A firm hand clapped me on my shoulder, shaking my knees. "Excellent work, Tisaanah. Incredibly impressive."

Zeryth stood beside me, greeting me with a pleasant smile. His hand remained around my shoulders. That otherworldly magnetism was gone, replaced with a much more comfortable, human friendliness. Still, I resisted the immediate urge to shrug away from his hands.

Get on your knees.

But I simply smiled — gave him one befitting of the sweet teenage girl that I was when I first met him. Insulting the Arch Commandant was not in my best interest.

"It's good to see you after so long, Zeryth," I said.

One telltale wrinkle flickered over the bridge of Max's nose, and I immediately knew what was coming.

"What the hell was that?" he spat. "Three high-ranking Valtain against one apprentice? In what world is that reasonable?"

I shot Max a warning look. As touching as it was that he was so angry on my behalf, I didn't need him undermining my success, even if his intentions were good. Besides, I wasn't afraid of being pushed hard. Not when it gave me that much more of a chance to prove myself.

Which I had. That was all that mattered.

"Maxantarius. What a surprise." Zeryth had remained on my arm. His easy smile hardened. "Are you finally attempting to rejoin society?"

"It's a temporary testing period. So far, my opinion is mixed."

"Really? A happy-go-lucky person like you?"

Max practically snarled. "You didn't answer my question. Do you want to explain why you thought it was acceptable—"

Shut up. "Max is a very loyal teacher," I said to Zeryth, infusing my voice with a shade of too-pleasant, too-sweet good humor.

Max caught my glare and shut his mouth, though doing so looked like it put him in physical pain.

Zeryth waved my comment away, chuckling. "We're old friends. Trust me, I'm very familiar with his charming idiosyncrasies." Then he turned back to me and his smile softened from hard-edged to gentle. "I can't tell you how happy I was to hear that you made it here, Tisaanah. But then again, if anyone could do it…"

I beamed. "Thank you."

I could hear Max's unspoken response, visibly thrashing behind his teeth: *Well, she would have made it here a hell of a lot sooner if you had*—

I gave him a Look — capital L — before it could escape, and he turned his face to the ground, scowling.

And then, my most sparkling gaze firmly planted back on Zeryth's lovely face, I finally asked the only question that really mattered: "Do you have any news from Threll?"

Zeryth's expression stilled in a way that made my stomach lurch. "Yes. We need to talk." He gestured to a small door off the main room, then turned to Max. "If you'll excuse us, Maxantarius. I promise I'll bring her back in one piece."

"I'm not worried. She already had you on your ass once today."

Gods, Max.

But Zeryth just let out a low chuckle. "We can't argue with that, can we?"

Then he turned to me and beckoned. "Follow me, Tisaanah. Let's talk."

We wound down white halls, narrow and empty. Zeryth was significantly taller than me, certainly well over six feet, and I had to crane my neck to look up at him as we walked.

"I apologize for my slow response to your requests," he said, casually. "I was, you see, preoccupied with quite a lot of travel."

"Of course."

"I was quite surprised when I first stopped at Esmaris's estate to find—" He let out a breath. "Well."

Every muscle in my body tightened. "Tell me." My saccharine facade was beginning to melt.

"Things there were in... significant disarray. Esmaris, as I'm sure you know, was dead." He glanced at me. I wondered if he knew or suspected what I had done. If he did, he didn't say anything about it. "His son was there to take his place."

"Ahzeen." I had met him only twice, and intensely disliked him. He looked just like Esmaris, and had inherited every bit of his father's ruthlessness, though none of his charm.

"Yes. Not a very friendly person, it turns out."

I shook my head. That was an understatement.

"While I was there, he was in the midst of a ruthless manhunt for his father's killer. And when I say 'ruthless'... I've never seen anything quite like it."

I could only imagine. No one did manhunts quite like the Threllian Lords did — all of those impeccable white outfits switched out for blood red. There was a ritualistic quality to bloodshed that they embraced, inhaled. And Ahzeen had a greater reason than any to throw himself into the bloodiest possible path. Esmaris had all but disowned his son. The final time he came to the estate, he and Esmaris got into a very loud, very public argument that escalated to such brutality that it ended with Ahzeen being dumped at the gates with *a missing eye*.

Ahzeen's reputation and respect would always be hampered by his father's very well-known distaste for him. But in Esmaris's death, he would have an opportunity to earn back the respect that came with the family name — without the inconvenience of

Esmaris himself. That is, as long as he proved himself to be strong and committed enough.

"I was there twice," Zeryth went on. "Once on my way out, when I arrived shortly after Esmaris's death. And then, once on my way back, after I wrote back to you last." We rounded a corner. "The first time, Ahzeen and his men were still frantically carving a path through Esmaris's enemies, slaughtering anyone and everyone who could possibly be connected to his death."

The hair stood up on the back of my neck. A perfect opportunity — excuse — to show dominance over rival families. That was a very dangerous game.

"But then, when I was there again a few months later, that wasn't the biggest concern. The estate was facing serious retaliation from the other Lords. I was hearing about it all over Threll."

My hands were trembling. With every new piece of this story, my vision flashed with another way that Serel could be killed — slaughtered in the initial bloodshed or rooted out in the internal manhunt or sent to his death on a bloody, impersonal battlefield in the name of a man he despised.

We came to a door and stopped. I put my hand on Zeryth's arm, at first for emphasis, and then left it there because I needed the stability. "Tell me. Did you find him? The— the person I asked for?"

Zeryth gave me a serious, unreadable look. He reached for the doorknob but didn't turn it yet. "I did everything I could. I know this is important to you."

Important to me? I wanted to scream. *Important to ME? You think this is about ME?*

As if this wasn't so much bigger than I was? As if this wasn't an imminent danger hanging over the heads of thousands and thousands of people?

My fingers tightened. Clenched until I could feel the muscled flesh of his forearm beneath my fingernails.

"*Show me.*"

Zeryth opened the door.

CHAPTER THIRTY-ONE

I steeled myself with such ferocity that it took me a moment to realize that the wisp of a body lying in the bed in front of me was not Serel.

No — that was a head of fiery copper hair, resting on that pillow, face turned away from me. And the arms that extended over the layers of blankets were long and gangly, not Serel's lean, tanned muscles.

My mind stalled, unsure whether I was disappointed or relieved. But whatever whirring thoughts began materializing within me froze when the figure in the bed turned their face to look at me.

I clamped my teeth down on a gasp.

For a split second, I didn't even think the face that greeted me was human.

But he was human. He was an old friend.

I swallowed my shock. Smoothed my voice into something so calm and melodic that I thought it had to belong to someone else. "Vos," I breathed, in Thereni. "I'm so happy to see you."

I saw only a glimmer of surprise in Vos's eyes. Even that was easy to miss, mostly because it was impossible not to be distracted by the two gaping, triangular holes where his nose once was. Or the burn withering the freckled skin of his right cheek. Or the scar that traveled across his mouth, splitting his top lip in two.

No. Eyes. Look at the eyes. Those are the same.

The same as the last time I saw him: when I lied to him about my departure at Esmaris's stables, tricking him into letting me leave.

Vos stared at me flatly, not reacting as I crossed the room and dropped to my knees next to his bed. I reached out to touch his mind, brushing my fingers against his thoughts, and was greeted with a searing wall of pain and fury that was so strong that I almost — *almost* — let my pleasant mask slip.

Vos's breathing, which came in whooshing gasps through the holes left behind by his missing nose, quickened. And his expression hardened.

"Vos —" I slipped my hand over his, and didn't show my surprise when I felt only two fingers beneath my touch.

"What are you doing here?" His voice snapped like a twig breaking in two, vicious and ragged. "It looks like you made it, then, didn't you?"

"You did too. You're in Ara. You're free now."

For a moment, he had no response. Then rage descended upon his features like a blanket of fire, muscles around his missing nose twitching into what would have been a sneer, that split lip curling. I had always loved Vos for his unabashed enthusiasm — the way every emotion danced across his face in illuminated colors. Now, the darkness of his anger, his agony, crossed him with the same intensity.

"Free?" he spat. "You call this *free?*"

"You're in the territory of the most powerful Wielders in the world. They can help you." I stroked my fingers across his hand, and across his mind. "It won't always be like this. I promise it won't."

I hoped I wasn't lying to him. Again.

"This happened to me because of *you.*" He yanked his hand

away. "Did you think of this when you lied to me that day? Did you think about what they would do to *me* when they found out you were missing?"

Yes. I did. The answer curdled in my throat. Did that make it better or worse? Did it matter?

My eyes burned. "Tell me what happened."

"What do you *think* happened?"

Interrogation — when Ahzeen realized that Vos was a witness, and a key part of whatever bloody story he wanted to tell. Punishment — for Vos's incompetence or his perceived betrayal. Probably some mix of the two. When it came to the lives of slaves, Threllians were not particularly discerning.

"I'm so, so sorry, Vos," I whispered. "I'm so, so sorry." Then I leaned forward, staring so deeply into Vos's amber eyes that our faces were only inches apart, every decimated scar on his face painfully sharp. "Please, Vos — what happened to Serel? Where is Serel?"

I didn't know it was possible for the rage to lurch deeper into Vos's face, but it did. "He was sent for to go fight Ahzeen's fucking wars. Before they took me. Before they questioned me. So I didn't get to see them drag him away when I named him."

My skin went numb. Vos's eyes burned into me.

"You did it, didn't you?" he hissed. "You or him. I know you did." His head dropped back against the pillow, as if all his energy left him at once, leaving behind only a residue of his fury. "I told them everything," he whispered. "Not that it made them stop. They didn't want the truth. Didn't want a useless enemy like some poor slave boy. They were looking for bigger game. But I named him anyway. And I hope that wherever Serel is now, his nose is rotting right next to mine."

I looked down at my hands. When I looked back at Vos, for a split second, it was Serel's disfigured face that glared back at me.

"Get out." Vos rolled, turning away from me so I was left staring at the back of a head of copper hair. "I don't want to look at you."

"CAN YOU FIX HIM?"

The moment Zeryth closed the door behind us, I threw myself into a solution. It was all I could do to keep myself from melting into a puddle of grief and terror. But I was still numb, my hands trembling as I twined them together.

"Willa has been working on it. But it's not an easy case. The scars, maybe. But the nose will be difficult. And the fingers are gone."

"I have Solarie friend. Healer. He maybe will help." Aran words felt awkward and clumsy on my tongue. That brief conversation in Thereni felt like it had knocked my Aran vocabulary back to where it was months ago. Or maybe that was just the fact that I couldn't think straight. Couldn't think at all.

"Maybe that would help," Zeryth said.

"Something must help. I will not let him stay in that way."

"Of course we'll do everything we can."

Everything they can. How many times had they said that to me? Did they mean it? Did those words mean *anything*?

I stopped short, turned to Zeryth. "When will we go to Threll?"

Zeryth's white eyebrows arched.

"This is not only about Vos," I said. "So many slaves have been hurt like him. You saw this. Yes?"

"Sadly."

I shook my head, one brisk movement. "I will not allow it."

"I can send out word through our networks to watch for your friend. Get him out as soon as—"

"This is not *just him*," I shot back, more sharply than I had intended. But names and faces welled up inside of me, honing the edge of my words. This was so much bigger than Serel. Than Vos. Than me. For each of us, there were so many equally broken souls — thousands who hurt and loved and grieved just as hard as we did. And for every Esmaris, for every Ahzeen, there were hundreds of other Threllian Lords who threw bodies into wars and beds and beneath whips like they were nothing but sacks of flesh.

It hit me all at once. A wave that threatened to knock me off my feet.

"There are so many more. We cannot allow it. They have no power." I looked up at Zeryth, softened my voice. "But we do."

Zeryth's brow twitched. "*We?*"

"You are strong enough to do it."

The things men will do in pursuit of their egos. If they'll tear down countries for it, maybe they could do something good with it, too.

But Zeryth shook his head. "It isn't that simple, I'm afraid." He said this dismissively, as if he were turning down an invitation to dinner instead of justifying the deaths of thousands.

"So what will we do?"

"Tisaanah—"

"We will do nothing? You will do *nothing?*"

Nothing, a voice whispered, *like you did when you met a pretty little teenager collared by a vicious man four times her age, and left her there?*

Zeryth's face hardened. "You're standing here in the Tower of Midnight right now," he said, sharply. "That's not nothing."

What was that even supposed to mean? I dragged myself here. Put myself through their demands. What had he done to help? Sent a flattering letter to Nura? Dragged back one injured slave who was useless to Ahzeen anyway?

But one look at Zeryth's face forced me to cull my anger. Too far. I was going too far.

"I— I'm sorry. You are right." I gave him a weak smile — gentle, girlish. "You've done so much for me. I don't forget that."

For a moment, he gave me a cold stare down his nose, and my heart clenched — terrified that in my inability to manage my anger, I had thrown away one of my greatest advantages.

Then his face softened, and I exhaled. He placed a strong hand on my shoulder.

"We got you out. That's a start. Patience, Tisaanah."

We? I got myself out. Serel got me out. And Vos paid for that with something more valuable than his life.

It is not enough, I wanted to say. *It is never enough.*

But I looked up at Zeryth with big eyes. "Patience," I echoed, and the word tasted like blood and treason on my tongue.

CHAPTER THIRTY-TWO

I didn't even trust myself to open my mouth after that, for fear of whatever would come tumbling out. I kept myself tightly bound, carefully wrapped, as I returned to Max in the tower lobby, as I nodded politely when Willa invited me to some ball or party or some other frivolity — I wasn't paying attention — and as Max and I left those oppressive Towers into the crisp almost-autumn air.

Max tilted his chin towards the city, a cluster of activity just down the hill. "I've already broken my record of time spent in polite society for the last five years. We could keep up the streak and have that promised celebratory outing, if you want. Get a drink or three. Talk about all of the ways in which that test was bullshit."

There was a certain veiled softness, a certain imploring question, to his tone that made it very clear that he knew something was wrong.

"No. Thank you."

"Do you want to —"

"No." I said it more sharply than intended. "I only want to go home. Please."

I want to go home.

I didn't even know which home I was talking about. Max's house. My room in Esmaris's estate. My little cabin in my village, beneath the wings of my mother's safety. A Nyzrenese city I barely remembered. All of them. Or none.

I just didn't want to be here, in the judging shadow of the Towers, when I fell apart.

"Of course," Max murmured. I closed my eyes, heard the welcome crinkle of paper and ink, and opened them to flowers. The sight of those wild, twisting vines was just enough to make every strained knot inside of me snap at once.

My knees hit the dirt.

MAX LISTENED in silence as the words spilled out of me. With each one, his mouth grew tighter, his eyes harder, the tight wrinkle at the bridge of his nose more pronounced.

"They are fucking with you," he said quietly, when I was done. "Don't accept that from them."

I drew my knees up, wrapping my shaky fingers around them. Even now, all of my muscles were still tensed, as if holding back something unpleasant that I couldn't allow to reach the surface.

Were they fucking with me? Or did they just not think of me — or anyone like me — at all?

"Why would they do that?"

"I don't know. But that? What they did to you during that evaluation?" He shook his head. One sharp movement that burned more than a string of curses.

"They needed to test me," I said, quietly. "And I did it."

"It doesn't matter. That was so far beyond the bounds of a typical evaluation. You were better than they expected you to be, but that doesn't change the fact that they stacked the deck against you."

"I'm not afraid of that."

233

Max let out a violent scoff. "So, to you, all of this is alright? It's alright for them to humiliate you this way? It's alright for Zeryth to leave you in slavery even though it would have taken nothing for him to get you out? It's alright for them to screw with your head for some stupid game? He tried to force you — *literally* — to your knees. That's fucking demeaning. And that's alright with you?"

No. Not alright. I swallowed a surge of rage.

But—

"I cannot change what they do. I can only change what they think of me."

"Right, because Zeryth Aldris's friendship has done so much for you, so far."

My head hurt. Heart hurt. I pressed my palms to the ground, soaking up the coolness of the damp earth. "I need his favor. You know this."

Max stared at me for a long moment, cold fire rising in his eyes. He stood up, paced, crossed his arms. And then turned back to me. "Do you know what I don't understand about you sometimes, Tisaanah? Why aren't you *angry?*"

That made me want to laugh. Why wasn't I angry? I wasn't angry because I devoted so much of myself into turning that energy into something else, stuffing it so deeply into myself that it lined the inside of my skin. "I can only control myself. That's all. No one has any responsibility to me."

"No. *No*, they *do* have a responsibility to you. They have a responsibility to be decent human beings." He let out a breath through tight teeth. "Sometimes— sometimes I look at you and I'm amazed at the sheer fucking scale of how people have failed you. Just utterly *failed you*. It's enough to make me sick, so what about you? How can you look at any of them and not want to claw their eyes out?"

"This is not about me," I shot back. "I want to make things change. And to do that, I need to use whatever tools I have."

"Whatever tools you have."

"Yes."

"And what is that, exactly? What is this tool that you're utilizing? You are more than your value to powerful men, Tisaanah, and those people will use you and throw you away."

I drew in a breath so sharp that it sliced me from my chin to my navel.

I heard that. I heard that shade of judgement. I knew it so well — whispered in hallways and corners and in the cloying tones of every man I danced for. I knew it so well it only had to lift its head from a mile away for me to catch its scent.

I jumped to my feet, fists clenched. "That is *not true*," I spat. "I had *nothing* more than that, Max. My value to powerful men is why I am alive. So don't you *dare* speak of me in that way."

His face immediately shifted, lips parting. "No, I—"

"You *do not* get to tell me how I should feel about what has happened to me. And what will anger do for me? Why do I need that? So I can drown in it? So I can use it as excuse to do nothing with my life?"

His mouth closed. Tightened. I saw a flicker of hurt cross his face, then felt it echo in my chest. "I'm guessing," he said, tightly, "that you're thinking of someone specific."

Silence. We stared at each other, both simultaneously wishing that we could inhale our words back into our lungs. My blood rushed in my ears. It drowned my words.

So I was relieved when Max's came first. "I would never, ever judge you. That was an ignorant thing to say." Most people averted their eyes when they apologized. But not Max. He looked right at me, unwavering, the corners of his mouth twisted. "I'm sorry."

Shame was an unfamiliar shade on his face, softening all those hard-edged features. He looked...sad. Just as drained as I was.

I watched him, a question stirring.

Once, in Threll, I was walking the bounds of Esmaris's estate and came across a dead bird in the street. It had been crushed to death by a wagon wheel — smashed right up its middle, glossy black fire-tipped wings splayed out against the white cobblestones. I knelt down beside it and examined the morbid beauty of the day-old blood against those shiny black feathers, the grotesque symmetry of the way it flattened in the street. I imagined it just standing there as the wheel rumbled over it. And I wondered, *How did you get here, little bird? Why didn't you fly away?*

Sometimes I found myself looking at Max, at the aftermath of all those hidden scars written across every inch of his body and mind, and wondering the same thing — *What happened? Why didn't you fly away?*

"You want me to hate the Orders as much as you do," I murmured. "But you won't tell me why. What did they do to you?"

He let out a quiet breath. "I can't give you those answers."

"You do not want to."

He gave me a long, considering look, brow furrowed. "You're right. I'm a mess. I know I am. I can't argue that." He shrugged. Its forced nonchalance only highlighted the rough weight of his voice. Anything but careless. "I do nothing because I already did everything and failed. And I couldn't take it. Just couldn't do it anymore."

Just couldn't do it anymore. I could feel that starting in my own bones. The crushing weight of that hopelessness. I looked down at the dirt, at the leaves covering my toes. The moss on the rocks reminded me of the burns crawling over Vos's face, the space between the leaves echoing the gaps of his missing nose.

I felt fingers on my chin, lifting my gaze. Max looked back at me with serious determination. "But I think you are better and stronger than I am in every way. That is the truth."

A lump rose in my throat. I waited for his fingers to leave my chin, but they didn't.

"Don't let them ignore you, Tisaanah. You're better than they are. They should be terrified of you. Make them scared. Be *angry*."

I blinked and saw everything — everything — in that split second of darkness: every wide-brimmed slavers' hat, every lash of Esmaris's whip, every one of Zeryth's condescending smiles, every injury that tore Vos's body. They dug their fingernails into me, clutching at my heart like desperate ghosts.

My answer shuddered in a broken breath. "I can't. I can't."

"Why?"

Because it's too much.

Because my fury petrifies me.

Because the last time I got angry, I felt a man's life wither in my hands.

I opened my eyes and looked into Max's, cloudy and blue, a reflection of my own. "Because if I allow myself to be angry, I will never stop."

He leaned closer. So close his nose brushed mine, so close I could count his eyelashes. And so close that I felt his warm breath across my face as he smiled and said, with the viciousness of smoke and steel, "*Good.*"

CHAPTER THIRTY-THREE

I stood at the entrance to the Towers ready for battle, watching the skyline of the Capital glow with the faint, failing light of dusk. I told myself that I wasn't nervous, even though I knew it was a lie.

I was alone, for now. Max had left me a Stratagram to get to the Towers but told me he had some errands to run and would meet me here later. Just as well. It was easier for me to get ready alone. Maybe he understood that, though I don't think he knew exactly what I was planning.

I turned and swept my eyes over the Towers' dazzling splendor. They were lit up so brightly that they cut into the sky like two infinite columns of light, glass glittering in sunset. Each tier was now decorated with clusters of overflowing flowers and spilling swaths of shimmering chiffon.

A little much, I thought. But still, it was amazing how much they had managed to do to decorate since just yesterday.

I heard a familiar voice call my name and turned to see Moth bounding towards me, Sammerin not far behind. Both were impeccably dressed — even Moth, to my surprise, who wore a double-breasted jacket rendered in a striking orange brocade, his blond curls tamed (however temporarily) into something that could possibly be described as "neat." As he approached, I could see that he had torn the edge of one sleeve. I was sure it would be ruined by the end of the night.

"You look very nice, Moth."

His eyes dropped. "Thanks. So do you."

I looked to Sammerin, who was just catching up. He really did cut an impressive figure when he wanted to. He was always neatly put-together, yes. But tonight, in a close-fitting coat rendered in amber silk, a black velvet cloak falling over one shoulder, he was downright striking. I hoped I would get the opportunity to witness his famous flirtations. He was certainly dressed for it.

"And you, Sammerin."

"Thank you." He paused, regarded me. I wondered if I should be insulted by the faint surprise that flickered across his face. I decided I wouldn't when he plainly stated, in that low, smooth tone, "You look beautiful."

I looked down at myself — at the blood-red silk that hugged my body all the way to the ground, the skirt just light and billowing enough to float around my feet with my steps. Airy fabric slipped off my shoulders and fell into a low neckline of flowing crimson, all supported by a golden chain that clasped around my neck. The necklace Max had given me was nestled against my collarbone.

I gave Sammerin a little smile of thanks, and then I turned in a circle, slowly. When I reached them again, Moth and Sammerin's faces were rendered in a shock that I found extremely satisfying.

That, after all, was exactly my goal.

My back was completely exposed, showcasing the full topography of scars over spotted skin. The fabric dropped so low that when a breeze blew, I got goosebumps at the dimples at the bottom of my spine — but I didn't care about decency. I wanted to make an impact. I wanted to *show* everyone who wouldn't listen.

That was why I'd taken the simplest dress I could find and slowly carved away pieces of it until it showed every single one of injures: removed the bottom of the sleeves to expose the scars on my forearms, dropped the shoulders to highlight the nicks at the crook of my neck. I swept my hair up so it wouldn't cover one inch of it.

They wanted to ignore me? Fine. I'd show them what they were ignoring. I'd show them what their complacency meant.

"What happened?" Moth asked, at last, in a small voice. "To your... to your back?

"I was a slave before I came to Ara. Did you know that?"

His eyes widened. "I— I didn't."

"And I got these scars when I tried to buy my freedom."

His mouth closed, puckered slightly in something between thought and realization — as if he had never considered the possibility of such things existing in the world. I wondered what that was like. To live a life so untouched by such ugliness that the very concept of it was startling.

"I think you look nice anyway," he said, quietly.

"Thank you, Moth."

Sammerin regarded me in silence. I could have sworn I saw a glimmer of satisfaction cross his face as he said, "I do too." Then he lifted his chin, gesturing to the Towers. "Shall we?"

As we started towards those foreboding gold-and-silver doors, I adjusted the white lily that I had tucked into my hair. It was a last-minute addition that I stole from the garden as I left. I figured that Max wouldn't mind, and besides, it all felt incomplete without it.

How poetic, after all: to wear Esmaris's sigil as I exposed every terrible thing that he did to me. As if I were carrying him with me, hissing into his ear: *Look. Look at everything you failed to destroy. Look at what your cruelty created.*

———

I COULD FEEL their stares on me. I could feel it as clearly as I could feel fingers brushing my skin, touching my face, running their hands over those ugly, ugly scars.

Good.

The lobby of the Towers had been completely transformed. Flowers and tapestries covered every surface, the light of hundreds and hundreds of candles dancing over them. Both sides of the lobby were combined into one giant room, the gold of the Tower of Daybreak on one side meeting the silver of the Tower of Midnight on the other. Music permeated the air, coming from everywhere and nowhere at once, mingling with voices and slightly drunken laughter. That mural of Rosira and Araich loomed over it all, their faces drawn to the ground as if casually observing the festivities.

There had to be several hundred people here. All were impeccably dressed — though most more modestly than I was. But that was for the better. With my Fragmented skin and my red dress and my scars, I stood out exactly as much as I wanted to.

Moth disappeared into the crowd almost immediately, wandering around to explore with wide-eyed fascination. Sammerin didn't try to stop him.

"I know he's going to get into trouble," he said with a twitch of a shrug. "Why fight nature?"

I chuckled. Indeed.

"Is every member of the Orders here?" I asked.

"Far from it. There are plenty who chose not to come. These things get a little tedious year after year."

It was easy to forget, sometimes, exactly how many Wielders existed in the world.

When I looked back at Sammerin, his eyes were drawn off across the crowd. I followed his gaze to a woman lingering near the wall, drink balanced in slender fingers, who sporadically peered back at him through chestnut waves.

I nudged his shoulder. "Go. I will be fine."

"Go where?"

I arched one eyebrow. "Go."

He paused, holding back a little smile. "Order events are a special kind of dangerous."

"So am I." I grinned. "I'm not afraid."

"You did come dressed to inflict some damage." He stepped back into the crowd, then hesitated and turned back to me.

"Max will be here soon, I'm sure," he added, raising his voice slightly over the crowd.

"Will he?" Max had said, somewhat begrudgingly, that he'd go to the event if I did. But now that I was here, I couldn't even imagine him *existing* in this environment.

"Oh, he won't miss it," Sammerin replied, and I caught only a hint of that familiar unreadable glint in his eye as he melted into the party.

With Sammerin gone, my eyes scanned the room again. Now that I was looking, it was easy to spot Zeryth — the whole room seemed to bend around him, like he was the center of gravity around which this entire affair revolved. He stood near that enormous mural, making exuberant conversation. He had the light of someone who was utterly in their element — and dressed in an impeccably tailored jacket lined with white silk and silver thread that glimmered beneath the lights, he looked the part.

Nura, on the other hand, lingered against the wall alone, nursing a drink. Her dress was an almost comically faithful adaptation of the outfit she wore every day — white, high-necked, with long sleeves that hugged her slender arms and a skirt that reached the floor.

I stepped out into the crowd. Necks craned to follow me, stares immediately followed by horrified gasps at the sight of my back. "Did you see *that?*" I heard one man whisper to his companion, and I held back a furious smirk of delight.

Look at me, I commanded, and they all obeyed. I felt every one of those eyes.

But I felt Zeryth's most of all.

And when I turned around and looked over my shoulder, pretending to be surprised to find his gaze meeting mine, I gave him a dazzling, vicious smile.

"Zeryth," I purred, by way of greeting. "Dance with me."

A dusty, well-worn metronome started in my head. I hoped I remembered my dancing steps after all these months.

"I'd be delighted." My arms were around Zeryth's neck before the words fully left his lips. His hand rose to my waist. In one smooth movement, he swept me out onto the dance floor. It was amazing how quick, how fluid, the whole transaction was — like we were two stars colliding and flying away. And if people were staring at me before... well, now they were *gawking.* Perfect.

1, 2, 3...

Zeryth's white hair was neatly tamed into a tail at the base of his neck, though a few strands escaped and danced around his face as we moved. He grinned at me.

"I always knew I'd see you at one of these things one day. And you're just as stunning as I thought you'd be."

4, 5, 6...

I returned his smile with my own — one I pulled back and dusted off for the first time in a long time. "I'm very happy I have made it here, too. It is an opportunity that most people like me never get to have."

Zeryth's face, ever the picture of pleasant charm, didn't so much as flicker. But I felt his fingers tighten slightly at the base of my back, as if extra aware of my scars.

"I'm sorry I couldn't give you the answer you wanted yesterday. Your friend has my greatest sympathy."

"That's very kind of you. We should be grateful to have even the thoughts of the Arch Commandant." *1, 2, 3.* We spun around the room, moving so quickly that the crowd smeared behind Zeryth's face. And my smile was so unwavering I thought it might crack. "What more could we ask for?"

A brief hesitation. "Well—" he started.

"What more could I have asked for, Zeryth?"

My smile disappeared, though Zeryth's only barely soured.

"I would have gotten you out if I could, Tisaanah," he said.

"I do not think that's true."

"I—"

But my words leapt up my throat like ropes of fire. "I think that you enjoyed the way I looked at you when I was fourteen and you were the only thing I knew of a world beyond Threll. I think it that felt good to you, and I think you liked me. But I do not think you wanted or cared to get me out."

"It is a complicated situation."

"That may be true. But nonetheless, my life was not worth your inconvenience. And that is what it is. But do not lie to me about it. I'm tired of lies and performances."

Zeryth's eyebrow twitched. With little warning, he launched me into a twirl. I managed to catch myself before I lost my balance, spun in a gliding swirl before he pulled me back against him. As I landed, he tilted his face toward my ear. "Isn't that what we're doing now? Performing?"

4, 5, 6.

"A performance shows people a pleasant lie," I replied. "Tonight I show them an ugly reality."

A cool breath of a chuckle caressed my cheek. "I see nothing ugly here."

I returned his laugh with my own. "Then you are not really looking, Zeryth."

"Aren't I?" He pulled back just enough for his gaze to meet mine, one eyebrow quirked. "You and I aren't so different. Lots of the people you see around you today were born with privilege, your instructor included. The world was theirs to lose. You and I, we had to claw for it. I look at you and I see a victor." His next words came closer, reverberating against the skin of my ear. "And that is very, *very* beautiful, Tisaanah."

For the first time, I allowed the sneer bubbling up within me to reach my face. "This is not a game, Zeryth," I said. "I have twenty-seven scars on my back from the night I tried to buy my freedom and Esmaris rewarded me by trying to beat me to death. I was beaten, I was raped, I was almost killed. It is written into my body and soul, just as your guilt in it is written into yours, whether you want to see it or not. But you cannot ignore it.

Neither can I. And neither can they, because I will not allow them to."

I lifted a palm, waving to the crowd that had gathered around us.

Zeryth's expression remained smooth, perpetually unrattled. But something — a certain spark of pleasure that I could not quite read or understand — leached into it as he said, "I have never ignored you."

"No. You'd just rather see me on my knees."

"I had to test you. And you passed."

Test me for what? I wanted to ask. *What would possibly excuse that?* But instead I only said, "I do not need you to apologize for the past. I have only one question for you. What will you do to help me keep others from meeting my fate?"

And there it was. A crack across his serene, smooth exterior — so delicately masked that I almost didn't see it. "Tisaanah, I'm—"

But before he could finish, I brought my mouth to his ear. And in a breathy hiss that sizzled into the air, I whispered, "I don't care if you're sorry."

4, 5, 6, and...

And I spun away from his hands, hurling myself back into the crowd. I didn't look back — I didn't need to know he was watching me go. The spectators parted as I slipped away from the dance floor. They were watching, too.

A little, satisfied smile tugged at the corner of my mouth.

And it was then that my eyes looked out across the room and immediately settled on a familiar figure. One that I recognized instantly, even through the throngs of people that separated us.

As if he felt my gaze, Max glanced up from a conversation that he looked like he would much rather avoid. And when he saw me, that expression of disgruntled weariness melted into a little, knowing smile that, I knew, was meant only for me.

And without thinking, I returned it.

CHAPTER THIRTY-FOUR

Max left his conversation so abruptly that it looked like he didn't even say goodbye, turning to glide through the crowd toward me. And even from this distance, when he stood, I was a bit stunned by his appearance. He wore a purple silk jacket that looked incredibly expensive, meticulously tailored to his shape, lined with gold buttons and thread that sparkled beneath the flickering blue lights of the party. His hair was unusually tamed, combed and parted.

He was, at first, so striking that he was almost unrecognizable as my disgruntled and vaguely disheveled friend. But as we approached each other, I noticed a smattering of little off-kilter elements — that his jacket was open a button too low, the collar curled on one side; that one rebellious strand of hair had already escaped the oils meant to keep it in place; that the white shirt beneath his coat that was slightly wrinkled.

I loved those little idiosyncrasies.

I loved all of it.

"Thank you for providing a much-needed reason for escape," he said to me, once we tucked ourselves into a quiet spot. We were relatively secluded, though stray glances still followed us. I wondered if they were intended for my scars or his reputation. Both, maybe.

"You are very late. I wasn't sure if you would come."

"Of course I would."

I watched the corner of his eyes crinkle, just barely. Watched his gaze hold on me for a moment before flicking away.

Oh, Sammerin had said, with that mysterious glint, *he'll be here.*

Then I ran my eyes again down his throat, over his shoulders, over sleeves crinkled as if they had been pushed up his forearms and then hurriedly straightened. And then I craned my neck, peering at his conversational companion, who now sat awkwardly alone.

"She was pretty."

"I didn't notice."

I certainly did.

And I also noticed the way that his gaze dipped down my body. Ran back up.

"This was smart," he said. Too casually. "The dress."

I batted my eyelashes. "Oh? Is that all it is?"

"Don't pretend that you need me to stroke your ego. You know you look good." Then he glanced over my shoulder and raised his eyebrows. "Everyone knows it, apparently."

I followed his gaze to a cluster of people who looked at us a little too long to be accidental before hurriedly turning away. "I think you're making an impression," Max said. His eyes flicked away, off towards the cluster of activity around Zeryth, and I wasn't sure whether I imagined the change in his voice as he added, "The dance was smart, too. You two put on quite a show."

"I do not know if it worked. If he'll listen."

"If nothing else, it got you plenty of attention. No one can count on Zeryth suddenly developing a sense of moral decency. But if your goal is awareness, you're making progress."

Progress. Was that enough? "I am not done yet," I murmured, and the hint of smile twitched at the corner of Max's mouth.

"I'd expect nothing less."

For a long moment, we just stood there, shoulder to shoulder, looking out into the party. The crowd was growing louder, the music more aggressive, the smell of perfume and skin more pungent.

I caught a glimpse of a familiar face on the outskirts of the dance floor and grinned, nudging Max's shoulder. "Look."

Across the room, Moth paced, hands awkwardly clasped behind his back, casting nervous glances towards a pretty Valtain girl in an atrocious pink dress.

"Ascended above," Max groaned. "Don't do it, Moth. Valtain girls are trouble."

I laughed. "Even me?"

"Especially you."

We watched as Moth approached the girl and, after a brief conversation that looked so awkward I felt myself physically cringing, the two strode off together to the dance floor.

"One day," Max stated, matter-of-factly, "he will look back at this as the beginning of his downfall."

I scoffed. "You are only jealous because no one would dance with you when you were his age."

"Only one poor soul," he replied — and my eyes inadvertently found Nura, across the room. "But to be fair, I was a bit chubby then and not nearly as dashingly handsome as I am now."

His lips curled around the words with the cloying coating of sarcasm. But when his gaze flicked to me, a lump that I didn't quite understand grew in my throat. There was something about the way that he looked at me — heavy with an unspoken question, blue lights dancing across his face, heat radiating from his skin even from inches away — that made warmth pool at my core.

I lifted my chin towards the open doors leading out to the gardens and the cliffs. "It's too loud," I said. "Come outside with me."

Together, we slipped through the crowd and out the doors. A

heavy fog had rolled in with the sunset, and the wall of cool, moist air felt like stepping into a cloud. We walked in silence down the weaving pathways, encountering fewer and fewer partygoers. Until finally, we were alone, standing on a stone patio that opened up to the cliffs and the sea.

The fog was so thick that it softened the moon to a thumbprint smear, blending the line between the sea and the sky. The Towers stood mournfully behind us, chiffon gliding in the slight sea breeze. Music warped through the mist in distant echoes.

We were still in the shadow of the Towers, but the party felt so far away.

And yet, even in this solemn solitude, even in this chilly night, that heat still remained.

I looked out over the sea and pointedly not at Max, even though I could feel his eyes on me.

"I'm a terrible dancer," I said. "Did you know that?"

"You were a dancer in Threll, weren't you?"

"I was, but only by memory. I counted the steps. Simple, if I practiced enough. I did not even need music."

He chuckled. "Brute force. I should have known." Then, after a moment, "I think that may be the first time I've ever heard you admit weakness aloud."

Gods. It probably was. I lifted my eyes to him and placed a finger over my lips. "Only for you to know. And I only tell you this because I don't want to embarrass myself when I ask you to dance with me."

Silence. Such deep silence that the vestiges of distant music mixed with the suddenly deafening pound of my heartbeat. Max stood there, back straight, hands clasped behind his back. For once, I could not read his expression.

"Or," I said, lightly, "will you look back at this as the beginning of your downfall?"

"I..." He let out a breath, a chuckle, tucked his hands into his pockets. Then removed them. "My answer hinges upon one condition."

"What?"

He took a step forward, and then another. I did, too, until our bodies were directly in front of each other, until I felt his warm hand slip into mine.

"No counting," he said.

"Only this once."

"Only this once."

And his arm was already around my waist, my hands at his shoulders, by the time I whispered, "Deal."

We swayed together, somewhat awkwardly, to distant music. My cheek just barely skimmed his. He smelled like ash and lilacs and the faint hint of the faraway sea.

"I did not think you would say yes," I murmured. "I thought you weren't made for social graces."

His chuckle was silent, but we were so close that I felt it reverberate through his muscles. "Firstly," he retorted, "we are alone. So 'social' does not apply."

True.

"Secondly." He attempted to launch me into a gentle twirl. We mistimed and stumbled, fracturing his next word with scuffed laughter. "There is nothing graceful about what we're doing here."

Very true.

He looked at me and raised his eyebrows, asking silent permission for a second attempt. I nodded, and we almost —
almost — managed an actual twirl.

Except, I slid on the damp ground and, in my distraction, hurled myself against his chest. We both let out *oofs* of impact and my awkward laugh was still dying on my lips when I suddenly became so acutely aware of the warmth of his body pressed against mine. Of how much I liked it. How much I wanted to envelop myself in it.

My arms slid around his neck. He lowered me into something slightly resembling a dip, and I curled against him. Every nerve in my body was on fire, set aflame at the brush of his mouth against my cheek, the barest whisper against my skin as it traveled to my ear.

"So maybe," he whispered, "I could be made for this."

Maybe I could, too. Made, or unmade. In that moment, I didn't care which.

———

WE DID, eventually — reluctantly, though neither of us admitted it aloud — return to the party. And I resumed my performance, collecting startled glances and horrified stares the same way that I once collected little silver coins. I told the truth to anyone who was bold enough to ask me, sparing no brutality, no ugliness, no responsibility.

Not enough. Never enough.

Those words still throbbed inside of me as Max and I finally left the party, long after the lights had begun to flicker out, long after Sammerin and Moth and most other guests had retreated. Since our one dreamlike dance, we had hardly spoken at all, right up until we stepped back into the familiar warmth of that cluttered living room.

In this setting, I suddenly felt ridiculous in my finery. Max must have too, because he immediately pushed his sleeves up to his elbows, releasing a sigh and another button of his collar.

"I have to say, Tisaanah, it was worth it to brave my first Order event in the better part of a decade just to see the looks on their faces when you were done with them."

"I'm not done with them. I have barely begun."

I had spent the night cutting myself up into little pieces for consumption, forcing people to acknowledge me, thrusting my pain into their faces. And now I felt like something in me was just... depleted. And for what? For their horrified stares? Was that enough?

Not enough. Never enough.

"The first step is to force them to confront the reality," Max said, as if he heard my unspoken doubts. "People don't like to do that, but I saw it happen tonight. Even in Zeryth, and normally his head is too far up his own ass to see much of anything."

"But I must decide what is next."

"You will. And you know I wouldn't say it if I didn't believe it."

He did believe it. I knew he did. And I didn't let our gazes hold long enough to see all of it — the depths of it — for reasons I couldn't quite understand.

Instead, I gave him a weak smile. "Right now, I just need to get out of this dress."

As soon as the words left my lips, I swallowed an odd buzz that rose to my skin at my choice of phrasing. And I wondered if I was imagining the timing of Max's extra blink, the slight shift in his stance.

But he just said, "Understandable. Get some rest."

"Goodnight."

I went back to my room and closed the door. Slipped out of my deeply uncomfortable shoes. Then I reached to my back to unfasten the clasp at the back of my dress —

And let out a grunt of pain. Strands of my hair had loosened over the course of the night and tangled themselves around clasps that held my dress around my neck. I fought with it for a few minutes longer, then, when I finally feared I might draw blood, I gave up with a flail of frustration and marched back out into the living room. "I am stuck."

Max put down his book. "You're stuck."

"Yes. My hair, and my dress—" I gestured to my neck. "Can you... uh... help?"

He stood there, still, for a second too long. And in that moment, an image flashed through my mind. Hands and skin. Red silk on the ground.

I shook it away. *Gods, Tisaanah. Control yourself.*

"Well," he replied. "You would have to get in line behind all of the other women who want me to undress them."

I rolled my eyes, turning around and lifting my hair. "Have I not earned first place?"

A soft chuckle. "I suppose that is undeniable."

I heard every step. And then his hands were at the back of my neck. My scalp tingled as he gently — so gently — pushed my hair away, smoothing loose strands against my throat.

My eyelids fluttered.

"Hold your hair further back." His voice just a little too rough.

I obeyed, and he set to work, tension lapsing into complete focus.

"Ascended, what did you *do?* This is all wound up —"

"*Ow!*"

"Sorry, sorry, I just need to get it off of this part and... fucking hell. You've got a loose thread all tangled up in here, too. Who *made* this thing?"

"I had to make some changes!" I said, defensively. "And I am not a... a...sewing person."

"Seamstress. The word is seamstress. Hang on... I have to..."

And I was not prepared for everything that shot through me, all at once, as I felt his breath against the back of my neck. His mouth so close to my skin that I could feel the barest brushes of his lips.

I drew in a sharp inhale.

The panful tension in my hair released.

He had been using his teeth, I realized — to break the tangled threads.

"Sorry," he murmured, "I had to cut it."

I let my hair fall, my hands moving to hold up my dress. I choked out, "Get the lower one too?"

His fingers moved down my back, falling to the delicate gold clasp that rested between my shoulder blades. "This one?"

"Yes."

He obeyed. But his hands stayed there, his thumb swirling one gentle circle that set a shock from my toes all the way up the insides of my legs. "It pinched you. You have a red mark here."

My laugh was weak, breathy. "It will fit perfectly with all of ' my other battle scars."

He smoothed his thumb over it again. Then let out a low, rough chuckle. "If tonight was a battle, Tisaanah, you conquered."

My breath caught.

"You were merciless." It was almost a whisper, heavy with a certain reverence, as if he didn't know he was speaking aloud. And he just stayed there, his knuckles brushing my back, as if we were both caught in some strange suspension of time.

Of their own volition, my eyes closed. I hoped he couldn't feel the shallowness of my breathing, the rise of my goosebumps.

I was no stranger to touch. It was a professional tool, one of the few weapons I could wield to keep myself alive. Before, it had always been a demand, an instruction, a means to an end.

But not this. This was a whispering caress that reached past the scars on my back, past all of those ugly hurts, something that was only about the here and now. One that asked for nothing.

How long had it been, since someone touched me that way? With purposeless affection?

My body didn't know what to do with it, except to fall against it, call for more. And gods, I wanted more.

I felt him begin to pull away.

"Don't," I whispered, before I could stop myself.

A pause. I could feel his breath again, against the back of my neck, the curve of my ear. "Don't what?"

Don't stop. Never stop.

I turned my face. His was so close that his nose nearly brushed my cheek, the space between us vibrating in a way that made my entire world narrow to those few inches where our breaths mingled. He looked at me with sharp, heavy-lidded eyes, utterly focused, and yet...

... And yet, I knew him well enough to see it.

That he was just as terrified as I was.

I had spent my life begging to be looked at. *Look at me,* I cooed at the men I danced for. *Look at me,* I demanded of Esmaris in my killing breath. *Look at me,* I commanded to every person who gazed upon my tattered back.

And I showed each of them pieces that were as Fragmented as I was, little carefully chosen parts of a whole.

But it was here, in this gaze, that I was *seen* — seen for every incongruous part of me. And nothing had ever flooded me with such sweet, agonizing terror.

I looked at his mouth and wondered what it would feel like to show him another vulnerability, another truth. To let myself want.

Don't what?

Don't stop touching me, seeing me, needing me.

But I forced a light smile back onto my face. "Don't flatter me," I choked out. "It's unlike you."

And then, all at once, he was gone. He pulled away so quickly I was left standing there before a sudden, gaping absence.

"You should get some sleep," he said, too quickly. And as I nodded my response, I clasped my hands together so he wouldn't see that they were shaking.

"Goodnight, Max," I murmured.

"Goodnight, Tisaanah."

And I felt his eyes follow me as I padded down the hallway. He was still standing there, unmoving, as I closed the door.

THAT NIGHT, I dreamed of a knock on the door. I dreamed of the searing warmth of skin — of lips against my throat and my breasts and my inner thighs, of an overwhelming ache between my legs, of the frenzied tear of clothing. I dreamed of a pair of familiar blue eyes heavy-lidded with want, of a voice that I knew so well rendered ragged and desperate in a moan against my mouth.

I dreamed of slick desire that consumed me, unmade me, destroyed me. Of the taste of his sweat, salty and iron and—

And *iron* and—

And in a moment, it was all gone.

I dreamed of a world suddenly cold, save for the burn of the blood that covered me — the fire of those goodbye kisses, crimson smears left by everyone I had abandoned. My forehead, my cheek, and a dozen more, a hundred more, where Max's lips had traced across my body.

Desire tore into terrible dread.

I screamed his name.

But he was already gone.

CHAPTER THIRTY-FIVE

W hen I rose the next morning, too early after a fitful, restless sleep, Max was already up.

He sat at the dining table with a letter in his hand. He slid it to me silently. *Tisaanah*, the front read, in perfect inked script. Grateful for the distraction, I opened it.

Tisaanah –

It was a pleasure to see you at last night's festivities. You certainly made an impact. It would appear that many attendees developed a sudden, pressing interest in Threllian humanitarian causes — interesting coincidence, no?

But alas, this is not the subject of my correspondence today. Instead, I would like to discuss your evaluations. Normally, results would be delivered by letter and would not be available for another week or two. However, I would prefer to deliver yours in person.

Please come to the Tower of Midnight for noon. My clerks will be expecting your singular arrival.

We have much to discuss.

– Z.

I read it, then handed it across the table to Max, who did the same.

"It seems I will be traveling to the Capital again," I said.

"It seems we will," Max replied, and we looked at each other, anxious curiosity unfurling between us.

I TOLD myself that I was not nervous.

I told myself that I was not nervous as I recited every word of that letter through my mind, as I flipped through possible outcomes. As I picked at my fingernails, watching the Towers rise into view.

Max and I both knew, of course, exactly what "your singular arrival" meant — *"don't bring Max"* — but since I couldn't reliably Stratagram myself to the city on my own anyway, he would accompany me to the Towers before my meeting. I was happy for his company.

"Perhaps they changed their decision," I said, allowing a note of tentative hope into my voice. "About sending support to Threll with me."

"Maybe."

I heard what Max wasn't saying aloud: that it seemed too easy. And as much as I hoped otherwise, I couldn't help but think so, too. I'd gotten plenty of attention last night, yes. But it still felt like the first step of a larger struggle, not a victory all its own.

A wrinkle of thought formed between my eyebrows as I revisited my memories of the night before. "Maybe there is something else."

"What do you mean?"

One sentence kept snagging in my mind. One thing that Zeryth had said during our dance that imbued me with a small, tentative hope. "Last night, Zeryth said he had to test me. And that I passed. I thought he meant the evaluations. But maybe he meant something else."

A second of silence.

"Test you," Max repeated. His voice was odd, quiet.

"Yes." I was lost in thought as I began to scale the steps to the Towers' entrance. "Maybe because of what I asked for, they—"

"He said that they had to test you?"

"Yes. What—"

A yank on my arm interrupted my thought. I turned, and one look at Max withered the rest of my question on my lips. In a matter of seconds, all of the color had drained from his face. A spike of panic leapt in my throat.

"What's wrong?"

He said nothing. Just stared at me.

"Max—"

"He said that they had to test you," he said, again.

I nodded, confused, and Max just stood there with his hand still around my wrist, brow lined, mouth tight, looking as if he had just made some terrible realization.

"What's wrong, Max?" I pressed.

But his gaze flicked back to me, eyes wide and piercing.

"Don't go, Tisaanah."

He said it so fast that the words blurred into one desperate sound. I didn't even know if I heard him right. "What?"

"Don't go to the Towers. To the meeting. Don't go."

"I—" The expression on his face, the sheer terror of it, gutted me. "I have to go."

He shook his head, one sharp movement. "No, you don't. You don't *have* to do anything, Tisaanah."

"But—" I was so confused. This was everything I'd worked for — wasn't it? "I don't understand."

"Listen to me." Max's fingers tightened around my wrist. He took a step closer, his eyes bearing into me with desperate intensity. "No matter what they offer you. No matter what they give you. Whatever they ask you to do. Say no. Alright? Even if they send an army to Threll today. Even if they give you everything you want. Say no."

His voice was *shaking*.

My lips parted, but it took a moment for the words to follow. "Because they will not fulfill their promises?"

He let out a sound that was almost a laugh, but uglier, rougher. "It's not about that, Tisaanah. None of this is about that."

I opened my mouth. Then shut it. Finally, I could only choke out, "Then why?"

Max looked at me in silence, jaw tight.

Of course. What else did I expect? "You will not tell me."

"I can't."

Acidic frustration ripped through me. Surely he understood the weight of what he was asking me to do, or not do. And still, here he was, guarding his secrets?

"That is unfair," I said, quietly. "I know you hate the Orders, but—"

"I will go with you." He said it fast, in one exhaled breath. "We can go to Threll today. We don't need an army. You and I could do it alone. We will find a way."

His words careened through me, slamming against my heart with a force that left me momentarily speechless.

"I mean it, Tisaanah. I'm serious. Right now. We can go right now." He lifted his palm, gesturing to the sea. But his eyes did not leave mine, and I drowned in that thread connecting our gazes.

"If the Orders offer me support, then I need it," I rasped. "I have nothing else."

And there was no hesitation, no pause, as he stepped closer and said, "You have me."

My chest hurt.

I wanted to smooth the desperate wrinkle between his eyebrows. I wanted to still the quivering muscle in his throat that betrayed the intensity of his anxiety. I wanted to take the kiss that I had left behind last night.

And most of all — more than anything, *anything* — I wanted to say yes.

But this was not about me.

And he knew that, too. I could see it in the anguish in his face: that we both understood that what he was proposing was a fantasy. The two of us alone could never do what I wanted — *needed* — to do.

I placed my hand over his. "You must tell me why."

What I meant: *Give me a reason. Give me any reason to say yes.*

The corners of his mouth tightened. "Do you trust me?"

Gods, I did. More than anyone. "I trust that you are trying to protect me above all else."

A flicker of hurt crossed his face. "What does that mean?"

"It means," I said quietly, "that I am willing to make sacrifices that you are not."

His fingers tightened around mine. He barely breathed, barely blinked. "He could be dead, Tisaanah," he murmured, and he sounded like it hurt him as much to say it as it did for me to hear it. "What if he is? Even if you go there, he could be gone."

Just to hear my worst fears condensed into words rose a lump in my throat. "I know."

And I did. I knew that it was unlikely that Serel had survived. I knew how fragile his flesh was, how easy it would be for one slave boy to be killed by the cruelty or malice or mere carelessness of the Threllian Lords.

"But it's not just about him," I whispered. "There are so, so many."

Because, after all, such heavy sacrifices had already been made for me. How could I not return them? How could I stop at anything that would ever repay them? That was all I was worth. Even though the part of me that lingered beneath all of that — the part of me that stood against the wall last night, drowning in the sensation of Max's breath — wanted nothing but this.

We stared at each other for a long moment.

"Tisaanah, *please*," he said, at last. "Promise me."

I extracted my fingers from his, then placed my hands on either side of his face. I drank in his features. Then I pulled his face toward me and pressed my lips against his forehead. Inhaled

261

his scent of ash and lilacs slowly, savoring it. And in my exhale, I whispered against his skin, "I promise you that I will be alright."

I turned away before he could say anything else, and I didn't look back as I scaled the steps to the Tower entrance. It was only as I opened those heavy doors that I cast one final glance over my shoulder to see Max still standing there, watching me go.

I lifted my palm in a wave he did not return. And as I curled my shaking hands around the handle to close the door behind me, I wondered if I had just made the biggest mistake of my life.

CHAPTER THIRTY-SIX

E very single thing in Zeryth's office looked too expensive to touch. It was large and vast and meticulously decorated — furniture crafted with accents of platinum, curtains of wafting white chiffon, beautiful classical landscape paintings clinging to the curved walls. The room was closer to the size of an apartment than a typical office. Half of the wall was one massive sheet of windows, exposing miles and miles of thrashing sea from a truly dizzying height. Zeryth's office was located at the second-highest floor of the Order of Midnight. The top floor, he told me amiably on our way up, was where he lived.

Now, I sat in a little white velvet chair in front of a desk made of marble and mahogany. Zeryth settled into his own chair, leaning back and propping his heels up on the edge of the desk, regarding me with that ever-present smile.

Nura stood in front of the window, back straight, hands clasped behind her back. When Zeryth offered her a seat, she merely shook her head. He shrugged and flicked an almost-roll of his eyes.

"So," he said to me. "Tisaanah. Thank you for joining us."

My fingers were twined together in front of me, the pressure slowing a heartbeat that threatened to race. I carefully guarded my mental barriers — I didn't need either Zeryth or Nura to know how nervous I was, especially not when I still could not get Max's face out of my head, the sound of his voice begging me to leave still echoing in my ears.

"We're here to discuss my evaluations, yes?" I said.

"Yes." Zeryth swung his legs off of his desk and leaned forward, grin widening. "Well, you passed! Congratulations."

I waited for more. He said nothing else. Nura paced behind him in long, slow steps.

"That's wonderful," I finally said, flatly.

"Are you pleased with yourself?"

"Yes. But I am more interested in what is next."

Nura continued to pace.

Zeryth looked pleased with this response. "Of course. That is why we called you to meet us here today, after all—" Mid-sentence, he whipped his head around to shoot Nura a sharp look. "Must you loom like that?"

"I am not looming," Nura shot back, looming over Zeryth's shoulder.

"You are testy today. Nervous energy?" He gestured to the empty chair beside mine. "Have a seat. Relax."

"I'd rather stand."

The thread of my patience was growing tighter and tighter. "What are we here to discuss?" I cut in.

Zeryth shifted back to me. It was amazing how quickly and seamlessly his expression changed, his hard-edged frustration melting away. "This is not yet public knowledge, but early this morning, we received some deeply upsetting news. Our Queen Sesri had to throw another traitorous noble family out of power. This was a Ryvenai one this time. Nearly two hundred soldiers and civilians were killed in the resulting skirmish."

Gods! *Two hundred.*

"There were Wielders involved on both sides," Nura added.

"And it will only get worse from here," Zeryth said. "There

will be retaliations. And it has become clear that a much larger rebellion against Queen Sesri is—"

"Civil war is an inevitability," Nura cut in. "We stand on the precipice of a war that stands to be as deadly as—"

Zeryth snapped his neck around again, his composure shattering into a glare. "Again, with the looming. And the interrupting."

"Again, I am not looming."

"Sit down."

A sneer twitched at Nura's lip. "I'm not a child."

"No, but you are my subordinate." Zeryth flicked his finger, and the other chair screeched across the tiled floor, as if sharply yanked by an invisible hand. "*Sit.*"

Nura fell heavily into the seat, her expression carved in ice.

I sat still, trying not to visibly react. I wondered if this show was for my benefit.

Nura cleared her throat, still glaring at Zeryth. "As I was saying…we are looking at a situation that could be as deadly as the last Ryvenai war."

"Nura and I both fought in that war. Neither of us wish to relive the things we saw or experienced." The edge in Zeryth's voice was gone as quickly as it had come. "I'm sure that Maxantarius has expressed similar sentiments."

I didn't even like the way Max's name sounded on Zeryth's lips. "That is terrible. But I do not understand how it involves me."

Zeryth leaned forward, smirking. "I told you we were testing you."

"For admission to the Orders." I had to fight to keep my voice level.

"For something more than that."

I thought of the things that had never made sense before. Their insistence that I march on Tairn. The incisions where Willa had taken my blood. Nura's unusual interest in me. My strange evaluations.

But I refused to let my expression change. "Then what?"

Nura and Zeryth exchanged a look. The smile stilled in Zeryth's eyes even as it clung to his mouth.

"To wield a weapon," Nura said.

And when Zeryth turned back to me, that smile was back in full, dazzling force, light glistening on his teeth. "To *be* a weapon," he corrected. "A weapon powerful enough to save both our country and yours."

I only blinked.

I had so many questions. They danced in front of my face in such a morass that I couldn't close my fingers around just one.

I decided on, "What sort of weapon?"

"It is a form of raw magic," Nura answered. "It is many times more powerful than any natural power of any Wielder that walks Ara, or beyond. Even rivaling the power of the extinct Fey."

"Powerful enough," Zeryth added, "to end a war before it begins. Without it, the Great Ryvenai War would have gone on far longer and far bloodier than it did."

"*Be* a weapon?" I echoed.

Surely I had misunderstood that — hadn't I?

"Yes. It will become a part of you." Zeryth said this so casually, as if we were discussing the weather. "Just as your own magic flows through your veins. But... more."

Oh, is that all?

"Forever?"

"No. It can, and will, be removed."

"Why do you need *me* to wield it?" I didn't understand. Why would they entrust me with something that was, supposedly, so powerful? Why would they want a Fragmented foreigner to come end their war?

Nura shifted in her seat. Then rose, as if she couldn't help herself, her arms crossed over her chest. "It is very... selective about its hosts."

Selective? *Hosts?*

"You talk about it as if it is a person."

"All magic chooses its Wielder in a sense," Zeryth said, casually, in what struck me as a very deliberate non-answer.

266

"But if it was used before," I asked, "then why do you need another Wielder?"

Nura had begun pacing again. "Our last host is no longer a willing participant."

There was just something about the way she said it —

Without it, that war would have gone on far longer and far bloodier than it did.

Puzzle pieces scattered across my vision. My mind rearranged them. Slowly clicked them together.

This man is nearly solely responsible for the end of the Great Ryvenai War.

My eyes snapped to Nura.

No matter what they offer you, no matter what they ask you to do, say no.

"Max," I murmured. "It was Max."

She lowered her chin, just barely. "Yes. The only one."

My blood went cold.

"We will train you in the specifics," Zeryth said. "But most importantly, this will afford you more than enough power to accomplish your goals in Threll. Far more than enough to free your friends, and anyone else you please. Even if it didn't, we will send support to travel with you. All of this in exchange for your service in our own conflict, of course."

"But I do not understand—"

"I think the most important thing that you need to understand, Tisaanah, is that I'm giving you everything you have fought so hard for." He leaned back in his chair. "What else is there?"

In a way, he was right. Support. Power. Resources. Everything I came here to achieve.

I closed my eyes, took in a breath.

Even if they offer you everything you want. Max's words beat in my ears. *Say no. Promise me.*

I wondered if he was still outside. I imagined myself standing, striding out of the room. Imagined myself embracing him at the doors, telling him I was wrong, boarding a boat on our own.

Say no.

I opened my eyes to Zeryth's expectant stare and parted my lips.

Say no.

"I want a blood pact."

And with those words, my fantasy disintegrated like ash scattering into the wind.

Zeryth arched his eyebrows and let out a short laugh. "A *blood pact?* Who's been talking to you about blood pacts?"

"You know exactly who's been talking to her about blood pacts." Nura did not seem to find this nearly as entertaining.

Zeryth shook his head, a bemused smirk playing at his mouth. "Ascended. That man is so relentlessly morbid."

I forced my voice into something calm and confident — just as I did when I was twelve years old and tried to buy my freedom for fifty pitiful pieces of silver. I felt like that little girl now, even if I would never, ever show it.

"I'd rather be morbid than betrayed," I replied, coolly. "If I do this for you, I want the terms clear. And I want to be certain they will be fulfilled."

Zeryth leaned back in his chair, gazing at me with a hungry kind of amusement. Then he opened a drawer in his desk and reached in once to produce a sheet of crisp ivory paper. Again, for a silver pen. And a third time — for a curved dagger. Its edge glistened beneath the sun streaming through the window as he unsheathed it, laying it neatly on the desk.

"Very well, Tisaanah." His eyes held that same glitter as he pushed the sleeves of his silk shirt up to his elbows. "Let's make a deal."

CHAPTER THIRTY-SEVEN

"Wait." I stopped Zeryth as he placed the pen to the page. "I have not yet defined the terms."

"I thought our terms were simple. You swear yourself to the Orders for the purposes of bearing this weapon. And once the war is over, you have our support in Threll."

"I did not agree to any of that." I stood, placing my palms on the edge of the desk and leaning, forcing Zeryth to look up at me. "And it is far too vague."

After that whole display with Nura, I expected to trigger some kind of reaction in him. But it didn't. He remained unaffected. "Fine. What would you prefer?"

"We go to Threll first."

He blinked. If he was taken aback, that one blink — one momentary pause — was the only sign. "We are on the brink of war. The Syrizen will never spare the support to go with you, and we can't spare the time or resources to start a whole other war in Threll."

"I understand. If this weapon is as powerful as you say it is, I only need a little bit of help for this trip. Then I will make use of their full support after our work in Ara is complete."

Another blink. "You're saying you want to go twice."

"Yes. I want to get my friends now from the Mikov estate. And then, later, I will return with an army to work on a much larger scale."

I said all of this as if the very idea of doing anything else was ridiculous.

There was a brief silence.

"We will need to test it out," Nura said, at last, to Zeryth. "She'll need to learn how to use it. We can do that in Threll. With the help of the Stratagrams you laid out, we could get there quickly."

Zeryth nodded, raising his shoulders in a hint of a shrug. "That is fair."

Should I be concerned, I wondered, that he seemed so unconcerned?

He lifted the pen, but again, I stopped him.

"Wait. Make a list."

"A list?"

"Yes." I straightened, crossing my arms. "We are going to be very, *very* specific."

"If it makes you more comfortable," Zeryth replied.

He dashed off, in beautiful script:

1.

Then looked at me, raising his eyebrows expectantly. "Where shall we begin?"

I LEANED on that desk and dictated my terms until my wrists began to go numb. I specified every word — forced him to cross out phrases that I determined to be too vague, deliberated over each letter, defined every time frame to close each possible loophole.

I knew that I was giving up something valuable, or at least, certainly more valuable than they'd like me to believe. And I would have been lying if I said that I wasn't choking back terror and uncertainty. But I focused instead on my straining fingers, painstakingly beginning to claw a grip around what I had come to Ara to do.

A blood pact could never be broken. The terms must be fulfilled. And if I was very, very careful, that meant I could ensure the safety of my friends and the fulfillment of my goals with one piece of paper. If I could do that, I didn't care what happened to me.

I defined the length and goals of my initial travel to Threll, specified that Serel needed to be recovered, that the search for him would continue when I had to return to Ara if I failed to find him during my two-week training period in Threll — though I swore to myself that would not happen. I defined the number of soldiers who would be sent with me to Threll after my time in Ara was over, how long they would stay there, that our mission would not be complete until the Threllian Lords were removed from power.

Finally, I straightened, masking a wince as a shock of pain encircled my stiff wrists. "And," I said, "I want Vos provided for. For the rest of his life." I paused, then rephrased. "I want Vos to receive one thousand Lys per month, for the next eighty years. And, he will have a home given to him, and all healing care and medicine that he may need."

"That's a significant amount of money," Zeryth observed, but he wrote down my words exactly without further complaint.

I paused at the window, looking out over that beautiful ocean. The sky had begun to tint orange, the light growing more intense and dazzling as the afternoon began to give way to evening. It had been hours. A thought crossed the back of my mind, something mournful settling in my stomach.

"Is that your full list?" Zeryth asked.

"One more." One of the most important. I didn't look away from the ocean. "Maxantarius Farlione will be released from the Orders. He will be released from all pacts or agreements or... any contracts. Anything at all that binds him to you."

Nura had been standing perfectly still this entire time, hands clasped behind her back. But at this, her head turned to me.

Zeryth chuckled. "My, that's sweet," he crooned, but I was listening only to the sound of the pen against the paper.

I thought back to the conversation we had with Willa when I first arrived at Max's home — the veiled threat of consequence, implying that he stood on thin ice.

"And," I added, "he will be pardoned for anything he did in the past. A fresh record."

"A fresh record," Zeryth echoed, the smirk twisting his words. "Wouldn't we all like one of those."

Still, he wrote it down.

And then we were silent for several long seconds, the tick of the clock echoing through the enormous room.

I flicked my gaze to Zeryth, who had leaned back in his chair, looking at me with pleasant patience. "Is that all?"

The papers were spread out in front of him. Three inky pages detailing everything that I have ever wanted. Three pages that guaranteed the safety of my friends and a chance — at least a *chance* — at a better life for thousands of people.

And three pages that sold me back into slavery.

"Those are my terms," I replied.

Zeryth greeted my response with an easy smile, twirling the pen between his fingers. "Excellent. Ours are simple. You will take on the weapon immediately. And once you return from your initial training in Threll, you will remain in service to the Orders for the duration of the war. Once we no longer need it and you have fulfilled your own mission, the weapon will be removed from you, and you will be free."

My brow furrowed. "Too vague. Wars can last forever."

The one that tore my own people apart lasted for nearly one hundred years. I wasn't about to sign myself into indefinite servitude.

"We have every intention of ending this one quickly. That's why we're doing this."

"If only our intentions mattered."

Zeryth laughed. "Fair. Fine." He pondered for a moment,

then offered, "Seven years."

"Four."

"After all this — " He gestured to the pages on the desk. "–you surely understand that we have to be certain that we get what we need. We're making a significant investment in you. Especially when you consider…" He tapped Max's name in the contract. "You're forcing us to give up our backup plan."

I tried not to show the surge of anger that twisted in me at that. Fine. If that was how it was going to be. When I blinked, I heard Esmaris's voice so clearly: *You are worth one thousand gold.*

"I have one more to add," I said, "and then I will give you an answer."

Zeryth raised his eyebrows at me expectantly.

"My terms will be fulfilled even if I'm dead."

I expected some kind of quip, some snarky response. But he only nodded and pressed the pen to the page.

"Five years," I said, when he was done. "Five *or* until the end of the war, or until the Orders choose to release me. Whatever one is first."

Nura turned to us. She and Zeryth looked at each other, as if having a silent conversation.

"Fine," Zeryth said, at last. And his hands looped over the parchment in smooth, sweeping movements. Then he stacked the three pages neatly together and drew a Stratagram over the top sheet, striking an elegant circle of ink over our contract.

"I take it," he said, "that you've never done this before."

He reached for the dagger and extended his forearm over the desk. With one strike, he drew blade across his skin, opening a trail of red that spilled over the Stratagram.

"Your turn." He flipped the dagger in his hands, extending the handle to me. The blade smeared blood all over his fingers. "We should only need a little — "

But I didn't hesitate as I took the knife from him, and I didn't break eye contact as I slashed it across my arm — not even as I struck too deep, splattering crimson across Nura's white jacket, across the page, across that beautiful, expensive marble.

273

CHAPTER THIRTY-EIGHT

Nura excused herself almost immediately after we left Zeryth's office, slinking off without so much as a goodbye. Zeryth gave me a cloth to press against the wound on my forearm, and as we walked down the hall, I watched red blossom through the white fabric. Neither of us spoke.

I was led into a small, sparse, windowless room, white walls upon white floors. Despite the lack of windows, it was brightly lit — how, I wasn't sure — and only two pieces of furniture sat at its center: two plain beds. On one lay a tall, thin man, perhaps in his fifties, wearing loose grey robes that blended with the bedsheets. He did not move at all.

The other was empty.

It became harder and harder to choke my fear back down my throat. Especially when I followed Zeryth to the center of the room and noticed that the man on the bed had restraints circling his limbs. His eyes stared at the ceiling, glazed over.

Zeryth motioned towards the empty bed. "Lie down."

I told myself that I was not afraid and did as he asked.

I turned my head. The man's face fell towards me, sightless eyes staring at me without blinking. He was completely limp, one arm dangling over the edge of his bed, his mouth hanging slack and parted.

Zeryth leaned over me. The ceiling was so starkly bright that it silhouetted him. "I'm going to be honest with you, Tisaanah. This is going to hurt like hell. But I promise that you're not going to die, even if it feels like it."

Well, that was comforting.

I nodded, even as I flicked my eyes towards the man lying next to me and wondered if whatever he was qualified as "not dead."

Zeryth stood between the two beds and took the man's limp forearm, pushing up its sleeve and revealing scars on top of scars on top of scars. Then he reached to his belt and produced the dagger. It was still damp with the remnants of both our blood. He did not hesitate as he opened another slice along the unconscious man's arm, leaving a streak of red.

I watched the man's cloudy eyes twitch, only just, *just* enough that it might have been an actual reaction, and my stomach vaulted.

Then Zeryth reached for me.

He removed the cloth that I still held pressed against my arm, laying it neatly beside me on the bed.

"Sorry about this," he said, and I winced as he widened the gash in my forearm.

His eyes flicked to me, and for a moment, we just looked at each other. "Are you afraid?" he asked.

"No," I lied.

He let out a small laugh, as if it were that obvious that I was not telling the truth. Then he rolled his head, releasing a shudder of cracks in his neck. "Ascended, I'm not warmed up for this. On three. Ready?"

I wasn't, but I nodded.

"One. Two."

And I know — I *know* — that he didn't say three before the world went white, and suddenly I couldn't breathe.

Pain raked through the insides of my veins, my muscles, my

eyeballs, as if creatures with razor-wire fingers were dragging themselves through me. I managed to lift my head just enough to look at my arm, perched in Zeryth's fingers. I wondered if I was hallucinating when I saw the vicious tendrils of red and black spiraling from my seeping flesh, rising into the air like hair floating underwater. Melding with the crimson silver from the man's own limp arm.

The bright whiteness — the nothingness — of this room assaulted me, choked me. I felt as if my organs were being peeled apart and reassembled inside out.

I didn't realize that I was screaming until I noticed that I couldn't hear anything and that my throat was raw.

I had only one thought: that Zeryth had to have lied to me.

Because this could not be anything but death.

My head lolled. My vision blurred. My screams faded as my throat lost its grip on my voice, even as it still grabbed it with a toothless bite.

And the last thing I heard before I slid into blinding darkness was a voice whispering, with manic repetition, *{Home, home, home, home.}*

{Home.}

PART TWO:
FANGS

CHAPTER THIRTY-NINE

MAX

If I was a smarter man, I would have known from the very beginning that it was all trouble.

Even when I had known her for mere hours, Tisaanah was wringing concessions out of me before I realized that I was making them.

I'm inviting you inside, but only because...

You can stay here for tonight. Just *tonight.*

I don't know why I believe you.

If you go, I go.

Always a step further, a step further. She drove forward with such relentless determination, always, no matter what. How could I not follow? And while every one of those steps hurt, like muscles creaking back to life after years of disuse, they still felt so *right.* A slow, tentative, utterly fucking terrifying return to a natural state.

Still, I didn't realize.

Not when I agreed to let her into my house, or my mind, or my past. Not even when I realized that every time I was without her, I found myself collecting little stories and oddities to tell her about when I saw her again, like stones that I slipped into my pockets.

Maybe just a *dash* of it seeped through my thick skull that night, when I stood behind her, barely touching and yet drowning in her scent and her skin and my own roaring blood:

Trouble, Max. Trouble.

But that was nothing compared to this moment. The moment that I stood there, watching her walk up the steps to the Towers, knowing that nothing I could say or do would stop her.

And could I blame her? There was still so much I couldn't tell her. And it was almost poetic: that the very thing that had made me let her in that night, nearly six months ago — that determination, that powerful tenacity that made me *believe* in someone for the first time in so long — that would be the thing to wrench her away.

Despite it all, I still admired it, even as I hated it.

And it was only then that it became clear: all of those little steps were leading us right over the edge of a cliff.

I didn't see any of it until it was too damned late.

———

"TELL ME THAT'S NOT HERS."

My voice came out in a frantic, desperate growl that I hardly recognized.

I am such an absolute fucking idiot.

I had stood there and stared at the doors long after she left, my fingers clenched at my sides. I felt like a piece of clothing with a loose thread, and she had taken it with her, slowly unraveling me. It seemed like hours before I could even bring myself to move. When I could, I went to the Tower of Midnight, stood in the lobby, and I waited. And waited. And waited.

Hours had passed. The daily hustle and bustle of the Towers thinned, quieted. I stood, then sat, then paced, then sat.

I'm such an absolute fucking idiot.

When the doors to the main column opened and a familiar face greeted me, I took one look at her and felt like all of the blood had drained from my body at once.

"*Tell me that's not hers,*" I said again, my hand catching Nura's arm.

Nura looked down at herself, taking in the spatters of red across her white jacket.

"It's fine. She got a little overly excited at her first blood pact."

She said this as if it was supposed to be a relief. A *relief*, instead of the confirmation of all my worst fears.

"A blood pact?" I rasped.

My fingers unintentionally tightened around Nura's arm. She looked at my hand, then my face, and sighed.

"Walk with me," she said, jerking her chin down the hallway.

"Nura, Ascended help me if—"

"Just— walk with me." For one brief moment, so brief it was little more than a brush, she laid her hand over mine. Then, she pulled away and started down the hall.

A blood pact. A fucking blood pact.

I felt like my body had forgotten how to move.

And then I followed.

———

NURA LED me down a series of twisting white hallways until we reached a plain door far, far from the activity of the lobbies. Her apartment, I realized, as she unlocked it and waved me inside. It was just as clean and sparse and oppressively empty as every-thing else in this damn place, all white furniture on white floors against white walls.

Nura nudged the front door closed, then crossed the living room and went to her bedroom. I stood in the doorway, watching her back as she began unbuttoning her bloody jacket.

"Where is she?"

Maybe there was still hope. Maybe there was still time. Maybe I was wrong.

Nura lifted one finger to point to the ceiling. "Up there. Recovering."

Recovering.

I had to force my next words up my throat.

"You gave her Reshaye. That's what you were asking her to do."

It was the first time I had said my theory aloud, and I wanted so desperately to be wrong.

But Nura said, "Yes."

Fuck. *Fuck.*

"She's a good candidate," she went on. "And we need it now. We're on the brink of something worse than the last one."

I couldn't speak. My hands clenched at my sides until they trembled. The room brightened in a grotesque lurch as all of the lanterns in the room flared at once.

I had never been this angry, this horrified.

"Even for you," I choked out. "Even for you, this is — this is —"

"Calm down."

"*Calm down?*" Another flare. "That thing should be *destroyed*, and you know it."

"It's too useful." Nura cast me a sidelong glance, and there was something about that look that I hated — hated how much it made her look like the girl I fell in love with when we were twenty and much happier and stupider than we were now. "It won't be like last time, Max. And she didn't do anything she didn't want to do."

"She doesn't *know*, Nura."

"She would have done anything to save her people. It wouldn't matter if she did."

She was right. I knew it and hated it. Because back then, I had done the same thing. I'd sat in the Arch Commandant's office as he offered me everything I'd ever wanted. Selfish things. Petty things. That's all it took, and I signed away my soul.

I'd deserved it, at least. But Tisaanah— Ascended above, *Tisaanah*, and her noble causes—

I didn't allow myself to think about the next words that flew from my lips.

"I'll do it," I said, desperately. "I'll do it instead. Take it away from her and give it to me."

Nura had been halfway down unbuttoning her jacket, but at this she froze, then slowly turned to me. For a moment, she looked genuinely sad, and the rawness of that glance might have been startling under other circumstances. "You don't mean that."

"I'll do it now," I said. My hands were already at my sleeve, exposing my forearm and the scar from the last pact I'd made all those years ago. "We have history. I'd be better at Wielding it. It will listen to me."

Nura was shaking her head. "Max…"

"Just *do it*." I staggered forward. "This is what you've all wanted anyway, isn't it? And I—"

"It's *too late*, Max." Nura's voice sliced through mine, loud enough to echo and hang in the air. She let out a breath and dropped her gaze. "It's too late," she repeated, more calmly. "And even if it wasn't…"

I was still clutching my sleeve. I looked down at my shaking hand. At the sun tattoo on my wrist, at the scar just below it. All the signs of the commitment I'd once had for the Orders, and marks they had left behind after they had taken everything from me and thrown the rest away.

Just like they would do to Tisaanah.

And the horrifying truth was beginning to sink in — that there wasn't a damn thing I could do to stop it.

I didn't look up, but I heard Nura let out a long breath. Heard her jacket fall to the ground. "And even if it wasn't," she muttered, "I don't think anyone wants to play with that kind of fire anymore, anyway."

Slowly, I lifted my gaze, only to avert my eyes again.

"Put some clothes on," I muttered.

"Why, does this make you uncomfortable?"

She turned to face me fully, presenting her naked body…

…And the burn scars that covered it.

Every inch of that albino Valtain skin was mottled with red and purple, melted into something almost unrecognizable. The scars ran all the way from her shriveled toes up past her collarbone, over her throat, ending behind her left ear. She covered them up with her high-necked, long-sleeved jackets, but you could see the edges at the back of her neck if you knew where to look. The healers only barely managed to save her face. Practically peeled off all the skin and regrew it from scratch.

I didn't answer.

I had seen her body like this only once before, after the end of the war — after Sarlazai, after my family. She showed up at the door of my apartment, and we practically devoured each other with frenzied, manic intensity. But everything about our tryst felt toxic, like we were trying to fuck something dead back to life and pretending we didn't both smell the rot. We didn't even speak. When we were done, she rolled over, put her clothes on, and I didn't see her again for years.

The truth was, it did make me uncomfortable to see her this way.

And that felt wrong, because I was the one who did it to her.

"We both made our sacrifices," she said, quietly.

I almost laughed. *Sacrifices*. If that was what we wanted to call it.

Murder. Slaughter. "Sacrifices." Sure.

Eight years ago, on the second-worst day of my life, Nura and I had stood in bloody chaos in the mountains, fighting a battle we could not hope to win. And she had reached into my mind and forced me to decimate the entire city of Sarlazai. A betrayal that won the war, killed hundreds, and completely eviscerated me.

And yet, sometimes I forgot that when she made that decision, she fully expected to die for it. *Sacrifices*.

Just the thought of that day made my nostrils burn with the

smell of burnt flesh. And we were about to step back into that. *Tisaanah* was about to be thrown back into that.

Nura approached me, her features imbued with a softness that I hadn't seen for many years.

"You and your bleeding heart, Max," she whispered. "I'm sorry. I really am."

I choked out, "I need you to tell me that this wasn't why you brought her to me. I need you to tell me that I haven't been *grooming her* for this."

Silence.

"Nura—"

"It's obsessed with you. We thought that a connection to you would make it easier for her to control it. Make it more likely to accept her."

I let out a strangled sound that was something between a bitter laugh and a grunt, as if I had been punched in the stomach.

"But I meant what I said, that day. I thought— I thought it would be good for you, to have something to do with your life." She tilted my chin towards her. "Help us help her, Max. You can guide her through this."

I pulled away. "Like hell I can."

Not after what that thing did to me. Not after what I, however unwittingly, did to Tisaanah.

I shot Nura a glare. "I'm sure you're about to tell me it isn't a request."

A little smile flitted across her mouth. "It has to be a request. Tisaanah wrote it into her pact."

"She— what?"

She strode back to her closet. "She was smart. Very specific in her requests. We couldn't get out of our promises if we wanted to. And one of them was about you." She selected another one of her identical white jackets. "That you're released from all Order obligations. Fresh slate. Congratulations. You're a free man."

Words abandoned me.

I didn't deserve her. No one deserved her.

Nura slid her jacket over her shoulders, covering her burnt

skin with spotless white. It hung open as she turned to me once more, pausing.

"I did try," she said. "I tried Wielding it. It wouldn't accept me." She said this as if it were some great shame, some terrible failure. "It wouldn't accept anyone — and we tried so many. But... then she showed up. And it was really just a hunch, at first. Maybe because she's Threllian. Maybe something else, I don't know. But the minute it tasted her blood, it liked her."

Her brows lowered over those sharp eyes, mouth tight. I recognized that look. She was jealous. *Jealous* – but not because of me. Because of *it*. She was *jealous* that Tisaanah got to have this thing tear her apart.

My anger devoured me so completely that it burned itself out, and suddenly, I was numb — like every emotion became the deafening ringing left behind after a loud noise.

I couldn't. I couldn't do this. I couldn't watch this thing destroy Tisaanah the way it had destroyed me — and it would, even though she was better than I was in every way, stronger, kinder, more deserving. Still just another light to be snuffed out. Another tool to be wielded.

And I, however unwittingly, had fed her right to them.

Nura buttoned her jacket, sealing away her scars, and with them, that brief glimpse of human vulnerability.

"She's made her choice, Max. Now you just have to make yours."

"There is no choice," I spat, and started for the door.

"Where are you going?"

Anywhere. Wherever was the farthest from here — wherever was the farthest from this damned tower and these people and that *thing*.

"I will not be a part of this, Nura. I won't do it."

I can't. I can't do it.

I threw open the door and started down those oppressive, winding hallways — hallways that drowned me in open space. It was silent save for my rapid footsteps, a reminder of everything I couldn't outrun. But all I could hear was Tisaanah's lilting voice, from our day in the city all those months ago.

I heard it over and over, following every step:

If I become lost, I will never be found again.

I will never be found again.

CHAPTER FORTY

TISAANAH

I remember only the dreams.

I lost myself in a gushing stream of vivid images, drowning in fragments of people that I didn't know and yet knew intimately. A blonde-haired woman wearing a beautiful purple cloak taking a bite of an apple. A pair of weathered hands wrapping around a door handle. The distinct rush of cold as I stepped into a pool of cold water in a place I'd never seen before, pressing my toes on intricate ceramic tile. My throat contracting around voices, voices, voices.

When I snapped my eyes open into black darkness, I inhaled so sharply that I sucked in beads of the sweat rolling down my face.

My head throbbed with such vicious intensity that I could practically hear it on the inside of my skull. Saliva pooled at the back of my throat. In a distant thought that was almost drowned out by my pulsating headache, I recognized that I really, really did not want to vomit in bed.

I slid back the covers and relished the momentarily distracting coolness of tile beneath my bare feet, then I staggered to the washroom abutting the bedroom and leaned over the sink, clutching the edges.

I flicked my head to swish a strand of dangling black hair out of my face. It fell immediately back where it was, directly in front of my vision.

Bare footsteps approached and a soft, white light slowly imbued the room, illuminating my face in the mirror.

My face. Max's face.

My face.

Only very distantly, very far away, did it occur to me that this was not what I expected to see.

"Max." A whisper, hoarse with sleep. I looked over my shoulder to see Nura lingering in the doorway, blinking at me blearily, hair falling in wild, loose curls around her shoulders. She looked so... young.

"Are you alright?" she asked.

I opened my mouth to respond, but instead, I woke up.

"YOU'RE ALRIGHT."

A hand rubbed my back in smooth, wide circles.

It was dark.

Everything hurt.

Max.

I didn't realize I said his name aloud until I heard the voice answer, "Don't talk."

My eyes slowly adjusted to the darkness, and I found myself looking up at dangling silver braids. Nura. I could only lift my head just long enough to recognize her. Then a spasm shot through my muscles, and I rolled onto my side, curling up.

I just saw him. I could have sworn I did. But that wasn't right. He shouldn't be here. Was it a dream?

"Where — is he?"

I barely got the words out.

"I don't know, Tisaanah," Nura murmured. "No one knows."

My stomach clenched in nausea, but my cheeks tightened. *Good.* "I hope he's far away…"

"Shh." Nura's touch smoothed away sweat with the cool skin of her palm. "Sleep. Your body needs to heal."

A blanket of darkness began to fall over my senses, and my chest leapt in panic.

No. No no no. I didn't want to go back into that river of dreams. Couldn't. It would kill me.

A wave of pain converged with my waning consciousness, momentarily drowning me. When I swung back into tenuous awareness, I was clutching Nura's hand so fiercely that our fingers trembled together.

I had lied to Zeryth. I was afraid. I was so afraid that I couldn't breathe. My wide eyes shot to Nura, and I knew she understood my silent confession.

"You're alright," she whispered.

I gripped her hand as if it were the only thing keeping me tethered to the world — until that, too, melted into darkness.

"You're alright, Tisaanah." Her voice echoed, fading with me. "I'm not going anywhere."

A DREAM. A MEMORY.

"I'm not going anywhere, Max."

I blinked. It took me a moment to realize what she had said from beneath the pounding of my headache.

The girl held out her hands and grinned from between sheets of straight black hair. A bright green snake coiled in her hands, looking at me with unnerving yellow eyes.

"You can look at me with that blank stare all you want. I'm not going anywhere. And neither is he." She looked down at her companion and made an exaggerated pout. "It's not his fault that you're afraid of him. Put out your hands."

We were in a small, dusty room, light streaming through one large window, walls lined with shelves that held gold wire cages and little glass boxes.

Kira lifted her eyebrows at me, the sarcastic point abandoned in favor of a curling smirk that was so uncannily my own that it still sometimes shocked me. Six months away and I had almost forgotten the degree to which we shared the same damn face.

"I don't like creatures that don't have the common decency to have limbs like the rest of us," I said.

"You don't like the centipedes either and they have lots of limbs.*"*

"Something between snakes and centipedes is acceptable." I eyed the snake, who stared back at me with equal trepidation. "Put that thing away."

Kira let out a groan, but slid the snake back into his cage. It obeyed so quickly that it almost seemed like it understood what she wanted it to do. She did have an uncanny affinity with the things.

"He's one of my favorite new ones. I've gotten so many more since you've been gone."

One look around the shed had confirmed that. It had been half as full when I left, but she'd only been getting started. Father agreed to give her the shed out in the woods in exchange for her promise to never — under any circumstances, even the small ones, especially the small ones *— bring any kind of living creature into the house ever again.*

It had been the first thing she wanted to do when I returned home for leave. She hardly let me say hello to anyone else before she dragged me into the woods to show me the new additions to her collection.

She slid the green snake's cage back onto the shelf, alongside at least a half dozen other serpents of various shapes, sizes, and colors. Then snatched a glass box from the shelf below it. "Look at this!"

I looked down at a giant, shiny black beetle, its shell reflecting purple and green against the light through the window.

"Nice."

"Do you know what it eats?"

I shook my head.

"Rotting flesh."

"That's charming."

"Don't worry, only the kind that's already dead."

"Oh, good, that was almost morbid."

I ran my eyes along the wall. She liked snakes more than anything, so there were many of those. But the lower shelf, it seemed, was the "bug shelf." Beetles, ants, little squirming maggots.

I paused at one glass box.

"This one," I said, pointing, "looks too normal and pretty to be a part of your collection."

She followed my finger to the quivering butterfly perched on a mossy stick, light reflecting off of shimmering burgundy wings. "Oh. I thought so too at first. But!" Her dark eyes lit up. "Did you know that when butterflies make a cocoon, their bodies totally dissolve? They just become sticky caterpillar goo with a couple of organs mixed in. They don't even have a brain."

I wrinkled my nose. "That's disgusting. How did you find that out?"

I was almost afraid of the answer — so I let out a small breath of relief when she replied, "I read about it."

Then she added, "But I didn't think that sounded accurate, so I cut a cocoon in half at Aunt Lysara's house. And it was right! Just goo."

"Mother and Aunt Lysara must've been thrilled."

"Mother said I lacked social graces."

"She says that to me too."

Funny, because our mother also lacked "social graces," no matter how much she tried to pretend otherwise.

"Oh! I almost forgot!" Kira put down the beetle, distracted, and grinned at me as she snapped her fingers. Then frowned when nothing happened.

Another snap.

And a third — which released a small puff of blue sparks. She repeated herself, creating a slightly larger cluster of light, like a little fragment of lightning.

"Good, right? I've been practicing."

I smiled, despite myself. The only other Wielder in our family. It seemed fitting. Fitting and slightly terrifying. "Have you started thinking about what you'll do for training?"

A wrinkle crossed the bridge of her nose, as if I was asking her a stupid question. Another expression that I recognized as one that belonged to me first. "I'll join the military, like you and Nura."

My smile faded.

Six months ago, I wouldn't have hesitated to encourage her to follow my path. Hell, that's exactly what I did when she first started showing signs of being a Wielder — I had no reason not to. I liked the military. Liked the structure, like the competition, liked the way that it drove me to push myself further and further and further until I clawed my way all the way up the ladder. Certainly much higher than if I were secluded in some poor Solarie's shack somewhere, wasting my time with pointless exercises.

But these last few months — the war, the battles —

"Ugh, it smells terrible in here." The door swung open and Atraclius poked his head into the shed, wire-frame glasses shifting as he scrunched up his nose. "I've been sent to retrieve you. Father's getting impatient."

He grinned. He had one of those smiles that split his whole face in two. Almost obnoxiously infectious. "Besides, I'm starving. And I've got a lot of stories to tell you, Max."

{I've got a lot of stories to tell you, Tisaanah...}

I opened my mouth to answer, but couldn't speak.

{So many stories.}

The world froze. Then dissolved into blackness.

{Do you like them? I'll have yours soon, too.}

CHAPTER FORTY-ONE

TISAANAH

I grew sicker and sicker. Had it been days or weeks or months? Years? Hours? I didn't even know who I was anymore. I felt as if my own body was attacking me, like my own thoughts were devouring themselves. My strange, vivid dreams grew so real that I didn't know at any given moment whether I was awake or asleep, myself or any of these strangers. Or, most vividly of all, myself or Max.

I spent most of my time sleeping or dreaming or vomiting. Nura was the only one who spent any significant amount of time with me, lulling me back to sleep or attempting unsuccessfully to shove food down my throat. She was in so many of my dreams, too, though she looked different then — rounder-faced, more expressive, her hair in loose waves instead of tamed into those many braids.

So many of my dreams were about him. In my dreams, I *was* him. Did I miss him that desperately?

{You like his stories the best. I like his the best, too.}

The voice curled in my thoughts, lower than a whisper, so faint that it disappeared into my mind like a furl of smoke — gone too quickly for me to identify.

"I'm worried about her," I heard Nura say one day, at the other side of my door. "It wasn't this bad when he did it."

"Worried?" Zeryth's voice was pleasant, disaffected. "If you are expressing an emotion beyond vague distaste, it must be serious."

"This isn't a joke."

"I know she can do this."

Can we do this, Tisaanah? Do we want to?

My consciousness threatened to slip away yet again, but I heard something that snagged my interest and I forced myself to stay alert.

"Maybe he can help. You've heard nothing from him?"

"Why would I?"

"My," Zeryth purred. "All that moral aggrandizing, and he just up and *leaves*."

"Don't sound so smug, Zeryth. Even you can't pull off that kind of hypocrisy."

Do you think he'll come back for you?

Gods, I hoped he didn't.

And this time, I could have sworn I heard a small, confused voice say, very clearly, "Why not?"

And it was only then, in the genuine confusion of that question, that I realized the whispers I heard were not my own garbled thoughts.

I sat up.

"What?" My voice was so hoarse that even that one word cracked.

{Why not?}

This time the voice came from *within* my head. I couldn't pin it to a sound — it was neither male nor female, unmarked by age, though the word was spoken with the confusion of a small child.

{You like him.}

Shattered pieces of memories ran through my mind, like pages in a book being flipped by a thumb, each visible for only a split second. The first chuckle Max and I shared together — *"He could be your apprentice!"* — the look he gave me when I saw his decision to train me snap into place, the first time I heard him laugh at one of my jokes. *"If you go, I go."*

The sound of his voice as he begged me to leave with him. *"You have me, Tisaanah."*

{And beyond that, you desire him.}

Another set of images, of sensations, now: my gaze sweeping over his body, the warmth of him the night we fell asleep beside each other in the garden, the trails of fire his fingers brushed on my skin when he gave me my necklace. His lips against the back of my neck. His chest against mine. *"I could be made for this."*

{So why would you not wish for him to return?}

My mouth opened.

I was going insane.

{You are not.}

My mouth snapped shut.

Silence, save for my pounding heartbeat.

I waited.

Nothing.

My head lolled, throbbed. But then, just as I felt myself begin to drift out of consciousness again, I heard it, as if coming from very far away:

{Perhaps he will return for me,} the voice mused.

"Who are you?"

Maybe the better question was… *what?*

{Reshaye,} it answered, simply. *{I am many things.}*

I was definitely going insane.

{You are not. Do you frequently repeat yourself?}

The weapon will become a part of you, Zeryth had told me. *You talk about it as if it is a person.*

A dawning realization bloomed, scalding up my spine.

{Have you been enjoying my stories? I still have many to tell.}

It swung in and out like a dangling lantern, the light casting garish, shifting shadows on the recesses of my mind. It was as tired and disoriented as I was. I could feel it.

{Yours feel familiar. You smell like a touch I knew once long ago. Or maybe a story that I have since forgotten.}

Images shuffled through my vision again — pausing at a brief memory of my hands running through those famous Threllian plains, letting the tall grass tickle my fingers. Backwards. Then again.

"You know Max?" I whispered. Stupid question. I knew the answer.

A purr of familiarity slithered in the space between my thoughts. *{You do know. So why you do ask?}*

Again, that childlike confusion.

{Why?} it pressed. I realized it wanted an actual answer.

"Don't you see my thoughts?"

{There are many things I see but do not understand.}

"Me too. And that is why I asked."

The presence sighed — or at least it felt like it. Like an exhale. It made my skin crawl.

{Maxantarius and I have nothing but each other.}

It sounded further away. Every word unleashed waves of pain, as if my own thoughts and blood were rebelling against me.

That isn't true, I thought.

{Perhaps not anymore. Now, we have each other and you.}

I blinked and struggled to open my eyes again. It took me a moment to realize I was looking at the ceiling. I didn't know when I had fallen back in bed.

{You and I both grow tired.}

Tired was an understatement. I felt as if I were dying, losing both my body and my mind.

{You are more concerned with what you are losing than what you are gaining.}

A manic smile twitched at the corners of my mouth. I thought of Serel. Of my friends in Esmaris's estate. Wrong. I was more concerned with what I was gaining than anything else.

I felt curious fingers pause at that thought. Turn it over. Freeze the image of Serel's face and replay the sensation of his goodbye kiss on my cheek.

I felt the question before it was solidified into words.

"You see but do not understand?" I whispered.

{I understand what it is to want.}

Not to want. To love.

{To love is to want.} The whisper dipped me into darkness. *{I loved Maxantarius very much.}*

The bed split beneath me, sending me falling, spiraling.

{Perhaps I could love you, too. What a story we would write together.}

Darkness and flames devoured me.

A DREAM. A MEMORY

Flames devoured me, licking my skin, filling my nostrils with the putrid scent of burning flesh.

Skin bubbled when it burned, and those bubbles burst and gushed beneath the rough grip of hands or the more vicious bite of a blade. This, I had learned, was universally true. It was true of Order Wielders, it was true of Guard soldiers, it was true of Ryvenai rebels, and it was true of the men, women, and children who were none of those things.

It was true of Nura, who — even after what she had done — was the first body I crawled to in the ashes of Sarlazai. I was certain that she had to be dead. When I handed her off to the healers, I was so relieved to hear her release a little, agonized whimper as sheets of her skin clung to the toothy fabric of my jacket.

Relieved. Ascended, what a fucking word to use.

I watched my fingers pick apart layers of fabric, threads fraying between my fingernails —

"Max, I thought you might want to see —"

And I was back. Back here, in my bedroom on the Western shores, lying on my stomach on my bed. Looking down at that red bedspread and melting right into it.

I blinked and looked up to see Kira standing in the doorway, smiling at me with an unusual hesitancy. She held one of her glass boxes in her hands.

"Look. I raised this one. Just came out of its silk today." She lifted the

box to show me a little red butterfly, fluttering anxiously at the top of its enclosure. I barely glanced at it.

"Pretty."

"I thought you might like it because it has a reasonable number of limbs."

Her words faded to the background. I made a noncommittal noise of acknowledgement.

Kira's barefoot footsteps padded forward. "You know…I'm happy you're home for a break," she said, quietly. "Even if you aren't."

Before I could stop myself, I let out a violent scoff. A break.

"A break" really meant, "You're clearly going to lose your mind at any moment and we certainly don't want you here when you do it."

"A break" meant, "You were responsible for the deaths of hundreds of Order soldiers, so go hide for a while, while we decide whether you're a hero or a war criminal."

But most of all, "a break" meant, "My name is Zeryth Fucking Aldris and I'm a power-hungry bastard who wants every other candidate for Arch Commandant as far away from the Towers as possible."

Well, that was fine. He could have it. Suddenly it seemed so damn trivial.

"How does it feel to be a war hero?" Kira asked. "He'll never say it, but even Brayan is impressed."

There was a very recent time when even Brayan's unspoken approval would have been worth more than gold to me. But now, like the title of Arch Commandant, it meant nothing. I wanted to tell her, "It feels like children's bones snapping in my hands. What a thing to be proud of."

{You should be glad that he's finally recognizing what you are capable of.}

My heart stopped.

I ran my fingers over all of my mental walls and doors. None of them felt as solid as they once were. Nothing ever seems quite the same in there after a Valtain gets in and starts moving things around — and even beyond that, my head had become a messier and more confusing place than ever in this past week.

"I need to be alone," I snapped, and I didn't look up to see whatever

pitying look Kira might have given me before I heard her pick up her glass box and back out of my room.

I stood. Closed the door. Locked it. Then crossed the bedroom and jammed myself into a corner, resting my forehead at the apex of two walls.

{You are angry,} *Reshaye observed.*

Of course I'm angry. *I tried to grab hold of that mental door, replace it, but it was suddenly impossible to find.*

{You are angry at me.}

You killed thousands of people.

Thousands. The scale of it still made my hands go numb. And, save for a too-small handful of people, the world thought I did that.

{I made us war heroes.} *Its unnerving, childlike confusion rippled across my temples.*

Us? *I spat a scoff aloud.* There is no us.

A spiral of hurt clenched around my mind — so genuine and pure that it threw me slightly off balance.

{Of course there is an us.}

Ascended, how I hated it. Hated *it. From the depths of that hate, my mental walls began to take shape. There it was. And if I could coax it back, swing the door closed —*

There is no us. You did that yourself.

Distract it. And then…

A sharp impact reverberated through the back of my skull. Like an abruptly-caught heavy door, stopped mid-movement. Then all of the hairs on my body stood upright at the sensation of fingernails dragged across metal.

{I gave you everything that you desired. I gave you the power that you so desperately wanted to fulfill your ambitions.}

I did not want that. That was— that was horrible. I didn't want that to happen.

{You can not lie to me.}

You used my body to do terrible things. MY body. This is mine. Now get out of my head and let me enjoy my time with my family.

I couldn't do this. Standing here in the corner hissing at myself like a lunatic, knuckles clenched against the wallpaper. No, this was not going to be my life, or anyone else's. The first fucking thing I was going to do when I got back to the Towers was get this monster out of my —

{Monster?}

The word shook me from the inside out, lit me on fire with fury and wounded hurt.

In a furious rush, I tried to hold onto control — tried to slam that door closed —

{I gave you everything. I took on your ambitions as my own. I swallowed your weaknesses. And I gave you love that you do not deserve. Even now, I do. Even as you call me a monster. If I'm a monster, what does that make you?}

White, eviscerating pain slid beneath my skull. My mind began to slip, but I fought it, throwing myself around every thread of control.

{You belong to me, Maxantarius. Me alone. And you prefer these people to me? These people who will never understand you the way that I do? These people who will never love you as deeply?}

I am not yours. I am not fucking YOURS.

Those were the only words my mind could form through that all-consuming effort, and they were quickly drowned out by a wall of rage and my own mounting dread.

I felt Reshaye rise and rise and rise, until we were at the same level. Until it was as if we looked at each other straight in the eye, perfectly matched for one terrifying moment. Each clawing onto control with equal strength.

And then it said, in a sad, slithering whisper, {You forgot what you are, Maxantarius.}

I felt my back straighten. My fingers unclench.

No.

A door slammed in my face.

Stop.

I had made a terrible mistake.

My feet crossed the room. My hands unlocked the door. Opened it.

{You force me to do this.}

I threw myself against my own mind with frantic intensity, meeting only a wall.

STOP.

The word echoed, first as a command, then a plea. I fought and fought and fought.

But the steps just kept going.

Atraclius's room was first, next door to mine. I would remember the perplexed grin he gave me as I first threw open the door, and the way it barely had time to sour into fear before his blood spattered the gold carpet. I would remember the crunch of his warped eyeglasses under my boot.

Marisca's came next, then Shailia. I would remember two sets of chestnut curls singed and burning.

Stop stop stop stop—

Still, I fought. I clung to my muscles desperately, clawing, leaving gauges of horror. You won't do this, you can't do this—

My father. I would remember how he grabbed the fire poker before he saw my face, raising it with a graceful hand molded by decades of his own military experience. How a morbid hope leapt in me at the sight of it, how I threw everything I had into grabbing one fraying thread of control and making my body seize for a moment — just one split second. Do it, *I prayed.* Do it fast.

But when he recognized me, he hesitated, only long enough to tilt his wrist and redirect the point from my throat to my shoulder. Too long. The thread slipped from me, and I would remember the sickening angle at which that poker extended from his throat.

Then Variaslus. I would remember the way he grabbed my wrist first, slender fingers too startled to push back.

My mother. I would remember the single confused wrinkle between her dark eyebrows, the way her fingertips brushed my face as she fell.

And then I walked out to the entryway and stood there in massive, echoing silence. My fingernails still weakly clawed at the glass wall that separated me from my body.

You killed them all. You killed them all.

The sentence looped in a frantic, lungless breath.

My eyes stared at the door, watching waning sunlight burn through the stained glass semicircle that adorned it. Together, we smoldered in the remnants of Reshaye's anger, standing on the precipice of eerie, tentative calm.

I hoped that my despair would mask my untruth.

But then it whispered, {You cannot lie to me, Max.}

And as my fingers curled around the front door, my fight started all over again, with renewed desperation — unrelenting with every step that my body took through the forest, towards that familiar shed.

Please. Please. *I had never begged anyone for anything before. Not once. Not even in Sarlazai.* I'm sorry. I was wrong. You were always right.

My hands threw open the shed door.

Kira sat on her knees on the floor, the green snake winding its way up her arms.

Please, *I begged.* I will never fight you again. Don't do this. I will do anything.

There was a moment of stillness. I felt Reshaye's attention shift toward me, in quiet consideration.

In that moment, I seized upon its brief distraction. Made a mad rush for control of my own body.

My left finger twitched.

My head snapped to observe that hand, lifting it to my face.

Anger. Rising anger. {I told you, you cannot lie to me.}

And a force pushed me back, shoving me to the back of my own mind.

I would remember that Kira was the only one who tried to fight back — the sting of the lightning that leapt from her fingertips the moment she hit the ground, even as flames crawled up her clothing.

I would remember how quickly that green snake lunged from her arm to mine, burying its fangs in my wrist.

Most of all, I would remember her face — my face — as she stared back at me through tendrils of long black hair.

And I would barely — only barely — remember the crushing weight of my own consciousness being thrust back upon me. The shiver of Reshaye's whisper, {Now you have no one but me.}

As we tumbled together into darkness.

CHAPTER FORTY-TWO

TISAANAH

I woke up gagging and sobbing at the same time.

It took me several seconds to realize where I was, and who. More than that to realize that the voice that was weeping their names was mine.

And longer to recognize that another person was holding a basin beneath my face, catching my watery vomit while another hand held my matted hair out of my face.

Gods, it hurt. It hurt so much I couldn't even breathe, couldn't think, couldn't navigate my own mind around that seeping grief. I had never met them. And yet, I *knew* them so intimately that I felt their deaths like acid in an open wound.

A low voice was whispering, "Breathe. Breathe. Breathe," as steady as a heartbeat. My hand reached out and found the warmth of skin.

I realized, all at once, who sat beside me.

I lifted my face to see the ghostly outline of Max's face in the darkness, those bright, unnatural eyes glistening. The sight of him drew a dagger from my gut up through my lungs.

My fingers tightened around his. Real. He was *real*.

I choked out, "They all— they are all—"

"I know." A low, pained whisper. "You talked in your sleep."

I let out a cry that scraped from deep inside of me.

And I felt arms encircle me, pull me into an embrace that I craved, even though it made me so, so sad.

"You should not be here," I wept against his skin. "You were not supposed to be here."

Fly away, I wanted to beg. Even as I, ever the traitor, pulled him closer. *Fly away from all of this.*

I felt his back shudder with a broken inhale.

"They have nothing holding you anymore," I said, between sobs. "There is nothing— nothing to make you stay."

"Don't." His whisper was raw and throaty. And I felt his tears mix with mine, hot against my cheek as our bodies folded around each other. "Don't be stupid."

CHAPTER FORTY-THREE

MAX

I had made it approximately thirty-seven minutes before I realized that I was lying to myself.

A week ago, I had stormed out of the Towers convinced that I had no choice but to sever myself from all of this. I refused to become a part of the Orders' scheming, and I refused to help them take advantage of Tisaanah more than I already, unwittingly, had.

I returned home. And I stood there at the edge of my property, staggering from my anger and despair and the addled disorientation of Stratagram travel, just looking at it. My little stone cabin, and that wild, overgrown expanse of flowers. It had been a beautiful day — sunshine, a gentle breeze, flitting butterflies and all.

Idyllic. A bastion of peace and tranquility.

And in that moment, I *hated* it.

After the deaths of my family, I lost years to drugs, wine, and aimless wandering. A slower kind of suicide, perhaps. And when I finally clawed my way out of that self-destruction, I built a cottage too far away from the world to be bothered. I planted hundreds upon hundreds of flowers and told myself they were all the company I needed. *Better than people anyway,* I'd mutter to myself. *Simpler to care for. More predictable. And much prettier.*

And, to be fair, the flowers hadn't done what Tisaanah had. They just sat there, swaying in the wind, with no intention of up and selling themselves to the organization that ruined my life. I didn't have to run around begging *them* not to make blood pacts with Zeryth Aldris.

But they were also static and silent. They were simpler, yes, but they wouldn't whisper stories of lost lands at night, wouldn't joke or laugh. They were more predictable, but they had no dreams for a better future, no ambitions, no hope. And they were pretty, but they had nothing on Tisaanah's lively beauty, the kind that changed a little each time I looked at her, as if I were discovering a new breathtaking facet with each of her expressions.

I just stood there, and all at once, I was struck by my own self-absorbed cowardice.

I'd spent years so smugly certain that I was somehow morally superior for opting out of a world that was cruel and imperfect and complicated.

Morally fucking superior. Me, sitting here alone with the flowers, while Tisaanah suffered. Me, living in this cottage that had become her home just as much as it was mine, going back to a meaningless life and telling myself, *"Well, it's the only thing I can do."*

I sank to my knees. And for thirty minutes, I sat there, coming to terms with what I was about to do.

When I stood up again, my decision had been made.

Now, Tisaanah lay heavy against my chest, sleeping. Though, I remembered enough about my time with Reshaye to know that it was really more like losing consciousness than "falling asleep." Every so often my fingers would drift down to the inside of her wrist, relief in the warm beat of blood beneath fragile skin.

It had taken me a week to put my affairs in order, gather the supplies I needed, tie up loose ends. In some ways, I had been dreading coming here. But there was another part of me that felt an odd, primal sense of relief in the weight of her against me. Like some missing puzzle piece had been restored.

I'd been surprised at how much I *missed* her. And here, in this moment, in the blur of my exhaustion and the pre-dawn silence, it was so unnervingly easy to forget why we were here.

So easy to forget that hours ago, I had listened to her live my most terrible memory.

To call it strange would be an understatement. To hear fragments of the worst day of my life whispered back to me from the lips of someone who had become so precious to me. To be reminded of everything I had already lost while looking into the eyes of everything I had left to lose.

I dreaded morning.

How would she look at me, I wondered? Now that she knew about what I had done, and about the monster that now lived inside her? That thought scared me.

But not as much as my next one: The creature that had ruined my life now lurked behind those captivating mismatched eyes. I was scared of how she would look at me, yes. But I was terrified of how *I* would look at *her*, and the things I would feel when I did.

And so, for now, I was alright with this — the silence.

I wasn't sure how many hours had passed when I felt her shift against me. I prepared to slide myself out from under her. I could only assume that the minute she was awake, this was about to get incredibly awkward. And we had damn more than enough to worry about already without addressing... whatever this was.

Tisaanah lifted her head and looked at me, and I froze.

I knew right away that it wasn't her.

The eyes moved too much. Tisaanah had a steady, piercing gaze, but this was all over the place, jumping from the ceiling to the floor to the blankets to me.

The corners of her mouth lurched into something only vaguely resembling a smile.

"Hello, Maxantarius." She had no accent. The sound of her voice without it sent fire spiraling up my spine.

"Reshaye." The word came out in a low, choked snarl.

That lurching gaze settled on me, and the way it suddenly went steady was somehow even more unnerving. "I have missed you," she whispered, rough and gasping. "I always knew our story was not...complete..."

She — *it* — had to force out the final word, as if it were already losing its grip on control. And before I could react, the expression fell away, her eyes rolling and fluttering closed. She went so still that I found myself questioning whether she had even moved at all.

I pushed strands of black and silver hair from her face. Out. Totally out. Somehow, she looked *more* peaceful than she did before.

I let out a sharp breath and slumped back against the headboard, my heart pounding. Of their own accord, my arms tightened around Tisaanah's shoulders.

Perhaps this could have been the part where I realized I'd made a terrible mistake.

Instead, I felt a different kind of fury scorch my veins, setting me alight.

Maybe Reshaye was right. Our story, apparently, was not complete. And I would be lying if I said that I wasn't afraid. But I was also *angry*.

My fingers wrapped around Tisaanah's. Squeezed.

If this wasn't the end, then I was ready to write a better fucking conclusion this time.

Whatever it took.

CHAPTER FORTY-FOUR

TISAANAH

My eyes were crusted shut when I woke up, and I nearly panicked in the darkness, terrified of what I might see or hear within it. But there was still no sign of Reshaye, to my relief. Piece by piece, it all came back to me. My dreams — my memories. Sarlazai, and what came after. Every dead Farlione face. And…

I forced my eyes open (*crack!*) to blinding brightness, and to the sight of Max pacing the length of the room, looking as if he had been doing so for a long time. There was something about his demeanor that was so different than the intimacy we shared last night — even compared to the typical, everyday intimacy of our friendship before this terrible week began. A certain removed, focused intensity.

He looked terrible. And yet, he was the most beautiful thing I'd ever seen. This second thought felt slightly traitorous, as it flitted through my mind.

I shouldn't be happy that he was here. He was, after all, sharing a room with the same thing that had killed his family.

The thing that now lived *inside* of me.

"You shouldn't be here," I told him. My voice was raspy.

He barely acknowledged me. Barely even looked at me. Instead he sat at the edge of the bed, placed his hand on my sweaty forehead, and practically interrogated me about how I was feeling. (Headache? Tolerable. Chills? No. Nausea? Moderate. Fever? Mild — on, and on.)

I answered him with increasingly curt responses. Then I ran my tongue over dry lips and whispered, "Why did you come back?"

He looked away. "Your energy needs to be on taking care of yourself. That's where you need to focus all of that relentless brute force, because you're going to need every bit of it."

A small part of me sank into the faint affection of the way he said, "relentless brute force," distant as it was. But that was quickly drowned out as a knot formed in my stomach.

"Max —"

"It took over last night," he said, abruptly. "Briefly. Just for a minute, while you were sleeping. But you need to be aware of it."

He said this all with strained, level factuality that I knew he had to force.

I felt like my stomach dropped through the floor.

"What — what *is* it?" I whispered.

But Max just said, "Can you feel it now? In your head?"

I started to shake my head, but he continued. "Don't answer so quickly. Really *feel* for it. Quiet yourself. Listen."

I paused. Closed my eyes. And, slowly, a glow simmered to life within me — my own mind, lighting up like a map, just as the souls in the tower of Tairn had that day of the battle.

I ran my fingers across all of it, every cluster of shadows. And I did find Reshaye — folded up in a corner, completely dark, completely silent. A... presence.

"It is as if it's sleeping," I murmured.

"It is as sick and weak in the beginning as you are. What it did last night took away all of its energy."

"The memories or —" I couldn't even figure out how to word it.

"Both. All of it." I opened my eyes, and Max was regarding

me quietly, sharply. "Pay attention to how it reacts to these things, and always, *always*, know where it is. Your gifts should make it easier for you than it was for me." The *"I hope"* was unspoken, but we both heard it. "Now we're going to take this opportunity to learn how to shut it out. It should be easy for you right now."

My head still pounded, but compared to how I had been feeling since receiving Reshaye, I felt ready to swim the Aran seas. Certainly more than well enough to throw myself into Max's instruction as he described how to bind Reshaye into its own little room, secluded in a separate corner of my mind. His, he told me, had been like a closet — a door he could imagine closing, then bolting shut. A rudimentary, simple image for a Solarie who had only limited grasp of mental magic.

But I saw things differently. My mind was not a maze, but a web — spools and spools of thoughts that grew more complicated the more I looked at them, my attention lighting up threads like clusters of fireflies. It was dark where Reshaye was, as if it had inhaled the threads down its throat. I imagined wrapping it in a series of bindings, shackling it, locked with a key that I hid within the recesses of my own thoughts.

But still, this seemed so... weak. I did not voice this, but Max must have seen my apprehension anyway. "Some of it might be a crutch," he said. "And no, this probably won't work forever. That's why you always have to be looking for it. *Always*. But it's a start."

A start. That was something. It had to be.

For a moment, we stared at each other. Something tightened in my chest as I took in the shadows beneath Max's beautiful eyes.

He held my gaze only for a moment before looking down at his hands, fidgeting.

"Max—" I started, but he turned away, reaching into his pockets and placing a series of rattling bottles on the desk.

"This one is for the headaches." Each sentence was punctuated by another pang of glass against the wood. "This is for the nausea." He continued down the line — for the chills, for the lack of concentration, to force a dreamless sleep. Then he paused before the two final bottles. "This one will knock you out in seconds."

He did not need to tell me why I might need such a thing.

"And this one will render your magic nonexistent for anywhere from minutes to hours depending on how much you take."

I strangled a gasp. I didn't even know such a thing was possible.

And then he just stood there, gaze drawn to the ground.

I wanted to seize upon this moment of silence, but I wasn't even sure what I would say.

A knock on the door interrupted my thoughts before I could clarify them, and Nura entered. "You look worlds better," she observed, then turned to Max. He barely looked at her.

"So," she said. "You came back after all."

"So it would appear," he said tightly.

Then her eyes fell on the bottles lining the desk and her eyebrows rose. "How did you manage to get these?" She paused at the last one and shot him a look. "Is this what I think it is?"

"You're the mind-reader, not me."

"Did you *leave Ara* to get this? Even Zeryth and I typically can't get our hands on this stuff."

He shrugged. "I have my connections." Then he tucked his hands into his pockets and straightened, flicking his gaze to me. "I have a few things I need to do. You'll be alright for an hour or so?"

Words that I could not untangle still coiled in my chest. So many things that I had wanted to say to him.

But I swallowed them back, and simply nodded. He gazed at me for just a split second longer before he turned around and slipped out the door.

NURA SAT beside me for a while, examining me, taking my pulse and checking my breathing. At her mere touch, a revulsion rose in me. When I looked at her, I saw flashes of memories that weren't mine. Most vividly, the image of her blood-stained face, palm raising to my temple, in a betrayal that would wreck Max's life and destroy the city of Sarlazai.

Perhaps she noticed me flinching away from her touch, because she gave me a long, quiet look, one that balanced on the edge of an unspoken question.

"Has it begun speaking to you?"

The memory of that voice slithered through me. "Yes," I said.

"Good. I think you've pushed through the worst of it, then. And you should be able to begin harnessing it soon."

Harnessing it. Is that what she told herself she was doing in Sarlazai that day?

"What *is* it?" I whispered.

"That's not an easy question to answer. The best we can tell, it is essentially raw magic — raw magic that draws from a deeper level than that harnessed by human Wielders, deeper even than that drawn upon by the Syrizen, or the Fey."

"But it... speaks."

"It is sentient," Nura said, lightly. "Yes."

"So what *is* it? Or was it?"

"No one knows. It was secured by Zeryth's predecessor, Azre. Somewhere past Besrith." She was quiet for a moment, her gaze slipping further away. "He died before anyone could find out exactly where. But it is very powerful."

Memories flashed through my mind. Memories of fire and blood and destruction, and above all, devastation. Memories of Max's family, and their dead, horrified faces.

"It showed me memories," I said. My gaze met hers, and I knew we both understood which ones.

Nura's throat bobbed. Her only hint of emotion. "It is a terrifying creature in many ways," she said. "But it is also incredibly powerful, and even in the horrible things it does, it saves many lives."

"It showed me what you did in Sarlazai." My fingers clenched, and Nura's eyes flicked away from me, suddenly preoccupied with the notes on her lap.

"I did what my position and my rank bound me to do."

"You *forced* him." My words came through clenched teeth. The betrayal that Max had felt that day still ached in my chest. I knew what that was — to feel like your body is not your own. And his memories of the city's destruction mingled with my own half-remembered images of the capital of Nyzerene burning. "And *so many* died."

Her gaze shot to me, sharp as the edge of a blade. "I did what I had to do, and I will carry that weight to my grave. Thousands and thousands more would have died if the war had continued. It would have gone on for years. And I saw it, then — an opportunity."

I could smell the burning flesh. *Opportunity.*

"You know as well as I do that sometimes, we have to do terrible things for the sake of something bigger. You knew that when you spilled your blood on that contract." Her mouth tightened, a sorrowful wrinkle forming between her brows. "Max was the most important person in my life. There was only one thing I loved more than I loved him." Her eyes flicked back to mine, brighter, colder. "Ara. Only Ara."

My stomach knotted. Love? Was that love? To betray someone's trust so viciously? To make sacrifices on the behalf of so many other people?

No. Never.

I didn't trust myself to open my mouth. Nura rose, wandering to the desk and looking at those little glass bottles.

"He came back last night, then?"

For some reason, my answer made my chest ache. "Yes."

I watched the corners of her mouth lift into a little, mournful smile. "I knew he would."

CHAPTER FORTY-FIVE

MAX

I strode through the streets with my hands shoved into my pockets. The sounds of the city did nothing to drown out my thoughts, and the fresh air did nothing to distract me. The memory of Tisaanah's voice when it was not her own still lingered constantly in the back of my mind, and with it came the looming dread of all that would come next — like an avalanche groaning above us, while I clutched the first broken stone in my palm.

I knew it would be bad. But I still had been caught off-guard by how hard it hit me — just to see Tisaanah when she awoke. How just looking at her made words tangle and fear tear through me like a mouthful of broken glass. I knew she had questions, and that soon, I would have to answer them. And I knew that I'd been too abrupt, too distant, this morning.

But I just... couldn't. Not until I figured out how to confront all of this, and scraped up the courage to pull the lid off the box I'd sealed shut for nearly a decade. *Soon*, I told myself. *Soon*.

But for now, I just walked.

The shop was in the outskirts of the city, where buildings were still nestled closely together but far from the hustle and bustle of its center. It was a little thing, squished between two much larger businesses, but had a stateliness to it — even the front steps were immaculate, the plants neatly groomed, the burgundy paint gleaming. *Esren & Imat* read a sign above the door.

It was unlocked. I slipped in quietly and leaned against the frame, feeling awkward.

The inside of the practice was just as neat and quaint as the outside. Immediately within the door was a small waiting area. Two folded paper barriers hid the entrance to the back section, and I could hear voices from behind.

"—still can't open these fingers, Healer." The first sounded as if it came from an older man, audibly anxious. "And I told you that if I can't do that then I don't know how I'm gonna keep at my work."

"I understand." Sammerin's voice. It couldn't be a starker contrast to his patient's brogue — smooth, steady. "And from the beginning, the goal has always been to make sure you regain full use of your hand. That's happening somewhat slower than I'd anticipated, but that is completely normal."

I took a step to the side, so I could peer around the barrier. I could see Sammerin's back, and the back of his patient's sun-spotted, balding head.

"There are twenty-seven bones in the human hand, and four major tendons," Sammerin said. "When you first came to me, twenty of them were crushed, and three of those tendons were totally severed. Not to mention all of the muscle and skin that had been torn apart. See?" There was a rustling of paper. "Today, you only have five fractured bones left, and the tendons are re-growing nicely. We just need to take our time to be certain that all of the delicate connective tissues reattach properly."

He said all of these things as if they were simply a collection of facts, steadfast and gentle. He was good at that. Taking the insurmountable and, quietly, making it surmountable.

It wasn't a surprise — or, shouldn't have been a surprise. But here I was, peering into the life of a man I called my best friend, and it hit me all at once exactly how selfish I had been, how uncompromising. I could count on one hand the number of times I had deigned to visit Sammerin's practice over these last years, all the while he dropped in on me four times a week just to make sure I hadn't hanged myself.

All the things I'd missed, just so I could lock myself up in a fucking cabin somewhere and pray at the altar of my own isolation.

Behind me, I heard a door swing open, and a familiar voice pipe up. "Max? What're you—"

But then, a *thump!*, then a *crash!*, then a shatter.

When I looked behind me, Moth was on the ground, surrounded by scattered instruments and broken glass, and an overturned side table.

"Hi, Moth," I said.

"Hi, Max," he replied, somewhat sheepishly.

"*Moth.* How many times have I reminded you to—" Sammerin appeared from behind the barrier, then stopped short when his gaze fell to me.

"Max."

His demeanor shifted, falling into seriousness, as if something about my face or posture alone told him that something was very wrong. And, of course, as always, he was right.

I gave him a smile that probably looked more like a grimace and a weak wave. "Hi."

———

SAMMERIN LISTENED, ever-patient, as I told him the whole sorry thing.

It all sounded so ridiculous. Borderline insulting, actually. After all, he had spent roughly eight years holding me together after the war and the Orders and Reshaye had all ripped me apart — holding me together as if I was just a collection of limp limbs, like any of his grotesque battlefield corpses.

And here I was. About to step back into it again. A slap in the face.

When I was done, he sat there silently, digesting everything he had heard.

"I knew something was wrong," he said, at last, "when you voluntarily appeared in public."

I mustered a weak scoff. "In my defense, I've been downright social lately."

Sammerin crossed his arms and watched me, a slight furrow in his brow. One would think that after all this time, I would be better at reading him, instead of just sitting here squirming under his assessing gaze like a child waiting to be scolded by a parent.

"So." I cleared my throat. "That's it. And you know. I mean. You know what I have to do."

He lowered his chin in the ghost of a nod. "Yes."

"Yes? I was expecting something more along the lines of, *'This is a terrible decision, Max, what the hell is wrong with you?'*"

A tiny, humorless smile. "I know exactly what's wrong with you." Then it faded as he asked, "It's done, then?"

My answer physically hurt. "Blood pact and all."

He winced. "This is ugly, Max."

Ugly was the kindest possible term for what this was.

When I spoke again, my voice was rougher than I had intended. "Those bastards should *know* better. They saw what that thing can do. I can't just let it go. And I can't just leave her there."

The wrinkle between his brows deepened. "You would be giving them exactly what they want."

"I know it." I shifted uncomfortably in my chair. "And... there is one other thing."

"You're asking me to go, too."

He said it as a smooth, matter-of-fact statement, not a question. Ascended, how did he *always* know?

I cleared my throat. "The thing is... if you don't do it, who will? I don't trust those people. But you know her. You know she's not— a tool or a monster."

Sammerin gave me a small nod, still unreadable.

"I know that this is a big thing to ask of you. And I would understand if you wanted to tell me to where to go."

There was a long, agonizing silence.

"There have been a lot of bad days," he said, slowly. "During the war. After. But the one I think about the most is the day after it happened."

He didn't need to say what "it" was. There was always only one "it," one event that loomed over them all. Even though we had never broached this subject. At least not so directly. To have it thrown out there in the open now left me momentarily off-kilter, especially in the wake of these last few days.

"I don't remember," I said. The days after my family's death were a smear of nightmares, dark and runny like bleeding ink. Hours, days, weeks. Gone.

"Good." His eyes flicked to me, and there was something in them that I rarely saw on Sammerin's face. Regret. "I hope you never do. But I think about it often. And I think about what would have happened if I had been there one day earlier."

He said this, as always, calmly. So calmly that it took me a minute to realize exactly what he was admitting. When I did, I was stunned. Speechless.

All these years, and I'd had no idea that he had been carrying that kind of guilt. He'd never told me. Never so much as revealed a hint of it.

"You shouldn't," I murmured, at last. "It wouldn't have made a difference."

But Sammerin just shook his head and said, "It was my job."

To keep me — to keep Reshaye — under control. His particular abilities, control of human flesh, made him the perfect failsafe. He could force my body down, force my lungs to shrivel or limbs to lock. Terrible. Humiliating. Painful.

But effective.

That was, after all, why the Orders had partnered us. He was the leash.

"I told you to go," I said, and even as the words left my lips, I

320

knew they were an understatement. I'd *forced* him out. I was grieving the lives lost in Sarlazai, horrified by myself and the creature that lived inside me, heartbroken by Nura's betrayal. And I let all of that consume me until I was cruel and selfish and fucking *stupid*. I just wanted to be alone.

Well. I got my wish, didn't I.

I leaned forward. "Listen, Sammerin. That day was a tragically perfect set of circumstances. A flawlessly aligned, cosmic event of cascading shit. It doesn't matter what might or might not have happened if you were there, because you weren't. But even if you were, maybe it wouldn't have changed anything. Maybe the shit would have just cascaded a little differently, and there would have been one more body dragged out of that house."

I blinked away that brief flash of possibility before I let it settle.

Because therein lay the one certainty: if that had happened, I wouldn't have made it through these last eight years alive.

He let out a long breath, but said nothing, his eyes lowered.

"Alright?" I pressed.

"Alright."

Then his gaze met mine, and the well of emotions in it was so unnervingly stark — the reluctant setting down of a weight.

"I never want to see a day like that again," he said. "So yes. I will go."

Relief flooded me.

"Thank you," I murmured.

The only words I could find, even though it was too weak of a response.

Sammerin shrugged. "You've saved my life enough times. And..." His expression hardened, just for a moment. "... Tisaaanh deserves better."

Then he cocked his head, smirking. "Perhaps next time, though, you could choose a more mundane paramour. Maybe a baker. Then we could just sit around eating pies instead of throwing our lives into such exciting disarray."

I barked a scoff, grateful to let the tension break. "It's not like that."

"Hm." His eyes narrowed. Then he added, "I expect to be paid exorbitantly, of course."

"Of course," I replied.

As if there was enough money in the world.

I HAD one more stop to make before I would return to the Towers, and I dully dreaded it. Yet another thing that I never thought I would have to do again. I wove through the dim alleyways of downtown, stopping at a familiar, dusty storefront. I couldn't help but eye the place where we had passed the man with the green coat and matching bird last time Tisaanah and I had come here. Nowhere to be found now.

Via looked thoroughly unsurprised to see me — so unsurprised that it was a little unnerving — and invited me in with casual nonchalance. She wore only a garish, silky robe tied loosely around her waist. As she led me back to her workshop, I earned a lazy wave from an equally half-dressed man lounging on a sofa.

I was glad I didn't arrive ten minutes earlier.

"So, Max. What can I do for you?" She lit the lights in the back room, one by one. With each new flame, more blades slit the darkness, cleaving through shadows with shocks of reflected gold.

"I need a weapon."

"I remember a time when you said you wouldn't need one again."

Ugh, don't remind me.

"Turns out I was wrong."

"I knew something was going on when you asked about the Chraxsylis. That's heavy shit."

"You're coming perilously close to asking questions, and I thought that went against your policy."

She cocked her head. The dim light enhanced her severe features, cutting shadows across the dramatic panes of her face. She looked downright otherworldly. Via wasn't a Wielder, but I'd bet my life that she had some kind of magic sensitivity. She needed it to make the kind of weapons she made as well as she did, and beyond that, her perception was nothing short of uncanny.

"It doesn't need to be anything fancy," I said. "Just something better than whatever standard-issue garbage they'd try to—"

Via padded across the room and opened a closet. My words were drowned out briefly by a series of clatters as she dug around — and when she turned, I forgot what I was about to say.

Ascended, I hadn't looked at that in years. Wouldn't have expected the sight of it alone to punch me in the gut quite like it did.

"You kept it," I breathed.

"You think I was going to let one of my best pieces get dumped in the trash or gambled away? Left in a brothel alleyway somewhere?" She clicked her tongue, shaking her head.

"You could have resold it."

"I knew you'd need it back one day. Besides, it loves you. Here." She extended her arm, holding the weapon out to me. "Don't be so scared of it."

Truth be told, I *was* a little scared of it.

I reached out, and my hands slid easily into memorized, well-worn position.

Via had crafted this for me almost ten years ago. It was the length of a spear, but double-ended, forged from bronze that was so lightweight that it seemed to stretch the bounds of feasibility, elegant swirls and scrollwork dancing along its length. The blade on one end was pointed, made for stabbing. The other slightly curved, for slashing. But more importantly...

I spoke to it as I had years ago, and it understood me just as easily. It would have been easy to mistake the divots that curled over its length for decoration. But with the addition of my magic, they lit up like trails of molten fire. Flames pooled along the blades' edges.

Another thought, and —

The staff split in two in my hands, separating in the middle into two separate weapons. I put them back together, melding them into one. Spun it. Separated again. Seamless.

"Need any tweaking?"

"No, it's…"

Perfect. It was almost terrifying how right it still felt.

"Of course it is." Via gave me a little, pleased smile. "And I have one for her too."

I must have looked as startled as I felt, because she let out a laugh. "The world isn't as unpredictable as you seem to think it is, Max. Besides, I heard she was going to go save the world or something, wasn't she? I thought she'd need something one day, and I felt… inspired."

Sammerin, you gossip.

The truth was, I was going to bring something back for Tisaanah. I wasn't about to let her walk into chaos with some clumsy, standard Guard sword. That would be downright insulting.

"You know," Via went on, returning to the closet, "women always come in here looking at the pretty silver bows or the little dainty daggers and those kinds of asinine things. But I thought… well. She seemed *interesting.*"

She turned around holding a long, curved, burgundy sheath. Then she slowly withdrew one of the most exquisite blades I had ever seen.

It was long and delicately curved, with an angled, pointed tip. But most strikingly, it was made out of two shades of metal, gold and platinum twining together in a wild, organic dance, like the roots of two trees tangling underground. In a few gaps between the two, I could see that the center was hollow — offering veins that would accommodate magic, like mine did.

She handed it to me, and I examined it. It was impossibly light, considering its length.

"This had better not snap in two on her."

"You insult me with that implication."

She was right. For all my grumbling, I had never known Via to produce anything less than an impeccably crafted weapon.

"Beautiful, isn't it?" she said, admiringly, and I had to nod.

Beautiful and functional. Just like Tisaanah.

"I named it," Via said. "Il'Sahaj."

"Il'Sahaj?"

"It's Besrithian. It means, 'blade of no worlds' or 'blade of all worlds.'" At my confused glance, she clarified, "In old-tongue Besrithian, 'aj' means both 'none' and 'all.'"

"That's impractical."

"Impractical, sure. But certainly poetic."

"Seems a little far up its own ass."

"My art pieces are my children, Max. I name all of my children. Even yours."

"I don't even want to know."

She smiled, shrugged. "Maybe one day I'll tell you. But I figure, you can't go around breaking chains and freeing civilizations with a boring weapon without a name."

I could hardly take my eyes off of it. It was, I admitted, the perfect thing for breaking chains and freeing civilizations. And it *fit* — fit Tisaanah so perfectly that it was hard to believe that Via had only met her once. She wouldn't know how to use it at first, of course, but what a thing to grow into.

"It's beautiful," I said. "You've outdone yourself. How much do I owe you?"

"Consider it moral reparations for all of those dirty, dirty weapons contracts I do," she said.

She ushered me to the door, waving away my further insistence on payment. "Go do something with your lives. And Max..." She paused at the entrance, mouth twisted in thought. "Try not to slide back into the shit."

No promises. "I'm doing my very best."

"Well, good luck. To both of you." And with that, she melted back into the warmth of her apartment, leaving me standing there holding two beautiful weapons that felt at once painfully familiar and deeply uncomfortable in my hands.

I dropped a bag of gold coins in her letter box before I left.

CHAPTER FORTY-SIX

TISAANAH

By the time Max returned, I was clawing at the walls.

It was amazing the sheer speed at which I swung from weak and ill to feeling like I was crawling out of my own skin. In fact, I felt *so* good, *so* energetic, that it edged on unpleasant — like something was just a little bit off, like my blood was running hot. My heart beat fast even when I was sitting still.

So when Max got back, when he showed me the weapons he had gotten from Via... I think I must have looked a little insane, because he hesitated to even let me hold the sword. He did, though, and I cradled it in my hands as if it were a child. It was the most beautiful thing I had ever seen. And that name... Il'Sa-haj. Blade of no worlds. Blade of all worlds.

Just like me.

If I had been able to stop myself, stop my thoughts, for even a fraction of a second, I might have been moved by it. I didn't think that Via so much as looked at me when I first met her, let alone saw me as worthy of something like this.

I unsheathed the blade again, feeling the carved bronze handle beneath my palms, trailing my eyes over the dancing silver and gold. Something inside of me purred at the sight of it.

"We haven't had very much training with swords."

Max had continued to give me some rudimentary combat training throughout our time together, but not very much of it, and always with much shorter blades than this.

"No," he said. "I probably should have… if I was thinking right, we probably should have done more. Considering your plans."

I looked up, and he looked away.

Our gazes still had only brushed each other's since I woke up. He wouldn't really *look* at me. And I supposed I understood that. Even those brief scuffs were heavy with words that weighed on my heart like lead.

I considered all of those words now, everything that I wanted to say to him. Considered how I might tell him how sorry I was for what had happened to his family; how to tell him how much it meant to me that he came back for me. Considered how I might ask him what might happen to me — to us — next, considering the creature that now lived inside my mind.

But all I could hear was my own rapid heartbeat pounding in my ears, my muscles twitching.

I could try to say all those things… or I could *move*.

I stood up, pacing, Il'Sahaj clutched in my hands. "We can begin now."

"Begin… training?"

"Yes."

"Are you feeling—"

"I'm feeling like I cannot stay still for another minute." I turned on my heel to face him. A wry smile tugged at one side of his mouth. The left, as always.

"You need something to throw yourself into."

I let out a small breath. He understood. Of course he did. I nodded, loosening a bead of sweat that pooled at my temple.

"Well then." He picked up his own weapon, curling his fingers around it gingerly. "Fine. If you can do it, I can do it."

I WAS SO SOAKED with sweat that the cotton of my shirt was plastered to my back, strands of loose hair clinging to my wet cheeks and neck. And my heart throbbed and throbbed and throbbed.

Once, as a child, I found a little baby rabbit — one left alive after the entire nest had disappeared. It was so small, so fragile, that its whole body trembled with its heartbeat. And each beat was so rapid they all blurred together like hummingbird wings.

That was what my heart felt like. A thousand beats for each breath.

I wasn't scared, though. Quite the opposite. I felt hungry. I felt *ravenous*. Powerful, like my blood was boiling in my veins.

Max brought me down to a training room, and I threw myself against that wall with everything that I had. Il'Sahaj sat unused against the door, a sight that infuriated me every time I looked at it. He had given me a sparring stick instead, which I now swung with as much force and precision as I could muster through a series of exercises.

"It's all about control," he told me, as he blocked one of my strikes. He used his staff, though he kept the blades sheathed, saying that he needed to get re-acquainted with it. "Just like magic."

Control. Control. Control. What *wasn't* about control?

I threw myself into it further — faster, harder, losing myself in the repetition and the scream of my arms, my back. If it hurt enough, I wouldn't have to think anymore.

A grunt escaped through my teeth at the impact as another one of my blows smacked against Max's bronze staff.

"Don't push yourself too hard."

I opened my mouth and let out a laugh. A laugh that sounded a little sour, a little acidic — a little too frantic.

Max hesitated just barely, a concerned wrinkle between his brows. I seized upon the opening to push forward. Another swing. Low. He almost missed it.

"Tisaanah—"

I nearly landed another strike. But just as quickly, he turned on his heel, flinging my own force against me, pushing us both against the wall. Our breaths panted and mingled into the air between us, where our staves collided.

He looked at me *now*. Looked at me with searching, wary intensity. Satisfaction slithered up my spine.

"You feel like everything is running too hot," he said. "Right?"

Right, I thought, but something inside of me devoured the word before I could acknowledge it. Something that lingered between rage and desire and *hunger.*

"I'm fine," I hissed. "You cannot be gentle with me. I'm not done."

I was capable of anything. I could do this. And he gave me this little wooden stick, as if I would hurt myself with something real?

Ha!

I slipped down, freeing myself beneath his arm, skimming his side and dancing backwards. Dancing— that's what it was. A series of steps. Deep in the back of my mind, a key slid into a lock. They all lit up against the whitewashed wooden floor, like the map of my mind had been laid out before me.

Max spun as quickly as I did, ready to block. He was fast. It was beautiful, how fluidly he moved. Almost predatory. I wondered what he looked like when he wasn't holding back. He had been holding back in Tairn. And he was certainly holding back now.

Crack.

Wood collided with metal, splitting the air as he blocked.

"That's enough. Take a break."

No.

Not enough. Never enough.

I was so focused that I didn't feel the grin split my face as I pulled back only to lunge again.

And again.

And again.

I knew exactly how to move, even in ways unfamiliar to my

muscles. My mind pulled the steps from somewhere, fed them to me in numbers like I had known so well in Esmaris's court.

1, 2, 3, 4...

The cracks of impact came faster and faster. He only blocked, never struck.

I let out a grunt as I surged forward with a particularly vicious leap, and as our weapons met, I could feel the strain of his arms absorbing the impact. I grinned at him, but he met me with scorching stone.

The whorls on his staff ignited with liquid fire, and the staff split cleanly in two.

He sidestepped in one smooth movement, sending me tumbling to the floor with a snarl that sounded nothing like myself. My sparring stick snapped as I collided with the floor.

As I fell, I flung out my arm and sent a spiral of air curling around his legs, sweeping his knees out from under him.

I pounced on him the moment he hit the ground, my skin relishing the coolness of the floor as I planted my palms over each of his shoulders, my broken stick still clutched in my hand. I had draped myself over his torso, our breaths heaving against each other.

"I won."

Gods, I forgot how much I loved exceeding expectations.

My hair dangled down, having escaped from my braid, now tickling the tip of Max's nose. I smiled and smiled, but he still looked at me with that solemn, searching look. I relished his gaze, then dragged my own over his jaw, his sweaty throat, down to the apex of his unbuttoned white shirt. So damp that it clung to his skin, revealing every twitch or ripple of the muscles beneath.

I felt no satisfaction from my victory. No, I was hungry, hungry, hungry.

Not enough. Never enough.

"That wasn't all yours," he said. "I recognize some of those movements."

I wasn't listening.

His hands gripped my shoulders — as if to hold me in place, stop me from moving any closer.

"Tisaanah, look at me."

Look at me, look at me, look at me.

My head lifted, slowly raking my way back up his body, all the way up to his face.

And with that same movement, I realized my hand was clasped around the broken sparring stick, the sharp end pressed to the underside of Max's jaw.

And I realized that it was not my voice — not *my* voice — that flowed over my tongue as I said, "I am looking, Maxantarius."

CHAPTER FORTY-SEVEN

TISAANAH

And just like that, all of the control was sapped from every thread of my thought, every line that connected me to my muscles. Like a wall jumped up from the ground, slamming me behind glass.

I tried to move my hand, tried desperately…

Nothing. Not a twitch.

"I still find it so strange," my lips said. My eyes still roamed across Max's face. A face that was so still, so pale. "Seeing you out here. You are so soft and mortal."

My hand pressed the broken stick harder against his throat, coaxing forth a single drop of blood.

His fingers dug into my shoulders, but he didn't move. He was so rigid that he could have been carved from stone.

Within my mind, my fingers clawed at that glass wall. Panic rose and rose and rose.

Let me back in.

{You have had your fun. Now I have mine.}

My left hand — the one not occupied with the stake — traveled up Max's body, trailing my fingertips across his chest, then shoulder, then throat with curious, feather-light touches. "I did not understand at first," my voice mused. "The nature of her interest in you. But now I see. It is a sex thing. Humans are obsessed with sex. I find it very strange, now, though perhaps there was a time when I did not." My head tilted. "I find myself curious. Do you think of her the way she thinks of you?"

I felt that curiosity — that genuine question — ripple through my mind. But I was too consumed with my suffocating paralysis to be embarrassed. I clawed at the force that trapped me. With every meaningless impact, I felt myself begin to question whether I existed at all.

Max's eyes bore into me with frigid fire. "I see you, Tisaanah," he said, quietly, deliberately. "I see you still. You're still there."

I clung to that brief reassurance even as my lips curled, letting out a wordless snarl.

"You speak only to me now."

"I speak to the only person here that matters."

A hiss. Another drop of blood. "You *abandoned* me, and you address me with such cruelty?"

"Are you trying to scare me?"

"I am showing you how I felt when you locked me away. What it was to be cast out." My knuckles were white around the wood, the muscles of my arm trembling. "What it is to be powerless."

I threw myself against the glass again, inhaled a terrible lungful of frantic panic —

A scoff. "Powerless? At a piece of broken wood?"

Powerless. Something clicked. I forced myself to calm.

I had spent my life being powerless. I knew how to find power where there was none.

And so, instead of reaching out to Reshaye with another strike, I reached out with a caress.

I see your wounds. I see how his betrayal hurt you.

No lies. It would know if I lied. Only the most carefully chosen of truths.

Its attention turned to me.

{I have indeed suffered many terrible things.}
I know you have.

It paused. And for one brief moment, I felt it cede to me, brush against my thoughts in an intimacy that made me force myself not to recoil —

In a sudden shock, a slice of terror shot through me, eyes blinded in a memory of *white white white* —

And then that was consumed by a burst of Reshaye's fury.

"Do you know what they did to me? Locked me up in a broken mind and a broken body. Nothing but white for so many days, so many days." My teeth gritted, lip curled. "You had no one left but me, and you still threw me away. Why would you do that?"

Power throbbed in my veins. Magic.

The lights in the room dimmed, growing hazy and dark like the red dusk before a sunset storm. The fingers that braced against Max's shoulder tingled, and a wince of pain flitted over his nose.

Slowly, so slowly, Max's left hand slid down my shoulder. Down my arm. "Find a foothold," he murmured, never taking his eyes off mine. "Find something you can grab and don't let go, Tisaanah."

"You speak to *me!*" I felt a wrinkle slice my nose. "Answer a question for me, Maxantarius. I know your body. I know what it is capable of. You could have her thrown across the room by now. You laughed at my broken piece of wood. But we are still here."

"That wasn't a question."

A laugh scraped my throat. "Perhaps you are right. Perhaps it is no question at all. I have, after all, always seen all of your weaknesses."

My fingers burned, sizzled over his skin. And a terrible smell coated my nostrils. Max's jaw strained, fighting back a wince. His hand curled around my wrist. And I knew he was waiting, waiting until the last possible moment —

The room grew darker and darker. My eyes, beneath Reshaye's control, flicked to Il'Sahaj.

No.

I fought back my own panic.

What would you gain by killing him?

A silent laugh snaked through my thoughts like a terrible shudder. *{Retribution.}*

But you say you love him. And if he is dead, you will never have him. And I'll tell you a hard truth, Reshaye — if you kill him, if you hurt him, you will never have me, either.

{And why would I want you?}

Because you wish to be loved, and I have loved many monsters.

Max's fingers tightened.

One terrible second of silence, a wave of fury cresting, cresting…

{Then you could love one more.}

The room plunged into darkness, and Reshaye thrust out my hand to receive Il'Sahaj as it flew across the room.

No.

Max twisted my wrist, flipping me onto my back, sending spirals of agony up my arm and through the back of my head as it cracked against the floor. But Reshaye didn't react, still ready for that blade—

Its gleeful rage tasted like blood on my tongue.

Stop! I threw myself one more time against the wall that separated me from my muscles —

And realized, all at once, that my mind was not a room. No, I had forgotten: it was a web.

I was not contained. I could go *up.*

My fingers closed around Il'Sahaj's hilt, straining as I raised it.

I crawled up the threads of my mind, inhaling them back into myself. I followed the paths that were dipped into darkness. Reshaye.

My arm lifted.

And just as my body had prepared to bring down Il'Sahaj's

blade across Max's throat, I dropped a razor across all of those infected threads of thought, severing Reshaye from my mind.

It let out a screech that clawed through my entire body, so consuming that it blinded me.

A crash.

My breath careened into my lungs as if I had fallen from a great height. And the light, which returned all at once, slapped me across the face.

I turned my head to see Max pushing himself up from the ground, Il'Sahaj on the floor beside him. My wrist was bent at a sickening angle, but I was grateful for the pain, grateful for the way it tethered me to my body.

"Tisaanah." My name was a ragged sigh of relief on Max's lips, so low it took me a moment to recognize it. He pressed his forehead against mine and said it again, as if he didn't realize he was speaking aloud.

For a moment, the sheer horror of what I had almost done paralyzed me. Gods, I had almost — that blade had been so close, *so close*, to his neck.

We were both shaking. I braced my palm against his face with my good hand, then my eyes landed on his throat — the one trickle of blood beneath his jaw. And then, three odd, gruesome purple-black finger marks at his shoulder.

What was that? A burn? I pushed back the torn fabric of his shirt, prompting a sharp breath through his teeth.

No, not a burn, not quite...

A low whistle cut off whatever poor attempt I was about to make at words.

"Am I interrupting something?"

Max and I pulled apart. I used my intact hand to push myself upright. Zeryth leaned in the doorway, gazing at us with one curious eyebrow cocked.

"Last time I saw you two, the mood seemed a little gruesome for this sort of thing, but then again, I suppose the threat of mortality can have that effect on people."

Before Max could let loose his inevitable snapping response, and before I could even begin to explain what had just happened, Nura appeared beside Zeryth. The somber look on her face froze the words in my throat.

"Get up. We don't have time to mess around anymore." Her voice hitched, ever so sightly, as she said, "The Capital has been attacked, so we need to get your contract underway. We leave for Threll at dawn."

I BARELY SPOKE, barely allowed myself to breathe as Max and I followed Nura and Zeryth down the static white hallways of the Tower of Midnight. My hands still shook, and I clasped them together to hide it. Even Max was uncharacteristically silent. Easy enough to pass off as shocked silence in response to what Nura was telling us. Which, to be fair, was deserving of it.

"Rebels, gathering from three houses that had been removed from power," Nura was saying, as we strode through the halls. Her voice was strained. "Bold of them. But for the first time, they have real backing. Three powerful families. A few thousand soldiers. Nothing compared to the Guard, but..."

We rounded a corner, reaching the outer halls of the Tower and a sheet of glass windows. My breath died in my throat.

"Gods," I breathed.

"Fuck," Max whispered.

"Exactly," Nura murmured.

The outskirts of the Capital, far in the distance, were bright with fire. As if the city was a living being, and a burning infection spread along its edges through flaming veins.

I stepped forward and pressed my fingers to the glass. If I looked closely enough, I could see torchlight rushing towards the outbreak of violence. Sudden darkness just beyond it, as those outside the fighting drew their shutters tight.

An old, old memory panged the back of my thoughts — an old memory of what was once Nyzerene falling into ash and flames, watching it with my face pressed against my mother's shoulder as we fled.

"They'll fall." Nura's voice was low, but firm. "Every damn one of them, the Guard will get. And then once we're back..." She levied one final stare out across the city. Then met my gaze as she lapsed into silence.

A shiver ran up my spine. I cradled my broken wrist.

Just as quickly, Nura turned and gestured for us to follow. "Dawn, Tisaanah. Be ready to leave. The sooner we go, the sooner we come back."

CHAPTER FORTY-EIGHT

MAX

Tisaanah drew in a hiss between clenched teeth as Sammerin held her wrist between gentle fingers.

"It's easy," he said, and in this moment there was nothing I was more grateful for than the unshakeable calmness in his voice. "Clean break. Simple fix."

He glanced over his shoulder at me. The reassurance was meant for me just as much as it was meant for her.

I shook my head, without entirely meaning to.

Even with everything else going on, even considering that creature looming over me and the darkness and the magic and that fucking *sword* —

It was the snap of Tisaanah's bones that filled my ears, drowning out everything else. That, and the crack of her head hitting the ground, so hard that I thought for one terrifying minute that she might not get up again.

I paced the outskirts of Tisaanah's room, like there was something I could keep from settling in my mind as long as I kept moving. Her eyes followed me. I knew it hurt like hell, to have your bones stitched back together, flesh forcibly repaired. But she didn't react. She just looked at me, in that particular way of hers, like she was not just seeing but *observing*. Peeling back layers with her stare.

I didn't realize that I had spent six months memorizing that look — memorizing the way I felt beneath it — until her eyes had landed on me in that training ring and I knew before she moved or spoke that it wasn't her.

I paused beside her bed. "Everything quiet?"

She nodded.

Sammerin gingerly placed Tisaanah's hand on her lap. "Be careful with it for a while. The joint will be weak for another week or so."

I looked at her wrist. Straight, unmarred, like it had never been injured at all.

A lump caught in my throat.

"I'm sorry."

"You should have done it sooner," she said, quietly.

"It didn't want to kill me. If it had, I'd already be dead."

Tisaanah flinched, her eyes landing on my shoulder. I kept my odd wound covered — I still hadn't quite figured out what it *was*, exactly, though I did know that it fucking *hurt* — but her gaze bore through the fabric.

I'm sure she saw the same thing I did when I looked at her wrist, but for me, this pain was only a reminder that Reshaye didn't need to waste time with broken sticks and magic swords if it really, truly wanted me dead.

No, what happened in there was a game.

I should've known that. I should've held out longer.

She opened her mouth, and I knew she was getting ready to tell me, yet again, for the hundredth time today, that I should leave.

"We know how this discussion goes, Tisaanah. Don't start."

"If I had hurt you —"

"It wasn't going to."

Sammerin stood and cast me one quiet look before he slipped out the door. If Tisaanah noticed him go, she didn't show it.

"If I took even *one more moment* longer to take back control —"

"You didn't. And now you know how to do it."

How strange it felt, trying to be optimistic about this, of all things. Optimistic or willfully ignorant. My most cynical, most obnoxious self would call the two the same.

"Besides," I added, "tomorrow we leave for Threll, and you'll be glad you have one of the best fighters in Ara with you when we get there."

The echo of a smile twitched at the corners of her mouth. "Are you bragging?"

"It's not bragging if it's true. And for once, I'm looking forward to watching those bastards burn."

I meant every damn word of it.

She lifted her face, and for the first time since I returned, I didn't pull away from the bare, electrifying force of her gaze. I wasn't sure, entirely, why it had made me so uncomfortable. Maybe there was too much I didn't want her to see, or too much I was afraid of seeing in her. Maybe there was just something about the way her face struck me, every single time, that terrified me beyond belief.

I pushed aside one strand of hair that cut across her green eye. "Show me that unrelenting brute force, Tisaanah."

She didn't move, didn't speak. But a fiery glitter seeped into her eyes, and I let their flames strip me, burn me, consume me, until there was nothing left but ash.

SAMMERIN CLENCHED his pipe between his teeth as he released a perfect ring of smoke.

His face never betrayed anxiety, never anything more than thoughtfulness. But I knew he smoked only when he was nervous.

We strode through the halls of the Tower in silence. Down and down.

"What is it, Sammerin?"

His eyes asked me a silent question, and I returned it with a knowing look.

"Whatever you're pondering. Just say it."

Another slow puff of smoke, through his nose like a dragon. "One day, Max. It's been one day, and we're already here."

"It wasn't going to kill me."

"That thing is unpredictable."

"She had it. I should have waited."

"A broken wrist was a small price, and it looked to me like she gladly paid it to ensure your safety."

"What are you saying, exactly?"

"I'm saying that I listened to you tell me for years how much you wish your father had not hesitated that day."

My fingernails bit my palms as my next words lashed from between my teeth.

"If you're implying that I should have —"

"No. Definitely not." He shook his head, releasing another unfurling breath. I wanted his reaction to be stronger than it was. "But what if it was more? If it was going to kill you, would you let it? Because that would be something she would have to walk with for the rest of her life, too."

I still saw the faces of my siblings every single time I blinked. Didn't I know it.

"It wasn't going to kill me."

"You need to think about what you'd do if it got there."

"We won't let it get there."

Sammerin gave me a look that veered infuriatingly close to pity.

"Don't," I growled.

"You're in an unwinnable situation. And it knows that, especially now. It will use it against you."

I hated how right he was.

We walked in silence, the smoke from his pipe clogging my lungs.

"I wish I could wrap this up in some kind of profound

conclusion," he said, at last. "Something more helpful than just telling you to be careful."

I did, too — even though I suspected that even if he could, I wouldn't like what it had to say.

CHAPTER FORTY-NINE

TISAANAH

I spent the night practicing the movements that I had brushed in the sparring ring, running my muscles over them again and again until I absorbed them into the core of my memory. Sleep held no appeal, even though I was exhausted. I thought, that after dragging myself across the ocean while I was actively dying, I knew what it was to be tired. No, that was nothing. This exhaustion drew from my soul.

Reshaye felt it too, apparently. It was silent. Good.

Max returned to my room after Sammerin left. He had his own quarters here, but he remained in mine, slumped in an armchair, critiquing my movements until his eyelids fluttered. Eventually, he was just a heap of limbs, head tipped back, snoring slightly — like his body had simply ceased to function.

We did not speak again about what had happened today, and for that, I was grateful.

I much preferred to think about the fact that, in mere days, I could see Serel again. Could have him back with me, safe.

If he was alive.

If I could find him.

If I could do any of it in the exceptionally narrow span of

time that I had at my disposal, or with the exceptionally limited resources, and, of course, with the exceptionally unpredictable factor of Reshaye.

If, if, if.

Somewhere in the small hours of the morning, I put down my sparring stick and went to the window, pressing my fingers against the cool glass. My room was not at the top of the Towers, but it was certainly high enough to loom far above the ground. The Capital spread out beneath me like a toy replica, reduced to distant streetlights and blocks of impersonal moonlight. Even in the darkness, the Palace glittered in the distance, reflecting light that did not exist — or perhaps it reflected the flames that still glowed like fireplace embers along the outskirts of the city.

I wondered if Nura and Zeryth were still out there, controlling the damage.

I wondered if lives were still slipping through their fingers, even now.

{Beautiful.} A faint whisper furled around my thoughts, shivering up my spine. *{I forgot how beautiful it could be.}*

My heart stilled.

I checked the threads of my mental web, preparing to push Reshaye back out if I needed to.

What? Engage, distract.

{The world. The air. Freedom. Fire. All those stories.}

I found it — faint, tired, weak, clinging to a few delicate strings.

{You treasure freedom as much as I do. No one desires it more than someone who has never had it.}

I felt it shuffle through my memories again. Memories of Esmaris the first day he met me, of the way his gaze unwrapped me like a gift.

Tomorrow we travel to my old home. You and I will give freedom to many people who have never had it, just like us.

{Threll.}

Yes.

{I knew that place, once.}

Again, the memory of grass against my hands. Backwards. Forwards. Again and again.

{Did you know that they locked me up for so many years? I had nothing, no one. I do not know how long. Many years. You would think it would be nothing for me. But even though I have lived so many lifetimes, I felt every second of it. They tried to give me many other bodies, many other homes. But I hated them. They felt like nests of broken steel.}

Its hiss raked down the back of my neck, then softened into a writhing caress.

{Not you, though. You are silk.}

I had to choke back my revulsion.

But I found myself asking, *What were you? Before?*

{I do not remember. Now I am only pieces of many things. Incomplete.}

Its pain rang out in my chest, a mournful, empty cry.

I am, too.

Fragments. Fragments of a Valtain, born of a country that no longer exists, bound to an Order that only partially accepts me.

{I know. Perhaps we will make each other whole, Tisaanah, Daughter of No Worlds.}

Perhaps. The lie took everything I had.

{What a beautiful broken butterfly you are.}

And I felt it touch the fingers of my mind, catch them where they sat poised to push it back into darkness, digging into them with bodiless claws.

{You betrayed me today.}

Panic lurched. It curled tighter around my thoughts. Pain sizzled in my spine.

{You cut me out. And if you do it again, my butterfly, I will open his throat and lick his blood from your fingers.}

And it melted back into silence, leaving my thoughts as I slid down the window into a shaking heap on the ground.

CHAPTER FIFTY

TISAANAH

I *will open his throat and lick his blood from your fingers.*
The next morning, I felt no sign of Reshaye in my head, save for the slight pressure lingering silently at the back of my skull. But it didn't need to speak to me now. The words it had said to me last night were more than enough to haunt me all day.

I could barely bring myself to look at Max in the morning. Not that there was much time to socialize, anyway. We rose at dawn and immediately began preparations to travel to Threll. The boat that would carry us there was a beautiful creation, low and slim, sails fanning out like the spines along a lizard's back. The rising sun seared through the white-and-gold fabric, emblazoned with a sun and moon, leaving little doubt as to who claimed it.

It looked nothing like the plain merchant's boat that had carried me across the sea more than six months ago. And yet, when I stood at the docks, pungent smell of the ocean in my nostrils and salty air stringing my cheeks, the scars on my back throbbed.

I was surprised to find out that *both* Nura and Zeryth would accompany us, at least on the first leg of the trip. In addition, we would also be joined by two Syrizen. I had to force myself not to stare at their neat, eyeless scars as we were introduced: Eslyn and Ariadnea. Eslyn, who was slight with sharp features and golden skin, seemed much friendlier than her taller, broader, fairer companion, but the two of them still were reserved and kept to themselves after greeting us.

I got the impression, based on their frustrated-sounding whispers and cold glances, that they were not particularly thrilled about coming on this journey. And yet, unnerving as they were, I was glad we had them.

Because that was it: just seven people to march into the home of one of the most powerful Threllian Lords on the continent. Or eight, I supposed, if we counted Reshaye.

Max stood against the dock railing next to me, and we both looked out at the sea, leaning into each other's silence. My anxiety choked me, and I knew that if I so much as glanced at him, it would all come bubbling up. I could feel him staring at me.

I will open his throat and lick his blood from your fingers.

"Tisaanah..." he started, but before he could speak — to my relief — a louder voice broke through the air.

"But when you get back?"

Max and I turned to see Moth hurrying after Sammerin as he crossed onto the docks.

"I don't know when that will be, Moth," Sammerin said. "Helene will be an excellent teacher."

"But when you do?" Moth pressed. "When you do come back, maybe then?"

Sammerin turned around, tucked his hands beneath his cape, and regarded Moth for a long, quiet moment. "Yes. When I come back, when I am no longer needed by the Orders, I will be your teacher again."

Moth seemed only slightly comforted by this assurance, giving Sammerin a skeptical glance beneath a furrowed brow. Then he caught sight of Max and turned to us, shrinking slightly under his gaze.

"I'm sorry again about the spyglass. And the flowers. And the—"

The left corner of Max's mouth raised. "What spyglass?"

"The one I—"

"I don't remember any spyglass."

"Remember, I broke it—"

Max sighed and pinched the bridge of his nose, and, despite everything, I found myself suppressing the tiniest of smiles. "Never mind, Moth. It's fine. It's forgotten."

"Oh." Moth looked down at his hands, fidgeting. "Well, still—"

"There was a time when I broke a lot of things I didn't mean to, too. Just keep working on it. You'll get there. When you do, I think you'll be a hell of a Wielder."

Moth looked so startled that his whole body lurched. "You do?"

"Maybe." Max shrugged. "Prove me right."

This statement seemed to rearrange Moth's whole world. Then he looked to me.

"Sammerin wouldn't tell me all of it, but you're going for the slaveowners, aren't you? That's why you're going to Threll."

"Yes," I answered, and a shadow passed across his face. Most people that I met in Ara knew how to shield their emotions, but Moth's still seeped into the air like a cloud. I knew he was thinking of my scars.

"I could help."

I shook my head. "Not yet. You still have many things to do here in Ara."

Things like learning and growing — slowly — I hoped. Things that had nothing to do with battlefields and war.

His brow furrowed. "One day I will, though."

"I believe you, Moth."

And, as I felt that cloud around him harden into resolve, I meant it.

A flush rose to his cheeks. He extended one hand and waited.

When I stared at it, confused, he muttered, "Your *hand*, Tisaanah."

I laid my palm in his and tried not to laugh as he planted a clumsy brush of a kiss against my knuckles. "Good luck," he said, then too quickly dropped my fingers as he gave the three of us one final, hurried wave and was ushered away with his new instructor.

"Moth, breaker of flowers, spy glasses, pitchers, and hearts," Max mused, shaking his head. "He *is* your apprentice after all, Sammerin."

"He's a little smitten, I think. But I suppose it can't be helped." And I tried not to notice how Sammerin's gaze slid to Max as he said, "When I saw that red dress, I knew we were all in trouble."

WE SET off so early that the sun was only just beginning to rise in the sky. No one seemed to feel entirely comfortable. We got through the day with tight, stilted interactions — easy enough, since there was so much to do. Long after the sun had set, we finally stopped to eat. Zeryth took his stew up above deck and dangled his feet over the edge as he ate at the front of the ship. Nura took hers off to a corner, alone. Max, Sammerin and I ate in long, awkward silence. That strange suspension still hung between us — not quite an absence of words but an overabundance of them — and neither of us, it seemed, were ready to confront it.

Instead, as I choked down bland stew, I couldn't help but watch the two Syrizen across the deck. For two people with no eyes, they moved with such precision. There was no stumbling over the location of the ladle or bowls. No second guessing as to where the pot was.

They couldn't be fully blind. Not really.

"You've never met a Syrizen before?"

My staring must have been obvious, because I turned to see Sammerin watching me thoughtfully.

"No. They're—"

But as if they sensed that we were talking about them, Eslyn turned around, gave us a half smile, and sauntered towards us with Ariadnea in tow.

"I've got to admit, Sammerin. I was surprised to see you here, of all places." The two of them settled beside us, and we scooted around to make room. Up close, everything about them seemed honed for lethal perfection. Their uniforms, crafted of black leather and stiff fabric, were identical and meticulous, their hair perfectly pinned, their spears gleaming beneath the lantern light. And of course, there were those scars — neat, straight, precise.

All of this seemed jarringly at odds with Eslyn's jovial friendliness as she settled down beside us. Even though there was even something about *that* that seemed... predatory.

She cocked her head towards Sammerin. "Been awhile. How're things?"

"Well enough, Eslyn."

"You know each other?" I asked.

"Many years ago," Sammerin said, just *slightly* too quickly, and Eslyn's eerie, eyeless gaze fell to me.

"Syrizen are recruited from the military, so once upon a time, we ran in the same circles. Didn't we, Sam?"

"One might say so," he said, mildly.

That tone was downright frosty, by Sammerin's standards.

"We had a mutual friend," Ariadnea said. She had a low, deep voice that reminded me of stone. Steady and heavy.

"Yes, one of our fellow recruits," Eslyn added.

"Mm," said Sammerin, looking down at his bowl.

Interesting.

"So you knew each other before—"

"Back when I still had those big beautiful blue eyes, yes," Eslyn said, and laughed while everyone else remained uncomfortably silent.

Ariadnea had not stopped watching me. "You have never met a Syrizen."

It wasn't a question, but I still shook my head.

Eslyn chuckled. "The staring made it obvious enough."

"I did not mean to be rude. I just..." Gods, it was impossible *not* to stare. "You are very... graceful."

"Expected us to be stumbling around like baby kittens, eh?" Eslyn chirped. "Well, we can see well as you."

"Just differently," Ariadnea added.

My gaze darted between them. "How?"

Eslyn replied, simply, "The layers."

"The layers?"

"Magic is a series of layers, far beneath the physical world," Ariadnea said. "Different layers, or streams, for different types of magic. Valtain magic, Solarie magic..."

I nodded. Common knowledge. The stuff of storybooks.

"It goes much deeper than those two threads alone. There are many, though those two are the only ones that human Wielders have been known to access. The Fey, for example, are theorized to have many threads of their own, inaccessible to human Wielders."

"Syrizen," Eslyn said, proudly, "are the only human Wielders able to tap into a deeper layer of magic."

"If only for seconds at a time," Ariadnea added. "And with great... concessions, in order to force a higher sensitivity." She gestured to her own eye sockets with a wry smirk.

A shiver ran up my spine. "With your eyes gone, you feel it more strongly."

"Exactly."

Out of the corner of my eye, I saw Max shake his head, and an echo of my own discomfort panged in my chest.

My next question was clumsy — impossible to word. "So... why you?"

"There are many very specific qualities one must fulfill to be capable of being one of the Syrizen," Ariadnea said. "We all are Solarie, because the more external, energetic magic of the Solarie is needed to give us the sheer power to push between the layers. But at the same time, we require a sensitivity to the movements of magic that most Solarie lack. There is a very intricate series of tests to determine each candidate. No one knows why, but overwhelmingly, only women tend to make the cut."

"There aren't many of us," Eslyn said, "but we're good at what we do. We may only be able to dip half a layer deeper, but even that gives us many unique powers." Her eyeless gaze fell to me, and her smile twisted, widened, with a hungry curiosity. She leaned forward. "Though I hear that the thing that lives inside of you draws from much, much deeper than that."

My mouth went dry.

{Me,} a whisper beckoned, from far, far away. *{She's talking about me.}*

The voice was so distant that it was barely audible, weak and tired, gone as soon as it had arrived. But suddenly, I found myself pushing back vomit.

"It turns out that when you become a Syrizen, you don't just lose the eyes, you also lose your ability to hold a conversation about anything other than your grand sacrifices," Max muttered. "Tiresome, Eslyn."

But I could feel his gaze on me, even though I could not look at him.

I stood up, politely excused myself, and turned away before I could hear their response.

EVERYONE RETREATED below deck to their makeshift, curtained rooms early. I lay there and listened to the sounds of the ship slowly quiet. I tried to sleep. But I couldn't stop running my fingers over the threads of my mind, again and again and again, checking for whispers and movement until I was about to drive myself insane.

And finally, when I couldn't take it anymore, I pushed back the curtain and padded barefoot up the stairs, exhaling in relief when I reached the deck and was greeted by an infinite blanket of stars. Like the whole world just opened up.

I stopped and took a breath, trailing across the deck —

— and stumbling as I almost stepped on a *face.*

Specifically, Max's face. Max, who was lying on the wooden floor, hands folded over his stomach.

He didn't flinch as I leapt aside and let out a Thereni curse.

He opened one eye. "Careful."

"*Max.* What are you *doing?*"

"Lamenting." He opened the other eye, both meeting mine in the darkness. "And, if I'm being honest, trying desperately not to hack my guts up. I'm not made for having anything other than solid ground beneath my feet."

I rasped out a chuckle.

It was amazing how good that felt. Just to laugh, a little bit, even though it wasn't really that funny. I clung to that fragment of our former intimacy like it was gold.

I lowered myself next to him, lying down on the floor. "I think it is more — wobbly down here."

It took me a moment to choose the word. As fluent as I was by now, my mind was muddy lately.

"Wobbly, huh?"

"Yes. Right word?"

I watched the corner of his mouth curl into a smile. "Excellent word."

At least down here, my whole body swayed with the rise and fall of the boat, instead of just my feet — and the expanse of stars stretched all the way across my vision. Breathtaking.

We lay there in silence for a moment, listening to the water lap against the sides of the boat and the masts creak with each gust of wind. The warmth of Max's body brushed my skin, though I was careful not to touch him. Uninvited, the memory of Reshaye's words flitted through my mind: *Now I understand. It is a sex thing.*

I shuddered. The longer I could ignore that, the better.

I wasn't sure how long it was before Max spoke. "You ready?" he murmured.

"Yes."

No. I am not ready.

"You will be," he whispered, and I felt my cheeks tighten. I did not dignify uncertainty aloud. But in some ways, it was nice to have someone who heard the things I didn't allow past my lips.

"Are you?" I asked.

"Hell, no."

"Yes, you are. You just do not know it."

A breathy scoff. I turned my head to see him already staring at me — a steadiness, an intensity, to his gaze that made me want to look away and fall further all at once.

Something I could not, or perhaps would not, identify ached in my chest. I looked away.

"So are we going to keep doing this?" Max murmured.

"What?"

"You know me well enough by now to know that I'm not stupid, Tisaanah."

I almost laughed. Stupidity had nothing to do with it. We'd simply moved past the point where either of us was capable of hiding from the other.

"I don't know. Are we? If you open a door, it opens both ways."

He scoffed. "What is that supposed to mean?"

A lump had risen in my throat, and when I turned to look at him, I felt it swell. "You should not have come back," I choked out. "After everything that it did to you."

Something tightened in his features. Almost a wince. "You should have listened to me."

He was right, a part of me whispered. *I should have.* "You should have *told* me."

"I couldn't, Tisaanah."

"Then tell me now," I said. "Tell me everything. I need to know, because we are *living* it."

My voice was still so quiet that it was barely more than a whisper. But the intensity of it hung in the words like smoke.

Slowly, he turned his gaze back to mine and held it. There was a part of me that wanted to break it, look away from those peculiar eyes. I didn't.

"Six months," he said, roughly. "I had it for six months. Maybe a little longer. I was in the military. A Captain. It was becoming increasingly clear that the war would not end easily or without significant blood. We'd been attacked. Azre, the Arch Commandant, wanted a successor chosen, in case of the worst. Me, Zeryth and Nura were among the candidates. And I wanted it. I wanted that title more than I'd ever wanted anything. So..." His voice trailed off, and when it resumed, it was rougher. "You signed that contract because it gave you the means to protect all the people you left behind. But me? I signed mine because I *wanted* to. Because I wanted *power*."

He spat the word, and I could *feel* his regret, his anger.

"For awhile," he said, "it seemed like I got that. Because Reshaye is wildly, insanely powerful. *Nothing* should be that powerful. My magic was my own, but... so much more. It was terrific, at first. But soon..." He let out a breath. Shook his head. "It's unpredictable. Possessive. Vindictive. And it's willing to crush whatever defies it."

Possess or destroy.

I shuddered.

"Inhuman," he muttered.

"Inhuman?" I shook my head. "Very human. The ugliest parts of humanity."

"I believed that if I tried hard enough, I could force it into submission. It didn't work that way. In Sarlazai, it all came to a head. And then..."

He didn't need to continue.

My hand slid into his before I realized what I was doing, and his fingers folded easily around mine. In the contact of our skin, I felt faint waves of his nervousness pulse from him to me, even from behind those carefully guarded mental walls.

"The thing was, only a very, very small handful of people knew about the existence of Reshaye. Which meant that most people believed — *believe* — that I was personally responsible for what happened at Sarlazai. And it was war, but that was…"

His gaze darkened, and as it did, the memories skimmed the surface of my thoughts, too — his memories, of the fire and the flesh and the burned-up too-little corpses.

"There were pre-trials," he said, "to determine whether I would be charged with war crimes. I wasn't there. I was… not in a position to testify on my own behalf. But Nura testified for me. For hours. From a fucking *wheelchair*. I'll never forgive her for what she did to those people, or, selfishly, what she did to me. But that… sometimes I still don't know what to make of it."

Nura. Ever the enigma. Every piece of information only made her more difficult to understand.

My fingers tightened.

"And they removed it then?"

"Yes. It was… bad. Like receiving it, but worse, because it rips out half your mind with it when it goes. And Reshaye very much did *not* want to go…" He lapsed into silence, then stared at me with a lowered brow. As if there was something else he might say.

But then he glanced away. Shook his head. "Well. It almost killed me."

A realization clicked into place. "And you didn't tell me any of this because you were bound to silence," I whispered. "You made a blood pact."

"Yes. They said that it needed to remain secret. And at that point, I would have agreed to anything to get it out of me. Hell, it didn't seem like such a terrible thing, to never speak of it again. And their final gift was the perfect cover story. My father was a Ryvenai noble who was a close personal friend of the king. There were plenty of people on both sides who would have loved to see the Farlione family wiped out for that alone. And just like that, the murder of the Farliones became just another unfortunate wartime tragedy."

His voice lowered, guttered, bit into the words like claws against stone. When he looked at me again, his eyes were serious and sad.

"I wish I could say," he said, slowly, as if he were making a terrible confession, "that I wanted to tell you. But I didn't, even if I could. I didn't want you to know any of it. Not until I watched you walk into those towers and I realized what not knowing would cost you."

His fingers tightened around mine until they trembled, folding me into a silent apology.

And I echoed it with one of my own. "I wish I had listened."

I meant it.

Because it could just be us, right now. And I knew it was unrealistic. But it was such an appealing fantasy.

I will lick his blood from your fingers.

The memory of Reshaye's words slithered through the darkness. I felt its presence in the back of my mind and shuddered.

"It hates you," I murmured. "It threatened you. It already hurt you. And Max, if—"

My words tangled. What ones could I possibly choose that would express everything that had been roiling in me for the last two days? How could I explain what it would do to me if I hurt him — more than I already had? How could I tell him how much it meant to me that he came back and yet how quickly I would trade that for the promise of his safety?

Words were nothing, compared to that. It would be like trying to move the sea with a spoon.

I lapsed into silence and didn't resume. But a wrinkle formed between Max's brows, and I saw the understanding seep into his eyes.

"When we were in Tairn, at the foot of that tower," he said, quietly, "and you asked me to let you help, my first thought was, *No fucking way. Too dangerous.* But it turned out that our only shot at beating that thing was doing it together."

Bittersweet warmth suffused my chest, punctured with a pang of guilt.

I didn't deserve him. Gods, I didn't. And yet, traitorously, the deepest recesses of my soul were so happy he was here.

The faintest beginnings of tears stung my eyes.

"It turned out that we were a decent team," I whispered.

A little smile warmed his voice as he replied, "Yes. We were."

CHAPTER FIFTY-ONE

MAX

With the help of the three Valtain moving the wind over the seas, we were set to arrive at Threll in a matter of a week instead of weeks, plural. I still found the boat, and all of the circumstances surrounding our place on it, simultaneously oppressive and terrifying. Yet, since our moonlight meeting the first night at sea, there was something that felt a little lighter, a little easier, about my interactions with Tisaanah. It had been the first time in eight years that I had carved those stories out of myself. There were still shards of it that were buried within me, yes, and there were still things that I hadn't been able to force myself to acknowledge aloud.

But still... she knew more than almost anyone else did. And I never thought that would feel good, but here we were.

Reshaye, mercifully, was mostly quiet. I suspected that its display a few days ago in the sparring ring had sapped its energy. It was early to be taking control like that, to be using magic. There were times when I'd see Tisaanah's face harden, her eyes go far away, and I knew that it was whispering to her. But days passed, and it didn't go further than that.

Tisaanah and I spent most of our time practicing her combat.

Reshaye's trace memories from previous hosts had given her some fragments of innate knowledge that, together, we pieced into something more complete. And at night, once everyone went to sleep, we would creep up above deck and sit beneath the sky. It felt cleaner up there. More free.

But on our third night at sea, she was so exhausted that she passed out the minute she hit the pillow. So I went up there by myself, drilling my movements over and over until my muscles reclaimed the memories.

I was out of shape.

These last few days of training had, embarrassingly, strained me to the point where the muscles of my arms and back groaned in protest every time I moved, unaccustomed to the way they had to work to control a weapon. Better now, I supposed, than a week from now.

"No apprentice tonight?"

I swore under my breath, whirling around. Nura stood there, looking smug.

"Ascended, Nura, don't do that."

"Pay closer attention."

I almost scoffed. That advice was almost poetic, coming from her. If I had, perhaps none of us would be here.

"You're out of practice," she observed, and I bristled.

"I didn't think I'd have to do this again, so yes, marginally."

Nura's face was a white, silent mask. Every time I looked at it, I had to fight the rage in my chest back until it was a faint pulse beneath my blood — rage on Tisaanah's behalf, yes, but also nearly a decade's worth of built-up betrayal. A strange, surreal thing to confront every day.

"Need a sparring partner?" She reached beneath her jacket to pull out two daggers and gave me a little smile. "I think we left it at a tie last time. But it's been so long."

I knew I should say no.

That I was too damn angry at her for a "friendly" fight to be a good thing.

But I didn't hesitate as I said, "Fine."

No magic, we agreed. Five paces away from each other. Turn. Position. And —

I had forgotten how fast she moved. Like she became shadow.

I had to block her immediately. And again, spinning on my heel to match the liquid speed with which she bent around me. She slid away from the impact as if my staff had merely pierced a cloud of unfurling smoke.

Block — again.

She paused only long enough to give me a smirk. "Try harder, Max."

I watched her silent footfalls, marked her speed, the length of each stride. Marked where she'd land two, three, four seconds from now.

And seared forward in one calculating strike.

That's how you had to be, with Nura — calculating. You couldn't wait for her to come to you or expect to beat her with scattershot strength. You had to attack, decisively. One perfectly calibrated movement after another.

I watched her feet and hands and blades all at once, turned, curled, angled the curved blade of my staff just the right way.

I could be fast too.

One strike, with everything I had, the same way a viper lunges with its entire body.

One strike, and one hit.

She let out a ragged breath, grace disrupted, feet sliding across the floor. She threw her loss of balance into a turn. Just like I knew she would. Just like I knew she'd strike low, then high, then turn —

I was ready.

A swing, a half-step, a counterstrike for each movement. We glided across the deck, answering each other's jabs and evasions with immediate responses, each growing shorter, sharper, angrier.

I watched her face in between the blurring movement of our weapons and saw the blood-spattered soldier who raised her hand to my temple seven years ago. I saw the sad, patronizing look she gave me when she told me about Tisaanah's blood pact.

My anger burned so hot that it turned to ice. I slipped further into my strikes, like putting on an old, comfortable jacket.

Nura's silver eyes glittered as she narrowly evaded one of my swings. "There you are, Captain Farlione."

There I fucking am.

I spun on my heel. Intentionally dragged my left side, only barely. Let my left ankle twist.

And when she saw that, when she lunged — because I knew she would — I was ready.

With one final leap, I cut off her movement with the length of my staff, knocking one of her daggers from her hand, pushing her to the ground—

— Only for her to roll, then spring forward. So fast I could hardly see her. So fast that she was behind me by the time I saw her forearm swing around my neck. She brushed the wound on my shoulder and for one critical split second, a wave of pain so powerful that it blinded me seized my muscles. I fought it.

No dagger. I could still —

And then she flicked her wrist, another blade sliding from beneath her sleeve. Poised at my throat before I could finish disarming her.

"I think that's your yield," she said into my ear.

"Ah, I see." I tried to pass off my breathless panting as an exasperated sigh, with only partial success. "Magic was off limits but hidden blades are fair game. So little has changed, Nura."

"That was always our problem, Max." She released me and stepped back. "You always thought I was more honorable than I am."

I let out a scoff through my teeth, resisting the urge to clutch my shoulder, which still throbbed viciously. "That's a generous way of framing it."

Her gaze fell on my wound — covered, but despite my effort, it must have been obvious where it was. "You should have Sammerin look at that."

"I'll take care of it."

"Put your pride aside. We need you in one piece."

I picked up my staff, pointing at her with one end. "We? Let's be clear, I am not here for you."

"So defensive. So protective." *Thwip* — as her knife retracted back up her sleeve. "I know I earned your distrust, but right now, we're on the same side."

"Says the woman shoving daggers up her sleeves."

That was Nura. All those hidden sharp edges, ready to slide between your ribs.

"Insult me all you want," she said, too casually. "I'm still glad that you came back after all. I love when Zeryth has to admit I'm right."

There was something about the way she said it that made my knuckles whiten with rage around my staff. I bit down so hard on the words jumping up my throat that my jaw trembled.

We stood there in silence. Then Nura let out a little sigh. "Well. Thanks for the practice. Goodnight, Max."

But as she turned away, I barked, "Nura."

She turned and peered over her shoulder, eyebrow raised.

"*Why?*" I spat. "You were there. Why?"

It was practically a jumble of words, none of them particularly specific or meaningful. But I saw her expression shift, and I knew she understood exactly what I was asking.

She had been there beside me through the whole thing. There was a time when I trusted her more than I trusted anyone — more than I trusted myself. And as much as I hated her, as much as I held her to unforgiving accountability for what happened in Sarlazai, I knew that she had loved my family almost as much as I did.

She was ruthless, focused to the point of callousness and cruelty. But she was not stupid. Perhaps not even selfish, not quite. She wasn't Zeryth, driven by ego to the point of reck-lessness.

So... why?

A faint smile. "What?" she said. "You still think better of me?"

"I want to know where you're hiding the blade."

"If I tell you that, what's the point of hiding it?"

I gave her a hard stare. The same one I used to give her all those years ago, when I needed to puncture through all of that ice.

And just as it had then, her expression flickered. "I wouldn't do it if it didn't need doing."

"For what? A petulant twelve-year-old's throne?" I shook my head. "No. That doesn't make sense."

"I wouldn't do it if it didn't need doing," she said again. Then, lower, "Trust me, Max."

I scoffed. Trust her. Right.

"I suppose I don't get to argue with that look." The final remnants of her smile disappeared. And I saw it — hesitation.

"There's something big coming," she murmured. "And none of us get to frolic in gardens with pretty Threllian girls until it's over."

A cold shiver ran up my spine. Not even at her ominous words, but at the look in her eye: ruthless determination.

I could think of few things that were more dangerous than that.

"Something big," I repeated. "Ah yes. That puts all of my concerns to rest. My trust is secured."

She didn't laugh, didn't smile. Didn't strike back. She only shrugged. "I've never been afraid to be the bad guy." And she turned away and threw up her hand in a lazy wave. "Thanks for the spar, Max. Tell our girl I said goodnight."

TISAANAH LOOKED SO *normal* when she slept. Well, maybe not normal, exactly — nothing about her was average, after all. But when I went back below deck and peered through the open gap in her curtain to see her face smooshed against the pillow, I let out an involuntary breath. No one would ever guess what was going on in that head. The beautiful machinations or the monster that consumed them.

I find myself curious, do you think about her the way she thinks about you?

The line popped into my head without warning, prompting a surge of uncomfortable disgust. No accent there, and no trace of Tisaanah, either. It was so far from her that I could hide behind my revulsion enough to keep myself from thinking about all of the curious implications of that line.

The answer, of course, was, *Yes, frequently, in great detail.* But I would pretend that wasn't the case as long as I possibly could. I was, after all, a well-practiced, world-renowned expert in denial. I was good at magic, good at fighting, good at gardening. But I was *excellent* at avoiding inconvenient truths.

I slipped through the curtain and settled silently onto a crate near the wall, leaning back against the wood, as I watched the top of Tisaanah's head. The steady beat of her breaths.

I blinked. The world was blurrier when I opened my eyes again.

Another blink. This time, they didn't open at all.

CHAPTER FIFTY-TWO

MAX

"**M**ax."
May-oocks.

I clawed my way through darkness. Turned in my dream and peered up to the cloudy sky. So did Brayan, his steel gaze turning and lifting as he lowered his sword.

"*Max.*"

I jolted awake. In the process, I moved my left shoulder without thinking and paid for it with a surge of blinding pain.

"You were talking in your sleep." Tisaanah's eyes were ringed with darkness and heavy with concern as they fell to my shoulder. "Still?"

I couldn't even unclench my teeth.

"It's nothing."

"*Stupid,*" she huffed, and drew back the curtain as she beckoned to Sammerin.

I SHIVERED and eyed the two Syrizen across the room through the open curtain. They were on the opposite side of the boat, but

I could feel them staring at me, a sensation that was no less uncomfortable due to their lack of eyes. Ascended, they were creepy. I resisted the urge to cross my arms over my bare chest.

"Can you close that, please? I don't like having an aud—" The rest of the sentence was lost in a clenched hiss between my teeth as Sammerin touched the skin around my wound.

He furrowed his eyebrows. "Really? I wasn't even close."

Tisaanah drew the curtain closed without looking away from me. "It smells very bad, too" she observed.

Despite myself, a smile twitched at my mouth. Tactful as always. Sometimes I wondered if I should be insulted that I never got any of that saccharine charm that she produced for everyone else, but I'd come to realize that this was really the greater compliment. No counting her dancing steps with me.

"Thanks, Tisaanah." I glanced at Sammerin, who now stared at the dark patch of my skin with stony concentration. "What *is* it, exactly?"

I still hadn't been able to figure it out. It definitely wasn't a burn, but it wasn't quite a cut either, and it hurt worse than nearly any other injury I'd ever received. That was saying something.

And, embarrassing as it was, Tisaanah was right — it had really started to *reek*.

"I've never seen anything like this before," Sammerin said. Tisaanah wandered back over to him, concern in her eyes. Concern and a shrouded touch of guilt.

"It's noth—" I started to say.

And then the whole world went white and my body folded in on itself.

"Mother of bleeding fucking hells!"

It was a solid ten seconds before I could even draw a breath, let alone open my eyes.

"Sorry. It's better without warning." When I did, Sammerin was gazing at his hands, rubbing his fingers together. "I needed to feel it."

"Creative cursing." Zeryth had pushed aside the fabric and

was leaning against a wooden pillar, watching me with lazy curiosity. "You have a way with words, Maxantarius."

"Fuck you." I was in too much pain to even wish that I could come up with something more inventive.

"And delivered with such enthusiasm."

"Don't you have something better to—"

"This is *rot*." Sammerin spoke quietly, focused only on his fingers. Zeryth and I both lapsed into silence.

I glanced at Tisaanah, who stared back at me with wide eyes. "Rot?" I echoed.

"Rot. Decay." He shook his head, still staring at his hands, then my wound, perplexed. "I can't even speak to the flesh. It's dead."

"Like an infection?" Tisaanah asked, hesitantly.

"An infected wound will start to decay if left unattended long enough, but this is *far* beyond that. Was it like this from the beginning?"

"It's gotten worse, but—"

"Was it black like this?"

"Yes." Tisaanah answered for me. "It looked the same."

"I've never seen anything like this," Sammerin muttered.

Neither had I.

In me, Reshaye had simply ramped up the scale of my natural magic ability, feeding my own powers back to me at a staggering scale. But as a Valtain, this kind of physical ability would be difficult for Tisaanah. And I'd never heard of any Wielder, Valtain or Solarie, turning something living to decay through touch. Not even a Wielder who controlled flesh, like Sammerin. He could tear it apart, deprive it of blood, strangle it and wither it slowly. But *rotting* it? Outright killing it? That was new to me.

Tisaanah paled.

"It appears I'm missing some background information. *You* did this, Tisaanah?" Zeryth's eyes had a certain sparkle in them, a certain hunger, as they landed on her and lingered.

"Reshaye did," she corrected.

I wished I could have reached into her lungs and stopped her before she replied.

"We-ell. That is *interesting.*"

Tisaanah's gaze flicked back to me and to that peculiar wound. But I was looking past her, at Zeryth, whose eyes roamed over her with eager pleasure, like he had just been presented with a gift that he couldn't wait to unwrap.

There had been many, many times over the years when I very vividly imagined how good it would feel to rip out Zeryth's throat, but this may have been the first time that I actively had to stop myself from doing it.

"You think?" I scoffed. "Honestly, it's a little underwhelming. Annoying more than anything. Let's just heal this thing up, Sammerin."

I knew it was unconvincing, but it was my best shot. My blood roared as a little smarmy twitch at the corner of Zeryth's mouth told me that he knew exactly what I was trying to do. It was so distracting that I almost didn't hear Sammerin as he said, "I can't."

My attention snapped back to him. "You can't?"

"Not easily. I can't talk to this. And the shape is…" His lips thinned in concentration. "I need to dig it out before I can try to bridge the damage."

Did he just say *dig?* I tried not to let myself blanch.

"Can you leave, please?" I snapped at Zeryth. "This is invasive."

It was amazing, how fast Zeryth's expression changed — like every muscle rearranged into a razor-sharp glare all at once. "This is *my* ship. I can crawl into the washroom with you and I'd be well within my rights. And that aside, I don't appreciate your tone. Remember who you're speaking to."

Right. Zeryth Aldris, Arch Commandant.

Zeryth Aldris, the man who once went out on a reconnaissance mission with five of his most talented military peers — his most talented *competition* — and, conveniently, was the only one to return alive. The man who forced me back to my family home to get me out of his way. The man who advocated for my imprisonment, even though he knew perfectly well the truth of what had happened in Sarlazai that day.

Zeryth Aldris, the man who "befriended" a teenaged Tisaanah in slavery and proceeded to leave her there, not once, not twice, but *four damned times*. And then had worn that lazy little smile as he tried to force her to her knees in front of everyone that she so desperately wanted to impress, just because he could.

And who now, after *all of that*, looked at her like she was a slab of meat ready to be quartered for his own purposes.

Oh, I knew exactly who I was speaking to.

I smiled at him through gritted teeth and said, "I could never forget."

Frankly, I was proud of my restraint. But clearly my tone was still not up to Zeryth's standards, because he straightened, shoulders squaring, head cocked. "Come here, Maxantarius."

"This is not needed," Tisaanah cut in, before shooting me a look that said, *Shut up and stop causing trouble.*

"*Stand up* and *come here.*"

Long, sharp fingers grabbed ahold of my mind and squeezed, squeezed—

I managed five long seconds before my legs betrayed me, rising from the chair without my permission and taking one agonizing step after another. I stopped a few steps in front of him and arched my eyebrows, as if to say, *Happy now?*

He raised a pale finger and beckoned. "One more step."

Bastard. I made the movement as tiny as I possibly could, inching forward only slightly, and he laughed. "You never make anything easy." His smile soured into something closer to a sneer. "You've always been so *mouthy*. But that willpower has never quite been strong enough, has it? Always failed you at the most important times."

Low. So fucking low, even for him. Fury clawed at every muscle in my body.

"This is your boat, but it is my mission." Tisaanah's voice cut from behind me. "And these distractions are not useful, Zeryth. This is not why we're here."

"Distractions?" His gaze lowered to my shoulder. "I only wanted to get a closer look at this. I like to fully understand the potential of the resources I have at my disposal." He examined the wounds, his nose wrinkling. "Disgusting. And fascinating."

Then he turned to Tisaanah, face drawn into overwrought concern. "It troubles me, Tisaanah, that you didn't feel comfortable telling me about this sooner."

Her face remained neutral, but I watched her expression steel in that particular way that told me that she was calculating the perfect response. Then her features settled into a well-practiced apologetic sweetness, and she replied, "There was just so much happening...so fast...I wasn't thinking properly."

It was so saccharine that it bordered on sarcasm, or maybe I only thought so because I knew her too well. But Zeryth, at least, appeared to buy it. One blink and that dazzling, effusive smile was back.

"We've all been a little distracted. It happens, in times like these. But, make no mistake — this *is* why we're here. None of us can afford to forget that." His breezy gaze flicked to me, gesturing to the wound. "Get that taken care of, then. Have fun with the...digging."

And just like that, he glided away, not so much as bothering to look back as he ascended the steps to the deck.

CHAPTER FIFTY-THREE

TISAANAH

"That went exactly how he wanted it to," Sammerin said, shaking his head, and Max scowled in a way that said he knew his friend was right.

I watched Max as he slumped back down onto that crate, my teeth gritted. *Stupid.* So *stupid*, in that uniquely male way, to sink to getting into a dick-waving contest instead of stopping to *think* about what that would mean. Gods, what a privilege that must be.

I may have had the ability to decay flesh — a thought that made me shudder — but I still lacked the freedom that would let me behave so carelessly.

Max caught my eye. "What?"

"You made it too easy for him."

"Trust me, I've known Zeryth long enough to know that he would have found an excuse for that display regardless. That was unavoidable. Now or later." A scoff. "Bastard."

"It doesn't matter. You cannot give him so much to use against you."

Max's face hardened. "That man treated you like an animal, and he was just looking at you like you were—" He let out a breath through his teeth. "And you're telling me that I didn't play nicely enough?"

I wanted to laugh. How could someone be so cynical and yet so naive? "Do you understand how many men have looked at me that way? Like a thing, not a person? I wouldn't have survived a week in Esmaris's court if I had—"

"But that's not *right.*"

"Of course it's not *right,* but it is the way it is. The only weapon I have is to use that."

Max looked down at his shoulder. At that glistening black rot. "I don't think that's even remotely true, Tisaanah."

A whisper, far away, as my eyes fell to that patch of rot: *{Look at what we can do together. Beautiful.}*

That one echo of a whisper, and it was gone again. It was always, always so tired.

"I am *bound* to the Orders," I said, to Max. "That is true whether I like it or you like it. And that...*rot...*" I lifted my hand to his shoulder, biting back my disgust at the word. "That does not belong to *me.* That belongs to *them.*"

Bound to Zeryth. Bound to Nura. Bound to Queen Sesri. And, of course, perhaps most dangerously of all, bound to Reshaye. All those ropes cutting into my skin. My skin that could *kill.* My hands that would *decay.*

It was easier, I acknowledged, deep in the back of my mind. It was easier to be angry at Max for doing what I couldn't than to think about all that implied — than to think about what those people made me and what my servitude, my slavery, would force me to do.

Because that? *That* just made me feel sick, no matter how many times I told myself that it would all be worth it if it meant freeing those that I left behind.

"But you are more than all of those things," Sammerin said, quietly. "Don't forget that."

"I will be whatever I need to be."

"What about what you *want* to be?" Max leaned forward, wincing at the movement. "What about *you?*"

What about me? I was a means to an end. My mother had sent her only child away. Serel had been ready to sacrifice his life. What they gave up for me to had to *worth* something.

"It is not the time for me to be selfish," I said. "Not yet."

And because I couldn't bear to look at it anymore — at Max and the way he saw me, at the wound I had given him, at everything that it implied I would be used for — I turned around and went upstairs, finding some small relief in the salty breeze and unforgiving stark sky. Zeryth lounged at one end of the boat. But I was drawn towards the back, where Nura stalked in circles.

Thwimp.

The sound was sharp and clean. Every three paces, Nura threw a little knife at the masts, buying glints of silver in the wood. I wandered to her and couldn't help but be impressed that her knives were lined up in a straight, perfect line, nearly touching, accuracy impeccable.

Her face lifted to greet me. That little movement startled me, despite myself. Sometimes, when I first saw her, it was like the sharp edges of my mind caught a fraying piece of fabric, snagging at threads of memories that didn't belong to me. Sometimes they were tinged with a bittersweet affection. Other times, furious anger. Most commonly, I saw the sad, determined, unapologetic look in her eye as her hand raised to my — Max's — temple in Sarlazai, paired with that devastating betrayal.

"I heard that mess downstairs." Her attention turned back to her throwing knives.

Thwimp.

"I forgot how entertaining those standoffs could be," she added.

"I would not call it entertaining."

She shrugged. "Either way, it sounds like that wasn't the most intriguing part." Her eyes flicked to my hands. "*Rot.* Interesting."

Self-consciously, my fingers curled. "Yes."

"Aren't you lucky to have that kind of power…"

I did not feel lucky. But I said — to her and to myself — "If it will accomplish my goals, then yes."

My mind ran over the memory of Esmaris's sneering face, and Reshaye's exhausted hiss slithered through my thoughts. I winced.

"We'll see what we can do with that," Nura said. "But that's impressive and unique. I'm sure it will strike fear into the hearts of your Threllian Lords. Into anyone, really."

Thwimp.

Her fingers moved so fast that they became slender white smears. This one buried itself into the wood a little off-center. She grimaced at it, then gave me a long, thoughtful look. It would have been easy to shrivel under that gaze.

What does Nura want? I asked myself. I was good at answering that question. But Nura — Nura was difficult. She was cruel and cold. But she had been so gentle with me when I was sick. And she had testified on Max's behalf when no one else would. She had damned him, but also saved him.

And yet she hadn't batted an eye to destroy an entire city, to kill hundreds of innocent people, to betray the person that she claimed to love the most in the most terrible way.

She leaned slightly towards me when she spoke again.

"Zeryth harasses Max because he sees him as a threat, and he needs to prove his dominance at every opportunity," she said, her voice low as she cast one brief glance to Zeryth at the other end of the ship. "He does the same thing to me, as is obvious. You are either Zeryth's friend — meaning, someone he can use — or a threat."

Possess or destroy. It was always the same.

"What he just saw will make you a threat to him," she said. "Be aware of that."

I almost scoffed. I would never allow Zeryth — or Nura, for that matter — to see me as dangerous. Not *really.* I would show them parts of my strength, yes. I would show them what I could give them. But even during my time in slavery, I never allowed myself to be seen as a threat. There was power in being underestimated.

"That would be silly of him," I said. "I am bound to the Orders. You know this."

"Just because he thinks he can use you doesn't mean he isn't also afraid of you. Be careful. You have too much potential to be eaten up by his primal temper tantrums. What a waste that would be." She gave me a quick, knowing glance. "Men want power because it makes them feel good. Women want power because it lets us *do* things. And imagine, Tisaanah, the things we could do with you."

Her eyes snapped back to Zeryth and didn't move, not even as she flicked three more blades from her fingers.

Thwimp, thwimp, thwimp.

This time, they were in a perfect line. And she gave me one little smile that unfurled over her face like frozen winter's breath — a little pleased smile that told me those knives landed exactly where she wanted them.

CHAPTER FIFTY-FOUR

TISAANAH

Four days. That's all the time we would have in Threll.

I was given two weeks total for my mission. Fourteen days. Five would be used to travel there, and five to travel back — maybe less, if we were lucky, but I couldn't plan for luck. As the days and hours and minutes ticked by, I found myself cursing the sun for rising too many times and the sea for moving us too slowly, even with the help of Zeryth, Nura and I moving the wind as much as we could to get us there faster. We were, after all, moving more than twice as fast as I did when I first came to Ara. Still, it was not fast enough.

The days ticked by.

We gathered to solidify the plan when we were less than twenty-four hours from shore, the misty outline of the Threllian continent barely visible in the distance. Once we landed, we could get to the Mikov estate very quickly, thanks to the Strata-grams that Zeryth had laid out over the course of his — apparently extensive — travels throughout Threll. We would not, I instructed, use force — not immediately. Not until I saw Serel and I had him in safety. I could not risk striking too early and having him suffer the consequences.

"And after that?" Max had asked, arms crossed as he leaned back against the mast.

"The whole purpose of this trip was to see what Reshaye is capable of," Zeryth added with a sharp smile.

I resisted the urge to correct him, or to allow myself to consider the fact that Reshaye still had hardly spoken to me since the sparring incident. Instead, I returned his grin with grim determination. "They will not let the slaves go easily. I'm sure that we will have our chance to fight. And to make sure that the estate will never hold slaves again."

"Excellent," Zeryth replied, sounding pleased with this answer, but it was Max's eyes that met mine across the room. Together, we dipped our fingers into a pool of nervousness and hunger and fire.

That night, our shoulders brushing as we watched the sunlight paint the sea with splashes of blood red, I could only think about time and our lack of it. *I was stupid. I should have asked for more.*

I did not voice that thought, but Max said quietly, "With the right kind of relentless brute force, four days is more than enough time to topple a Threllian Lord or two." As if, as always, he heard my buried doubts. And even though I didn't totally believe him — not completely — I still let out a slow exhale of relief, just to hear that hope solidified into words.

"It will have to be."

I COULDN'T SLEEP that night. I was so nervous that I could hardly breathe. Nervous just to exist in that space again. Nervous that I would fail. Nervous that I wouldn't. Nervous to see Serel again, after it had taken me so long to come back for him. And nervous that he wouldn't be there.

Throughout this trip, I had been constantly aware of the web of my own thoughts, forever conscious of Reshaye's cold darkness. I'd felt it moving and shifting and whispering, but nothing more, not even when Max was near me.

For a while, that had been a relief. But now, on the eve of our arrival, my own fragility loomed. I had one shot. Just *one*. And without Reshaye, I was nothing.

And so, alone above deck, I stood beneath the milky moonlight darkness. In the distance, I watched the outline of Threll grow closer and closer.

And I did what I never thought I would:

I tried to wake Reshaye up.

When I touched it, I was hit with a wall that sent me staggering — a wall of white and bright, unforgiving light, a flash of golden hair, the bite of fingernails into flesh. And, above all, *terror*, like I had reached into the thick of someone else's nightmare.

When I opened my eyes, I was on my knees, and Reshaye curled around my thoughts, scaling the web of my mind like a spider leaping from thread to thread. The remnants of its fear twined with mine in my veins. I forced my own back as I whispered quiet comforts to the quivering presence in my head.

Shh. You are alright. You are safe.

A growl rippled up my spine. *{Never.}*

You're safe.

{They did such terrible things.}

I wondered who "they" were. Zeryth? Nura? Max, even?

Or were "they" dozens of people spread over decades or centuries, the collected aggressors of a million fragmented moments? Perhaps Reshaye didn't even know.

I fed it my forced calm. *Many people do terrible things. But we can either eat our anger and make it fuel us or we can let it eat us alive.*

Reshaye inhaled the memory of my mother, her stern and beautiful face as she told me those words, then blew it back to me like smoke through its nostrils. I felt its unspoken question.

That is my mother. She told me that, many years ago.

{She is gone.}

Yes. She died a terrible death, just like the rest of my family.

I let it see the ropes, the chains, the wide-brimmed black hats. I let it see the broken bodies I saw come through slave marketplaces, people too old or weak to work in the mines to be sold off for scrap. I let it see the scars.

I felt it pick up and inspect each image like a curious child examining a new toy, intrigued but unmoved.

Fine. New approach.

Tomorrow, we go back to my homeland. And I want revenge. That was a concept I knew it grasped. It killed Max's family to punish him. It understood anger, even if it wouldn't understand my love. *Is that what you want, too? You know what it is to be angry.*

A skittering chuckle. *{Yes. It is the only solid thing that remains. Everything else has rotted away.}*

My memories withered like Max's flesh beneath my fingers. I had to fight my revulsion.

Then help me. I'll need you, when we get there. Only you. When I call for you, will you come for me?

And Reshaye shivered, shuddered, writhed, sinking further and further into my terrible memories until it hit the sharpest one of all: Esmaris's face, his sneer, the blood flecking his cheeks. It watched the images again and again, agonizingly slowly, as if dissecting them.

{You were betrayed by someone that you thought loved you.}

I could not bring myself to voice my confirmation, even though I knew, in a terrible, twisted way, it was true. Instead I asked again,

Will you help me when I call for you?

A long consideration.

{Yes,} it whispered, and slithered back into darkness.

CHAPTER FIFTY-FIVE

TISAANAH

The Stratagrams that Zeryth had laid out were staggered throughout Threll, intended to give him a network of touch points that he could leap between for quick and flexible travel. Still, "quick" was relative. We jumped to so many that my head was spinning by the fifth leap.

"When you're unfamiliar with the land," Max explained, between stops, "you can lay out Stratagrams to use as hooks to grab onto between jumps. But they can't be very far apart, a few miles at most." Even he, at this point, was starting to look a bit pale.

The first jump took us through the port city. The second, through the rocky ravines. The third, into a lush, looming forest.

But I didn't think it would hit me so hard, so deeply, when we made what must have been close to our tenth leap and we were greeted by rolling grasslands. Land that once, long ago, would have been Nyzerene.

The sight of those grass-covered hills, golden with brushes of autumn's mortality, dusted with distant hints of wildflower color, stole the words from my head and the breath from my lungs. If I squinted enough, I could see my family in the distance. Little silhouettes of a village brushing the horizon, a waving figure calling me home from miles away.

My home, I thought, the words lonely and mournful. *How could I have forgotten?*

The rest of the group shuffled away, moaning about their headaches or preparing for the next leap. But I just stood there, staring.

I felt the familiar presence of Max halt beside me.

"Welcome to Threll," I murmured. "Welcome to Nyzerene."

"It's beautiful."

Pride and sadness melded in my chest.

"I'm glad you got to see what I see when I remember my home. Before we go witness all of the terrible things that it has become."

"Me too," Max said, and we stood there for just a moment longer, letting the ghosts wrap around us, sinking into the beauty of my sad lost world.

Just for a moment, before we turned around and made another stomach-churning leap.

THREE MORE LEAPS.

By this time, my head spun every time we landed. To make things worse, Reshaye was growing more and more agitated.

{Now?} it asked, impatiently, with every landing.

Not yet, I would reply, with as soothing a tone as I could manage. But I was beginning to wonder if I had made a mistake by rousing it the night before. It did a tenuously good job of listening to me... so far. But I dreaded what would happen if it got fed up with my rejection before I was ready.

When we landed this time, it took me a moment to clear my spinning vision, to push Reshaye back, to put the rest of my head in order.

When I did, I blinked and found that we were standing on a long, dirt road. The path led up to a rising hill, upon which sat a building. Not enormous, but certainly imposing — constructed of golden brick that seemed to rise directly from the amber grass surrounding it, spires topped with rounded points that came to a curled tip like the dollop of frosting on a pastry. Perhaps it had once been beautiful, but now it crumbled and peeled with superficial neglect.

Activity surrounded it, people and horses bustling around its base. At the other side of the hill, I could see lines of figures making their way to its entrance.

My chest guttered as I realized what I was looking at.

"This was abandoned last time I was here," Zeryth said, frowning.

"This building is Nyzrenese," I murmured.

The architecture was very similar to that of the Threllian Lords, but the little differences were easy to spot if you knew where to look — the narrower windows, brighter shades of paint, square doors instead of rounded. One of our old governmental buildings, left to rot. Now used to cage and torture the people it once served.

I looked again to the lines of people traveling the paths and furrowed my brow. Walls and walls of terror hit me, shaking my knees. I had forgotten how powerful the emotions of large groups of unshielded minds were. And these? These slid between my ribs and clawed at my insides.

"Hey!" Two men on white horses trotted towards us, shouting in sharp Thereni. One raised a scimitar above his head, a clumsy threat. "What the hell do you think you're doing?"

Two men on white horses.

Two men wearing wide-brimmed, black hats.

My blood turned to ice. "Slavers." Of course. They did this — took up abandoned buildings to use as trading and transport hubs. I had been in many myself.

As if fueled by the shock that ran through me, Reshaye banged at my thoughts, eager.

{Now, we end them.}

Not yet.

385

The men rode closer, approaching us down the dirt road.

"If we Stratagram out, we do it now," Ariadnea said.

Zeryth gave me a curious look, unfazed, one eyebrow tweaked. "We don't *have* to go, if Tisaanah would rather intervene."

"There are maybe fifty men up there," Nura said. "Plus the slaves."

"For us? Easy," Zeryth purred. "What a wonderfully noble way to see what Reshaye can do."

The string of furious Thereni curses grew louder, coupled with hoof beats.

I looked up at the building, landing on a small figure in the approaching line. A child, with her wrists bound in front of her.

{Yes, yes, now!}

Not yet, not yet.

"It's up to you, Tisaanah," Max said, quietly. "One word and the place goes up."

We were so close to Serel. So close. And the odds here were not in our favor. Fifty men, compared to the seven of us.

But—

I looked at that child, her head craned up to squint at the building before her. I tasted her fear down to my bones. Her blood ran through my veins, and mine in hers.

And then my eyes fell on one of the many black-clad figures, a tall, thin man who turned to look over his shoulder at us, and my breath caught. Even from this distance, I knew that figure.

You ever buy unripened fruit at the market? he had said, looking at me like I was something to be devoured, in words that I would hear repeated in eight years' worth of nightmares.

"One of the men who took me as a child is here."

When I met Max's stare, fury rolled over his features like storm clouds, dark and cold and lethally still. He drew his staff from his back and readied it, warmth pulsing faintly where his fingers crossed its designs. Coiling. Waiting for my permission. "This belongs to you. I only move when you tell me to."

The hoof beats were nearly upon us.

I reached behind my back and wrapped my fingers around Il'Sahaj's hilt.

I saw those hats, their assessing gazes, the bodies of my slaughtered kin. And I was *angry*.

{Now? Now?}

"One word, Tisaanah."

My blade was out, the edge as sharp as the terror of the girl I was and the rage of the woman I became.

My eyes snapped to that one slaver and stayed there.

"Yes," I breathed.

Reshaye let out a triumphant laugh.

"Are you fucking deaf—" The approaching Thereni voice rose to annoyance, then sliced to sudden silence. Max's staff seared through flesh as if it were paper, a wicked, eager satisfaction settling into his face as we all flung ourselves into hell.

CHAPTER FIFTY-SIX

TISAANAH

The two approaching slavers fell as if they were made of sand. And just like that night, it was quieter than I expected it to be. Their words strangling into silence, their bodies falling with dull thumps onto the ground.

For a few seconds, everything was suspended. Me and my blade, Max and his, the Syrizen and their unsheathed spears. Sammerin, Nura, Zeryth poising for action — all of us ready.

And then, all at once, something snapped, and we plunged into dirt and blood. I buried myself into it with unexpected glee. I had not killed since Esmaris. Even at Tairn, I had managed to avoid it. But as my eyes snapped to that one man and stayed tethered to him, I wanted nothing more than blood.

I screamed out a rough, frantic command to protect the slaves, praying that it didn't get lost in the snap of chaos. Out of the corner of my eye, I saw Eslyn grab Sammerin and disappear with him, reappearing fractions of a moment later near the glut of terrified slaves. Good. Because I couldn't think about them.

There was only one place I wanted to go.

I relinquished just a few threads of my mind to Reshaye. Just enough that I felt its power cackle through me, rising the hairs of my arms, twining with the intoxicating, overwhelming emotion that I sucked through every breath.

I grabbed minds like handfuls of skinned grapes. And I relished the way that the slavers' terror ran down my arms just like their blood did when I rammed Il'Sahaj through their chests. Every strike of the blade left rotten smears of decay, even shallow near-misses blooming with putrid black flesh. Reshaye threw itself into every shred of control I gave it — first with glee, then with impatience.

{More,} it demanded.

Not yet.

This was mine. Mine alone. And I needed the power over my muscles that I maintained with such desperate mental energy — with so many innocents here, I could not risk that.

Still, maintaining that control grew more and more difficult as I drowned in the agonizing, bloodthirsty euphoria that was solely mine, and the confused terror that wasn't. Max was beside me, filling my nostrils with the scent of burning flesh, and he sank into this brutality with a precise grace that was darkly beautiful.

There was nothing graceful about what I was doing. If he was a dancer, driven by years of training and lethal precision, I was an animal drunk on hunger and instinct. But he protected me, covering up the sloppy mistakes of my rage, responding to every silent request of my movements.

I looked at no one but that one tall, thin slaver. He grabbed for his scimitar, but scampered along the walls of the building, ducking through the door like a terrified rabbit seeking its den.

I fought my way to him. I hardly felt the blood spatter across my face as I struck down the guard in the doorway, or the wound that he slashed across my arm when I failed to hit my target. For one split second, the slaver's fat fingers curled at my arms. I ceded more control to Reshaye and let it wither his hands until he screamed — until Max tore him off of me and threw him against the wall, opening him from his navel to his throat in one slash and letting his mushy, smoldering gore spill over the floor.

My body shivered with Reshaye's laughter, with its pleasure, with its unsatiated desire.

{More, more, more,} with every beat of my rapid heart and every inhale of rage, hands yanking at my mind with increasing desperation.

I hardly paused at the dead guard, flying into the house with a lurch only to stop short. It was so dark inside that my eyes struggled to adjust. And the *fear* hit me all at once, as thick in the air as the sweaty scent of bodies and urine. Through every open door, I saw the glimmering whites of eyes and fingers that trembled around ropes and rusty shackles.

A ragged breath tore through me. Gods, it was just — it was too much. My memories of my time in places just like this burned my throat like acidic bile. I stumbled. Nura and Zeryth flew past, sealing those rooms, clearing the hall. They killed so easily.

Max's hand brushed the small of my back. A wordless note of concern when he couldn't stop moving or fighting long enough to speak.

{Do not stop!}

I wasn't.

Couldn't, even if I wanted to.

I stood in a large lobby, a sweeping staircase opening before me. The steps were already filling with the frantic bodies of the remaining slavers pouring downstairs, blades drawn. One lunged for me. One touch — one brush of my sword — and his flesh turned to ribbons of pus and rot.

His body had not hit the ground when my eyes once again found who I was looking for. The tall, thin man had retreated to a corner beneath the stairs, his black hat discarded to reveal pitifully thin hair on the head that he bowed, as if keeping his eyes to the floor would keep him from being seen.

Him. *Him.*

All of my exhaustion faded away into the background of a single memory: that night, again and again.

Too young to whore. By some standards.

One surge through the mass of bodies, and I was upon him. I grabbed him. Threw him to the stone ground. Felt my throat release a wordless, groaning cry.

I wanted to watch him suffer the way I had suffered.

{More, more!}

Reshaye gulped my anger, still begging for more control. Holding it off grew further and further from my thoughts.

The slaver's arms shielded his face — already marred with rotted handprint wounds from my touch — mouth flapping in gummy pleas. "Please, please, don't— *Please —*"

My people had begged too.

I stood over him, feet on either side of his hips, Il'Sahaj in my hands. "Do you remember me?"

"Please, please..." His face lolled, pressing against the floor, eyes squeezing shut.

"Look at me!" I thrust Il'Sahaj's blade in his face and used it to turn his cheek. The flesh of his face withered into decay where the metal touched it. I relished his squeal of pain. His fear pulsed through me like a hideous, intoxicating drug.

"Don't kill me," he wept.

Bastard. *Bastard.* There was no recognition in his eyes — nothing but that cowardly panic.

He took everything from me. Killed my family members in their beds. Sold a child to a terrible fate. Me, and so many others.

And he didn't remember.

{It is not enough,} Reshaye hissed.

"Remember me," I snarled. A command, not a question, as I opened my palms to release streams and streams of butterflies — crimson, putrid wings spewing into the air as violently as the spurt of blood and the smoke of funeral pyres. They kept coming, surrounding me even as I closed my hand around my sword's hilt again, as if they were peeling from my skin.

I heard my name, faintly, far away.

I ignored it.

"Please," the man moaned.

391

He did not remember. He did not care to remember.

I was nothing to him. Invisible and unseen, just another body to use and sell and ruin, the same as so many who came before and after me.

And maybe it was the same for me. I looked down at the old man cowering on the floor and noticed the pudge to his cheeks, the sharpness of his nose. Was this really the same man that I had met all of those years ago?

Did it matter?

The bloody red butterflies clouded the air, sticking to the floor, the ceiling, the walls and to my soul.

Not enough. Never enough.

{More!}

I let my rage consume me.

{NOW!}

An animal cry escaped my throat as I raised Il'Sahaj over my head.

And when the blade came down — when it spread lightning-fingers of decay over the slaver's body — my hands were no longer my own.

Tears streaked my cheeks as Reshaye lifted my chin and let out a manic, howling laugh.

CHAPTER FIFTY-SEVEN

MAX

I was no longer looking at a woman.

I was looking at a fucking goddess. A goddess of death and vengeance and utter, indiscriminate destruction. She could be nothing else – standing there in her white jacket so spattered with blood that it soaked crimson, sword raised, those scarlet butterflies forming a cape around her shoulders.

"Ascended above," I rasped to Sammerin. "Did *I* look like that?"

"Yes," he said. "You did."

The butterflies clogged the air, spreading down the halls. And when Tisaanah straightened, the wooden floorboards blackened beneath her every step.

The slaver that I was fighting blanched and stumbled, eyes wide. I took the opportunity to run one searing slash across his throat, never looking away from her.

"Incredible," I heard Zeryth gasp.

The remaining slavers, at least the ones close enough to get the full effect of what they were up against, began retreating.

Or at least, trying to. They didn't get far. She dragged them back with yanks of invisible hands, withering their flesh with mere brushes of her sword.

And her expression —

It wasn't Tisaanah's rage or her pain or even her angry satisfaction that greeted me when those mismatched eyes flicked to me. No. It was empty, glazed-over glee.

That was Reshaye. That was *all* Reshaye.

Those putrid butterflies grew so dense that I could only see her in flickers through their wings. One hit Sammerin's arm and he hissed as he wiped it away to reveal a smear of rot.

I grabbed Nura's arm. "Get those people out of here." I jerked my chin down the hall – to the rows of rooms that I knew held the slaves. "Through a window if you have to."

The tail end of my words were drowned out by a howling screech as Tisaanah – Reshaye – rotted out another slaver alive. There were only a few remaining now.

I issued the same command to the two Syrizen, who went flickering off into the opposite direction.

Tisaanah turned around. I saw those empty, unfamiliar eyes settle on one of the ajar doors. I heard the whimpers of fear coming from inside.

And I didn't – couldn't – give myself one sorry second to think before I leapt in front of her, my staff crossing her path.

Her beautiful mouth spread into a bloody, furious grin as her accentless voice hissed, "Move, Maxantarius."

CHAPTER FIFTY-EIGHT

TISAANAH

I was being ripped apart, and I loved every eviscerating second of it. I smelled nothing but blood, could feel nothing but the withering of my enemies' skin beneath my own. I sank into it and let myself drown — turned myself over to my pain and my vengeance.

And it took me too long to realize exactly what I had relinquished. That I not only didn't *want* to stop, but that I *couldn't* stop. My attempts to control my own body were met with that same thick glass wall, just like they had that day in the sparring ring with Max — but more painful, more vivid, because I was drunk on Reshaye's euphoria, like every one of my nerves were firing at a hundred times their typical strength.

I fought the fog and pounded on the glass.

Let me back in.

{No.}

I threw myself at it, dragging my fingernails down it like claws. *Let me back in!*

A wave of suffocating pleasure clouded my senses as another body hit the ground, withering beneath my hands. *{You asked for my help. This is what I give you.}*

But even its voice sounded slurred and drugged. It gulped every scrap of emotion, of terror, like shots of liquor.

Body after body hit the floor.

No. No, I couldn't let this happen.

I forced myself to calm, to breathe. Not a wall, I reminded myself. A web. A breath, and the layout of my own mind once again spread out before me in threads of glittering silk. But— but this time, something was wrong.

The threads weren't arranged in complicated but neat clusters. Instead, they tangled. And they weren't alight with delicate white light. They were on *fire*. Blue, black fire that crawled down the threads, as if drawing them into a closing fist.

I tried to sever them. Tried to push Reshaye back into its secluded corner. But I was greeted with a vicious strike, as if I were being slammed into a wall, then bound, ropes tightening around my throat.

Except, the ropes were my own memories.

The blurry, half-remembered image of the capital of Nyzerene burning.

The burn of my mother's goodbye kiss on my forehead, and of Serel's on my cheek.

I don't need your money.

Hands — hands on my wrists, my body, my breasts, the whip that sliced my skin again and again and again.

Panic. Panic rising and rising, rising so high that I almost didn't even see Max's face before my eyes.

Don't, I begged, before Reshaye let out a withering snarl and slammed a blanket of black over me.

Shutting me into darkness and drowning me in my own terrible past.

CHAPTER FIFTY-NINE

MAX

I searched her face for some sign of my friend, but I saw no trace of Tisaanah in those features or that voice. My stomach sank.

Come on, Tisaanah. Come back.

"You're done," I said.

A pained sneer formed over the bridge of her nose. "It is not enough."

"You're done," I repeated. The red butterflies still streamed from her skin, clustering around her like wings and rising to the ceiling. But they were deformed now, little more than flapping blobs.

"Come back, Tisaanah. You're still there."

For one moment, she stared at me, and hope leapt in my chest.

And then the sneer deepened.

"*We* are not done," she snarled, and lifted Il'Sahaj into a vicious slash.

Fuck.

I blocked her, then again, and again. Every time her sword clashed against my staff, black crept up the liquid fire that pooled in its divots. Her magic was overtaking my own, hijacking the veins built into my weapon. My palms began to burn where my skin touched the metal. A butterfly collided with my forearm and I winced at the ensuing pain.

I thrust the metal back in one violent push, hurling her against the wall. She hit it, then stumbled, taking a moment too long to find her footing. The way her legs lurched told me that Reshaye still did not have complete control of her body.

A perfect opening. The part of me that was a trained fighter knew the movement so well that it twitched in my arms. Any other opponent, and that would be the end.

But this was not any other opponent. This was Tisaanah.

And all I could bring myself to do was pray that the moment of stunned impact might give her the opening that she needed to seize her own control.

Instead, her head lolled for only a moment before her eyes settled on me and she lunged.

I blocked, wincing as the skin on my palms burned.

Where was Sammerin? I couldn't even see through these fucking butterflies. I could only take my eyes off her for split seconds at a time, but when I could, I searched over her shoulder into that morass of red.

Another lunge. Another block. Another rush of decayed black.

"You stifle yourself, Maxantarius." Her nostrils twitched. "Why are you so afraid?"

I pulled away. My feet danced over dead bodies, each step deliberate to avoid slipping on a floor covered in gore and oily rot. Only for us to clash together again, her mouth offering a small, thoughtful smile.

"I already know what you really are. I know everything about you." The smile soured. "I gave you those gifts. And yet, you never—"

The black crawled further up the veins of my staff.

Ascended, my fucking *hands*—-

She went for another slash, and again, I evaded her.

"Would be an excellent time to come back now, Tisaanah," I barked.

Please, Tisaanah, I know you can do this.

The world went red, then white. Suddenly my back was against the wall and my side was on fire. When I opened my eyes, I saw fresh blood dripping from Il'Sahaj's glittering blade. A blade that she raised, and then —

I ignored the scream of my body as I rolled out of the way.

She lurched again, her movement sloppy and too slow. And there it was again, an opening: I could slash the backs of her calves. It would force her down. Easily repaired, if I was clean about it.

If I was clean enough. If I wasn't, she might never walk properly again.

I raised my blade, setting up the movement. But then my eyes met hers for one moment, and my heart lurched, and my hand paused for a moment too long.

And then another figure appeared out of nothing, flickering to life like a shadow emerging from those red butterflies and striking Tisaanah's back with lethal precision.

I heard only my friend's voice as she let out a cry of pain. And I knew I should take the opportunity as I saw her fling Ariadnea off of her, as I saw her stumble as blood ran down her back. But my hands were still. Even as she straightened and turned to me with a frenzied glare. Even as she raised her blade again with a shriek.

But then, she froze. Her body twitched, and then lurched. I'd only lived this, never seen it from the outside, but I knew exactly what was happening.

I didn't need to look to know that Sammerin was beside me, one arm raised, his brow knotted in concentration. He drew his fingers into his palm. Tisaanah's body let out a sickening series of cracks as it lurched to the floor, her limbs askew.

The butterflies were dripping down the walls like thickened blood.

Her eyes clung to mine. Fury melted into terror. She let out a strangled sound that didn't sound human. Probably because Sammerin was tying her muscles into knots, forcing her lungs to shrivel until her brain relinquished consciousness.

I dropped to my knees beside her. Rot was still pulsing across the floorboards, softening them beneath our feet. I didn't notice. I didn't notice anything but the way her terrified gaze found mine and looked nowhere else.

I'm sorry, I wanted to tell her. *I'm so sorry.*

Her breathing convulsed, fighting the whole way as her eyelashes fluttered.

Crack!

If I'd been able to look away, I would have seen that the wooden beams of the building were beginning to give beneath the tendrils of decay.

"This is coming down." I heard Nura's footfalls land beside me. "Time to go."

I scooped Tisaanah up in my arms and stood, and I didn't look at anyone as I carried her out of the building, her limbs suddenly limp as Sammerin released her body from his control.

CHAPTER SIXTY

TISAANAH

To call them nightmares would be like calling a typhoon a "light drizzle."

I spent hours tangled within the worst of my memories, all mashed together, all attacking me and strangling me at once. They were reality, but worse — my mother saying goodbye to me as her flesh withered and eyeballs fell from her sockets, Esmaris raising his whip as his skin turned to shadow and flames. And no matter how I clawed and fought, I couldn't get out. They dragged me back every time.

By the time I awoke, it was past sunset. I was in a makeshift bed in a tent, Max at my side before I was even aware enough to recognize him. An encampment, apparently, had been set up relatively quickly. Zeryth, Nura, and Max explained to me what had happened. I listened, numb.

"You were *spectacular*," Zeryth said, smiling.

I didn't feel spectacular. I had been shut out of my own mind.

I looked at Zeryth, but didn't reply to him. Instead I turned to Max and stood, ignoring the way the ground shook and slid beneath my feet. "Show me."

He obeyed. Together we walked up to the top of the hill

where the Nyzrenese building had stood. *Had* stood. Now, it crumbled. Half of it remained upright, barely, while the other side toppled into chunks of stone and wood. One of the remaining columns stood precariously off-kilter. Patches of red crawled over some of the stones, stark and aggressive even beneath the moonlight.

I looked down the other side of the hill, to plumes of black smoke in the distance.

"Bodies," Max stated, following my gaze.

"Slavers?"

"Yes. Every last one of the bastards."

I thought I might feel more. "And the slaves?"

"We have more than one hundred and fifty people in that camp." He pointed back towards the encampment — tents and campfires dotting the hillside.

"Was that all of them?"

I hated his ensuing silence. A lump rose in my throat.

"*All* of them?" I pressed.

"One was hit by falling stone when the building came down. Sammerin did his best, but he died."

He died. I appreciated the straightforwardness of that statement. No "he didn't make it." No "we couldn't save him."

He died. He died because of my lack of control. And the only reason why more didn't was because Max had stopped me, and Sammerin had forced me down.

My numbness cracked, but didn't shatter.

"I want to see them," I said, gesturing to the camps, and Max nodded.

He took me down to walk through the clusters of people. There weren't enough tents for every person, but the night was clear and temperate, so many people set up around little fires. They weren't all Nyzrenese. The Threllians, after all, had conquered and enslaved nearly half a dozen countries, and I could tell from the various accents dotting the air that nearly all of them were represented here. But though they may have been born into different nations, they might as well share blood now.

They all gathered together in exhausted peace. Comfortable, at least. They had managed to save a good number of supplies from the slaver hub, Max told me as we walked, which explained the tents, food, and sleeping arrangements.

I heard wails punctuate the quiet conversation and stopped. My head turned to figures gathered near the edge of the camp.

A warm hand pressed my shoulder. "That won't help anything," Max murmured. "Trust me, I know." But I pulled away anyway, and he didn't try to stop me.

The body was bound in tatters of white fabric in a makeshift Nyzrenese shroud. It was small and slim — perhaps a teenager. A selfish part of me was grateful that I couldn't see his face.

A middle-aged woman wept over his body, flinging herself over him, frizzy brown hair shaking around her face in time with her sobs.

My numbness broke, and her grief assaulted me in a wave so strong that it drowned me.

I opened my mouth, but said nothing. What would I say? That I was sorry? That I offered my condolences, my prayers, my respect? What value would that be to her — prayers from the woman who had killed her son, blessings from the gods that had allowed him to die?

My throat shuttered. I turned away before their eyes could find me, but I was a little too slow. I heard the whispers start as I took my first steps away from the fire. And I felt their recognition rise from the camp like steam as eyes, one by one, flicked towards me.

I kept my gaze straight ahead as Max and I walked back to my own tent. But I didn't have to look at them to feel it, and I didn't have to listen to them to hear their whispers. They were afraid of me. *Witch*, their shuddering thoughts said. *Monster*.

THE RIPPLING GRASSLANDS were just as beautiful beneath the moonlight as they were under the amber glow of the sun. I let my back sag against smooth tree-trunk bark and watched it flow.

I had stared at the roof of my tent until the hum of activity outside lapsed to silence. Then I rose and tread with bare feet through the camp, all the way out into the plains. There, I settled by a tree and several wildflower bushes to look out over the rolling lands and *think*.

I was not surprised when, not long after, I heard quiet footsteps approach. I didn't have to look to see who it was. There was, after all, only one person who ever joined me for my midnight thoughts.

"You too?" I asked, and Max let out a scuff of a laugh.

"Me too."

He settled beside me. I heard rustling and glanced at him to see him pinching dead blossoms from the wildflowers, then crumbling them to ash in little bursts of fire within his palms. Just as he had in his garden — just as he had the first time we sat together at night in the aftermath of a too-close brush with death.

"Sorry." He folded his hands in his lap when he noticed my gaze. "Habit."

"No, I—" *I love it.* "It is probably good for them."

He squinted down at the flowers, cerulean blue with white-tipped petals. "I wonder if I could get these to grow at home."

"The weather is very different."

"Nothing the right spell couldn't fix."

My eyes slid down the hill, falling on the distant tents and sleeping figures sprawled around smoldering fires. One hundred and fifty people with no homes. Some had asked to return to their own townsteads, or what was left of them. But many had chosen to travel back to Ara under the official protection of the Orders. Ara, a country where they could be free — but a country that was so wildly different from their homes, where they had no property, no friends, no money, and no language.

If only it would be as easy to help them take root.

"Wherever they go will be better than where they would be

right now, if you had not helped them," Max said, following my gaze.

I thought of that shrouded body and his mother's wails. *Not all of them.*

"The last thing I remember," I said, softly, "is my hand on the door, and your face. Nothing else. Only... pictures here and there." Flashes of blood, rot, red butterflies. Frames of my fight with Max. My eyes fell to Max's side and ran up, reliving a memory I barely grasped of my sword snaking along his ribs. "I know you're hurt, even though you did not tell me."

He looked away. "I'm fine."

"But what if you weren't? What if *they* weren't? What if —" I shut my eyes and in that moment of darkness, I relived Reshaye's frenzied, all-consuming hunger. "It was like it was *drunk*. It felt every death, and it..."

"It thrives on it," Max finished.

"It would not have stopped." My throat tightened. "And I had no control. I was so far from control that I don't even *remember*. What if that happens again?"

"We won't let it."

Was that enough?

The things that I could have done... the thought of it strangled me with petrifying fear. My eyes burned, blurred. And then I said something that I had never, ever said aloud before. "I don't think I can do this. I don't think I'm strong enough."

Silence. I traced the abstracted shapes of the grass and gravel, mostly because it seemed like a much more manageable alternative to looking at Max's face.

"I want to tell you a story," he said, at last. "After the war ended, after... everything... I was a mess for a long time. Years full of cheap alcohol and Seveseed dens and aimless wandering and not much else. And one night, I started a typical miserable fight at a typical miserable pub and got my typical miserable ass kicked out on the cobblestones. It was a frigid winter that year, so I was wandering around the streets of the Capital shivering like a drowned rat."

I'd drawn my legs up to my chest, rested my cheek on my knees to look at him. His gaze slid to me, and I was a little startled by the fact that he looked almost shy, embarrassed. "And, as we all know, I'm not made for that."

I chuckled.

"So," he went on, "I stumbled into the next open door I could find. It was this — this little bakery that had been set up for the night to show off these paintings..."

His gaze drifted farther away, sliding into the memory. I wondered if he knew how much his expression reflected his thoughts when he spoke. Or how much I loved that about him. "They were nothing special, to be honest. The artist mostly painted his wife lounging around in a garden, and let's just say it was easy to tell that he was an amateur painter. But there was just something so *genuine* about them. I could just *picture* him slaving over every little blobby line." He gave an awkward chuckle. "I was *very* drunk."

I let my eyes close, and I was there with him.

"But what really did me in was when I was looking at this one enormous painting. A real labor of love. And the date written on it..." He cleared his throat, a little, strangled noise. "It was the same day as Sarlazai. While I was off in the mountains, doing... well, *that*... Somewhere, miles away, this man was just sitting in his garden, painting his plain wife with the reverence fitting a fucking goddess. And that just... *hit* me. It hit me so hard that I wept like a heartbroken fourteen-year-old girl. Because I had forgotten."

"Forgotten?" I whispered.

"I had forgotten that people could be that way. I had forgotten that someone, somewhere, was painting terrible pictures of their wife in a garden. I was so far gone that I didn't even remember that that kind of mundane contentment actually existed, least of all in the same moments as such terrible things."

My heart clenched. I nodded.

"I didn't exactly have a wife I could ask to flop around on benches for me, and I can't paint for shit. But after I cried myself to depletion and sobered up, I thought to myself..." His shoulders rose in a tiny shrug as his gaze slipped back to me. "I thought, 'Well. I can make a garden.'"

Planted every flower. It was obsessive, Sammerin had told me, once. An understanding clicked into place. I closed my eyes as my fingers found the necklace around my throat, my thumb pressing against the third Stratagram at the back. The one that would take me back there. "It was a very nice garden."

"The best damn garden in Ara."

Gods, I hadn't known how much I would miss it.

There was a long silence. And then Max's voice was more solemn, most hesitant, as he said, "You gave me that same feeling, Tisaanah."

My breath stilled.

"Not right away," he went on. "Though, I will admit, '*It says snp snp*' was fairly charming from the beginning. But a couple of weeks later, when you told me why you had come to Ara and what you planned to do... I'd just forgotten that people could *be* that way. That there were people who just wanted to do something good for the world."

My eyes burned. I had wanted that — desperately, I wanted it, even though now that goal felt so far out of reach. My mother and Serel had sacrificed for me because they believed in the greater things I could become. But with the echoes of that woman's sobs scarring my ears, I felt nothing but shame.

I glanced at Max, at his solemn stare, and there was something about the way he looked at me that pierced through all of that — all those doubts, all those insecurities.

"But you are so much more than that, too, Tisaanah," he said, softly. "I think you forget that. You pushed as hard as I did and saw everything worth seeing and regaled me with your, frankly, *terrible* jokes, and... you became my friend. Your goals made me respect you, yes. But it was everything else that made me —"

He shut his mouth, cleared his throat, looked away. Then back. "I told you that together we would find a way to do this, and I meant it. But I stand with you until the end. *You*, Tisaanah.

If you wanted to run, I swear we'd find a way out. And if it all goes up in flames, I'll burn right beside you and it will still be the best thing I — "

I didn't realize I was crying until I tasted salt.

"Stop."

Suddenly, it made sense.

What do you want? I had asked Max, so many months ago. And I had never quite managed to answer that question, not completely. But now I understood. I understood why he believed in me so much. Because more than anything, Max wanted to believe that one person was capable of making something change. Because —

If you can do it, I can do it.

I choked out, "You can do it even if I can't."

A wrinkle formed between his eyebrows.

"It's easy to die for someone," I said, "but it is so much more valuable to live. I do not give you permission to fail if I fail. Do you understand me?" When he didn't answer, I pressed, "Do you understand?"

"Yes," he whispered.

"I don't believe you." I placed my palms on either side of his cheeks, resting my forehead against his. He still smelled like ash and lilacs, like he had carried the remnants of his garden all the way across the sea. "You are the best of men, Maxantarius Farlione, no matter how much you try to convince the world otherwise. Promise me that you'll keeping fighting your battles even if I lose mine."

"You won't — "

"*Promise.*"

His fingers found my face, tracing a warm trail down my cheek. And then, as if a thread had snapped, he pulled me into a sudden, fierce embrace. I sank against it so smoothly, my arms sliding over his shoulders, my knees adjusting so that I curled around him.

"I promise," he murmured into my hair.

I hoped he wouldn't expect me to let go, because I wouldn't. I wanted to drown here, in the way his chest and heartbeat and breath felt against mine. A desperately needed reminder: *We are still alive, and we are still together.*

I turned my head, just slightly, so that my face was pressed to the smooth skin of his neck, so that I could breathe him in and hold his smell in my lungs.

I brushed my lips against his throat.

His fingers tightened at my back, and that touch seared up my spine, heartbeat rising to the surface of my skin. And in that moment, a truth solidified in my heart, my soul, my blood — a piece of me that wanted nothing more than to seize this chance.

Because I wanted *him.*

I wanted him in so many ways. As a friend, as a kindred soul, as a fierce teammate. As skin and lips and teeth. As a hitched breathless moan in the darkness or a lazy embrace in the sunrise. I wanted that. I wanted it all.

I grazed my mouth over his skin again, relishing the sensation of the silent groan that dragged through his breath. I followed it higher, to the corner of his jawbone, skimming my lips over the angle of it, over the raised texture of the little scar there.

A silent question.

He shuddered.

Shuddered and jerked away from me, just far enough so that his eerie, bright eyes bore into my own —

As he blurted out, "This isn't what I want."

CHAPTER SIXTY-ONE

MAX

T*his isn't what I want.*
It all depended on the definition of "this" — whether those words were unshakably true or the biggest fucking lie I had ever told anyone else or myself.

Still, the sentence leapt out of me before I could stop it. And the hurt that careened across Tisaanah's face gutted me. "Oh."

Her mouth turned down. She had a perfect mouth, with a top lip slightly fuller than the bottom, and corners that always, always curled up just a little at the very edges. Even now.

It was an effort not to stare at it. It always had been.

Right. It all depended on the definition of "this."

If "this" was the sensation of her lips against my neck, or that little sound that I suspected she didn't even know she'd made, or the way that she felt enveloped in my arms…

If "this" was the sound of her voice, or the way she saw the world, or her stupid jokes…

"I never expected this from you, Tisaanah," I choked out. We were still so close. Our noses almost touched. I could barely focus on the words I forced out of my mouth. "Almost every single person in your life has used you. And I'm not— This isn't—"

And I wouldn't be another one of those people, unwittingly or not.

This isn't what I want.

If "this" was her lips, her body, her kiss, her touch, I would be lying if I said I hadn't thought about those things. If I hadn't had to shove them into a dark corner of my mind, never to be disturbed, never to be addressed.

But if "this" was her friendship, her companionship, her trust? Her happiness? Her safety?

Those things were worth more to me than anything else ever would be. Downright precious.

And for that, I would throw everything else into a box and lock it away never to be acknowledged, permanently, if that's where they needed to be. I had already been prepared to do that.

My thumb swept over her left cheek, where gold skin met white. "We can erase the last minute and a half, Tisaanah. Never speak of it again."

She whispered, "Is that what you want?"

"Is that what *you* want?"

We were so close that our breaths mingled. Hers was trembling. Or was it mine?

There was no hesitation as she whispered, "No."

Something wrenched in my chest. Something I couldn't, or perhaps wouldn't, identify.

"Today was a hard day," she murmured. "I saw things that scared me. I did things that scared me. I want to claim you tonight because maybe we won't have tomorrow. So, no. It isn't."

Claim! I was not even remotely prepared for the reaction that inspired in me, a dizzying, near-primal desire that scorched my every muscle. I never thought that word would sound so appealing.

"Is that what *you* want?" she asked. "To forget it?"

The moonlight glinted in her eyes as she stared at me — those stunning, mismatched eyes, that now, as they always did, saw right through me. Her gaze was tired, her hair tangled and messy, her clothing oversized and simple. And yet, I suddenly found myself unable to breathe, because to call her beautiful would be such an understatement that it was downright insulting.

My chest tightened again, and I realized what it was that I'd been feeling:

Terror. Sheer terror.

This isn't what I want.

Because that look always pierced through every lie.

And it went so far beyond a kiss, or a touch, or an embrace, or sex. If I opened that door, I would be handing her something so much deeper than that. And I knew the opposite was true, too — that I was being entrusted with something precious.

"Max?" Her fingers were at the sides of my face.

I shook my head. "No," I murmured. "No, that isn't what I want."

And with those words, the tension snapped.

We both moved at once. She fell forward against me, and I slid my arms around her, pulling her closer, my mouth lowering to meet hers. First as a caress, just testing the way her lips felt against mine. Then in something deeper as we settled into the same silent language — a brush of her tongue sending a shudder up my spine, and the reply of my own teasing a tiny, wordless groan from Tisaanah's throat.

Ascended fucking above. That sound. I decided that I could spend my whole sorry life learning new ways to coax it out of her.

I felt her lips warm into a smile. "Tent," she whispered, though she could barely get the word out because we didn't stop kissing long enough. "Now."

Hell. Who was I to question?

CHAPTER SIXTY-TWO

TISAANAH

One glance from Max, and the lanterns all flickered to life at once, bathing the tent's spare interior with a delicate orange glow. The door had hardly closed behind us before we yanked each other back into an embrace.

I had never kissed anyone like this before, and now, I never planned to stop. It was like walking into a world of color when all I'd ever seen was black and white. I loved the way he tasted — loved the way his mouth offered me long kisses and short ones, teeth occasionally claiming my lips in little, affectionate nibbles, tongue skimming mine. When his mouth moved to my cheek, I mourned it only for a moment before he trailed kisses down to my chin, to my jaw, lighting fire to my neck.

My knees were going to give out.

I — somewhat ungracefully — dropped to the ground, falling over my bedroll, Max's hand still in mine. He followed with a movement that was far smoother, lowering himself to his knees and crawling over me. Gods, I had never seen anything so beautiful — the grace of the movement, the intensity of his focus on me. It was so wrenching that I wished I could capture the image and save it forever.

And then his weight was on top of me, and his mouth smashed against mine, and I once again lost all capacity for thought. No, I was nothing but nerves, impulses responding to his touch, back arching against his body.

My hands raked over his back. I could feel his muscles, his movements, beneath the thin cotton fabric of his shirt, but I wanted skin. I only managed three buttons before Max yanked the shirt off over his head.

"Wait," I whispered, stopping him as he began to lower himself to kiss me again. He straightened, and I took the opportunity to just *look* at him.

"Well, *this* isn't fair," he said, raising a pointed eyebrow as his eyes fell to my shirt.

"Be patient."

I ran light fingertip touches over the line of his shoulder, down his chest, up the other side. I paused at the scar on his left shoulder — where I had wounded him in the sparring ring. Then I trailed my hands over the lean muscle of his abdomen, across the ridges of his ribs. He let out a hissing exhale that may have started in arousal but ended somewhere closer to a hitched chuckle.

"I can't remain appropriately seductive if you're going to tickle me. It's going to ruin my image."

The scar over his ribs was longer, fresher, still mottled with angry purple. I only vaguely remembered running Il'Sahaj's blade across his side. This wasn't even a clean cut, the scar thick and wavy. With the rot, I'm sure that Sammerin probably had to remove all of the decayed flesh before —

"I see you, Tisaanah." Max caught my hand in his. Then lowered himself over me and pressed his lips right between my eyebrows, where the tension of my thought had pooled. "No thinking," he whispered, against my skin.

And just as I was about to wonder how, exactly, I was going to fulfill that request, he gave me a kiss that made it all too easy — impossibly easy — to comply.

The warmth of his body hit me through my clothing, but still —

His hand slid up my side, pausing at the button at the apex of my neckline. Waiting for silent permission.

My hands met his, tearing it off me, and then there was nothing between us but our skin.

I still could not pull him close enough. I wanted to touch him everywhere, wanted to drag my nails across every muscle.

When his hand ran up my side and settled over my breast, his whole body shuddered. So did mine. Desire burned in my core. Suddenly, I was unbearably conscious of his weight between my thighs. Of the touch of his fingertips as they ran up the insides of my legs. Not as high as I wanted them to be.

Not enough. Never enough.

I yanked at the button of my breeches. Max sat up, straightened, helped me pull them off. Captured my leg and planted a kiss on the inside of my knee. Then further up, on the inside of my thigh, this one punctuated with a gentle close of his teeth, a rough curse beneath his breath.

Need, new and unfamiliar and utterly consuming, overtook me.

Then he sat up, straightened. The world suspended for one long moment, silent save for the quiet cracking of the lantern wicks. I felt his gaze sweep over my body, slowly, as if drinking in each inch. Felt it, not saw it, because I turned my face, self-conscious for reasons I couldn't totally understand.

My body had always been one of my most valuable commodities, and I used it as such. It had never bothered me to be looked at.

But then again, Max wasn't just *looking at* me. He never had. This was being *seen*, barer than I ever had been before. No counted dancing steps. No costumes. No false confidence.

"I wish I was better with words," he murmured. And when I could finally bring myself to turn back to him, the sight of him caught in my chest and squeezed — that face, the gaze that met me with such bare, raw honesty.

I was in love with him.

The thought floated through my mind, simple and unshakeable. Undeniably true, even though I couldn't bring myself to say it. Even if maybe, in the end, I wouldn't be able to keep him.

"You do not need them," I whispered back. A truth we both understood for fact. Especially when I looked at him and saw my silent confession reflected back at me.

My fingers ran down Max's sides, settling at narrow, muscular hips and running along the waistband of his trousers. Unbuttoning. He let out the most beautiful sound I had ever heard, a heavy exhale that dragged its claws over me with the hint of a groan.

That one movement broke the thread of tension as we fell upon each other again. I tasted every inch of him, every expanse of skin, and relished the way he unraveled as I traveled down his chest, over the cords of his abdomen, and lower and lower, until he grabbed my shoulders and dragged me back up to his face. "Not now," he murmured, the words muffled by an impatient kiss as he flipped me beneath him.

I hardly had time to prepare myself before his fingertips slid between us. Slid into me. My back arched. The world went white.

Gods below.

"Not now," I whispered, and his hands didn't stop as the breath of his chuckle unfurled against my mouth.

"Maybe I want to take my time with you."

"Just like you." I had to focus very, very hard on forming each word. "It always takes you so long to do things."

My breath hitched. I heard the smile in his voice as he responded, "And you're always so demanding."

Demanding!

I dragged my fingernails down his arm, shifting my hips lower. And then I finally hooked my legs around him — finally felt him settle at my entrance. I pulled away from him enough to meet his gaze.

"I win," I whispered.

"My ego will never recover."

The smile faded, and he smoothed tangled hair back from my face.

"You're sure?"

I was sure of nothing anymore, except for this.

My teeth skimmed his ear as I answered, "Yes."

He gave me one long, passionate kiss, and pushed into me.

And my whole world unraveled, expanded, narrowed. My back arched. Awareness was limited only to this. To the places where we were connected. Where he was inside me, yes, but also every inch where my arms wrapped around him, my legs, our stomachs. For a moment, he just held himself like that, pressed within me, and I could feel him trembling. Our lips were against each other's, sharing ragged breath.

Nothing — *nothing* — could ever feel this good. This right.

I let out a little moan, dragged my fingernails over his back.

And something about that snapped some invisible thread of tension.

He withdrew, then plunged back into me. I met each stroke, my hips rolling against his. Our bodies asked and answered, ceded to each other, moved with unhindered intuition.

Together, we burned.

I rolled over him, pressed myself against his chest, and he clutched at me like he still couldn't decide which part of me he wanted to touch most, taste more. He settled for all of it: my lips, my neck, my breasts, his hands running up and down my back, my legs, the growing heat where we were connected.

My thighs clenched around his hips, as if I could pull him deeper. I felt myself building, rushing to a wild edge, and for the first time in my life I relished that utter lack of control, threw myself into it. And I knew he was, too, because his movements were faster, thrusts wilder. He sat up so that he could pull me to him, and I lost all capacity for words, for thoughts, for anything but instinct.

Maybe I said his name — whispered it, or moaned it, or

shouted it. I wouldn't know, because the end obliterated me, a pleasure so intense that I shattered.

And he followed me over the edge of that cliff, his fingers in my hair, his lips uttering a groan against my neck. His hand grabbed mine and squeezed, fingers intertwining just as our bodies did. He clutched me like he would never let me go.

And he didn't. Not even as the wave crashed over us, as the pleasure subsided into a numb, beautiful tranquility.

We fell back amongst blankets and lay against each other, our panting slowing to something deeper and smoother. Max lifted a lazy hand to lower the flickering of the lantern flames. I nestled my head against his chest and watched his knuckles around mine dim beneath the lowered light, our skin falling into the cool silence of shadow.

Still, he did not let me go. Not as his breath deepened. Not as my vision blurred. I never looked away from those hands.

My last thought, as sleep took me, was that I wouldn't mind at all if I was tethered to his harbor forever.

CHAPTER SIXTY-THREE

MAX

I was caught in quite a predicament.

On one hand, I had a beautiful, nude woman draped over me, her face nestled against my neck and slow breaths tickling my skin, and I felt truly content for the first time in weeks — hell, years. It would be so easy to curl up with her and fall into an enticing rest, clinging to the wonderful notion that she would be there when I opened my eyes again.

On the other hand, I had a beautiful, nude woman draped over me, her fingers drifting sleepy circles over my chest, and neither of us had any idea what would happen to us come sunrise. Maybe one or both of us would not make it out alive. Or maybe we'd immediately be whisked back to the Orders to go fight the next war, once this one was over.

Maybe Reshaye would tighten its hold on Tisaanah and steal any promise of future moments alone together, which was a prospect that terrified me so deeply that I pushed it from my mind.

Either way, who knew how long it would be before we could be this way again? And maybe I *needed* sleep, but did I really need it any more than I needed her? Than I needed to spend every possible second inside of her, or touching her, or watching her, or listening to her? I wanted to memorize every sound she made, every expression, every freckle or mole, like I was a cartographer tattooing a map of her onto my soul. Still so many paths to chart.

Sure, I was tired. But there was *work* to do.

Tisaanah's circles drifted, turning to lazy S shapes over my stomach. I bit back a twitching laugh. Not well enough.

"What a beautiful giggle," she teased.

"Letting you find out that I'm ticklish will be the biggest mistake I've ever made."

Her fingers drifted lower. Ticklishness was no longer my problem.

I craned my neck to look down at her. She blinked back at me with one green, half-open eye, her hair a flurry around her face, kiss-swollen lips twisted into a mischievous little smile. Ascended, that smile. Maybe I knew from the beginning that it would be my undoing.

I raised my eyebrows, as if to say, *Really? Again?*

"Too tired?" She lifted her head, letting tendrils of black and silver hair dangle over my face. "You would rather sleep?"

My hand ran down her side, following the warmth of her skin and the curve where her waist met her hip.

What a predicament, indeed.

I pulled her face to mine, resigned to my noble sacrifice. "If you can do it, I can do it."

———————

I DID, eventually, have to pry myself away. The sun had not quite risen when I defied my every instinct and removed myself from Tisaanah's arms, throwing my clothes back on and giving her a — fine, two; fine, three — goodbye kisses. We were in mutual agreement that it was better to avoid the awkward questions that would come with my leaving after sunrise.

The dusky darkness met me with a wall of cool air that was

one part refreshing, one part depressing, like a physical manifestation of how different the inside of that tent was to the rest of the world.

In there, I could remove myself from reality and think about nothing but Tisaanah for five blissful hours.

Out here, we were surrounded by displaced people whose homes had been destroyed, and we were on our way to fight the most powerful house in Threll.

Well, that was more effective than any bucket of cold water: *Oh, yes, now I remember. Everything is terrible.*

I kept my steps silent as I moved across the path to my own tent, glancing to the other darkened tents and sleeping bodies to my left. Tisaanah's tent sat on the outskirts of the camp, beside mine, so it wasn't far. Still, I was careful not to wake anyone as I opened the flap—

"You smell like debauchery."

I jumped so high that I had to bite back a curse, whipping around to see Sammerin seated cross-legged beside the path, in front of his shelter. With his dark clothing and his typical quiet demeanor, he practically melted into the dusk.

"Shit, Sammerin, don't do that to me." I stepped towards him, examining his face while trying not to let him know I was doing it. "Don't you have more productive things to do? Like sleep, for example. Perhaps that would be a better use of your time."

Even in the darkness, it was easy to see that shadows pooled beneath his eyes, his quiet amusement weighed down by exhaustion. Yesterday had been a long, hard day for him. Lots of people to heal — and, of course, putting down Reshaye took a massive amount of energy. When I last saw him, he was so spent that he practically had to drag himself back to his tent.

Sammerin just looked at me, that knowing look sparkling in his eye, and raised his eyebrows slightly. "Have fun?"

"I don't know what you're talking about."

"Max, what's this?" He pointed to his tent.

I knew this was not going anywhere in my favor. "I'd love to play this game, but I have all kinds of important things to do."

"This is a tent. A shelter constructed of fabric. Fabric is a material not known for its sound dampening qualities." He said all of this in that perpetually smooth, calm voice, but his tired eyes glittered with laughter. "You're lucky that I'm the only one close enough to hear."

The thought of Zeryth — or *Nura* —

I cringed and tried not to show it. "Firstly, I am a gentleman and therefore, again, I have no idea what you're talking about. But secondly, if I did — *theoretically* — I'd find it highly, highly suspect that you listened to that."

"Be assured that I tried very hard not to. But at least we got the inevitable out of the way." Then, something shifted in his expression. The amusement faded. "I hope you're both ready for today."

A knot formed in my stomach. Right. In hours, Tisaanah would be walking back into the home of the man who had — well, I didn't even want to think about all of the things that those people had done to her. She — *we* — were about to take on the most powerful house in Threll. And I'd have to watch her put herself in that kind of danger. And, of course, Reshaye…

"I'll be more ready after another hour of sleep," I grumbled, shoving my anxiety down my throat.

Sammerin stared at me with that searching concern for a couple of seconds longer, then shrugged. "At least if you die, you'll die happy."

"Fuck you."

"I don't need anyone's leftovers."

I stifled a chuckle as I went into my tent.

CHAPTER SIXTY-FOUR

TISAANAH

He had been gone for minutes, and I already felt his absence like an aching emptiness in the center of my chest. The tent was colder without him. Goosebumps were forming on my naked skin. And I could already feel the looming shadow of anxiety encroaching at the edge of my thoughts.

Anxiety. Reality.

But I tried to take just one more moment to lie there in the afterglow. I flattened my palm against the bedroll beside me. Warm. His scent — our scent — still hung in the air, sweet and familiar and unfamiliar all at once.

I'd heard about it, of course — all that sex could be. But sex didn't even feel like the right word for what this had been. Sex was the tool I had wielded for survival, practiced and impersonal. This was... more. It wasn't just about the bodies, or even the physical pleasure of it. It was vulnerable. It was trusting. And I never thought that it could feel so good to open myself up that way.

But gods, it had. So good it was terrifying.

I was still lying there like that, my hand pressed to those sheets as I begged them not to cool, when I felt it.

A voice. *The* voice.

{You got what you wanted.}

Reshaye was weak and tired, its words gritty with exhaustion that echoed in my own bones.

That brought me back to reality, fast. It hit me so suddenly that I didn't have time to steel myself before my body stiffened, the memories of yesterday and the nightmares I had endured careening into me like a physical force.

My stomach turned and I prayed that it wasn't talking about Max.

{Revenge,} it whispered. *{I gave you what you wanted.}*

My relief was only momentary. The image of those nightmares, of my hand on the door, of Max's face, of the mother's wails —

{Yet, you are angry with me.}

My heart stopped.

No.

{You are. I smell it. I taste it.}

It turned colder and colder, coiling around my thoughts like a snake.

I am not angry with you.

{You cannot lie to me.}

Its confused hurt seeped into my blood, tainting it in unfurling tendrils. I hated the way that it turned over all of my thoughts, encroaching dangerously close on the ones that I wanted only for myself.

Please — I began.

But then, everything stopped.

And I felt a sudden jolt of sharp, furious betrayal.

It brushed a memory of last night — the faint image of Max's hand running over my stomach. I yanked the memories away from it before it could see more, stuffing them into the back of my mind.

But it clung to the image. That one little fragment. Max's fingers on my skin again. Backwards. Again. Backwards. Again.

{What is this.}

A daydream.

{Show me what this is.}

It embarrasses me for you to see my fantasies —

{You cannot lie to me! You cannot!}

The words shook me, a roar that tore from inside my body.

{Now I understand. You are abandoning me just as he did. The two of you, together —}

No! Never —

But its next words hissed through me with the acid green of jealousy.

{I gave you everything. I gave both of you everything. And you betray me, too?}

I —

Gods, I was tired. I was so tired, and so afraid, and my mind couldn't form the right words — and all this, when it had *locked me up —*

{I DID lock you up! Just as you did to me!}

You were going to kill innocent people, and you were going to —

{I was giving you what you had asked of me. I gave you what you wanted and you gave yourself to HIM. The two of you conspiring against me.}

Fingers on skin. Two seconds of memory, over and over again, cycled obsessively.

{Show me the rest.}

No. I couldn't. I wouldn't. That was the only thing that was real, the only thing that was *mine.* I forced myself to calm down. This was dangerous. I needed to be careful. I needed to count my dancing steps.

You gave me gifts beyond my imagination. I would never —

Pain crackled at the edge of my vision, stealing the breath from my lungs. My fingers tightened around fistfuls of linen.

It slammed itself against my thoughts, raking fury down the back of my skull, flooding over my tongue with the sharp pain of heartbreak.

All I could think about were Max's memories. His memories of Reshaye, the day it had taken everything from him.

All I could think about was everything I had to lose, here on sheets still warm from everything precious to me.

And in my panic, I threw at it the only thing I could think to offer. The thing it wanted most of all. The thing that I had always sold in exchange for the safety of myself or the people I cared for:

I love you. I love you, Reshaye.

One terrible moment. Fingers on skin, again, again, again.

{You cannot lie to me,} it hissed, as it fell back into silence like a wave retreating from the shore, leaving behind nothing but the scarred remnants of its fury.

I NEED you! I cried.

Raw. Honest. The ugliest truth of all.

But by then, it was gone.

CHAPTER SIXTY-FIVE

TISAANAH

My encounter with Reshaye echoed in my head long after sunrise. It lapsed into total silence, so still that I could only assume that it was still recovering from the day before, but that didn't mean that it didn't still loom over my every thought.

I felt ill.

Especially when I left my tent beneath the harsh light of sunrise and saw Max for the first time since everything had changed between us. He had stopped in his tracks and just stared at me, somehow managing to look serious despite a tiny reluctant smile quirking at the left side of his mouth, and my chest had tightened and all I could think about was the way his skin tasted.

But only for a split second.

And then my thoughts had turned to Reshaye and its jealousy. I hated that its fury and its absence both frightened me equally. And above all, I hated the way that fury had latched onto Max.

Selfish. I had been so selfish. Because if Reshaye hurt him because of me — if it hurt him with *my* hands —

I had managed only to give Max a distant, weak smile before

launching myself into logistical preparations for the day. We
gathered the camp in early morning, and even though they were
terrified of me, I had to direct the people we had recovered.
Zeryth and I were, after all, the only ones who spoke Thereni,
and Zeryth's accent was far worse than I'd remembered.

Halfway through this process, Max snatched me away in a
brief quiet moment, pulling me behind one of the remaining
tents. His hand remained on my arm, thumb swiping in the hint
of a caress. He regarded me with a wrinkle of concern between
his eyebrows.

"What's wrong?"

"Nothing is wrong."

"Don't patronize me." The wrinkle deepened, and he hesitated before asking, "Is it— are you having doubts about–"

"No," I said, quickly. "No, never."

He looked visibly relieved, though only for a moment. "Then
what?"

I didn't say anything. The thought of tainting what had
happened between us in his mind, too, made me feel even sicker
than I already did. And worse was the thought that Reshaye
might witness my confession somehow—

"Do I need to start guessing? I've always been bad at that,
but–"

I swept my fingers over my mind once, twice, three times,
checking for any activity before I lowered my voice and whispered, "Reshaye knows."

Every muscle in Max's face hardened at once. "What did
it do?"

"Nothing. It— nothing." Checked again. Nothing but darkness. "I will not let it do anything."

I wish I believed that.

"None of us will," Max said.

I wish *he* believed *that.*

He slid his hands around my waist. I wanted nothing more
than to sink into that warmth, retreat back to last night and
never return to reality.

Instead, I could barely make myself meet his eyes.

"Listen to me, Tisaanah. I mean that. We controlled it yester-day. We'll control it again. *You'll* control it again."

I didn't control it yesterday.

I was silent, leaving my uncertainty undignified.

His arms tightened around me, breath skimming my ear. "We walk in together, and we walk out together."

He was trying to convince himself, I knew, his desperation merely masquerading as certainty. My chest ached. My hand slid up to his shoulder, and I could feel the raised texture of the scar I had given him through his shirt. Merely a scratch compared to what I *could* do.

If Reshaye came after him using my hands, my body, would he let it happen?

"You made a promise to me last night," I choked out. "I need you to keep it. Whatever that demands."

And before he could say anything else, I yanked him towards me and gave him one long, hard kiss.

Then I pried myself away and returned to the preparations without another word.

THE PREPARATIONS WERE WELL under way and hours had passed — hours of torturous doubts — when Zeryth beckoned to me from across the camp. When we were out of earshot of the others, he informed me, far too casually, that he would be returning to Ara with the refugees.

My heart sank. "Why?" I asked, sharper than I had intended.

"Someone needs to escort them. I speak Thereni." He slipped his hands into his pockets, breezy and casual. "And, I have Order business to attend to at home."

He spent almost six months traipsing around Threll, and *now* he needed to rush back to his office?

Anxiety had gnawed at whatever was left of my patience. It took palpable effort to control my tone as I said, "You are very respected. It would be helpful to have your skills and reputation with us today."

He just smiled that forceful, dazzling grin. "You don't need me. At least, if what I saw yesterday was any indication, you're more than capable of doing what needs to be done."

That was with Reshaye, who might not even help me anymore. Who might be too dangerous to unleash so close to my friends.

"But in our pact—"

"Our pact mentions nothing about *me*. It offers you support. Which, clearly, you have in spades." The pointed glance that Zeryth shot across the field, to Max, was not lost upon me.

I made my eyes wide, dipped my chin, cocked my head. "But you are *important*."

Desperation was making me lose my grip on subtlety. I was certain Zeryth would see my behavior for what it was. If he did, he didn't show it. He just gave me a dismissive pat on the shoulder.

"You do what you need to do here. I do what I need to do there. And then I'll see you back at the Towers." The hunger that glinted in his eye almost made me shudder. "I'm sure you'll have plenty of fun at the estate. In fact, maybe even more than you anticipated."

I raised my eyebrows in a silent question, and Zeryth's smile glittered. "I took the liberty of writing to Ahzeen Mikov to tell him of your arrival today. He is always so eager to have important guests, after all."

Of course. Ahzeen cared about nothing more than status, and hosting high-ranking members of the Orders was certainly an honor — especially if it came at the personal behest of the Arch Commandant.

"In fact," Zeryth went on, "he was *so* glad to be receiving such honored visitors that he wrote back with invitations to an event he's hosting tonight. A celebration of victory, apparently, over one of his enemy Lords. Receiving the generals home, flaunting his great wealth and vast power, all of that."

I was very familiar. I had danced at so many of those parties, flirting for silvers at a time. But my mind snagged on one particular phrase: *receiving the generals home.*

Serel was a guard. Serel was fighting Ahzeen's wars. And Serel, perhaps, would be among those returning.

"This is your mission. It's your choice how you want to approach it." Zeryth shrugged. "But, if you wanted to attend..."

He reached into the inside of his coat and pulled out two folded pieces of paper. One was a Stratagram, presumably the mate to the one Zeryth laid out at the Mikov Estate. And the other was a foiled invitation with words inscribed in flowery Thereni script.

"If I recall correctly, you're very fond of dramatic statements at fancy parties."

He offered me nothing more than a shrug and a smirk as he turned and sauntered off, leaving me standing there, looking down at that platinum paper and running my thumb over the raised lily sigil.

Every powerful Lord in Threll would be there. All in one room, ready to bear witness to what one former slave could become. And how poetic it would be, to devour Esmaris's legacy where it had once devoured me, little by little, night after night.

I'd be lying if I said that wasn't appealing. But Zeryth underestimated me by implying that the spectacle of it all would be my main draw. The party offered that, yes. But it also offered something much more valuable: the opportunity for the most beautiful of distractions.

The corners of my mouth began to curl as an idea unfolded.

I could do this.

I could free the slaves of the Mikov estate, and I wouldn't even have to use Reshaye to do it.

Somewhere deep inside of me, beneath the unease and anxiety that had plagued me all day, a wicked flower took root.

CHAPTER SIXTY-SIX

MAX

I looked down at the guard's outstretched hands, only barely hiding the twist of distaste that tugged at my lip.

"Don't make such a sour face." Tisaanah crossed her arms, arching an eyebrow at me. "You know we have no choice in this."

Fine. Unsuccessfully hiding.

Reluctantly, I unstrapped my staff from my back, casting one more glance out over the city as I turned.

Everything about this place put me on edge.

I wasn't sure what I was expecting, but it wasn't quite this. When we first arrived at Mikov's Court, I realized why people spoke of the lands of the Threllian Lords with such awe. This wasn't an estate. It was a *city*. A city that rose up from the grasslands like a gleaming ivory mountain, tiers of white marble cascading up until they culminated in Ahzeen Mikov's palace.

It was beautiful, yes, but in the ugliest of ways. I looked at all of that finery and I wondered how many tattered backs it took to build it, and how many sparks it would take it bring it back to the earth.

And I lingered particularly long on that last part, especially

when I saw the way that Tisaanah's demeanor had shifted, ever
so slightly, the moment we Stratagrammed into this city. Back at
the camp, I was relieved to see her light up again with that
particular relentlessness once she figured out her plan — that
woman did, after all, *love* a plan. But that force dulled a little as
soon as we stepped foot here, even though she tried not to show
it. She still held herself like a queen, but she was afraid, and I
hated that this place could do that to her.

Especially as we met slave after slave in the shadows —
friends of Tisaanah that had agreed to help us with our little
project, a risk to them that was not lost in any of us for a second
— and I was reminded over and over again the past that she was
confronting.

Now, we stood in the shade of the gates surrounding Ahzeen
Mikov's home, nestled into a tiny nook of privacy between buildings as activity buzzed just feet away. The party had already
begun. Two guards stood with us. One shifted uncomfortably
from foot to foot, looking anxious. The other, the one trying to
take my weapon from me, regarded us with fascinated interest
that made me feel a bit like a caged curiosity.

"We can't exactly walk into a party armed to the teeth," Nura
said, unstrapping the daggers from her hips. Easy for her to say.
She probably had seven hidden blades shoved into her under-
wear alone.

"I don't see why not," I grumbled.

I did, in fact, see why not. I was just being difficult.

I sighed and handed my staff to the guard's waiting hand,
eyeing it as he placed it against the wall.

To be fair, the Syrizen looked even more uncomfortable with
the prospect than I did. Ariadnea and Eslyn clung to their spears
until the last possible moment, relinquishing them with the reluc-
tance of a parent turning over their firstborn child.

"We will get them back when we need them," Tisaanah reas-
sured us.

My gaze flicked to her, and I managed to be startled, yet
again, by the way that she looked. She wore a red silk dress that

wrapped and tied around her waist, shimmering fabric closing billowed sleeves around her wrists and the skirt falling into a loose pool around her ankles. Simple, but *distractingly* striking, especially since the fabric was so light and delicate that it settled into every peak and valley of her body. And the whole damn thing was held to her only by that one knot at her waist.

Despite the circumstances, I still couldn't help but imagine tugging on one end of that bow and watching all of that fabric slide over her skin and settle onto the floor.

Apparently, it had been hers when she lived here. A maid friend of hers had left it for us, among other supplies, in a hidden package beyond the gates. "It was actually a nightgown," she told me, sounding somewhat embarrassed, when she first put it on and twirled. "Can you tell?"

Yes. But in the best of ways.

But later, I caught her rubbing the silk between her fingers, brows furrowed, lost in thought. And I realized all at once who gave her that nightgown, and under what circumstances she had probably worn it, and I wanted to tear it off her for a very different reason.

Tisaanah thanked the guards in Thereni, exchanging some words that I didn't understand but sounded encouraging. The nervous one kept glancing to the throngs of people in the street in a way that unsettled me.

She turned back to us, letting the guards depart first. "We are ready," she declared.

I watched our weapons disappear with the guards as they rounded a corner. "You're certain we can trust them?"

"Yes." She followed my gaze, a little smirk tugging at her lips. "Don't worry. Pieces of metal are not our most dangerous weapons."

True. The one that lurked in Tisaanah's mind scared me more than any of the people we were about to face.

When an appropriate amount of time had passed, we went to the street and approached the estate gates. As planned, we were quite late for the event, so the entrance had begun to empty, only a few straggling guests lingering outside.

The gates parted like giant, golden jaws.

I stayed beside Tisaanah. I didn't need to look at her to feel the way she stiffened as we passed beneath the shadow of the marble archway. I caught her hand briefly in mine and squeezed before letting our palms slide apart.

We would walk in together and we would walk out together, I swore. And in between, we would do what we came here to do. It just had to be that simple.

I rubbed my fingers together, reassuring myself with the warmth of flames that licked my skin.

Right. The metal was not my only weapon. And if it came down to it, maybe it would be nice to rip these bastards apart with my bare hands. All the better to go a little slower.

CHAPTER SIXTY-SEVEN

TISAANAH

The walls of the Mikov Estate closed around me like teeth, threatening to crush me back into the girl that I had been six months ago. I hadn't been prepared for the sheer physicality of it — the way that simply seeing those white columns, those white-clad bodies, those golden lily sigils would strike me the way Esmaris's whip had, opening wounds in my soul that I thought had long ago healed.

Every muscle in my body was tensed as we were led through that familiar archway, into the den of luxury and excess that had once been my home. And the party was the same as they always had been, the present superimposed over the past. I found myself instinctively looking for Esmaris, ready to defer to him, to play to his moods and expectations.

Yet... I had stepped into a surreal, inverted mirror image of my memories. When I attended all those identical affairs, I had been a slave. But in this one, guests watched us pass with gazes of wary respect. Servants bowed their heads. Maids stepped aside and averted their eyes. And the horns lifted, and the page's voice raised to announce us as we walked in. Not as servants, but as guests of honor.

"Announcing the most honored and esteemed guests of Ahzeen Mikov, the representatives of the Orders of Midnight and Daybreak!"

Hundreds of pairs of eyes turned towards us, perched atop swathes of billowing white fabric. But I didn't look at them. No, I looked only at a single familiar figure across the room, lounging at a table that sat several feet higher than all the others: Ahzeen Mikov. The sight of him hardened my fear into fury.

His gaze settled on us, and he smiled.

"Ah, yes! Representatives, let me express what a deep honor it is that you were able to attend. We are all very excited to have you here."

Gods, I had forgotten how much he looked just like his father. Yes, he was younger, thinner. Yes, there was that eyepatch, gold and glittering beneath the moody candlelight. But when he looked at me, I still felt as if I were withering beneath Esmaris's identical gaze.

I don't need your money.

Twenty-six.

Crack!

Reshaye writhed through my thoughts, as if the burst of adrenaline had shaken it awake.

Ahzeen stood at the head table, arm raised, a glass of red wine perched in his fingers. Everyone, in fact, was holding red wine. A room of billowing white marked with splashes of crimson.

"Your timing is excellent," Ahzeen said, beckoning us further into the room.

I smiled. "It is our honor to be here, Lord Ahzeen."

I braced for the impact of his recognition. Surely, he — surely *someone* — would know who I was. But his expression didn't change. I waited for something that did not come. Ahzeen simply regarded us with the sharp interest befitting a group of very important guests, not the shock befitting a former slave.

We were led to a table near the center of the room, wine glasses handed to each of us. I had to hold mine steady, even though my hands desperately wanted to shake — first with nervousness, and then with mounting indignation.

I really was nothing to him. To any of these people. I had always known that slaves were given little thought or consideration in this world, but it was only now that I fully realized exactly how *nothing* we were. I had, after all, *met* Ahzeen, twice. He had once thrown me against the wall, reeking of wine, too drunk to even effectively paw at my dancing costume. Esmaris had yanked him off me before it could go any further. At the time, I thought he was protecting me. Now, I realized that he was merely defending his property from a lazy and undeserving son.

That was the night that had ended with Ahzeen being thrown out of the gates, eye gouged out. A night I remembered so vividly that I still knew exactly how the damp warmth of his breath felt against my cheek.

And he had no idea who I was.

"Please, join us." He lifted his eyebrows, raising the glass once more. A ripple of red whispered through the room as the guests did the same.

I did too. Out of the corner of my eye, I saw my companions follow my lead, even though I knew they couldn't understand what was being said.

I could practically feel Max's revulsion. And even though I was glad that he hid it for the time being, something about it still comforted me.

My eyes swept across the room, and my heart stopped.

There, near the second entrance, nearly lost behind the bodies of white-clad guests, I caught a glimpse of golden hair. Golden hair and a pair of wide, watery blue eyes.

Serel.

"To our honored guests, who grace us with their presence today from the faraway towers of Ara," Ahzeen began. "To my honored Generals, who led us to victory yesterday against the house of Rivakoff."

Serel. Scarred, tired-looking, thinner than I had left him. But alive. And *here*.

Even through all of these people, even from across the room, I felt his emotion hit me and meld with my own. Shock drowned out by relief drowned out by profound, unwavering *love*.

He was *alive*.

My eyes burned as I watched his face twitch, the corners of his mouth wavering between a smile and the grimace of tears. I could only chance little glances at him. Too many eyes were on me. And I didn't trust myself to look at him for more than a fraction of a moment without letting my composure crack.

Still, I gave him one glance — one little glance — that reached across the crowd to whisper, *I told you I would.*

And he returned it with one that said, *I knew you would.*

He stood shoulder-to-shoulder with Ahzeen's other guards. I recognized many of them, and their recognition reflected back at me. They saw what the lords did not.

"...to the memory of my great father, Esmaris Mikov, whose legacy we gather to avenge..."

Reshaye stirred, inhaling the strength of my emotion.

My relief.

My love.

My fury.

This — *they* — were the reason why I was here.

"...and, above all..."

My eyes found Ahzeen again, and for a moment, through the flickering candlelight, I saw his father.

I saw the man who had raped me, who had whipped me, who had nearly killed me.

I saw the man who had sent my friends to their deaths. The man who had sanctioned the torture and rape of dozens of slaves.

I saw him, and I smiled.

Reshaye purred.

He smiled back, and I drank up his satisfaction from across the room as he thrust his glass higher into the air. "Above all, to *victory*."

I threw my head back and drank the wine, wiping the

crimson that stained my red lips with the back of my hand. And I let the glass shatter onto the marble floor as I strode into the center of the room. The dancers – my replacements — awkwardly stepped aside, casting uncomfortable glances to each other.

"Ahzeen Mikov." I cocked my head and gave him my most enrapturing smile. "Have we met before?"

The musicians had gone silent. I felt the attention of the crowd like a physical force wrapping around me. I grabbed it and drew it closer.

Ahzeen's eyebrows furrowed, an uncomfortable smile at his mouth. His bemused confusion tasted sour and sweet at once, pungent in the space between us. "I do not believe so, my lady."

The room began to darken.

I smiled and pulled on the sash at my waist. The silk of the nightgown rippled like water as it slid over my body and pooled around my feet, revealing one of my old dancing costumes — one swath of fabric over my bust, a floating skirt low around my hips.

I stepped forward and planted my palms on the head table, leaning over Ahzeen. I was so close that I could smell the saccharine scent of his cologne and the oils that had been worked into his hair, which hung in a neat black ponytail over one shoulder.

"What about now? Do you remember me now?"

The wrinkle of confusion deepened. "I—"

1, 2, 3...

I sucked the light from the air, coating the room in a hazy mist as I stepped backwards with light, lilting leaps. I opened my palms to release a cacophony of sparks. Silver butterflies danced from my fingertips.

4, 5, 6...

"And what about now?" I purred.

Look at me, I commanded, just as I had when I had stood in this very room, hundreds of times before. *Look at me like I'm the last thing you'll ever see.*

And just as they had then, they all obeyed.

CHAPTER SIXTY-EIGHT

MAX

No one was looking at anything but her. Even I struggled to tear my eyes away.

I had never seen her like this before. It was incredible, the way she summoned their attention and refused to let it stray. Tisaanah unleashed spectacle after spectacle, body writhing, feet bare against the smooth stone floor, a smear of color in a world of white.

"Now," I whispered to Nura, who nodded. Slowly, we fell to the outskirts of the ballroom. Easy. No one so much as glanced at us. They were all too enraptured by *her*.

I pressed myself against the doorframe and kept one eye on Tisaanah as I watched Eslyn and Ariadnea inch along the back of the room and out the door. In the back hallway of the servants' entrance, slaves were lined up against the opposite wall.

As planned, the two Syrizen began to take hold of slaves, one by one, and flicker away into nothingness. There were wards surrounding the Mikovs' city that prevented the use of Stratagram travel — basic security, after all. But the Syrizen moved through layers of magic much deeper than Stratagrams...

making Eslyn and Ariadnea two of very, very few people in the entire world who were capable of slipping those locks.

Now, they were silently taking slaves and depositing them at a rendezvous point outside the city gates. All while the most powerful people in Threll stood mere feet away, utterly entranced by Tisaanah's performance. The perfect distraction.

Unease still stirred in my stomach, leaving me slightly dizzy. But I'd be honest: I didn't think we could get this far.

I watched Tisaanah unleash wave upon wave of translucent butterflies, climbing onto Ahzeen's table as the room grew darker and darker, eliciting gasps from the audience.

If I hadn't been so nervous that she would get killed at any moment, I would have laughed at her exaggerated dramatics. But then, they were no surprise. Tisaanah never did anything halfway. And if she was going to create a distraction, she was going to create the most distracting distraction ever to distract.

In the servants' hallway, slave after slave disappeared.

Ascended above, I thought, *this might actually work.*

I found the guard boy across the room who had taken our weapons. Made eye contact, preparing for the signal.

Any minute now.

CHAPTER SIXTY-NINE

TISAANAH

I was drunk. Drunk on the glass of wine that I had gulped down, yes, but also drunk on the attention of the crowd. A buzzing headache throbbed behind my temples, but I didn't have to fake my grin as I rolled off of Ahzeen's table and twirled to the center of the room.

"And what of these?" I said, gesturing to my scars. "Do you know how I got them?"

I didn't dare chance even a glance at the servants' door, or what happened beyond it. But I did catch Max's eye, just once. I loved the way he looked at me.

Reshaye's delight had begun to sour, hissing and spitting like a cat at the back of my skull. Still, it ignored me, refusing to speak.

That was fine. I was doing quite well without it.

I smiled at Ahzeen, even though my headache spiked. "Your father gave them to me. The night that I killed him."

Ahzeen's one visible eye widened.

A shocked wave of whispers rippled through the crowd.

I didn't stop dancing, basking in the scale of what I had just said.

Ahzeen leapt to his feet, his furious recognition rolling over me all at once. Oddly enough, it didn't hit me quite as hard as I would have expected it to, considering the fierceness of his reaction.

"A mere *slave whore* could not have killed Esmaris Mikov," he snarled.

"A slave whore did indeed."

I scanned the room, watching the other Lords and ladies whisper furiously to each other. Odd that I didn't taste their reaction in the air — but I could see it, the scale of their surprise and their judgement.

Ahzeen Mikov, I knew, did not want to remember me, even if he could.

Vos had already told me that Ahzeen had all of the information he needed to at least suspect that I was responsible. But it did not help Ahzeen politically to punish some faceless, nameless slave. No — Ahzeen needed power. He needed respect. And in the world of the Threllian Lords, respect was earned through honor and dominance.

"Liar," Ahzeen hissed.

"Which one of us is the liar?" I stopped at his table, blinking sweetly up at him. "How many wars did you use your father's death to justify? How many Lords did you kill in his name?"

If I had not been so transfixed on the delicious rage on Ahzeen's face, I might have noticed that the room was beginning to brighten again.

I might have noticed that, beneath the pounding of my headache, Reshaye had gone silent.

I might have noticed that I couldn't hear or feel the rippling emotions of the party guests.

Instead, I watched Ahzeen's lips curl into a sneer.

"Fragmented cunt," he spat, sending flecks of spittle across my face as he bore down on me. "I knew the Orders were threatened by me. But I thought more highly of them than to send some wench to topple the most powerful family in Threll."

And *then,* as that sneer split into a terrible, cold smile, I noticed.

I saw his hand raise, and in the split second before he brought it down, I tried to shoot a gust of air at him to push him back.

I tried, and nothing happened.

His hand collided with my face with such force that I went careening to the ground. But I didn't think about the pain. I only thought about one terrible realization as my blurred vision settled on the broken remains of my empty wine glass:

The world had gone dull, like half of my senses had been cut off.

I had no magic.

CHAPTER SEVENTY

TISAANAH

"When I heard that a group of Order Wielders would be coming here, well, of course I had to take my precautions, considering that the Orders had been quite uncooperative in offering their assistance."

I let out one steady, long breath as I pushed myself up from the ground. Ahzeen paced circles around me. His voice was too loud, too confident. He was showboating.

"But *this*. This is more than I expected. A spy and a seductress come to turn my allies against me. Or, my stolen property returned to me. *Get up.*"

His fingernails bit into my skin as he yanked me to my feet. I was so dizzy I could hardly steady myself, but I straightened my back through sheer force of will.

For the second time in my life, I saw my plans topple before me.

What was I going to do?

My eyes found the slaves gathered at the edge of the room, looking on in veiled horror. The expression on Serel's face cut a dagger through my guts. I couldn't bring myself to meet their gazes. Instead, I looked only to Ahzeen, meeting that one dark, hateful eye with equal intensity.

He smiled at me, an ugly, joyless movement. "I do remember you now. You and your beautiful dances. Why don't you perform for us, whore?"

Whore. I hated him. Hated that word. Hated the anonymity of it all. "My name is Tisaanah."

"Your name is whatever I want it to be."

Commotion drew my gaze at the other end of the ballroom, and my chest seized as I saw the fight break out — guards trying to capture my companions. Glimpses of blood.

No. I would not let this happen. It would not end like this.

Think, Tisaanah —

A vicious impact struck my face, and my body once again collided with the stone ground.

And another one — a kick to my stomach that sent me curling in on myself.

Something stirred weakly at the back of my mind.

"Get up."

I did, even though my body screamed. I didn't let it show. As soon as I hit my feet, he struck me again.

Pain bloomed through my skull, but I straightened as if it were nothing, locking empty eyes back on Ahzeen.

Uneasy whispers ran through the crowd. *How unseemly,* they were muttering. *How uncouth.*

My vision swam, and it was a struggle not to laugh. Two-faced hypocrites.

Ahzeen had always lacked restraint. And that was his greatest crime: not beating me, but that he did it out here, in front of them. They were too civilized for such things. They beat their slaves in private. They raped behind closed doors.

"Perform," Ahzeen commanded.

"No."

Another stirring in the back of my mind — gone before I could understand what it was.

He grabbed my arm, fingernails digging into my skin, eye baring into mine.

"Do you think the Orders can protect you? Do you think they make you any less of a slave? Do you think their power is greater than mine? Clearly, that is not true." He gestured to the door. "I have taken your companions, including the Second of the Orders, captive quite easily."

There it was again: the performance. We were all just pieces to illustrate his dominance to all these people he so desperately wanted to impress. I bit the inside of my lip so hard that blood flooded over my tongue.

I didn't look, even though he clearly wanted me to. I looked only at him, and I *hated* him.

I hated all of them.

"You try so hard to fill your father's name," I spat. "But everyone in this room knows that you never will."

Another strike to my face before the words were even out of my mouth. I hit him right on that nerve, just as I had intended.

"You forgot your place," he snarled. "But I will remind you."

You forgot what you are, Esmaris had said to me.

I smiled a serene, bloody grin. "If you want to kill me, then kill me."

Ahzeen's one exposed eye glinted with an anger that rivaled my own. His fingers tightened around my arm.

"Fine," he spat. "I'll finish what my father started."

And dragged me through the parting crowd, to the entrance of the ballroom, down a white hallway that was all too familiar.

CHAPTER SEVENTY-ONE

MAX

I realized too late. I had been dosed with Chryxalis before. The headache. The numb, tingling sensation at my fingertips. I'd barely touched that wine. The dose had been powerful, perhaps even coated on the outside of the glass. Not that the details mattered now.

I snapped my fingers and yanked forth only the tiniest of sparks.

No.

I spun around just in time to see Eslyn flicker away — slowly, too slowly — before I could stop her. Ariadnea grabbed for her a split second too late, making the same horrifying realization that I did. She could have been caught between dimensions, if her magic failed her before she and the boy she carried could emerge.

I saw Ahzeen strike Tisaanah, heard her hit the floor, and my vision went red.

"Weapon!" I whirled to the guard boy we had met earlier, my hand outstretched. *"Now!"*

He wouldn't understand my words, but he clearly understood

my tone. I only glimpsed him dive for the corner of the room before my attention was yanked away by the telltale *whoosh* of a raised blade.

I evaded just in time.

But half a dozen guards were upon us like flies to carrion. Where I dodged one, I nearly ran into another. And the effects of the Chryxalis seeped far beyond the surface, stripping my wits and my reflexes from me just as it stripped my flames.

I caught a wrist swinging towards Sammerin's head, twisted until I felt a crack, prying the sword from the guard's limp fingers. In that moment, I had never loved my brother more for every miserable night he spent running me through drills on far too little sleep all those years ago, no magic allowed.

But even that could only get me so far.

Bodies closed in on me, more and more. I slashed, I jabbed, I evaded, until blood spattered across my face. But it wasn't enough. There were always more.

Through them, I caught a glimpse of Tisaanah pushing herself up from the ground. Ahzeen standing over her.

A weak, pitiful cry rang out as the slave boy who had helped us fell to his knees, his throat slashed before he could reach our weapons.

A blunt impact struck the back of my head, but I surged forward, fighting arms and weapons and hands that tried to drag me back.

The forms closed in, blocking Tisaanah from view as she was struck again.

Beside me, I heard Sammerin let out a muffled grunt — the one sound that yanked me from my focus. I spun around to see him double over, clutching his side as one of Ahzeen's soldiers held a bloody blade. *Fuck*, that left knee, I should have been watching —

In that moment of distraction, another pair of hands grabbed me, and another blow struck my head. I tasted blood.

The last thing I saw, through blurring vision, was Tisaanah being dragged from the room.

And the last thing I thought was that I was going to kill every last one of them.

CHAPTER SEVENTY-TWO

TISAANAH

E smaris's office looked exactly as it did the day that he
almost killed me. When Ahzeen threw the door open and
yanked me inside, for one split second I could have sworn I saw
Esmaris's unmistakable form in front of the window, shoulders
square, hands clasped behind his back.

"I hesitate to say that you and I have anything in common,
but it seems that we do both love putting on a performance." He
sent me hurling against the desk. I stopped myself from falling
with my palms.

Gods, I was so dizzy. I thought it would stop, but it was like
my consciousness just kept draining and draining. I turned and
straightened, even though it took all of my strength.

At least we were alone. I had killed one Mikov in this room. I
could kill another.

"What is it that you want?" I asked. Time. I just needed time.
"The Orders can give you funding, if you wish."

"I don't need your money."

I don't need your money.

Crack!

There it was again: a faint, faint lurch at the back of my

thoughts. This time, it was pronounced enough that I understood what it was, and my heart leapt.

Reshaye, I whispered, but received no response.

But if it was still there — I could draw it out. I could *force* it out.

"Influence," I said, to Ahzeen. "You said you had requested the assistance of the Orders. They will give it to you in exchange for our release."

"*Your* release? I have the Second to the Arch Commandant locked up. I already have influence. Besides, slaves do not get to drive bargains." He grabbed my chin, fingers pinching my face as he turned it, examining me. "I *do* remember you. You were his favorite. I didn't understand why, even then. You look like a piebald cow. And yet— he protected you over me."

He released my face, only to grab my shoulder and spin me around. My skin crawled as his hands raked down my back, lingering over my scars. "But he rendered you useless with these ugly things."

A plan unfurled in my mind.

"But in the end, he couldn't kill me."

Ahzeen was so, so easy to bait. He struck me again, sending my face slamming against the desk.

As I pushed myself up, I imagined what his life would feel like withering beneath my hands, just like his father's had. My eyes bore into the desk. That *white* desk. And I threw myself into my fear, into my anger, until it consumed me.

Reshaye, I whispered, again.

I felt it move, prodded by my anger and pain.

"You aren't the only one with a penchant for the poetic," he spat. For one moment, my eyes lifted out to the window, looking out over the stepped marble of the Mikovs' beautiful city, blocks of silver and shadow bathed in moonlight.

I listened to Ahzeen's footfalls cross the room. Open a closet that I knew very well. I wondered if my old clothes still hung there.

Do it, I dared him, as his steps returned to me.

As the whip sliced through the air with a lethal whistle, and lit agony across my back.

Crack!

I forced my eyes open. I forced them to stare at that gleaming desk, filling my vision with white.

Nothing but white and white, for so many days, Reshaye had wept. I forced my face into everything that terrified it.

Crack!

Nothing but white and pain.

I thought of Esmaris, of his cold hatred, at the way it had struck betrayal into my chest. I flooded my thoughts with the agony of it.

Reshaye!

{Stop.} Its pain twined with my own. Distant. Faint.

The magic inherent in my blood was rendered useless, perhaps. But Reshaye *was* magic. Maybe it pulled from something deeper.

And I would not — *would not* — allow Ahzeen Mikov to destroy me or the people I cared for. I didn't have time to be afraid of the monster I'd have to summon to do it.

Crack!

Warmth spilled down my back.

{Stop!}

If you want it to stop, then MAKE it stop.

Heat flooded my veins.

I began to taste Ahzeen's rapid fury, putrid and metallic. A frenzied smile spread across my lips.

Crack!

I felt Reshaye roar to the front of my thoughts, lighting up the threads of my mind with power that stole the air from my lungs.

The world snapped back into focus.

I felt Ahzeen's aura solidify. The moment I did, I grabbed onto it with razored claws.

I spun around just in time to see him with his arm frozen. The anger that pinched his face shifted to confusion, then fear.

The last time I stood here in this room, with a man's life in the palm of my hand, I had been terrified of what I had done.

Not this time.

I drew the fingers of my magic around his mind and squeezed. He dropped to his knees.

A wave crested inside of me. Blood rushed through my ears as I bent over and grasped his face with one hand. His flesh withered around my fingers, spiders of black decay crawling over his cheeks.

I brought my face so close to his that the smells of his wine-sweetened breath and putrid rot mingled in my nostrils.

"Tell Esmaris I sent you," I whispered, and drew the fingers of my magic and of my hand together until both his mind and his rotting jaw were crushed to jelly in my hands.

The wave broke, and Reshaye screamed a terrible, wordless screech as it drowned me.

CHAPTER SEVENTY-THREE

MAX

The impact of my body falling against the wall and a loud *bang!* snapped me back into consciousness.

It all came back to me in pieces: the party, Ahzeen Mikov, the Chryxalis — and, most vividly of all, Tisaanah's body hitting the ground.

I jerked myself upright, trying to leap to my feet and stumbling as I found that my hands were tied behind my back. I was in a small, expensively furnished room, maybe some kind of library or sitting room. No guards.

"I need you to get your bearings fast." Nura's voice, low and calm, snapped my eyes to my right, where she stood against the wall.

My eyes fell past her, to Sammerin, and my heart stopped. He offered me a faint smile, as if anticipating my reaction, but he leaned heavily against the wall. Blood soaked through his jacket.

Beside him, Ariadnea didn't look much better. Her back was straight, shoulders square in the stance of a highly trained soldier. But she touched the side of her arm to the wall and to the edge of the end table beside her, betraying uncertainty that was hard to miss. Because, after all, a Syrizen without magic was simply blind.

Ascended above. We were in trouble. And all I could see, over and over again, was Tisaanah's form falling.

"Where—"

"I assume they *were* taking us to the dungeons. But something happened. A lot of commotion back towards the ballroom."

My blood went cold.

"They shoved us in here and just ran off to go investigate, but I doubt we have much time before they return."

Tisaanah. It had to be.

I only barely choked back a wall of furious terror.

Step back. My mind recited a series of commands from many years ago, reverent like a prayer. *Evaluate. Judge. Act. Leave no room for anything else.*

My gaze snapped back to Nura, settling on her forearms, tucked behind her back. It had to be her and me. Sammerin and Ariadnea were too compromised.

"Remember Albreit?"

A smile glittered in Nura's eyes. "You read my mind."

And right on cue, the door opened and two of Ahzeen's soldiers rushed back in. They were sloppy, frenzied, practically stumbling back into the room. Whatever they had seen had spooked them.

I didn't give myself time to dissect that.

Instead, I threw myself against the larger man and shoved him towards the wall, where Nura had turned, back to us — a dagger flicking from the inside of her sleeve. At my shove, the guard careened into her and let out a yelp as the blade buried itself into his gut.

The other one dove for me. Out of the corner of my eye, I saw Nura kick the first guard off of her blade. I narrowly evaded the swing of a sword. The frenzied momentum of his strike sent him stumbling, tripping over a coffee table.

Sloppy, sloppy.

I leapt over him before he could get up. One foot on his chest, the other coming down hard on his throat. He wheezed.

"Nura, *hands*."

Impact and pain lit up my wrists. I winced. Well, she didn't have to fucking *skin* me —

My annoyance was cut short by a crash to my left.

I whirled to see Ariadnea and Sammerin pushing the wounded soldier against a wall, cornering him.

I tried unsuccessfully to pull my hands apart. I could feel the fraying rope beginning to give.

The other guard, the one I had tripped, struggled to climb to his feet.

Nura pressed herself against the wall, bracing against it as she sawed at her restraints.

Another yank, and my hands finally broke free. I dove for Nura and grabbed the dagger from between her wrists, ignoring the pain that lit my palms as I pulled it by the blade.

The soldier stood upright, swaying as his arm raised.

To my left, I heard Ariadnea let out a muffled grunt as the other guard threw her aside.

Four seconds. I had four seconds, maybe.

With vicious force, I drew the dagger over Nura's bound wrists.

It had to be enough. I had time for only one stroke before I leapt for the man cornering Sammerin, yanking him back and drawing the dagger across his throat.

And I looked away from the man's gargling wound just in time to see Nura let the other man drop, a second bloodied dagger protruding from beneath her sleeve.

"It was smoother in Albreit," she panted, as I freed Ariadnea and Sammerin's hands.

I hardly heard her. Sammerin visibly struggled to remain upright. Blood now dripped from his jacket and formed a slick pool on the floor. Ascended, he shouldn't have been involved in that fight —

"Sam —"

"Listen." Ariadnea cocked her head, raising a finger.

We went silent.

And a beat later, the sounds of distant screams unfurled through the air. Quiet, but unmistakable.

My heart turned to lead and dropped all the way through my stomach. I leapt to the door. When I threw it open and stepped through, a curse flew from my lips.

Because this building was on fucking *fire*.

And it was no fire I'd ever seen before, either. One end of the hallway, the one that would eventually lead back to the ballroom, was crawling with glowing *blue* licks of flame. They moved slightly too slow, skipping like light reflecting through swaying glass.

The image I'd nursed in the back of my head — the image of Ahzeen beating Tisaanah to death in the middle of that revolting party — was replaced with something even more terrifying.

The distant shouts morphed into unmistakable echoes of the ones from Sarlazai. The ones that scarred the insides of my ears.

I nearly didn't hear Nura's gasp beside me. "Even with the Chryxalis? That's... remarkable."

Remarkable? *Remarkable?* It was *horrifying*.

Dread rolled over me as I thought of the look on Tisaanah's face when she was in Reshaye's clutches, cold and brutal and distant. And I thought of how different it was from the face that looked up at me in that tent, demanding promises of me in the moonlight.

"What is it?" Ariadnea asked, frustrated, twisting her eyeless face in one direction and the another. "What do you see?"

"It's not fire," Sammerin rasped. He sagged against the doorframe, clutching his torso. I looked at my friend and silent fear passed between us.

Only for a second, before he began to keel over. I caught one arm, and Ariadnea caught the other.

He was losing so much blood.

And Tisaanah was losing herself.

And I could be losing both of them.

Everything was going to hell, and I had never — *never* — been so afraid in my entire sorry life. For one moment, I breathed that terror in as deep as I could.

And then I exhaled it into savage resolve.

"Find a way out. Take everyone who will come with you, and get out of here."

Nura's eyebrows lurched. "And what about you?"

"I'll catch up."

She looked at the flames, then me, then the flames. "Don't be an idiot," she spat. "I told you the next time you tried to kill yourself, I wouldn't stop you."

I almost laughed. If only it were that simple.

It is easy to die for someone, Tisaanah's words whispered, *but so much more valuable to live.*

"Then don't," I said, and I turned towards those flames.

Sammerin's hand caught my arm, his fingers digging into my skin.

He didn't speak, but then, he didn't have to. His serious stare told me that he knew what I was going to do, and why, and that he couldn't stop me.

It took palpable effort not to let my voice tighten as I said, "I know you want to have a *moment,* you romantic bastard, but no time for that now. When this is all over. Sunset and all."

His eyes only barely crinkled. Weakly, he removed his hand from my arm just enough to form a particularly vulgar gesture.

I let out a laugh that was really a sigh of relief. "That's the spirit. Now get the hell out before you bleed to death."

I didn't give anyone else time to respond before I turned away, starting down the hallways in a brisk walk that quickly turned to a run. It was easier to look at those strange blue flames than it was to look at their faces. By now, the end of the hallway was consumed by it. I was running into a wall of flickering blue light.

I was running towards Tisaanah.

I do not give you permission to fail if I fail.

All I could think was that I loved her.

I hadn't told her that, but as that unsettling blue light grew closer and closer, I'd never felt any greater certainty. I loved her for her strength, for her beautiful brute force, for seeing what no one else did. I loved her for everything the world constantly used against her. I loved her for continuing anyway.

Promise me that you will keep fighting your battles even if I lose mine.

I stood with her, only her, until the end of our stories. But I refused to allow hers to be a retelling of mine. She deserved better than a lifetime of bloodstained hands and a tale with a bitter ending crafted from Reshaye's terrible acts. She deserved *epics.*

And I loved her so damned much that I would fulfill the promise I made to her, even if it became the hardest thing I ever did.

Even if it meant embracing a part of myself that I would rather pretend didn't exist.

The blue flames engulfed me. They were lightly cool, and they burned a slow, strange pain over my skin that rattled through me like lightning.

I waited until I couldn't take it anymore before I did something that I had sworn to myself I would never, ever do.

If Reshaye was drawing from a deeper power, then so could I. For once, I wasn't holding back.

My second eyelid slid open, and my body unraveled into fire.

CHAPTER SEVENTY-FOUR

TISAANAH

I was falling so fast that the world smeared around me. I reached for control and groped at nothing but darkness and shadow.

I had no control over my body as I strode down the hall, to the ballroom.

The ballroom where hundreds of people, including many of my dearest friends, awaited.

I was so afraid.

It's alright, I whispered to Reshaye, as soothing as I could manage through my rising panic. *It's alright.*

{I have told you so many times. You cannot lie.}

Even its voice sounded different, warped with strange, flickering power. Cold light that resembled flames surrounded me, clawing across the floor and up the walls with every step I took.

{You betrayed me,} it snarled. *{They all have. They always do.}*

The image of Max's fingers over my stomach flashed through my head again, two seconds repeated at a dizzying frequency.

Dread closed my throat. Max. Max who had believed in me so strongly. Where was he? Was he dead? Were they all dead?

I had failed them. Gods, they had followed me, and I had so deeply, utterly failed them.

Please, I begged.

{Silence.}

I turned a corner, and I was in the ballroom. The music overwhelmed my ears, throbbing into my head. The room was still packed full of finely dressed guests, though many of them had turned to filter from the room, whispering to each other in hushed voices and no doubt gossiping about what they had witnessed.

At least, they were, until I entered.

The corners of the room dimmed. Flames and rot spread spidering fingers across the floor. The guests froze and turned to look at me, eyes wide with shock or narrowed in confused disgust.

Reshaye turned my head and skimmed our vision by the slaves, too — guards lined up against the wall and maids who sank into the corners, terrified.

{Look at the way they look at us.}

Monster. Like I was a monster.

For a moment, I stood there, staring at them.

We need to find the others. I chanced a whisper. *They need—*

Then pain lit up my back, searing through still-seeping wounds, and my throat released a ragged screech. Cold embers erupted around me.

I spun around to see one of Ahzeen's generals upon me, bloodied sword clutched in his hands. My hands grabbed his face and watched it rot before he even had the chance to move.

But then there was another one, and another. A Lord eager to boast of his combat skills; a hired mercenary looking to do the same. Their strikes landed across my back and my shoulder.

Reshaye wailed, in a cry that rattled both my thoughts and my throat. I swung around and clawed at them. They died beneath my hands.

One of Ahzeen's generals let out a shout across the room, mobilizing the hesitant waves of slave warriors.

My lips curled into a snarl as my hand shot into the air, calling for Il'Sahaj. My fingers soon wrapped around its hilt.

Gods, no. No. I would not fight these people. I couldn't.

I grabbed for control. Grabbed for it and failed to find hold. Reshaye yanked my own muscles from my grasp, shoving me further into darkness. My vision blurred.

I tried again, and again, and again, to no avail.

And I screamed a wordless, voiceless plea as those soldiers rushed towards me, as Reshaye raised Il'Sahaj in a lethal battle cry.

No!

But then, before I could bring the sword down, I was blinded. Blinded by *fire* — real fire, the kind that seared the hairs from the tips of my nose, the kind that embraced me with such vivid heat that it sent my body staggering back against the wall.

At first, I didn't know what I was looking at. It took a moment for my eyes to adjust, and to realize that the fire was moving, and fast. Not moving like flames, but like a creature.

Reshaye's delighted smile spread slowly across my lips.

And my heart stopped.

It was a serpent. A massive serpent that wove through the air and the crowd, its body made of flames that ran together like water, sparks glinting as scales on its skin. It had no wings and no legs, but it moved uninhibited all the same. It lurched through the air in movements that were at once exquisitely graceful and wildly untamed, as if it, too, struggled to fully control its body.

And yet, it was still so *beautiful*. Warmth and light and power surrounded by cold magic and deepening shadow.

Its head turned towards me, and the realization hit me so hard that it took my breath away.

Those eyes. I would recognize them anywhere. The shape of them was seared into my soul. Even though now they were dark, veering on black, instead of their usual cloudy blue.

Reshaye's smile spread into a grin. "Oh, Maxantarius," I breathed. "You are even more beautiful than I thought you would be."

The serpent paused for a moment. Then, in one wild surge, charged towards me.

If I had control of my body, I would have cringed for an inevitable impact.

But before it reached me, the snake compressed, flames reforming into the ghostlike shape of a man. Claws of heat prickled my skin as I stared into a face that was so familiar, even as it was so terrifyingly strange — Max's face rendered in flame and rippling heat, dark eyes cutting through light so bright that it hurt to look at him.

Then, membranes slid from the corners of each of his eyes, transforming them back into the peculiar cool gaze that I knew so well. The flames withered, leaving behind sweat-slicked skin.

And it was this image, of Max in his normal, unremarkable human body, that nearly pushed me over the edge.

"It's time to stop," he said.

"Look at what we made together. You finally—"

"It's time to stop. We need to get these people out of here and leave." He placed his palms on either side of the wall above my shoulders, leaning over me with a wrinkle between his eyebrows. The desperation in his eyes gutted me.

He was talking to me, not it.

And Reshaye made that realization at the same time that I did.

{The two of you. Of course.}

My blood turned cold with Reshaye's anger and my dread.

No, I begged.

{I have had enough.}

"I have had enough." My palms pressed to either side of Max's face.

{You chose him over me.}

No!

{You already did.}

Max winced as veins of blight slithered across his cheeks. His fingers clutched my shoulders. "I need you to come back, Tisaanah."

I made a mad rush for control. And I felt it, for one moment — for one moment I felt the warmth of his skin beneath *my* hands.

But then Reshaye grabbed me and threw me back.

{No. You have made your choices.}

I fell further and further into the web of my own mind, where the shadows and the memories grew darker. Threads bound me, strangled me.

My vision began to go dark.

The last thing I saw was a grim determination on Max's face as those eyelids slid back and he dissolved into flames.

CHAPTER SEVENTY-FIVE

MAX

The world was blinding and bright and too damn fast. Every movement was a deliberate attempt to temper the sheer power that burst from my every muscle. Every breath felt like I was inhaling lightning. I was everywhere and nowhere. I was free for the first time and more trapped than I had ever been.

I spun away from Tisaanah, coiling through the air over the heads of petrified partygoers. Pain still radiated through me, even though my body was a very different form. Her magic seeped into my blood.

The room grew darker and darker. Tisaanah drew herself up, death trailing her feet across the floor. The blue flames burst forth in gushing waves, but they weren't hot, and they didn't give off light. Still, they devoured the curtains, the walls, and the flesh of the guests.

"You abandoned me." Her voice leeched and echoed with unnatural, unnerving bite. "I gave you everything and you threw me away."

She paced forward. Decay and blue flames slithered closer to the guards and the guests, who were by now climbing over each other for escape.

I threw myself in front of her, separating her from them with the wall of fire that was my body. A smattering of ill-advised soldiers — *idiots!* — made a dive for us, though many of their companions instead turned to flee.

I dove in front of her, coiling to surround her with a shield of my body. But I was not accustomed to controlling this form. I couldn't evade the way I normally would. A shock of pain ran up my spine — a slash far down my body.

What the hell is wrong with you?! I wanted to snap. *I'm trying to help!*

A hiss graveled from my throat as I shoved the soldiers against the wall with as much force as I could muster. But I was in an impossible position here, protecting her from them and them from her, like there were two sets of teeth clamping down around my throat.

Another screech cut through me as I was hit with another strike. This one so much worse than the first. The kind of pain that took my breath away, sending this unfamiliar body spiraling and lurching.

I glimpsed my tail to see blackened blood glistening through the flickers of fire. Tisaanah stood there with Il'Sahaj in her grasp, Reshaye's agonized fury etched deep into her painfully familiar features.

I had hoped that seeing the world this way – through a screen of red and blaring light – would distance me enough to make this easier.

It didn't.

I rushed her, pulling up at the last second so that she went stumbling back against the wall. Every time I came close to her, no matter how fast I was, she swung for me. Each time, she hit.

It was now completely dark save for the glow of my flames and the garish blue shadows cast over her face by hers. Deep, vicious cracks split the marble floor, the softened flesh of the stone finally giving out.

DAUGHTER OF NO WORLDS

There were still dozens of people in this room, trapped by cracks in the floor or simply too terrified to make themselves run. But even beyond that, this estate was massive. Surely there were many hundreds of people in this building. Many of whom were probably Tisaanah's friends.

I coiled around her again.

Another slash, another cut, another wave of rotting pain.

Come back, Tisaanah. Show me that brute force. Show me you can do this. Show me that I won't have to walk out of here without you, you stubborn shit.

I couldn't lose her too. I couldn't.

I pulled myself into a human shape. I stood directly in front of Tisaanah, who stared up at me with wild eyes and tear-streaked cheeks.

"You *traitor*," she wailed, in an accentless voice.

She looked utterly inhuman, bathed in blue ribbons of light, covered in blood. I noticed for the first time that her face was badly beaten, and that her clothes were in tatters.

Anger made the flames around me flare.

Tisaanah. My Tisaanah, picked apart by so many monsters.

I grabbed her shoulders and pushed her against the wall, ignoring Reshaye's growl of protest and the pain of the rot that sizzled my palms.

I held her there, trapping her. And then I wrapped my arms around her.

This couldn't be it. I couldn't let her go like this.

Decay rippled over my body and flames rippled over hers, a battle of blue and black dancing across our skin. I buried my face against her neck, even though the skin of my forehead screamed at the contact.

"Come back," I whispered. "You still have so much to do."

Reshaye growled, its fingers clawing at my back. My eyes began to water as ribbons of rot opened across my skin.

Her body shuddered.

"Why do they always do this to me?" her voice wept. "Why do they always use me and discard me?" It wavered so much that it could have been her – it could have been the trace of an accent that I heard. My heart leapt and broke at once.

I heard the deafening sound of cracking marble, felt the floor begin to melt beneath my feet. Distantly, the sound of terrified people shuddered through my ears. The same as they sounded in Sarlazai.

The edges of my vision were beginning to blur. The pain was becoming unbearable. I felt her begin to sag in my arms.

She was killing me. We were killing each other.

And if this was how it had to go, then I wanted — I wanted so fucking badly — to burn up with her here. Let our bones lie together.

But.

Promise me, she had demanded.

"You are *not fucking done,* Tisaanah, so *get back here.*"

And then I turned her face and pressed my mouth against hers — because I was desperate, because it was the only thing I could think to do — and I prayed to any god that was listening that it was not a kiss goodbye.

CHAPTER SEVENTY-SIX

TISAANAH

My mother's face became a desecrated corpse, Serel's screamed into Vos's disfigured features, Esmaris's rose and melted into a demon in the shadows. The scars on my back multiplied and opened and seeped and healed and split, over and over and over again.

I watched my family being whipped to death in the mines. I watched Serel crumble beneath falling marble, just as that boy had at the slaving hub. I watched Max's perfect face dissolve into ugly decay under my touch.

The silver threads of my mind wrapped tighter and tighter around me, binding me in my ugly past and my ugly future like a fly caught in a spider's web.

You could never do this. You brought death to everyone that you've ever loved. You let them sacrifice for you and you repay them this way?

I didn't know if it was Reshaye's voice or my own.

I saw only flashes of what was happening out there — flashes of blue and orange and flames and rot. With each glimmer of sight, I desperately tried to free myself, only to be pulled back even deeper than before.

The web of my mind was going dim, consumed by that blue fire.

It was all going to hell. It was going to end this way. With Reshaye, using my body to kill, to destroy. And all I could think, between the terror and the nightmares, was that I hoped Max would kill me before it happened.

Then, I saw another flash. An image — a memory, though not one that belonged to me — skittered through my head. A little girl with long black hair holding out a butterfly in a jar.

Did you know that when caterpillars make a cocoon, their bodies totally dissolve? Kira. Max's sister.

They become nothing, before they become something else.

And all at once, the idea hit me. I was fighting and fighting to get *out* of my own head, but Reshaye lived *within* me. It pulled from a deeper level of magic. And some part of that was inside of me, even if it was buried far beneath my consciousness. Even if I had to claw through the pits of darkness to get to it.

The threads pulled tighter, calling me, strangling me.

It will kill you! a part of me screamed.

But I didn't give myself time to listen to my fear. When the next wave of terror came for me, I hurled myself into the darkness.

I OPENED my eyes to a vat of dust-scattered ink and pain so intense that my vision throbbed.

The world solidified. Split. A sky. And a ground. And a horizon line.

Plains, I realized. I stood in the center of silent plains, miles and miles of nothing but faintly waving grass. Moonlight cast silver shadows across their wheat-frayed tips and wildflower petals. Their movements were odd, choppy, like the breeze was skipping and lurching. The flowers bloomed and wilted and died in strange succession, backwards, forwards, again and again.

I looked down at my hands to see that they, too, were changing. Like the boundaries between my form and the world were strange, ill-defined. I was naked, but my skin bled out into the sky like the translucent flesh of a jellyfish.

All around me, bleeding threads of light reached from the ground into the sky.

Only one, far in the distance, was searing violet, plunging all the way through the ground through a vicious weeping tear. One pure streak of magic.

Max.

I knew it immediately. The only other person who would be drawing from magic so deep. And beyond that, I felt him — an echo of a presence that, by now, I knew as well as my own.

And then, looming over me, I felt another presence that I knew too well.

I lifted my chin, up to the sky. Realized that there was a stream of light pouring from *me*, too. But mine clotted above me into a cloud of bloody crimson.

And it had *eyes*.

The eyes opened. And I recognized the thing that stared back at me, though I couldn't quite say how: Reshaye.

{You!}

The word was a roll of thunder. The ground shook. And suddenly, before I could speak or move, Reshaye dove for me, surrounding me. Its form shifted, morphed, into something almost resembling some grotesque variation of a human — long, spindling limbs that moved in fits and starts. A cloudy face. A pair of white, savage eyes.

And long, bladed fingers that were suddenly at my throat.

{You betrayed me!} it wailed. *{After everything I did for you, you betrayed me!}*

The pain hit me all at once — pain so intense I could barely breathe, barely think. Images bombarded me. White, white, white. Flashes of long blonde hair.

{I gave you EVERYTHING!}

One strike with those inhuman, powerful fists, and I was on the ground. Its claws dug into my shoulders. I felt the burning warmth of blood running down my back. And when Reshaye pulled back, it now wore Esmaris's face.

A flare of fury rose in me.

No. I was *done*.

"No," I snarled. *"No more."*

No more of *any* of it. No more dividing myself up as an offering to more powerful monsters.

No more sacrificing those I loved in the name of their own safety.

And no more would I fail to unleash the full potential of the power — *my power* — at my disposal.

Reshaye's fingers tightened around my throat. I looked into those empty eyes, those eyes that were somehow nothing and everything all at once.

It is a form of raw magic, Nura had told me, once. That's all it was. Magic to be Wielded.

And Wield it, I would.

I plunged my hands into the misty form of Reshaye's smoky form.

It let out a bone-piercing screech, but I barely heard it, because the pain was so intense that I momentarily lost my grip on my senses.

I thought I knew pain. I had been wrong. Nothing, nothing, would ever compare to this.

Through the agony, I pulled Reshaye to me. I Wielded its murky form the way I once Wielded water in a pond, so many months ago. It fought me every step of the way, sinking its teeth into my soul.

My own life flashed before my eyes in bloody fragments. A little faceless girl playing with flowers and paper butterflies in her village. A scared almost-woman sitting in the back of a rolling cart. Esmaris's home, my solitary dancing practice, my nights in his bed. A teenage girl weeping as her friend tended to her wounds and her heartbreak.

DAUGHTER OF NO WORLDS

And then, of course, some years later, the crack of a whip, the sails of a ship, the stark gleam of two towers on a rocky shore.

Reshaye wailed. Thrashed.

{You betrayed me, you, you, you...!} it wept, voice dissolving, unraveling.

I grabbed onto Reshaye the way I had grabbed onto Esmaris's mind, the day I first killed. And that was when I felt it: the agony of it. Not only my own pain, but Reshaye's, too — the agony of being so many different pieces stitched together, shattered remnants of half-lost memories, grief over faceless deaths and nameless betrayals.

White walls.

Golden hair.

Bright eyes and champagne feathers.

A forgotten name, screamed over and over and over again, until it was swallowed by stone.

Weeping.

{Stop,} Reshaye whispered, and it was the voice of a child. *{Stop, please, stop...}*

I pushed deeper.

And I reached the center, and the world went suddenly quiet, save for a rhythmic beat: the beating of a heart. There, at the core of Reshaye's magic, was a formless, pulsing mass.

I closed my fingers around it. It wasn't just one core, one heart, I realized — it was pieces of many. They were warm, throbbing in time with my own heartbeat.

"...We carry many stories..." I glanced up, through all of this rushing magic, and saw the faintest outline of a figure standing with me. Blurry, faint, the shadow of a shadow of a shadow. *"...So many stories, you and I..."*

The thunder roared. The sky flashed. Reshaye's wordless screech filled my ears. The pain grew so intense that I could barely think. I was being torn away, but that shadowy slip of a figure reached out and grabbed me.

"...It was never meant to be this way..." it whispered. *"...Take it, please, take all of it, take it away..."*

It shoved that heart into my hands — that mass of magic and power and broken memories. And in that same moment, I looked up through a vicious thunderclap to see two silhouettes engulfed in blue and red, burning in silent flames, locked in a kiss.

"...Someone calls for you..."

Max. The name lurched through my soul. I felt that kiss burn on my lips. It was joined by my mother's on my forehead and Serel's on my cheek.

Scars left by everyone I had left behind. Everyone I had sacrificed. Everyone I had lost.

No. Not again.

I would not accept another kiss goodbye.

I looked down at that core of power. Magic to be Wielded.

The figure lurched towards me, shredding and desperate. *"...Now!..."*

And at that exact moment, just as I felt its claws rip into the back of my skull, just as I felt myself lose my grip on reality, I took that heart and swallowed it. Inhaled its power. Felt it flood my veins.

Gods, power like this — how could it be anything but right? How could it be anything but good?

Light flooded from my fingertips, my eyes, my mouth as I opened it to let out a roar or a laugh or something in between.

I reached for the sky. And the world dissolved in white, and white, and white.

———————

You are not fucking done, Tisaanah, so get back here.

I heard him.

I felt him, felt his kiss, felt his breath reach for mine.

I threw everything I had, all of this new power wrapped around my fingertips, into one vicious slice. The nightmare images dissolved with wild screeches.

My mind snapped back into place. I was thrust back into a world of light and color and overwhelming sound. My body was in shambles, blood rolling down my skin, burns crawling over my flesh.

But I just clutched Max and pulled my lips away from him long enough to look into those dark eyes, into that face crafted from curling flames.

"You look beautiful," I whispered.

Shock careened across his features. Shock, then a shattered relief.

Translucent eyelids slid from the inner corners of his eyes. And then the fire was gone, and the rot was gone, and we were two humans of broken flesh and blood collapsing against each other and onto the floor.

Everything hurt.

Max's forehead was pressed to mine, hands clutching my face as if he couldn't believe I was here.

"You scared the shit out of me," he breathed, at last.

"Sorry."

In a daze, I removed his left hand from my cheek and flipped it palm up. Dragged a circle through the blood.

I could still feel my connection to that one deep, deep pool of magic, though the thread that tethered me to it was quickly growing thinner and thinner. I had one more thing I needed to use it for.

One line, then another.

"Tisaanah."

Max was beginning to sway.

"What?"

I drew the final line of my Stratagram.

"I love you."

We crashed upon the cobblestones outside of the Mikov estate. I collapsed to the ground, as did Max. And around us, dozens and dozens of slaves joined us. Every slave in the Mikovs' city, drawn to us like flower petals in the best damn garden in Ara, far across the sea.

But I didn't look at them. I looked only at Max, our cheeks pressed against the stone ground, my hand still cupped around his. The thread tethering me to the deep well of magic finally snapped, leaving me in my fragile mortal body, magicless.

The world dimmed.

"I love you," I whispered. And I curled my hand around his, squeezing as tightly as I could as unconsciousness took us both.

CHAPTER SEVENTY-SEVEN

TISAANAH

I woke up with a start from a dreamless sleep, air sputtering in my throat. Everything assaulted me at the same time: my body, my senses, the memories of everything that had happened at the Estate —

"Take deep breaths." It took me a moment to become aware of a presence at my side, a low, calming voice murmuring soothing instructions. "Careful, careful. Don't take it all in too fast. In, out."

A hand moved over my back in time with the commands. Soon, my breath and heartbeat slowed.

I was in a small but well-furnished bedroom. One look at the furniture told me that I was still in Threll — probably some-where expensive. But that was the last thing I was thinking about. I whipped my head around to look at Sammerin, who sat at the edge of my bed.

Sammerin. Looking at Sammerin made me think of Max, and thinking of Max made me think of the way he had looked the last time I saw him, the depth of his wounds —

"Max," I blurted out. "Is he — ?"

"He was in worse shape than you were, but he's fine. He's

still unconscious, but that's to be expected and probably the best way for him to heal, considering how he abuses his body when he's awake." His voice sounded like the earth, comforting and stable even through that quip.

"I want to see him."

"You will. How are you feeling?"

My head throbbed. The room spun. But when I looked down at my palms, there was no trace of the burns that had almost covered me. "Awful, but alive."

"To be expected." He stood, crossing his arms as he gave me a searching stare. "From what I hear, you went through quite a lot."

Images flashed through my mind. The flames, both blue and red, the rot, Max going up in fire — Gods, *that* was something that warranted more discussion — and of course, Reshaye—

Reshaye.

With a start, I paused and searched my mind for it. I found nothing. No movement, no whispers, no sign of it within the web of my thoughts. This was not totally surprising, considering how Reshaye disappeared shortly after a large display of magic. It was probably just as exhausted as I was.

And I wanted the break. Needed it. Who knew what I would face when it returned.

My head swam with questions.

"Where are we?"

"The Mikov estate. One of the guest houses."

I must have looked visibly alarmed, because Sammerin quickly added, "The Orders have taken power here now that the Mikov line has ended."

"The *Orders* took power?" I rubbed my temple. That was odd. Why would the Orders have any claim to the city? And why would they *want* it?

"I don't entirely understand it, either. From what I've heard, it sounds like they made some wise investments in the land and wealthy businessmen here, so when Ahzeen was killed—"

"They *bought* the city?"

We stared at each other in silence for a moment. My jaw worked.

"I find it suspicious, too," Sammerin said at last, quietly.

"And the slaves?"

As long as the slaves were freed, I didn't care what happened to the Mikovs' wretched city.

"We have them." He gave me a small, quiet smile. "I would call this a successful journey. And... there is someone here who is extremely anxious to see you." Sammerin went to the door, then paused, fingers on the handle, and turned back to me.

"You did well, Tisaanah."

My eyes dropped to the bedspread. "Everything went wrong."

"Almost," Sammerin said, "but not quite."

"I'm sorry that you had to experience this."

He lifted one shoulder in a shrug. "I'm not. Perhaps I was a bit concerned in the middle part. But some things are worth it."

He motioned to the door, raising his eyebrows as if silently asking, *May I?*

I nodded, my heart crawling to my throat.

Sammerin left the room. I let my eyes drop down to my hands.

Until I heard footsteps.

"Tisaanah."

Gods, it had been so long since I had heard my name said like that— with the sharp lilt of my mother tongue.

I watched my fingers clasp around each other, the image blurring.

Two more footsteps, approaching the bed.

"Tisaanah."

I couldn't bring myself to look at him, for so many reasons.

Because I knew my heart would just combust when I saw him.

Because I took so long to come back for him.

Because he saw me at my worst in that ballroom, saw my failure, saw the monster that Reshaye made of me.

"Look at me."

Look at me. Look at me. Look at me.

Warm fingers tilted my chin, just as they had on that terrible day seven months ago.

And just as they had on that day, clear blue eyes greeted me like a gulp of water in the middle of a desert.

Serel smiled at me, and something inside of me split open. I threw myself against him and buried my face into his tanned neck, into skin that smelled like my home, into an embrace that felt like dreams solidified.

And with all my body and soul, I wept.

CHAPTER SEVENTY-EIGHT

MAX

I stood in a familiar little shed that smelled like animals and rustled with the sounds of tiny feet. Kira held a little blue lizard in her palms. It skittered between her fingers and over the backs of her hands as she excitedly told me about everything that made it revolting and beautiful.

" —and *after that* is when it vomits up the carcasses to feed to its babies."

I leaned against the wall and made a snort of disgust.

"That's pleasant," I said, my voice dripping with sarcasm, as if I wasn't exactly where I wanted to be.

I had been listening to her go on for hours. Normally by now, I would be looking for excuses to leave. Today, for some reason, felt different. Something about this chilly afternoon seemed fleeting, like a ghost was about to slip through my fingers. I couldn't pinpoint the sensation until Kira stopped talking and turned around to look at me, dark eyes that were a reflection of my own peering through sheets of black hair.

Her image flickered, as if for one brief moment it was made of smoke, then solidified so quickly that I thought I was going insane.

A lump rose in my throat. A distant reality began to encroach on the edge of my thoughts, but I willfully ignored it.

"Show me the next one," I said.

"You don't like this one."

"Show me anyway."

Don't stop talking.

She knelt down and pulled out one final glass enclosure from the bottom shelf, opening it and reaching inside with the gentle touch of a mother picking up their precious child.

When she turned around, she gave me a mischievous grin. "Are you sure? I wouldn't want to *scare* you."

She held out her hands. The green snake regarded me with a wary stare as it wound around her arms.

There it was again. A flicker of smoke.

No. Stay.

"If you're feeling brave, you can even hold it," she teased.

The sight of the creature did coax forth some unease in my stomach. But I wasn't afraid of it. Not like I once was.

I extended my hands and let the serpent slide from her fingers into mine, coiling easily around my forearms.

"Huh. It likes you."

Her voice sounded far away. But I lifted my eyes and she stood directly in front of me, looking at me with a twisted nose and a strange sort of pride. An expression that, like so many of hers, I recognized as my own.

My chest hurt. Reality banged on the door.

But I wanted to be here for one more minute. Even though she was starting to float away, layers of her dissolving into mist.

"Tell me what revolting things this one does," I said, desperate to call her back.

"I don't think this one is revolting at all."

A wind blew, somehow, even though we were inside. It pulled her hair into puffs of dust. I reached out with my free hand to grab her, only to pass straight through her skin.

The shed dissolved around us like shredded parchment, revealing a stormy sky.

"Stop," I begged. My fingers closed around one solid handful of fabric at the edge of her sleeve.

She shrugged, a cheerful, ungraceful movement. "It's fine. I'm sure there's lots of interesting stuff out there."

No. I wasn't ready. There were still so many things I wanted to tell her — all of them, Atraclius, my parents, the twins...

I blurted out, "It wasn't me. I need you to know—"

She let out a scoff. "Ascended above, shut up, Max. We always knew it wasn't you." She looked over her shoulder. "I've got to go. And so do you. Try not to be so scared of everything all the time, alright?"

I wasn't ready.

But I opened my fingers anyway, and let her go.

———

MAX.

My dream relinquished me in slow, agonizing bites.

Maaaay-ucks.

Shit. I was dead.

We were both dead. Tisaanah and me, burned up together. There were worse ways to go, I supposed.

Maaaay-ucks-un-tar-ee-uuuusss —

First came the sound, my name in that melodic voice. Then came the pain, a faint buzz that sank into every inch of my skin, every muscle, every bone. And a faint tickling sensation across my cheeks.

I opened leaden eyelids.

Tisaanah's face hovered over mine, her hair spilling against my face, backlighting forming a golden halo around her contours. She was so beautiful that she could not be human.

Definitely dead.

Apparently I said that aloud, because Tisaanah replied, "You are not dead."

As I settled further into consciousness, the pain grew more intense. Well, that confirmed the truth of what she was saying. A dead man would probably feel less. I groaned. "How did we manage that?"

"I know only some of that answer. Some, you will have to explain to me, mysterious snake man."

I chuckled. The vibration of it ached. "Mysterious snake man. You shall now always address me by this title."

That part of it still felt like a dream, not a memory, or a page stolen from someone else's tale. I couldn't believe that I did that. I had spent the last decade avoiding what Reshaye had created in me when it was pried from my soul, refusing to acknowledge that a piece of it had forever changed me. And I had not only acknowledged that power but *used* it.

I didn't know whether that was terrifying, or freeing, or both. Maybe freedom was always a little bit terrifying.

Tisaanah let herself fall sideways, collapsing onto the bed next to me. I turned my head so that we stared directly into each other's faces, our noses almost touching. With great effort, I lifted my hand and ran knuckles over the side of her face, tracing the line of her jaw and the soft warmth of her cheek.

Real. She was real.

For a while there, I didn't think that this reality would exist again.

"*So?*" she said, expectantly.

"So what?"

"So, mysterious snake man—"

"Ascended above, give me a minute, demanding rot goddess."

"A minute for what?"

"A minute to be glad that we have one.—"

The joking smile faded at the corners of her mouth, sinking into something gentler and more pensive. My own mind reassembled the blurry, scattered pieces of what had happened at the estate. The plan, the dinner, the kidnapping, Nura and the Syrizen and—

I bolted upright. "*Sammerin—*"

"He is fine." Tisaanah stopped me, gently pushing me back to the pillow.

A breath of relief.

"And the others? The slaves? Serel?"

She nodded.

"So we did it."

She nodded again.

I let out a long breath. That was mind-boggling. That six people in five days managed to free hundreds of slaves and take down one of the most powerful houses in Threll. Sure, even if it took a brief detour through hell.

But then, if anyone could do it...

I thought of Tisaanah's contract with the Orders, of the war back in Ara, and a knot choked my throat. I could see a thousand machinations beginning to turn inside of her head. The wrinkle between her eyebrows told me that she was thinking about the same thing.

I smoothed it with my thumb, pushing away my own anxieties with the movement.

"Just one minute," I murmured.

"Only one."

And our faces moved towards each other at the same time, my fingers curling around her cheeks, hers sliding over my shoulders. Our mouths met in a kiss that said everything we couldn't quite put into words, one that started as a gentle whisper and quickly rose to a more passionate song. I reminded myself of the way her lips moved, the way her tongue tasted, the mild scuff of her teeth over my skin.

The last time I kissed her, I thought I never would again. And I was so damn happy to be wrong.

She pulled away, nose tickling mine, eyes smiling. And in that low, erotic voice, she whispered, "Your breath smells very, very bad."

I scowled and blew a puff of air directly into her face, prompting her to let out a giggle that was possibly the most welcome sound I had ever heard. And apparently my breath couldn't have been all that bad, because she stifled that laugh with another kiss, and another, and another.

And all I could think, through it all, was one thing: Ascended fucking above, I was *alive.*

I WOULD HAVE BEEN content to go on for at least a few more hours like that, but Tisaanah was, unfortunately, not as easily distracted.

I had no choice but to give her the whole story. The one final thing that I had not told her — told *anyone*. I knew I would have to eventually. But this was a secret that I had buried even deeper within myself than the truth of Sarlazai or the deaths of my family — perhaps because it was one that still stared back at me every time I looked in the mirror.

Now, though, I had opened a door that I couldn't close again.

"It happened when Reshaye was removed," I began.

"After my family, I needed to get it out of me. That was just non-negotiable. And the Orders were in serious disarray at that point, so there was no one left to give me too much of a hard time about it. Zeryth was all too eager, since the war was over anyway and frankly, I think the bastard was mostly scared that I had all of that power."

"He thought you would use it against him?" Tisaanah asked.

"I couldn't, since I was bloodbound to the Orders. As long as Zeryth acted on behalf of the Orders, I couldn't harm him, at least not intentionally. But the title of Arch Commandant is fought and bled for, and he didn't like how my having Reshaye affected him in that fight." So fucking trivial. Zeryth Aldris, forever concerned with his own position even when real people were dying. "And Nura — she wasn't about to argue."

That, I would never fully understand. I'd known Nura since we were both children, but even then, I never saw her cry. Not until my family's funeral, where I watched their pyres burn from a distance. She was the only one that saw me, the only other one hiding back in the shadows, her cheeks slick with tears.

I had pretended I didn't see her and walked away before she

could approach me. But the next day, when I had again showed up at the Towers borderline hysterical, demanding to have Reshaye ripped out of me, she didn't so much as say a word.

"But, like everything, it wasn't that easy," I went on. "They had pulled Reshaye from many bodies before, but bodies that it rejected. It had wanted to leave just as much as they wanted it gone. In my case, Reshaye definitely *did not* want to leave. I spent hours bleeding on that slab while they worked on prying us apart, all while Reshaye and I were fighting these ridiculous battles within my head. It didn't want to let me go. But I wasn't about to let it keep me."

I still shuddered when I thought about it, the way Reshaye had clung to me like a desperate lover.

Tisaanah had edged closer, her body pressed against mine and her hands wrapped around my arm. And for a moment, I was struck by how much I deeply appreciated this alternative.

"Eventually, it got so bad that they told me that if they went any further, they would probably kill me. I told them that was just fine with me."

I let out a breath, took a moment to ground myself in Tisaanah's attentive eyes.

"And I did die. Just for a few minutes. Short enough that it wasn't a done deal. And as Reshaye was being pried away from me, it's like it dug all of its claws into me to pull me back."

{You wish to be rid of me so badly?} it had hissed. *{You'd rather die than stay here with me?}*

"Reshaye *saved* you?" Tisaanah whispered.

Well, "saved" made it sound so damned righteous. "It cursed me with a life I didn't want out of spite. It dragged me back just as it was ripped from my veins. But it kept me alive by giving me a... *gift.*"

{Our stories are bound together forever, Maxantarius. Yours is not over yet, and you cannot discard the pages already written. It is burned into your soul, and now it will be burned into your body as well.}

The last thing I remembered, in those murky memories, was the agonizing pain of Reshaye being finally cleaved from me.

And its final, fading whisper: *{Enjoy the gift I have given you. You will always be followed by what you fear.}*

"I was unconscious for days. Sammerin was the only one there when I opened my eyes for the first time. I almost burned the house down and I didn't even have my wits about me enough to realize that I wasn't dreaming until he was screaming at me to snap out of it."

A wrinkle had formed between Tisaanah's brows. One of her fingers brushed the corner of my eye, tracing the outline. "You have another eyelid."

"Right." I blinked, suddenly conscious of the thin membrane that covered my eyeballs. Closed. Always closed. "It took me way too long that day to realize that it was there, and that by closing it, I could close the well of magic that transformed me." I let out a small scoff. "Did you know that snakes have eyelids like this? For a creature that fails to understand the nuance of human emotion, Reshaye does have a penchant for dramatic justice, doesn't it?"

"So when it is open—"

"You saw."

A hint of shame seeped into those two words.

I had spent nearly a decade aggressively ignoring that part of myself. It was a reminder that Reshaye had won — that it had changed me forever and turned me into something that was no longer even fully human. When it lived in my mind, I could tell myself that it was the monster, not me. But it had made me one, too, in its final slight.

And there was a part of me that hated for her to see that.

"You never told me," she murmured.

"I never told anyone. Only Sammerin knew, and I wouldn't have told him either if I'd had the choice. It was clear from the beginning that I couldn't control it. And anything from Reshaye is just... tainted. I wasn't going to use or even think about it ever again."

I chanced a glance at Tisaanah, cringing in anticipation of

what expression might greet me. But she just looked thoughtful, sad. "But you did it this time."

"You needed me."

Her arms tightened around me, her face burying against my shoulder. "You controlled it."

I had. That thought still boggled me. I wasn't ready to address the possibility that I could *use* this thing.

"So did you," I said. She had done what I never could: brought Reshaye back from the brink of a breakdown. And thank the Ascended that she did.

Our fingers slid to each other and intertwined.

"You were perfect," she murmured.

And we lay there for another moment, allowing ourselves to ignore the looming shadows of vanquished monsters.

CHAPTER SEVENTY-NINE

TISAANAH

Nura was waiting for me when I returned to my own room, her hand on the doorknob.

"You're up. I was just on my way to see you." Her eyes ran from my toes to my face, cold and analytical, as if inspecting me for damage. "Recovered?"

I shrugged. "Enough."

"Good. Because we can't afford to stay here any longer." She looked down, and I noticed that she was holding a crinkled envelope at her side. Her fingers tapped the edge of the parchment.

"Has there been news from Ara?" I asked.

"It's war," she snapped. "There will always be news."

Well, that answered my question. She was in a worse mood than normal. Which meant yes, there had been news, and it was bad.

"We leave first thing in the morning. We can't afford to waste time, and at this rate, we'll surpass the time you were promised. So, get your bearings together."

Her abruptness was jarring, especially considering that I hadn't even seen or spoken to her since before we entered the

Mikov estate. But I just nodded, even though the thought of returning to war made my palms sweat. "Fine. I will be ready."

She began to walk away, but I called out, "Nura."

She stopped. Looked over her shoulder.

"I have been thinking," I said. "About the party."

"What about it?"

"Ahzeen and Zeryth had met before. And I think it is obvious now that they did not part on good terms."

Not a very nice person, it turns out, Zeryth had said of Ahzeen, once. What felt like a lifetime ago. And something more than a desire to prove his power had prompted Ahzeen to attack us the way he had. He was brash and arrogant, yes, but not mindlessly stupid.

Nura let out a small scoff. "Obvious indeed."

"Zeryth sent us there knowing that Ahzeen was hostile towards the Orders. Towards *him.* I think that he knew there was a high chance things would be... violent." I leveled a steady, piercing gaze towards Nura. "Did you?"

She didn't shy away from my stare. Didn't look away. And didn't answer — but the sneer that barely twitched at the corner of her lip told me everything I needed to know.

No. She was just as blind as we were. He had set her up too, just like the rest of us.

"Then why?" I asked. "Why would he do that?"

"I warned you about how he is."

Possess or destroy. You're either a tool or a threat — and in this case, we were all both. He knew that I — that Reshaye — would make it out alive, but he didn't want or need to care whether any of the others did.

But...

"There must be more than that," I said.

"He has his goals, and that's all that matters to him."

"And what goals are those?"

Nura's mouth tightened, and I did not miss the way her fingers clenched around the letter in her hands. She turned to face me fully.

"When we get back there," she said, quietly, "I hope you're ready to fight like hell."

I almost laughed.

I thought of Max, of Serel, of the Threllian refugees who would be traveling back to Ara with us. I thought of all those precious souls that I had to protect. I'd been fighting like hell since I was shackled to that cart all those years ago, utterly alone. And since long before that, when I fled a crumbling homeland that no longer exists. I was born fighting.

Of course I wasn't going to stop now. Not when I had so much to lose.

I didn't so much as blink as I gave Nura a small, serene smile. "Oh yes," I said. "I know there are still many battles to win."

Maybe I imagined the faintest echo of a smirk that brushed her eyes. But she turned away too quickly for me to tell.

THAT NIGHT, Serel and I spent the night lying on the floor of my bedroom, just as we had hundreds of times over the years. We laughed and cried together, then laughed again, and cried again. I felt his pain with him when he told me of the wars that he had been sent to fight, how the estate had crumbled into chaos and paranoia after I had left. He held my hand as I told him of my training, of the battles, of the pact I'd made. His face lit up with shock and confusion as I told him about Reshaye — in the loosest possible terms — asking questions that even I didn't totally know how to answer.

I told him about Max, though I left out some details about the nature of our relationship. For some reason, I still wanted to pull those moments close to my chest, only for me.

But the topics of our conversations drifted far beyond our sad stories, which was what I had always so loved about Serel. He found the joy and the beauty in everything. He could tell me of the heavy loss of a bloody battle, and in the next moment, light up when he told me of how wonderful it felt to return to his friends. Once, many years ago, he had told me that his grandfather used to say that every moment in life was a coin with one dark side and one light. They fell on the ground with one side facing up, but the other always lay beneath it, there, but hidden. Serel always saw both sides of the coin, even when fate handed him nothing but darkness.

Finally, when the night grew so late that it was on the cusp of morning, I asked him, "Will you be returning to Ara with us, or will you stay here?"

He didn't hesitate. "Ara. Definitely. I need a change of scenery."

I let out a sigh of relief, then immediately felt selfish. Ara was at war. At least this city was now under the jurisdiction of the Orders. As ridiculous as it sounded, perhaps this was now the safer place for him.

When I voiced this thought, he let out a scoff.

"Please. You won't get rid of me again so easily, Tisaanah." He gave me a little smile and a wink that was so aggressively *him* that it knocked the air out of me.

For a moment, words evaded me.

How many times had I dreamed that I'd see him again? How many times had I been so certain that I wouldn't?

"You have no idea how much I've missed you," I murmured, fighting a lump in my throat.

He smiled, and said, "I do, actually."

————

{...SAW...}

It was late, when I heard it. A voice. *The* voice. I opened my eyes into darkness, into the old, familiar image of the white expanse of Threllian ceilings.

Beside me, I heard Serel's low, slow breaths.

My own pounding heartbeat.

For a moment, it was all silent — I wondered if I had imagined it.

And then, there it was. A voice, different than it had been before in ways I couldn't quite describe, closer and farther away all at once.

{You saw me.}

I felt it more than I heard it. It matched my own breath, my own heartbeat.

Yes, I whispered.

I felt it roil within me, a shudder that lay between a sigh or a laugh or a moan. It all felt so much closer than it once did, a power that moved in my blood.

{Our story is not complete, Daughter of All Worlds.}

A caress writhed against my mind. And my lips twisted into a smile. Not long ago, I would have been afraid.

Not anymore.

Good, I whispered. *I haven't decided how I want it to end.*

And I could have sworn it chuckled, as it slithered off into darkness.

CHAPTER EIGHTY

MAX

F ive damned days on land, and I had already forgotten how much I wasn't made for this. We were barely forty feet from shore, and I was ready to retch.

Or maybe that was just the physical reaction of returning to Ara, which I desperately did not want to do. Mostly because I had no idea what would be waiting for us there.

I pushed myself up from the rail and turned around, running my eyes across the crowded deck of the ship and up those spine-like sails. We'd had to charter a larger boat just to carry all of the people who were coming back to Ara. Most of the former slaves had chosen to remain in Threll, but many still would return with us.

I watched them hustle and bustle across the deck, leaning excitedly over the edge of the boat, pointing, laughing. Tisaanah had mentioned that most of them would not have ever seen the ocean before, and I had to admit that it was charming to watch their excitement. Even if another part of me wanted to say, *Give it another three hours and see how you like it when you're vomiting your guts out.*

"You are famous." Nura appeared beside me, so silently that

497

she seemed to fold from the air. She smirked and raised her eyebrows, nodding to a group of people across the deck.

I followed her gaze and sighed.

The sea was not the only subject of the former slaves' wide-eyed amazement. Faces turned constantly to shoot curious, awed glances to me and Tisaanah. This particular group looked away hurriedly as soon as they noticed my stare.

"You two put on a show. I'm sure none of them have ever seen anything like it." Her gaze flicked to me. "Neither have I."

"You didn't see it."

"I heard enough." She lifted her hands, fingers spread to mimic dazzlement. "*A great serpent of fire.* Interesting."

"They exaggerate."

"Probably. But you *did* manage to use magic while dosed with Chryxalis. And you went up against Reshaye. So I know that no matter how stories grow, something remarkable happened in that ballroom."

"The only remarkable thing that happened is that everyone managed to make it out alive."

A small, humorless laugh. "That is remarkable. We're in agreement there."

My eyes found Tisaanah, who stood at the head of the boat, body pressed to the edge of the rail, chin lifted. As if she were throwing herself into the ocean air. Remarkable indeed.

Nura followed my gaze.

"You know... I do want you to be happy, Max."

She said it quietly, almost under her breath. The statement was so jarring, so uncharacteristic, that I had no choice but to whip my head around to look at her.

I scoffed. "What, are you suddenly desperate for forgiveness?"

"You don't have to believe me." Her gaze slid to me. Serious. "But it's the truth. And no matter what happens when we get home, it still will be."

There was something about the way she said it — *no matter what happens when we get home* — that made me suddenly uneasy.

But before I could ask her what, exactly, that was supposed to mean, I turned around to see that she had already drifted away, melting into the crowd like another shadow.

Still, I turned those words over in my head as I settled back against the rail. My eyes found Tisaanah again. She was still in the same spot, leaning over the edge of the deck, looking out at the shore.

I started to approach her, and then stopped myself. Stopped myself, and just watched her, framed against the image of the sky and the sea and the distant Threllian hills.

Less than a year ago, a young woman in a ridiculous dress had been abandoned at my cottage and refused to leave. And now, absolutely everything was different. All of my certainties had been rearranged, some destroyed, some new ones built in their place.

And for the first time in so long, something new altogether had begun to grow in the space between those certainties, something harder to see but more powerful, more dangerous, more beautiful:

Possibility.

I slid my hands into my pockets, lifted my chin to the cold caress of the ocean air, and stood there for a moment longer.

TISAANAH

I clutched the side of the ship and swept one final glance out over the distant Threllian shorelines.

Hours ago, I had watched the Mikov estate unravel before my eyes as we Stratagrammed away. The home that had broken me and built me, and that I had broken in return, disappeared into nothing but smoke before my eyes.

I thought I would feel something more poignant in that moment, but I hadn't. It wasn't until now that the wave crashed over me. Now, as I stood on a boat packed to capacity with former slaves going to a new life, I whispered goodbye to Threll for perhaps the final time. Maybe I had felt nothing when I said goodbye to Esmaris's city because it had never been a home, just a prison.

But here, I could see the hints of flowing plains, far, far in the distance. I could feel the faint, echoing call of my home. Of my mother and the salty smell of her skin, cool and refreshing in her embrace. It hurt to say goodbye to that.

I looked down at my hands, two-tone skin pressed over the damp wood of the rail.

I felt different.

I had not heard Reshaye speak again, but I could feel it within me as if it were coursing through my blood. Certainly, its power, if not its voice. I had thought of my vision many times since I awoke, running through it step by step. I told Max about the whole thing, too. Neither of us understood, exactly, what I had done, if anything. Maybe it was just a waking dream, a vision like the nightmares Reshaye thrust upon me.

But it felt more real than that.

I curled my fingers together and pressed my hand over my heart, grounding myself in the faint pulse beneath my skin.

The cadence of familiar footsteps approached and Max leaned against the railing beside me.

"The last time I said goodbye to these shores," I murmured, "I thought it would be a miracle if I made it to the other side alive."

"At least we can be glad the circumstances are different this time."

"And I was alone."

I had been so, so alone.

I didn't pull my eyes from the shore, but I felt his gaze drag over my skin like a caress.

"I'm glad those circumstances are different, too."

My hand slid over his, and his fingers easily rearranged to accommodate mine.

Seven months ago, I stood on the deck of a much smaller and much dirtier boat, blood running down my back, three desperate sentences running through my head over and over again. The ghost of that girl still lived inside me somewhere. She had what it took to survive, and I had what it took to live.

I had Wielding skills honed by months of relentless brute force and instruction by the best damn teacher in Ara.

I had magic running through my veins that could destroy and create and rebuild.

I had the ability not just to look at people, but to *see* them, and to carry their stories with my own.

And, most precious of all, I had people to protect — love that burned for all of them like an enduring flame deep in my chest.

"We're not done," I whispered.

I didn't even realize that I'd said it aloud until I felt Max's fingers squeeze mine.

"Barely gotten started," he said, and a smile tugged at my mouth.

The Threllian shore grew farther and farther away. And within my thoughts, I whispered to myself just as I had seven months ago.

My name is Tisaanah. I am a free woman and yet still a slave. I am fragments of many things but a whole of only myself. I am a daughter of no worlds, and all worlds.

And I am not done yet.

EPILOGUE

This, Zeryth thought, was quite unfortunate.

He pulled his brow into a thoughtful furrow, doused his voice in well-meaning concern, and leaned forward in his chair. "My Queen, I still do not understand this change of heart."

Queen Sesri sat across from him, her hands folded delicately in her lap, swathes of velvet and cascading blonde waves falling over her shoulders. They were in one of the Queen's private meeting chambers, a small room that was still opulently decorated, and her seat was raised so that she looked slightly down on Zeryth despite her small size.

She did, Zeryth had to admit, look the part of a princess. Perhaps one day she would look the part of a Queen, too, though she was probably close to a decade away from really seeming like she belonged anywhere near a throne.

"I have told you my reasons," she said, haughtily. "Is it so strange to think that I have reconsidered whether fighting blood with blood is the best approach?"

She *sounded* confident, or at least, her words were even if her voice wavered slightly. But the real giveaway to her uncertainty was the way she shot a little glance at Tare after every sentence.

Her Valtain advisor sat beside her, unsettlingly quiet as always, sheets of straight silver hair framing his face.

Aw. How cute.

"The House of Laurel is not loyal to you," Zeryth said. "Lord Laurel is a known rebel conspirer."

Sesri looked at Tare, who nodded. "He is."

Her brow wrinkled. "Perhaps there is another way."

"Force, my Queen, is the only way to deal with such things." Zeryth gave her a comforting smile. "Though it is very admirable that you have such a benevolent heart. Just like your father did."

The mention of the late king, predictably, sent grief spiraling across Sesri's face. She looked down at her hands, frowning.

Zeryth took that opportunity to shoot Tare a pointed look, arching his eyebrows. Tare stared back blankly, offering — as always — no expression. But he turned to the queen.

"There is no other choice, my Queen," Tare said, gently.

Sesri pondered for a moment, then she shook her head. "There must be. I do not want to inflict suffering on my people this way. It has gone too far."

Hm. Interesting.

Sesri had expressed these kinds of sentiments before, but she had never gotten this far with it. Never remained steadfast once her father was brought up, or once Tare began pushing her.

Zeryth gave Tare another sharp glance.

"Sesri." Tare's voice grew more pleading. "I urge you to consider what the Arch Commandant is saying."

"I have. I will not attack the Laurels. We will have to do something else."

She shook her head again, more firmly this time.

She wasn't going to change her mind.

But that, Zeryth decided, was just fine with him. The timing was acceptable. Ideal, even. In fact, he would be lying if he said that a part of him wasn't hoping that this would happen.

"Very well, my Queen." Zeryth stood, then dropped to a low bow. "The Orders of course support whichever course of action you wish to follow. I shall begin working on some alternative plans."

He excused himself, and Tare followed to escort him from the Palace. The two Valtain strode down the hallways in silence, Zeryth's footsteps echoing with commanding force and Tare's so light that they were nearly silent. As they walked, Zeryth ran his eyes down the hallways, taking in the elaborate mosaics and gold filigree that lined the walls. So much gold. He preferred platinum, himself. A little more elegant and understated.

"I take it that we're at a clear understanding, correct, Tare?"

"Give her time."

"We don't have time, and even if we did, there's no reason to waste it."

Silence. "Would it be better to wait until Nura returned?"

Zeryth almost laughed. Oh, Tare. So sweet. So naive.

No, it certainly wouldn't. In fact, he considered the fact that Nura had *not* yet returned to be of very deliberate benefit to this situation.

"She'll understand," he said, and gave Tare a confident, sparkling smile.

NORMALLY, Zeryth would have chosen to use a Stratagram to get back to the Towers. On foot, the journey took close to a half hour, and Zeryth rarely found himself inclined to waste that kind of time. But today was a beautiful day — brisk, crisp, with a particularly salty breeze off the sea. He decided to walk. He could spare the extra time.

Today, after all, was lining up perfectly.

He had received a letter from Nura that morning detailing the — rather exciting, by the sound of it — events that had occurred at the Mikov estate. Tisaanah had proven herself to be every bit as powerful as he hoped she would be. So powerful, in fact, that he was actually *glad* that she had proposed a blood pact. Normally, Zeryth tried to avoid getting himself wrapped up in

DAUGHTER OF NO WORLDS

such things. But after what he had seen in Threll, he now found himself awfully relieved that she was bound by blood not to act against him.

But it was the bit about Maxantarius that Zeryth found especially intriguing.

He had not wanted to involve Maxantarius in this at all. He was too unpredictable, too unabashedly vitriolic towards the Orders, and, most importantly of all, Zeryth found the idea of spending extended time in his presence to be about as appealing as the idea of stabbing both of his eyes out and then eating them.

For the life of him, Zeryth had not been able to understand why Nura would bring Tisaanah to *Max*, of all people. And once Tisaanah had proven herself, he had been adamantly opposed to allowing Max to remain involved, at least not without *many* precautions. Zeryth was not about to let himself get stabbed in the back by Maxantarius Farlione, of all rutting people. It would just be too great of an indignity to lose a decade-long feud on top of the already significant indignity of being dead.

But then, the night of the ball, Nura had returned to the tower and calmly stated that they *had* their precaution: Tisaanah. "If you have her," she had said, "then you have him. It's just how he works. And we'll have a grip on her that's ironclad."

It was so shamelessly cold that Zeryth had to admire it.

And as much as it pained him to admit it, she had been completely right about all of it. Maxantarius was turning out to be a good investment after all. All the pieces were lining up perfectly.

He now had not one, but two outrageously powerful weapons at his disposal. And he finally had a real foothold in Threll, a coveted step that he had been working towards for years now. Ara was divided by a deeply unpopular ruler, all while the ruling Lords were slowly, one by one, replaced by Order allies.

And, best of all, his surly and untrustworthy Second was far across the ocean for at least five more days. Nura had always been an ally of necessity in this scheme. She was brilliant, and she hated him. A combination that made Zeryth all too happy to set this all in motion while she and her hidden knives were far across the sea.

Zeryth reached the Towers and hummed to himself as he went to his office. He took a moment to admire the thrashing sea, more vividly beautiful than ever in the shadow of a distant storm, before sitting down at his desk and composing a letter to his dear Second in Command.

By the time you read this, he wrote, *Sesri will be dead...*

END of BOOK I

Tisaanah and Max's journey will continue in Book II, Children of Fallen Gods, coming in July 2020 and available for preorder now.

AUTHOR'S NOTE

THANK YOU FOR READING!

Thank you so much for joining Tisaanah and Max on the first leg of their journey! I hope you enjoyed it.

Please consider leaving a review on Amazon or Goodreads. I can't overstate how much they mean to us authors, and you would earn my eternal gratitude!

Speaking of eternal gratitude... keep reading to find out how you can get a free prequel novella, following Max's time fighting the Ryvenai War.

ASHEN SON: A 4-PART PREQUEL

GET IT FREE!

Maxantarius is a skilled magic Wielder and a military rising star. But in one terrible night, he has learned that glory is bloodier than he ever could have imagined.

War has broken out, thrusting his family into the center of a savage conflict. In its wake, Max is chosen to compete for the title of Arch Commandant.

The title is all he has ever wanted. But the competition is merciless, and victory will mean fighting against his love... all while he must navigate a war that threatens to destroy those he treasures most.

As allies and enemies alike draw blades at his back, Max learns that no victor walks away with clean hands.

It's only a matter of how far he's willing to go.

Sign up to my mailing list to get all four parts of Ashen Son for free! Part 1 is now available:

carissabroadbentbooks.com/ashenson

ACKNOWLEDGMENTS

First of all: Nathan, thank you for being the love of my goddamned life, for listening to me whine and complain and work through plot knots, for keeping me caffeinated, for keeping me loved, for being the best brainstorming buddy, and for generally being the most incredible life partner. I am not at all exaggerating when I say that you're the best thing that ever happened to me.

Thank you to my writing group, Stephen, Michael, Noah, and Tom for being such a huge, formative piece of creating this story. Like I said, this book is really yours. The best part of writing this book was reading it to you every week.

And on that note, extra thanks to Noah for the herculean effort of beta reading all 600 pages of this monster in 4 days. That was, genuinely, some impressive shit.

Thank you to Kate for the wonderful editing. I'm so glad that our paths crossed and I think this may be the beginning of a beautiful friendship.

Thank you to Nick, for three previous books of editing work and for the many Skype calls. I'm sad to see you leave the fiction world but I hope that your new adventures are everything you dreamed.

Thank you to my family for always encouraging my writing and for the boundless support.

Thank you to Calcifer for keeping my toes warm during long nights of editing.

And finally, thank you to you, whoever you are, because it honestly just tickles me to think that anyone out there wants to read anything I slap on a page. You're the friggen best.

ABOUT THE AUTHOR

Carissa Broadbent has been concerning teachers and parents with mercilessly grim tales since she was roughly nine years old. Since then, her stories have gotten (slightly) less depressing and (hopefully a lot?) more readable. Today, she writes fantasy novels with a heaping dose of badass ladies and a big pinch of romance.

Carissa works as a cybersecurity marketing professional during the harsh light of day, and is also a visual artist. She lives with her partner, one very well behaved rabbit, one very poorly behaved rabbit, and one perpetually skeptical cat in Rhode Island.

Come hang out with her at www.carissabroadbentbooks.com.

facebook.com/carissabroadbentbooks

twitter.com/carissanasyra

instagram.com/carissabroadbentbooks

Made in the USA
Middletown, DE
07 December 2022

17266404R00307